WORLDWIDE PRAISE FOR THE AWAKEN SAGA

"Kept me on the edge of my seat the whole time."

goodreads

"Popa seamlessly blends international intrigue, criminal machinations, and family secrets to captivating effect."

booklife.

"Exceptional book! Lots of twists and turns."

goodreads

"Ellis K. Popa (delivers) an amazing story full of mystery, intrigue and romance."

— JOHN BENEDICT, BESTSELLING AUTHOR OF *ADRENALINE*

"Popa's prose is smart, arresting, and tightly woven."

— THE BOOKLIFE PRIZE

"This is an absolutely delicious book. I both devoured it in one day, and savoured every word!"

— CHARLOTTE, BLUE FAIRY BUGS BOOKS (UK)

"...this book is simply one of the best books I've ever read. The writing is sharp, concise, and instantly engaging."

— HEATHER, BOOKGIRLBROWN REVIEWS (US)

DAWN TO DUSK

THE AWAKEN SAGA
BOOK TWO

ELLIS K. POPA

It's always Darkest
Before the Dawn

And Fire Books
PO Box 223
Mountain Home, TN 37684
United States of America

PUBLISHER'S NOTE

Dawn to Dusk touches on sensitive subject matter such as kidnapping, violence, substance abuse, and teenage pregnancy. Young readers or those sensitive to such material should be advised.

ABOUT THE FRENCH WORDS

Several French words and phrases are found in the book, some of which are slang or colloquial in nature.

Readers will come across what may seem like oddities—for instance, *allez* in place of *allons* (let's go) or *chépa* in place of *je ne sais pas* (I don't know).

This was done intentionally to aid in authenticity, specifically with the regard to the way one character speaks. Francophiles, please be advised.

A SPECIAL NOTE

Dawn to Dusk contains fictional places and characters named after readers, fans, and supporters. This was one of the ways we expressed our gratitude for their support. Other bonuses included...

- access to the premiere of the new trailer
- a virtual party where we recreated a scene from *Dawn to Dusk*
- custom bookplates with limited edition artwork
- bonus character art + so much more!

These extras aren't available through retailers and only happen periodically.

To be notified of the next opportunity, **become an Extraordinary Reader**. It's FREE, and you'll receive twice-monthly emails with the latest news, bonuses, and events, including these special campaigns. You'll also get access to FREE BOOKS from other amazing authors...

SubscribePage.io/JoinReadersClub

THE PLAYLISTS

Check out the playlist for *Dawn to Dusk: The Awaken Saga, Book 2...*

LinkTr.ee/BookishMood

To access the special character playlists for Dom and Émilien, go here...

LinkTr.ee/D2DCharacterPlaylists

They are smashed to pieces from dawn to dusk; they perish forever while no one notices...

-IYOV, CH. 4, V. 20

O my little star, O daybreak,
how great you are!
Blind the eyes of the Germans!
Draw them along the wrong paths!
Show them the wrong way,
So that the Jewish and Gypsy children can live.

The golden winter is closing in,
Snow is falling to the ground,
on our hands like little stars.
The black eyes are freezing.
The hearts are dying.

— BRONISŁAWA WAJS ("PAPUSZA")

CONTENTS

This is the Sequel   xiv

PART ONE

Preface   2
Prologue   3
Begur   13
1. Hiding Place   14
2. Silent Tempest   21
3. Unplanned Plans   26
4. Stow Away   34
Barçelona   42
5. Special Delivery   43
6. Damage Control   53
7. New Plan   59
Begur   64
8. Silent Goodbye   65
El Prat   72
9. Toot Sweet   73
10. Intelligence Service   77
Corbera de Llobregat   86
11. Old "Friend"   87
12. Illustrious Guest   91
12½. Distress Signal   100
Orléans   103
13. Patron Saint   104

PART TWO

Paris   114
14. Final Destination   115
15. Long Lost   121
16. Long Last   128

17. Bastille Day — 136
18. Secret Message — 145
18½. Light Show — 151
19. Unveiled Secret — 156
20. Dress Rehearsal — 164
21. Unexpected Detour — 170
22. French Cop — 175
23. Secret Admirer — 181
24. New Route — 188
24½. Torn Apart — 197
25. News Report — 200
26. Evening Wear — 205
27. Yield Sign — 213
28. Unexpected Detour — 220
29. Renewed Hope — 228
30. Enemy Friend — 234
31. Friend Enemy — 243
32. Toute Suite — 252
33. Judas Iscariot — 258
34. Wolf's Lair — 265
35. Operation Valkyrie — 271
35½. Hour Glass — 277

PART THREE

36. Mission Failed — 283
37. Mega Lomaniac — 290
38. Get Away — 296
39. Vanishing Act — 302
40. Bicycle Kick — 310
41. Dig Deep — 318
42. Last Chance — 322
43. Happen Stance — 332
44. Blind Justice — 341
45. Saving Grace — 351
Gentilly — 357
Epilogue — 358

From the Author & Illustrators   371
Kickstarter Backers   379
The D2D Team   382
About the Author   384

THIS IS THE SEQUEL

This is the **SEQUEL** (Book 2) in The Awaken Saga.

Book 1 - *Awaken the Dawn*
Book 2 - ***Dawn to Dusk*** *** (this book)

If you prefer to read the books in order, you can grab *Awaken the Dawn* from these retailers...

Books2Read.com/Awaken1

PART ONE

Maksim's Rules of Survival

Rule 1: Be aware.

Rule 2: Be discreet.

Rule 3: Think logically.

Rule 4: Listen to your instinct.

Rule 5: Always be ready.

Rule 6: Avoid unwanted attention.

Rule 7: Assume you're being tailed.

Rule 8: Note every possible exit.

Rule 9: Assess every possible threat.

Rule 10: Never, ever reach the second location.

PROLOGUE

"You are certain you do not need medical assistance?" Mr. Amsel set a glass of water on his desk and settled into his plush chair. "I am able to call an ambulance," he said, situating his spectacles.

"No, no. Just... give me a moment." I reached for the water. Pain pinched at my shoulder blade—same spot where I'd been hit by shrapnel—and my hand trembled as I lifted the glass.

This injury wasn't the only reason I felt weak. After talking and verifying and signing paperwork, Mr. Amsel—the bank president—had finally disclosed how much money I'd inherited.

And I had nearly fainted.

"It is such a pleasure to have you as a friend of this institution, Fräulein Barrett." His mouth stretched wide, revealing sparkly white teeth. I could practically see euro signs glittering in the smile. "You can take your business anywhere. We here at Kopernikus-Bank understand this, and we thank you for entrusting us with your sizable assets."

"Uh-huh." I reached for the water again but thought better of it. "And when will the funds be available?"

"We are able to release twenty thousand euros today." He

swiped several pieces of paper from a sleek printer. "After you have signed these forms, I will issue your girocard—debit card—and those funds will be available immediately." He hesitated. "Unless this amount is insufficient for you, Fräulein?"

I gave a swift shake of my head. Maybe too swift.

Maksim had warned me that my funds wouldn't be accessible all at once. There were processes, checks, transfers that had to happen. "The employees may appear relaxed," he'd said, "as if this is an everyday type of transaction. I can assure you it's not. Don't do anything that may prompt them to call the police."

"What would make them do that?"

"Appearing frazzled, rushed. Not playing the part. You're the granddaughter of a billionaire. You'll have to act like it."

I peeked down at my black slacks and dressy blouse. I never wore stuff like this, and the frumpy heels rubbing blisters on my feet reminded me why. But at least I looked the part.

I signed the papers and returned them to Mr. Amsel.

"Thank you, Fräulein." He reached into his suit jacket and pulled out a business card. "Please do contact me should you have any questions."

"That's awe— I mean, thank you very much." I'd been about to say "that's awesome" but decided on something more proper. Billionaires said "thank you very much," didn't they? I'd have to check next time I googled *things rich people say*.

I tucked the business card in my purse and showed myself out of the office. My heels thumped as I followed the staircase down to the foyer. The building opened up, and sunlight poured inside through the vaulted glass ceiling.

A receptionist manned the front desk, taking calls and typing on her keyboard. She peered around her computer and smiled. "Goodbye. Be careful." She didn't sound German. Actually, she sounded... French?

I offered a halfhearted wave. "Thanks. You, too."

"But you should be very careful."

My feet stalled. I turned away from the revolving door and stared at the woman. "S-sorry. Did you say *very* careful?"

She focused on her screen, seemingly unaware that her words had affected me.

Probably a translation issue. That was possible. She could have meant something different.

"Fräulein Barrett!"

I wheeled around. Mr. Amsel was hurrying down the staircase. "Fräulein," he called. "You forgot your girocard."

"Mr. Amsel." I placed a hand to my chest, heart thumping full speed. "You startled me."

"Forgive me, Fräulein." He stepped off the staircase and crossed the foyer. His dress shoes clacked over the sleek tiles. His tie glistened in the sunlight.

He closed the gap and held the card toward me. I reached for it, planning to put it in my purse—but I couldn't pry the card out of his grasp.

I tugged again. He wouldn't let go.

"Mr. Amsel?"

"Be careful, Fräulein." His bright mood turned stone-cold sober. "There is danger."

My attention snapped to the receptionist. She was working away, her fingers clicking across the keyboard. That was the only sound. There were no other customers or employees in the lobby.

"Did you need something from Lilian?"

I focused on Mr. Amsel.

"She is our *Empfangsdame*. Receptionist." His smile returned, and he released the debit card. "Do you need something from her, Fräulein?"

"N-no."

"Then... is there anything else I may do for you?"

"I'm good." *I think.* "Thanks."

"Thank you, Fräulein. Goodbye." He waved as I turned away.

What in the actual hell?

The revolving door was big, wide, and I didn't recall it being so heavy. I grunted, pushing.

The enclosed space opened up, and I finally reached the sidewalk. Glass towers climbed into the sky. Exhaust fumes blended with the stench of hot pavement. The hum of motors created a backdrop of white noise.

I trekked up the sidewalk, heading for a nearby café—a.k.a. the meetup spot. Something brought me to a dead stop. I glanced around.

Dusty purple twilight settled on the city, but... there was no way it could've been this late. Could it? Had I been in the bank all day?

I pulled out my phone, planning to check the time. The screen stayed black.

Crap. The phone was dead.

I stuffed the device in my purse and hurried up the sidewalk. Maksim had been teaching me his rules of survival, and I tried to think of the one that'd be best for navigating this situation.

I couldn't, and a burst of panic fluttered.

"You're fine," I told myself. "You don't need a rule. Just get to the café."

That was probably true, but as I continued up the sidewalk, I realized just how dark my surroundings had grown. My attention trailed up the nearest skyscraper. Not a single speck of light glowed, and the top of the building disappeared into thick shadows.

The same was true for the building next door. And the buildings across the street. My only source of light was a lamppost that cast dim yellow over the sidewalk.

But... what about the cars in the traffic jam? Shouldn't they have their headlights on?

They should have—in theory—but the traffic jam had vanished. Silence crashed into me. A shiver dragged up my spine. Something was very, very wrong.

"Bonsoir."

The familiar voice slid into my ears and twisted through my psyche. *Oh, no. No. Please.*

"Did you miss me, *ma petite belle?*" A pause. A chuckle. "I think you did."

The urge to scream swelled.

Émilien stood beneath a lamppost, directly across the street, and he was smirking. Light glinted off something in his hand.

Cuffs.

"No," I whimpered, taking a measured step back. "Stay away from me."

"*Au contraire, ma chérie.* You"—he held up the cuffs—"are mine."

I whipped around, legs exploding in a sprint. Warm air rushed over my face. Flat pavement stretched beneath my feet.

I staggered, despite the smooth sidewalk, and nearly face-planted. Stupid heels. Why the hell had I worn these?

The bank building appeared on my right. I ran that way.

"Help!" My hands slammed against the revolving door. I pushed, expecting it to move.

It didn't.

"Mr. Amsel?" I pressed my face to the glass. Shadows encased the foyer. Mr. Amsel and the receptionist were nowhere to be seen.

I banged on the glass, screaming, begging someone to let me in. There was no movement inside the foyer. And no matter how hard I pushed, the door wouldn't budge.

Émilien tore across the street, head down, arms pumping. His face morphed into something vicious, animalistic.

I abandoned the bank building.

"Help! Someone help me!" My legs carried me up the sidewalk. I was heading in the opposite direction of where I needed to go. *Away* from the café.

"Maksim!" Tears blurred my vision. "Maksim, I need help!" My cries were frantic yet strangely hopeful, as if my voice might reach all the way to the meetup spot.

That hope fizzled the farther I ran. Still, I screamed for him. "Maksim! *Maksim!*"

My feet thrashed, longing to go faster, when a dark chuckle penetrated my senses. Émilien didn't sound like he was struggling or out of breath. Actually, he sounded like he was pacing me.

Because he was. He'd caught up easily, and now he was hanging back. Why?

He's enjoying this.

The epiphany rocked me. He wasn't chasing me to catch me. He wanted to mess with me first—a predator toying with its prey.

A circle and slash glowed red at the next crosswalk. *Don't cross.* That was the message, but there were no cars coming.

I barreled across the street.

A blast shuddered the air, and gray pavement erupted. I screamed and dove, rolling. Chunks of cement rained down.

I jumped up and kept going.

The ground rumbled. Cement exploded. I covered my head, running. Still running.

The explosions continued as Émilien closed the gap. His fingers brushed my neck before clamping down.

I stumbled and hit the ground. My arm and shoulder scraped. My body rolled.

I skidded over a bump in the pavement, and a burst of light flared. An explosion barreled into me. My back slammed against something, and pain seared every part of my body...

I SUCKED IN A BREATH AND SHOT UPRIGHT. STALE HEAT greeted me. My heart thudded as I took in my surroundings.

Silky sheets in bright, blazing white tangled my legs. Wooden posts stretched up from the bed, connecting to metal rods, and sheer curtains fell in long, flowing panels.

Relief swelled. I was at the rental house.

The first rays of dawn spilled through the windows, creating a natural nightlight in the otherwise dark room. "Maksim?"

There was no answer, and my panic ticked up. This was what happened in the dream. I'd been alone, and Émilien had been waiting for me.

But Émilien didn't know we were here. Maksim had taken precautions to ensure that.

I untangled my legs and drew the bed-curtains aside. Metal scraped metal as the rings slid across the rod.

I padded to a leather chair and reached for my robe. "Maksim?" I donned the lump of velour. The supersoft material slid over my arms and rested against my tank top and shorts.

I gathered my hair, pulling it from beneath the collar, and crossed the room. I reached for the door and hesitated. What if something happened to Maksim?

"You're being ridiculous." The words escaped as a shaky whisper. Clearly, I didn't believe myself.

I cracked open the door and poked my head outside. Shadows greeted me, and the flow of running water reached my ears.

I exhaled a laugh. Maksim was in the bathroom.

"Scaredy-cat," I muttered at myself.

I padded down the hall and stopped in front of the bathroom door. Light leaked under the bottom. "Hello?" A quick double-knock. "Maksim?"

The water stopped, and the door eased open. I peered inside.

Maksim stood at the sink, shirtless, a razor in his hand and slivers of shaving cream on his face. His jeans hung loose, revealing carved abs and V-shaped hip lines.

My attention moved to the scars from his motorcycle accident. They covered the right side of his body—arm, shoulder, back, even down to his hip and leg. The scar tissue looked dull under the bathroom lights, his skin pale and crinkly.

I gravitated to him. He tensed at my touch, my fingers gliding along the tough, uneven skin.

"Something's wrong." He cast a questioning glance over his shoulder.

I slid my hands around his lean waist, hugging him. "Bad dream. Just making sure it's you in here and not—"

When I didn't go on, he said, "Not someone from your dream?"

I peered out from behind him. My blue eyes and puffy black hair appeared in the mirror. I nodded.

He lowered the razor. "Who was it?"

I gripped my robe, pulling it tighter, and averted my eyes. "Émilien," I whispered. "You think he's still in jail? What if Vladimir got him out?"

Maksim stripped a hand towel from the sink and wiped his face. Bits of cream remained, but his skin was otherwise clean.

He tossed the towel and wrapped me in a hug. My emotions swelled as he rubbed a gentle hand over my back, steering clear of my shoulder blade. The bruises had yellowed, and the stitches were gone. Still, the six-week-old injury was tender.

"Do you remember what I said before we came here?" Maksim's deep voice reverberated against my cheek. "The promise I made to you?"

I peeked up at him. "That you wouldn't let anything happen to me."

"That's right." He cupped my face, drawing my focus to his eyes. The fluorescents highlighted the many shades of brown—from gold to dark chocolate—layered into his irises. "Have you been following the guidelines I've laid out?"

I nodded.

"No hints to Brandy about where you are? No pictures or audio?"

"None."

"And you've been using the double VPN I set up?"

I nodded again. "Every time I email her or go online."

"What about spending?" He tucked a frizzy curl behind my

ear. "You're using cash only? Not the debit card you received from the bank?"

"Only the cash you've given me. I haven't touched the card since Germany." That was a month ago.

"Then it was only a bad dream, and we have nothing to worry about." His eyes twinkled. "Kat, nobody knows you're here."

I exhaled my worry. "You're right. Nobody knows—" I hesitated. Nobody knew I was here. That was by design, of course, but I had never said it out loud.

Something about it sounded... wrong.

"Nobody knows you're here." Maksim sang the words, the hard edge of his Balkan accent smoothing into a silky blade. His hands moved to my waist, and I found myself walking backwards. "Isn't that convenient?"

I stared at him. His features, so familiar to me, suddenly looked different. His eyes held a new glint I hadn't seen before.

A sinister glint.

The bathroom lights flickered—once, twice. Each time, his irises flashed a whole different color, going from brown to...

"No," I whispered.

Flick, flicker. Flick-flick.

The lights kept struggling as Maksim backed me against the wall. Everything about him shifted—his height, build, hair.

I grabbed his arm, expecting scar tissue. There was none, and fear choked me.

I lunged for the door. He caught my robe and hauled me back. *"Oh que non, ma chérie."* He sang the words, and they weren't Romanian.

They were French.

I threw a punch. He caught my fist and laughed. The lights kept flickering, kept threatening to dump me in darkness, and panic tore through me.

He's not real, my darling. Dad's voice coaxed me from somewhere in the depths. *This isn't real.*

"This isn't real," I repeated. "Y-you're not real."

"But I am." Émilien—*not* Maksim—leaned in until the tips of our noses touched. He redoubled his grip, fingers wrapped around my wrists, and pressed his full weight, jamming my bad shoulder against the wall.

I whimpered.

The bathroom lights flashed, casting a sheen over Émilien's raven hair. His silver eyes burned with more than desire or lust.

They burned with vengeance.

"I will find you"—he placed his mouth by my ear—"and you *will* be mine."

BEGUR

I. HIDING PLACE

THURSDAY, JULY 11

"Don't let him take me! Maksim!" The screams burned in my chest and scraped at my throat. My eyes burst open to darkness.

A shadowy figure stood over me.

"No!" I scrambled to get away.

"Shh, shh. It's all right." The baritone voice came softly, urgently, as the figure caught my hands. *"Sunt aici." I'm here.*

"Maksim?"

"Da." Strong arms closed around me. *"Eu sunt, drăguță." It's me, sweetie.*

I buried my face in his chest. Tears poured into the soft fabric of his undershirt. Those were the kinds of shirts he always slept in. Because of his scars.

He whispered to me, rubbing my back and holding me close, until the first rays of dawn peeked inside the room.

I peered up. Slivers of pink daylight fell across him, highlighting his broad shoulders and chiseled arms. I eased closer. My feet slid beneath the sheets, aching to connect with his.

He wasn't under the covers.

I glanced across the room, and my midsection tightened. The door was open, as if he'd just come through it. "Did you sleep on the couch again?"

"I was reading last night. Fell asleep while I was out there."

I squinted, trying to read his expression. The room was too dark.

"What was the dream?" His matter-of-factness hit me like a baseball bat. "Who was in it?"

My eyes widened. That was what he asked me in the dream. Right before he morphed into—

"Kat?"

"Émilien." Tension wound around my heart and squeezed. "I-I was in Germany, at the bank, and he was waiting for me. Landmines started exploding. Then I woke up and—"

Realization dawned. I gasped.

He sat straight. "What?"

"Are you... real?" I groped in the dark. My fingers settled on his chest.

He tensed and grabbed my hand.

"Maksim?"

"Yes. I'm real."

"But you felt real in the dream, too." I scooted closer and nuzzled the back of his hand.

His hold loosened.

My fingers found their way to his arm, bumping along the rough surface until they disappeared beneath his sleeve. I wasn't always allowed to touch his scars. The nerve damage was extensive, and some days he couldn't bear the pain. Other days, he handled it fine.

I wondered if he'd tell me to stop now.

My fingertips glided over the uneven surface, along his biceps, around to his triceps.

He made a funny noise, something between a grunt and a moan, and swallowed. "Why do you do this?"

"It's hard to explain." I kept exploring, fingertips brushing over his shoulder. "Somehow, it always feels brand new, like I'm discovering fresh patterns in the scar tissue or... I don't know."

I drew a line along the border of his undamaged flesh. Silky softness grazed one side of my finger; roughness grazed the other.

I paused. "Does it hurt today?"

"No." His answer seemed to catch.

He cleared his throat and dragged himself out of my grasp. Disappointment slinked through me. "We need to get up. It's time to begin the next phase of your training."

He padded across the room. The overhead light doused me, and Maksim entered the closet.

I squinted. "I'm not up for training today."

Maksim reemerged wearing black workout shorts and a gray sleeveless shirt. He crossed the room and slid the bed-curtains aside.

Metal scraped metal like it had in the dream. I cringed.

"Think about your father's old saying, the one you told me about." He extended a hand. "'Desperate times make for desperate people, and desperate people are capable of anything.' Vladimir is desperate to find you. Your desperation must rival his."

"Okay, but... I'm so tired." I flopped over and hugged my pillow. "Can't we be desperate tomorrow?"

He hooked my torso and hauled me out of the bed.

"Hey!" I kicked, searching for the floor. "I'm serious. I'm really tired."

"And what will you do if you're tired while you're being pursued?" He set me down. "Rest? Take a nap?"

"I'm not being pursued. Not right at this moment."

His expression fell grim.

"Wait a second. We haven't been discovered, have we?"

He broke eye contact and crossed the room.

I chased after him and pulled him to a stop. "Is there something you're not telling me?"

"There was chatter on the Dark Web last week. Someone

mentioned Émilien." Maksim's gaze wandered the room, first to the window, then to the door. "I think we're fine, but I'd like to make sure he's still in custody in Romania, especially after your dream."

"You can do that?"

"I can ask Daniel to do it. I'll be able to call him from Barçelona."

"Barçelona?" My mouth popped open. "You're going back to that hacker girl's apartment?"

"Ivy. Yes." He returned to the closet.

"Can I go with you?"

He emerged, carrying his running shoes. "No," he said, brushing past me.

I tugged on his shirt until he stopped. "You promised I could call Brandy. I've only been able to send messages and emails so far. Maksim, I need to talk to her. Like, *talk* talk."

"You'll have to wait a little longer."

"But why?" My voice fractured. "You get to talk to Daniel every time you go over there."

"Do you think we're chitchatting?" He squared up to me. "Ivy is a high-level hacker. I'm in her good graces only because of the lucrative jobs I've secured for her in the past. It's the reason I'm permitted to go over there."

I opened my mouth. He held up a finger.

"Hackers want privacy. Hackers like *her* want extreme privacy. She can't afford to be compromised."

"But I'd be with you." Tears leaked into my voice. "Can't you at least ask?"

"I've mentioned you. She did not extend an invitation." He reached for my hands. "I will try again tonight, *dragă*. That's the most I can offer." He gave my hands a squeeze. "You've been very good about trusting me. Will you continue to do so?"

My head gave a slight down and up, but my heart wasn't in it.

It took a few minutes to find clean workout clothes and brush my teeth. By the time I finished, Maksim had rearranged every piece of furniture in the living room. The sofa rested against the opposite wall. The side tables and dehumidifier sat in the dining area.

Blue mats carpeted the floor.

"Where did you get these?" My gaze traveled to Maksim. He was barefoot, stretching, with one arm pulled across him. "Is there a gymnastics center around here?"

"Boxing gym. The owner sold them to me."

My gaze fell to my shoes, which were laced up. "I take it we're not going for a run?"

"We're going to practice the defensive techniques I've been teaching you." He nodded toward my shoes. "Keep those nearby. We'll be going for our run after."

I peeled off my shoes and socks and tossed them.

As soon as my feet touched blue, Maksim started toward me. "I'm the attacker. What are you going to do?" He snatched my wrist and then stood there, waiting. "Kat."

"Oh. Right." I cleared my throat. "Stop! Back up!" I widened my stance. I was supposed to put my hands up, but he already had possession of my wrist.

I tugged and twisted. He exerted zero effort and still managed to hold on.

"Can we start over? I-I wasn't ready."

"You must *be* ready. At all times." That was a reference to Rule Five: *Always be ready.*

He hauled me forward. I was about to collide with him when he stepped to the side, allowing me to stumble past. Then he chained me from behind with both arms.

"Ow!"

"What's your move?"

I tried to remember. My mind blanked.

"Rule Three," he said. "What is it?"

"It's—" Crap.

"Think logically," he said, answering his own question. "Don't panic, but you're losing precious time." He walked me forward. "We're moving. Now you need to worry about Rule Ten."

I squirmed, struggling. My feet slid off the mats and onto the stone tile.

"Imagine there's a vehicle in the dining room. That's where I'm taking you. *That* is the rule you're forgetting."

Rule Ten: *Never, ever reach the second location.*

The second location was a place that offered isolation and more control to the criminal. The chances of getting away dropped by the time a victim arrived—the reason it was so much more dangerous than the initial encounter.

"What do you do?" Maksim jabbed the back of my knee. It buckled, and I cried out. "Focus!" He pulled me up. "What do you do?"

"I-I have to escape before we get there."

"Do it."

I locked my knees and extended my legs, bracing myself. The effort slowed Maksim down—until he picked me up and carried me across the living room.

He set me down by the dining room table.

I cringed. "Whoops."

"Kat, come on. You're not taking this seriously."

"I am. I swear. It's just that—"

"No." He held up a finger. "You have been actively learning these moves for a month. We began watching self-defense videos five weeks ago. Six. While you were still in the hospital. You said everything made sense."

"It's different when it's happening in real life."

"You've experienced this in real life." He tilted his head. "Remember?"

My stomach bottomed out. Ștefan had done this very thing in Romania—grabbed me from behind, pinned my arms, all while pushing me toward a helicopter.

That was how the crime boss planned to kidnap me. The helicopter had been the second location.

The epiphany plowed into me. I slumped forward.

Maksim caught me.

"I-I was almost kidnapped. Maksim—"

"I know, *dragă*." He guided me to the couch and eased me onto the cushions. Dizziness spun through me. I swallowed bile, lips clamped together, and held my head.

"Had you known these moves," Maksim began slowly, "you could have broken Ştefan's hold much sooner. Do you understand why this is important?"

I nodded.

"Good. We'll come back to it." The cushions jostled as he moved from the couch. A moment later, he placed my running shoes next to me.

My attention traveled to him. "I really don't feel so good."

"You can walk if you're not up for jogging." He held out his hand. "It can be an easy day, but we're not going to stray from our routine. We can't afford to."

2. SILENT TEMPEST

P ale daylight greeted us outside. Maksim plodded down the colorful tile steps and headed for the stone path that led to the street.

I lagged behind.

The rental house overlooked rolling hills. In the distance, a bit to the right, the Mediterranean sparkled silver, filling the air with a salty tang I could taste from our doorstep.

My mind rewound to a few weeks ago. We had just arrived in Begur and had decided to walk to that beach. The views were amazing, but the sand had been brutal, slicing into my feet and toes.

Maksim had offered to carry me. I liked the idea—in theory— but he'd been beaten up pretty badly in Romania. Most of the blows had been focused on his right arm—same one he'd injured in a motorcycle accident. That was his "Achilles heel," so to speak, and our captors had exploited the weakness.

"I'm much better," he'd insisted. "As good as new. See?" He took my hand and placed it on his biceps. The muscles flexed. "Let me carry you."

I'd hopped onto his back, and he had indeed carried me... straight into the sea. With all our clothes on.

That was the first time he'd kissed me in this beautiful, magical place. My lips tingled as I remembered.

"Let's go." Maksim's voice boomed, intruding on the memory. He waited at the entrance to the property, his attention on me while he held the gate.

I followed the path he'd taken—down the stone walkway, past the pool—until I reached street level. "Sorry, I was—"

"Distracted. I know." He pulled the gate shut, and the hinges groaned. "Shake it off. We're already behind."

I'd been planning to share that sweet memory, to ask if he remembered it, too. His coldness plunged a knife straight into my heart. Why was he acting like this?

I started to ask, but... I knew why.

Seven weeks ago, I'd been traveling in Romania, trying to solve a scavenger hunt my dad made before he died. That scavenger hunt took me on a crazy journey that led to Maksim, a crime syndicate, and the truth about who we really were—our true identities.

Maksim had grown up in the Răzvan crime family, but not because he was related to them like he thought. Like he'd been *told*. He'd been kidnapped when he was three and raised by Vladimir Răzvan and his son, Ștefan.

As it turned out, *I* was related to this crime family. Vladimir was my uncle—my dad's older brother—but I hadn't known because Dad fled to America in 1989 and never talked about his family.

In the end, Vladimir and Ștefan killed Dad along with Dad's estranged father—my grandfather, whom I never even met. They were also the ones who killed Maksim's parents in the nineties.

Maksim and I had bonded over this common thread in our lives, but the same thread had formed a rift. Because now Vladimir, the man Maksim had thought was his uncle, the man who actually *was* my uncle, was hunting us down to the ends of the earth—partially because I had inherited my grandfather's estate, but mostly because he blamed me for Ștefan's death.

I hadn't meant for Ștefan to die—I had almost died, too—but Vladimir didn't care about the details. "He will never let this go," Maksim always reminded me. "In his eyes, you killed his son."

So money wasn't Vladimir's endgame. It was revenge, an eye for an eye. Hiding had been the only way Maksim and I could be together, but the pressure added one more complication to our relationship. Whenever things got hard, I had to remind myself...

There was a good reason for the additional stress and all these extra precautions. Maksim was taking things seriously. I needed to, as well.

The narrow street dumped us onto a larger road that curved around. Drought-tolerant evergreens, their leaves tiny and plump, filled the space on our left. Stucco homes in mustard yellow, brick red, and burnt orange spanned our right.

I followed Maksim to the far side of the hill. The street hooked left, and a galvanized barricade ran alongside a drop-off.

I paused and looked down. Dusty green blanketed the hill, nearly down to the seashore, while terracotta roofs peeked through the foliage.

A boat skimmed the distant waters, churning up foam and leaving behind a trail of white. My attention drifted to a bulk of dark clouds packed along the horizon.

Flick-flicker. The clouds brightened in sharp flashes, and a static charge hung in the air. My arm hairs rose to standing.

Heaviness, thick and uneasy, coagulated in the pit of my stomach. I held up my arm, staring at the staticky hairs, while a breeze that was far too cool kicked up.

The wind caught my hair and swirled it around. Shivers crawled through me.

"A storm is coming."

I spun around. Maksim stood two feet away, staring out at the water. His words echoed with a soberness that didn't match his bland expression.

"What did you say?"

"I checked the weather." He looked at me. "Forecast calls for rain later this morning."

My attention returned to the storm. The clouds were gray now, not so big. I waited for the flashes, but they never returned. Neither did that static charge.

My arm hairs lay perfectly flat.

"Come on." Maksim reached for my hand in a way that seemed mindless, like he was on autopilot.

He hesitated.

As my hand slipped toward his, he pulled away and started up the narrow street. My insides twisted. I wasn't imagining things. He'd become emotionally detached.

The road sloped down and carried us into something of a canyon—a small one—where a forest sprouted around us. The breeze stilled. The humidity thickened.

"I'm going to start my run." Maksim jammed an earbud into one ear. "I'll loop around and catch up."

"Sure." I offered up a weak smile. "See you in a few."

The path continued for four hundred yards before intersecting with the main road. Maksim jogged that direction, trees rising on either side of him.

I watched him become a speck of black and gray. He reached the road and turned left, heading toward town.

Eerie silence settled around me. Was it always this quiet? I couldn't say for sure. This was the first time I'd been down here without Maksim. Normally, we ran together.

Well, he jogged while I ran as fast as I could, trying to keep up. It was weird being down here by myself. Too weird.

I picked up the pace. My stomach churned, but I did my best to ignore it.

The gap between myself and the road shortened—little by little—until I reached the trailhead. "Finally," I said, hanging a left. I was on the road Maksim had taken.

He was nowhere to be seen.

I slowed my pace and started up the windy hill. My shoes

crunched over dirt, gravel. I was on the right side of the road, and a rock wall climbed beside me.

I was admiring a flowery vine when I realized someone was behind me. Not on foot, but in a car.

I scooted to the side and motioned for them to go around. They didn't. I crossed over the narrow road and motioned again. They had the entire right lane to themselves.

The driver pressed forward, passing me at a sloth's pace—and that was when I noticed how dark their windows were. I couldn't see the driver as the car rolled by.

I racked my brain, wondering what to do, when brake lights burned red. The driver stopped.

There was no way we'd been discovered, right? That couldn't be one of Vladimir's men?

My pulse stammered. I reached for my phone, intending to call Maksim. My hand found nothing but an empty pocket. Hadn't brought my phone.

I did an about-face and fast-walked in the opposite direction. My plan? Return to the trailhead and hide in the forest.

Wait. I couldn't do that. Shouldn't. Being in public was my best shot at survival. But there weren't any other cars, so this wasn't the most ideal of public places.

"It's a workday," I reminded myself. "Someone will be along any second."

But no one else came. And the next time I looked, the car was reversing toward me.

3. UNPLANNED PLANS

I rounded a bend. The car rounded the same bend.

I picked up speed. The car picked up speed.

"Dammit." My legs exploded in a run. The walking trail lay ahead and to the right. I angled for it.

Someone shouted. A honk followed.

I glanced, and my legs slowed to a jog. The driver was climbing out. He was Dad's age with salt-and-pepper hair and a medium build. He didn't strike me as the criminal-type, but that could have been exactly the way Vladimir had intended it.

I took up my defensive stance, hands out. "Stop! Back up!"

The man made a calming gesture. "I am a nurse. I work for a private clinic."

He wasn't wearing scrubs, which plunged me deeper into doubt. My gaze darted left and right. Still no other cars. "Wh-what do you want?"

"As I am driving, I see you, and I think you seem sick. You are very white. Pale," he amended, gesturing toward my face.

"I'm fine."

He started to say something else when another car appeared, then another. They followed the bend in the road, coming down the hill, and headed out of town.

I soaked in the rush of relief. Traffic was picking up.

The man jogged forward. We ended up three feet apart before I realized what was happening.

"Stop." I took up my defensive stance. "Back—"

"Please, *senyoreta*." He used the Catalan word for *miss* and held his phone toward me. "Call my clinic. They will confirm I speak the truth. The receptionist is Ginebra." He said the name *hee-NEH-brah*. "Because, really, I am concerned—"

"*What are you doing?*" Feet pounded the pavement. "Don't touch her!"

Black and gray flew from my left. Maksim slammed into the doctor. "Oof!" The man hit the pavement and rolled.

"Maksim, wait!"

"Go." He pushed me toward the trail. "There."

"H-he's a nurse. He thought I was sick."

Maksim returned to the man, who was scrambling to get up. A car cruised around the bend and skidded to a stop.

The nurse—supposed nurse—shouted. Maksim shouted back. The driver in the other car climbed out, cell phone in hand.

Oh, no. He was going to call the police.

"Can everyone wait a second? Please?" I raced over to Maksim and placed a calming hand on him. "Sir," I said to the nurse. "This is my boyfriend. He thought you were trying to hurt me."

The nurse glared.

"Everything's okay," I continued. "You were right that I'm sick. I-I need to go to our house—"

"Hotel." Maksim let a surly gaze fall on me. I wasn't supposed to tell anyone where we were really staying.

"Right. Hotel Catalina," I lied.

"I'll have the hotel doctor attend to her." Maksim wrapped an arm around me. "I apologize."

The nurse said something in Catalan.

"*Entenc,*" Maksim replied. "*Ho sento.*" Pretty sure that was an apology.

The man dusted himself off and returned to his car. The other driver kept glancing between us and his phone.

Maksim faked a friendly wave and then led me to the trail. "What happened? Tell me everything."

I gave him a rundown. "When he started backing up, I couldn't see inside the car. Seemed like he had blacked-out windows."

"Did he?" Maksim shot a look over his shoulder. "Were you even paying attention?"

"I was trying to." Tears plucked my eyes. "It all happened so fast."

"When you're captured, that will happen fast, too." He exhaled, rubbing his neck. "We're finished here."

"What do you mean?"

He didn't answer.

"Maksim?" I touched his arm. "What do you—"

He shrugged me off, and my feet went static. His gaze met mine, and I saw something I was deeply familiar with.

Regret. He regretted bringing me here. The epiphany filled me until a steady stream spilled over and dropped down my cheeks.

"I'm sorry," he said, reaching toward my shoulder. He hesitated. "Please don't cry. This isn't your fault. It's mine." He withdrew his touch, and the tears ramped up. "Kat, I thought I could turn you into something you're not. That's my fault, not yours." He scanned the area. "We should get to the house. We'll talk there."

He broke away and continued up the trail. He wasn't going especially fast, but he also wasn't waiting for me.

Yellow light penetrated the forest, casting a soft glow across his broad shoulders. Everything about him seemed tense.

I wiped my face and started after him. The rising sun must have cleared the hills by now, because my surroundings suddenly brightened... or was that just me?

The light collected into pinpricks all across my vision. The dots pulsed. The forest darkened, fading.

Blackness swallowed me.

"I ALREADY TOLD YOU. I'M FINE." I PARKED MYSELF IN A patio chair. The Mediterranean sun burned at midmorning, and I squinted against the blast of light.

"Then you won't mind having your vitals checked." Maksim stood, hand on hips, across the patio. His expression said *you're not getting out of this.*

I focused on the doctor. He was an older man—sixties, salt-n-pepper hair—and Maksim had convinced him to make a house call. The man had even brought one of those black leather bags.

"It's extra humid today," I said, "and I'm tired. That's all."

The doctor injected a smile into the awkwardness and knelt. "I must ask for privacy when I see a patient." He turned the smile toward Maksim.

"Of course. Excuse me." Maksim opened the French doors and slipped inside.

The doctor waited until the doors shut. "Are you normally so tired as you have been today?"

"Not usually, but I've been tired all week."

"Fatigued?"

I shrugged. "Sure. A little nauseated, too, come to think of it."

He donned his stethoscope and placed the bell to my chest, listening. When he seemed satisfied, he plucked out the earpieces and draped the instrument around his neck. "How long were you unconscious?"

"Not long. A second." Sixty seconds, actually. Maksim said I was out for about a minute.

The doctor dug through his bag. "And what part of Canada are you from?"

I stiffened. Maksim had told him I was Canadian? "Uh, Toronto. Thereabouts."

The doctor arched an eyebrow and sent a fleeting glance to the house. Maksim paced the living room.

"I'm going to ask you something," the doctor whispered. "Ethically, I'm required to ask this. Are you being kept here against your will?"

"No, sir. Not at all. Actually"—I slumped, propping an elbow on the table—"I get the feeling my boyfriend doesn't want me here anymore."

"I see. So he *is* your boyfriend? Not a friend as he told me over the phone?"

My mouth tumbled open. Maksim had called me his *friend*?

"Another question," the doctor said, "and forgive me if it seems intrusive. But is there any chance you may be pregnant?"

I snorted a laugh. He pointed a look at me.

"Sorry. It's just that—well—" My gaze traveled to the glass doors. Maksim had moved to the couch, elbows resting on his knees while he stared at his hands. We'd been in Begur for three weeks, and he'd been sleeping on the couch for most of that time.

Most. Not all.

Then there were the weeks before that—my outpatient recovery in Romania, the road trip across Europe. It'd been six weeks since the first time we'd ever...

"*Senyoreta?*" The doctor held me with an expectant look.

"It's definitely possible." My heart galloped. "You think that's why I fainted?"

"It could be why you've felt fatigued and nauseated. I suspect you fainted from overexertion. You'll want to lessen the exercising."

My insides sank, an anchor searching for rock bottom. "I'm supposed to start my period in a few days. I kind of feel like I'm going to start."

"You'll know soon enough." He stood. "Until then, I suggest a pregnancy test along with plenty of water and rest."

The French doors opened, and Maksim stepped through. "Everything all right?" His gaze traveled between the doctor and me.

"We were just finishing up," the doctor said.

"Thank you." Maksim extended an envelope stuffed full of euros. "For the house call."

The doctor said *gràcies*—Catalan for "thank you"—before making his way around the side of the house. The gate clanged, and a car motor whirred to life.

"Well?" Maksim stood in front of me. "What's the verdict?"

I might be pregnant. That was what I wanted to say. What I *should* say. Instead I said, "Twenty-four-hour bug. There's one going around."

"That's it?" His eyes narrowed. "Why haven't I been sick?"

"Better genetics? Luck?" I stood and squeezed past him. "I'm at the tail end of the virus. Probably why I'm feeling better."

Maksim drew me to a stop. "The doctor didn't say anything else?"

"Nuh-uh, no. Why?"

His brow dipped a degree more. "You're lying to me."

"I'm not." I reclaimed my arm. "He... Actually, he thought you might be holding me captive."

Maksim's skepticism lifted. He sighed and wiped a hand down his face. "I trust you put his mind at ease?"

"I did. But he was suspicious because our stories didn't match up." I fidgeted. "Is there a reason you called me your friend instead of your girlfriend?"

That made him pause. "Semantics," he finally said, stepping inside.

I followed him. "Okay, but—"

"I need to run to the supermarket before the rain hits. Are you well enough to deal with dinner?"

I blinked. "Huh?"

"What do we have? What do we need?" He said it more to himself as he headed for the kitchen.

"You're thinking about dinner? Already?"

"It's going to be an early one. We'll have to be finished by eighteen thirty at the latest."

Eighteen thirty was six-thirty p.m. Normally, we didn't eat dinner until eight or nine, sometimes ten.

"Fine by me." My gaze settled on the dirty dishes. Pots and pans littered the counter. "But why so early?"

"Kat, I'm going to Barçelona tonight."

My mouth dropped open. He was still going to Barçelona? An argument pressed forward. I was about to vocalize it when something occurred to me.

"I need time to prepare, plan my route." Maksim checked his phone. "That will tie up most of my day. If you could at least handle dinner—"

"I can." I stepped up. "I'll do the dishes, too. And go to the store."

He tilted his head. "You can manage all that?"

"Mm-hm, yep. Told ya I'm feeling better." In reality, I felt weak, tired, and a little bit nauseated—but the doctor had suggested a pregnancy test, and I could buy one at the store.

Maksim held me with a watchful gaze.

"Any, um, special requests?" I reached for the nearest pot. Meat sauce crusted the inside. "I could make another pasta dish."

"Make whatever you want, but be sure you visit the supermarket across town." He gave me a once-over. "Wear a hat. Keep to yourself. Don't draw any more attention."

"Are you really that worried?" I slid the pot closer to the sink. "You think that guy from earlier called the cops?"

"There's no way to know. We need to maintain a low profile until—" He stopped himself.

"Until what?"

His gaze connected with mine. His Adam's apple dipped.

I walked forward. "Until what?"

"This isn't working, *dragă*." His eyes skimmed over the room.

"These are dangerous waters, and you're not navigating them well."

"But—"

"Even if you were, we would have to leave, anyway. Because of what happened today."

"Leave... where?" Tension knotted in my throat. "You mean both of us?"

"Just you. It's time for you to go home."

4. STOW AWAY

The owner of the rental house was letting us rent his car, too. It was a Peugeot, and it was really nice—black, sleek, fast. The perfect getaway car, according to Maksim.

He wasn't planning to use it for that, but it was something he'd thought about. In case we were ever found. I assumed he was being overcautious, but now I wondered...

Could Vladimir find us? What would happen if he did?

I drove the Peugeot to the supermarket. There was another store closer, but Maksim preferred this one because it was always dead. Fewer people meant fewer potential problems.

The store's sign came into view. SUPERMARKET T.

I parked the car, hurried through the parking lot, and crossed over the quiet street. An old beggar woman sat on the front steps.

Her body moved slowly, her head coming around. She said something indiscernible and held out a shaky hand. I pulled out a five-euro banknote and passed it to her.

She called after me—probably saying thanks—but I didn't wave or smile like I normally did.

This is why you're going home.

My heart sank. It'd been twenty minutes since Maksim had

given me those instructions—simple, basic instructions about *not* drawing attention to myself—and already I wasn't following them.

Warm, stale air greeted me inside the store. Sweat beaded on my scalp.

I grabbed a red shopping basket and set it on the floor. These weren't buggies or carts, but more like plastic wagons that could be pulled through the store.

I rolled my basket toward the feminine hygiene products. Pads and tampons appeared on my left. Heat flooded my face as I reached the contraceptives.

The pregnancy tests were next to the condoms.

I snatched the nearest test. I didn't look at the price, nor did I bother to read the brand. Almost everything in the store was in Catalan. The rest was in Spanish.

"It'll be fine." I dropped the test into the basket. "I'll look up a video."

My knees trembled as I continued up the aisle. Needed to remember what was in the pasta sauce recipe, but all I could think was *pregnant.*

Pregnant pregnant pregnant.

Then another word flashed. *Home.*

Maksim wanted me to go home. That didn't necessarily mean we were breaking up—that I knew of—but the thought of being pregnant all the way in America, while Maksim was here in Europe, sent a crack straight through my heart.

Bright wigs and costumes and appeared on my left. Probably leftovers from a Catalonian festival. Barçelona was the nearest major city, and they had tons of events, some of which involved costumery.

The thought of Barçelona chilled my insides. Ivy—aka I.V.—was the hacker chick Maksim had tracked down when we first arrived in Spain. He'd said it was important—something about needing to use her system—but I noticed a shift in his behavior after that.

After going a second time—this was a few days after we came to Begur—I'd noticed a bigger, more dramatic shift. That was when he started sleeping on the couch.

You're imagining things.

You're insecure.

You're being paranoid. These were the things I'd been telling myself. But there was no mistaking his behavior now. He didn't want me here anymore.

Why?

I grabbed what I needed for pasta, garlic bread, and parmesan roasted broccoli, then headed for the checkout. A girl waited there. Her name tag read COLETA.

She gave me a once-over, as if searching for something.

Reusable bags, I realized. That sort of thing was encouraged in Europe. Highly encouraged—a.k.a. it would have been better to rob the old beggar woman than to not bring my own bags.

Crap.

Catalan was the main language in this part of Spain. Maksim had described it as a mix of French and Spanish, so it came easily for him. Not so much for me.

"*Bolsa plastica,*" I said, reverting to Spanish. *Plastica* was "plastic." *Bolsa* meant bag. That was the best anyone was getting out of me.

She punched in the cost. I rushed to bag my items, not daring to make eye contact, and all I could think was *Be discreet. Don't draw attention.*

As I left the store, carrying two grocery bags, an epiphany crash-landed on me. Maksim had said these were dangerous waters and that I wasn't navigating them well. Something like that.

The thing was, besides today, I'd been doing great. He said so himself. We had crossed the entire continent of Europe, mostly undetected, and I had even pulled off a disguise in Germany.

Something seriously changed after we arrived in Spain. *After* he'd gone to Ivy's. But what could have happened over there?

My insides skidded into the bottom of my stomach. *He cheated.*

"No." I shook my head. "He wouldn't do that." *Would he?*

"No," I repeated even though everything within me said otherwise. Ty had exhibited this same behavior—growing detached, distancing himself.

I thought back to January, to the way that relationship had ended. The nausea that had been swirling through me all morning returned.

I forced one foot in front of the other until I had crossed the parking lot. A tremor settled into my hands as I fumbled with the key fob.

The locks disengaged. The alarm deactivated.

My mind spun as I popped the trunk and loaded the groceries. I thought about Ty and all the horrible things I'd felt— before *and* after finding out he'd cheated. I felt the exact same way now.

My attention gravitated to a white object dangling in front of me. It was more of a milky white, actually, with hints of yellow.

The pull-lever attached to the trunk lid.

The color looked weird because it was glow-in-the-dark. If I was ever stuffed into the trunk of a car, I was supposed to look for that lever.

"Don't give the person time to escape onto a highway. You could be on the road for hours and never be able to jump out." Maksim's lesson rushed back. We'd gone over different scenarios, and he made me practice some of them.

That's right. I'd been inside this very trunk *while* the car had been moving. Crazy, I know, but I managed to pop the lever and jump out, and I'd done it without getting claustrophobic.

I bit down on my lip, teeth scraping the soft flesh. Something was up with that Ivy chick, and I had to know what it was. I had to know why Maksim was going over there, what was really going on.

Tonight might be my last chance.

I pivoted on my heel. The grocery store sat across the street, and as I stared at the bland gray building, the next part of my plan clicked into place.

The costumes. The wigs.

I closed the trunk lid and cut through the parking lot at a fast clip. A minute later, I was inside the store.

"THAT WAS AMAZING." MAKSIM WIPED HIS MOUTH. "You made that sauce from scratch?"

"Mm-hm. Brandy's dad is Italian, and he taught Brandy some of their family recipes. She taught me, so..." I propped an elbow on the table, using my palm as a chinrest. "What time ya leavin'?"

"Soon." Maksim pushed back from the table.

"Were you able to plan your route? Parking?"

He grabbed his phone. "I did."

"Cool." Time for my next set of questions. "So... how long would you say it's going to take this time?"

He sent a fleeting glance. "For which part?"

"Getting there. Coming back." I lifted a shoulder, blasé. "Barçelona is a straight shot down the coast—hour-and-a-half max—but when we came here, it took us three-and-half hours."

"I've mapped out better routes since then. I'll be in Barçelona in less than two hours."

Two hours wasn't terrible. I supposed.

He held me with a watchful gaze—so watchful, in fact, I wondered if I had said the last part out loud.

Had I? I didn't think so.

My pulse thrummed. "Something wrong?"

"Not particularly." He tilted his head. "But you never inquire about my routes."

"Oh, that." I feigned a laugh. "I'm asking because—well—" I stirred up the sweetest smile I could conjure. "I guess I was hoping you might be home early." I flitted a finger and placed it on his forearm. "Is that, you know, possible?" I drew a line while fluttering my lashes. "Maybe?"

His eyes just about popped out of his head. He stood up so fast his chair threatened to topple backwards. "Perhaps," he said, dropping his napkin on the plate.

As he turned, I wrinkled my nose and mouthed a sarcastic-but-silent "perhaps." Jerk.

He headed for the living room. I was a millisecond from entering phase two of my plan when he did an about-face. I drew back, surprised, as he stooped.

"I'm sorry I have to go." He planted a tender kiss on my cheek. "I wish I didn't have to."

Tears shimmied into my eyes. I clamped down on my emotions. *Focus, Kat. You have to focus.*

He gripped the key fob and strode for the front door.

"Maksim?" My voice threatened to crack. I squeezed a fist under the table, holding fast to my composure.

He turned on his heel. "Yes?"

"Since I'll be alone tonight—" I peered in the direction of the patio. My mouth was open, like I had more to say, but then I frowned. "Never mind."

"What is it?"

"I had a hard time locking the French doors. It's happened a couple times now. Felt like the latch was loose."

His eyes flashed toward the doors. "I haven't noticed."

"I usually don't, either... except these two times." I pushed up from the table. "It happened again today, and the idea of being here alone—" I pretended to shiver. "Would you mind checking them?"

Maksim pocketed the key fob. "I'll get the tools."

"Thanks. I know you're trying to hit the road." I followed him. "I'm exhausted after making that sauce. Had to chop and sauté onions, mince the garlic, make my own Italian seasoning..." I rattled everything off while he retrieved a toolbox the owner had left for us. "Anyway." I faked a yawn. "I'm beat. Going to lie down for a bit."

"Uh-huh." He sifted through the tools.

I walked away—but instead of going straight to the bedroom, I went to the living room and unplugged the dehumidifier. "Air's been moist since the rainstorm. Think this'll knock out the humidity?"

Maksim sent a fleeting look. "That's what it's for."

"Cool. I'll give it a shot." I hauled the dehumidifier into the bedroom, shut the door, and then eased the lock into place.

The latch groaned, but not so loud that Maksim would have heard. I hoped.

I plugged in the dehumidifier and turned it on. It hummed louder than a newer model would have—and that was exactly what I wanted.

After grabbing the spare key fob, which I had stashed in my room, I shouldered my backpack and pushed open one of the windows.

I slipped through and closed the pane behind me. Couldn't lock it from this side, but this was a pretty safe area. I hoped for the best, scooted between the hedges, and sprinted across the lawn.

The gate was the trickiest part.

My heart thundered as I lifted the latch. The hinges were usually noisy, and I hadn't been able to find a normal lubricant. Just olive oil. While Maksim had been planning his route earlier, I had snuck outside and greased the hinges.

It worked. The gate opened without groaning.

I eased it shut and raced to the car. Could have sworn I heard Maksim by the time I opened the trunk. I hopped inside and pulled the lid shut... except it didn't shut all the way.

"Dang it," I whispered.

Light seeped through the surrounding crack. I was about to tug again when footsteps approached. *Clang!* The metal gate slammed shut, and the footsteps drew closer. The lock on the driver's side door snapped.

It wasn't until that moment, that *very moment*, I wondered if Maksim could have a reason for opening the trunk. What if he'd brought a bag, something he didn't want out in the open, and decided to store it in here? How would I explain myself?

Before I could think of a solution, the footsteps came to a stop on the driver's side. The handle popped, but I failed to hear the next logical sound—his door opening.

Crap. Crap!

The footsteps rolled my way. I recognized the heavy tread of Maksim's boots, the way the chunky soles scraped the pavement.

I squeezed my eyes shut and prayed a silent prayer—a mix of I'm-sorrys and I-shouldn't-have-done-this confessions.

The trunk lid jammed shut. I blinked against the darkness. He must have noticed the trunk was ajar. Ugh, he probably thought I'd left it that way earlier.

The driver's side door opened. The car jostled, and the engine purred to life. Then we were moving.

BARÇELONA

5. SPECIAL DELIVERY

M y phone's backlight seared my eyes. I squinted, turning the screen brightness down, and checked the time.

8:16 PM

We'd been driving for a little less than two hours, and a burst of panic fluttered. I stilled it, thinking through this situation the way Maksim had taught me. Logically, without emotion.

First, I might've grossly underestimated how stuffy this trunk was going to be.

Second, Maksim was the expert at tailing people, not me. I had no idea how I was going to pull this off.

Third, if Maksim wasn't already planning to break up with me, he would if he caught me. I needed to prepare myself mentally.

That said, this wasn't the worst situation I'd ever been in. I could breathe—sort of—and I'd thought to bring water.

I groped for the plastic bottle. My fingers made contact, and the plastic crinkled.

I winced. Maksim hadn't turned on the radio this entire time, and I hoped really hard the whir of the engine was loud enough to mute any sounds I'd been making.

Slowly, cautiously, I lifted the bottle upright and unscrewed the lid. A couple of swigs later, I was carefully closing it.

The car veered right and then ground to a standstill. Then we were moving again. We turned... and turned... and turned. Felt like we were going in a circle.

Because we were. Catalonia had a lot of roundabouts, even more than I'd seen in Romania, and we were likely going through one.

I pressed a hand to the roof, trying not to slide around.

This same pattern repeated itself countless times. I was about ready to barf when we straightened out again and then stayed that way.

The car picked up speed and cruised. We had to be nearing Barçelona, right? After an hour and forty-five minutes of driving?

Sweat dripped from my hairline and slid down my face. Drops landed in my eyes, and I rushed to clear them. "Please, please get us where we're going," I whispered.

It wasn't exactly "your wish is my command," but fifteen minutes later, we slowed enough that I felt sure we were about to park. The sounds of the city, muffled by the trunk lid, hummed around me.

Maksim circled the block multiple times. At least, I assumed that's what he was doing. We would proceed forward, scooting through traffic, then hang a left and continue down the next street.

Then another left. Another. This went on for eighteen excruciating minutes.

Just park the damn car! The words burned within me, begging to come out.

Finally, a soft *tick-tick-tick* reached my ears. The turn signal.

The car reversed—slowly, at an angle—until we reached a stop. I made sure my phone was still on silent, slipped it into my backpack, and pulled out the wig.

I was stuffing my curls into the cap when Maksim killed the engine. I froze, listening past the other sounds—traffic whirring, some kind of bus or large truck motoring past, people speaking in Spanish.

Pop. That was the door handle popping open. The car jostled, and then...

Snap. Maksim was out of the car and had pushed the door shut.

Click. The locks engaged, and a quick *beep-beep* followed. The doors were officially locked. The alarm was armed.

I clutched the spare fob.

Maksim's boots scraped the pavement, moving away from the car until they blended with the other sounds. He was gone—or was he? Just because he'd walked away didn't mean he was out of view. Maybe he was on the sidewalk, checking for anything suspicious.

But why would he linger if he didn't want to be noticed? That was the point of all this—planning the route, choosing the right parking. He'd worked all day to ensure he wouldn't be noticed.

Plus, if I waited too long, I might not be able to find him. That would suck worse than the ride here.

I pressed the key fob, disarming the car. I could have punched the *trunk* button, as well, but instead I pulled the trunk release.

"Come on," I muttered, tugging harder.

The trunk popped. I held on to the string, ensuring the lid didn't lift too much or too quickly. That part was important. I mean, how many people would call the cops because they saw a girl jump out of a trunk?

At least a few. For me, that was a few too many.

Sunlight seeped through the tiny crack around me. I pushed the lid higher and peeked out. The nose of another car sat two feet away, and the sounds I'd been hearing roared to life.

"You can do this." I exhaled and pushed the lid all the way. Maksim had parallel-parked next to a row of restaurants. People traipsed up and down the sidewalk.

So far, nobody noticed me.

I swiveled around, bringing my butt to the opening, and slipped my feet out one at a time. I was lying on my stomach and did a pushup.

My legs slid out of the trunk. My body followed.

As soon as my shoes touched pavement, I shuffled my hands, like I was searching through the trunk rather than sliding out of it.

A quick side glance revealed a Spaniard, twenty-something, with a crinkled forehead. Thankfully, he continued up the sidewalk.

Maksim was nowhere to be seen—on this side of the street or the other—by the time I was ready. "Crap." I locked the car, shouldered my backpack, and moved up the sidewalk at a fast clip.

At the next cross street, I peeked around a stucco building. Some kind of wine shop. La Botiga Leezanne. Needed to remember that. I could always use the shop as a landmark for locating the car.

Sunset wasn't until 9:30, so there was plenty of daylight left. Unfortunately, it was getting close to the dinner hour, so there were also plenty of people.

I scanned the crowds.

Maksim was striding up the sidewalk at a steady pace. He had on a ball cap, something he never wore, but he stood a head taller than everyone else, which made him easy to spot.

"Speaking of cap." I reached into my backpack and pulled out a trucker's hat—something I'd found at a novelty shop in Begur —and pulled it down over the long, blond wig. It wasn't the most natural shade—pretty darn close to yellow, actually—but the other wigs had been bright red and orange.

My scalp baked under the layers.

I added my sunglasses—pink-tinted, so I could see after dark —and scurried after Maksim. Our training hadn't covered tailing someone, but I'd seen enough movies to know I needed to hang back.

Throngs of pedestrians hustled up and down the sidewalk. Maksim brushed past people at a bus stop.

Brring-brring! A delivery girl on a bike pedaled through the masses. Maksim stepped to the right and turned, doing a head-check as she cruised past. His gaze swung in my direction.

My pulse jumped.

I flung myself into the nearest shop. My running shoe caught on something—a step?—and I stumbled through the open doorway and careened into a rack.

Postcards flew. Magnets rained down. I skidded across the floor and landed in a heap mere inches from shot glasses and coffee mugs.

A woman dressed in a sari scampered over. She carried a stack of bags stamped with a round logo. Regalos de Kala. Gifts by Kala.

She dropped the bags and gasped.

"I am so sorry. Here, let me..." I swept my hand across the floor, gathering postcards and magnets, until I remembered Maksim.

Had he heard that? Worse, had he seen me?

"One second," I whispered, holding up a finger. Then I crawled across the shop and poked my head outside.

A familiar baseball cap stood head and shoulders above the crowd gathered at a crosswalk. The cap moved. He was scanning the area.

I pulled my head in. If he *had* seen me, surely he would have marched over and demanded to know what I was doing.

Right?

I poked my head out. The baseball cap moved farther away. He was continuing up the block.

I spun around, still on my hands and knees, and swept as many postcards and magnets into a pile as I could. Then I darted out of the souvenir shop and raced up the sidewalk.

Plenty of foot traffic moved between the baseball cap and me, and I was able to close the gap. But then the crowds grew sparse. The space between us cleared, and I was suddenly in plain view.

He paused at the corner, scanning like he'd done before. Shoot. Not again.

I spied a fancy restaurant with outdoor seating. DELICIOSO BY KAITEE & KELLY. I slid into an open seat on the patio. "Dammit," I muttered, checking for the baseball cap.

Still at the corner.

My surroundings grew awfully quiet. I glanced around. Everyone on the patio was staring, including the people whose table I'd joined. They sat across from me, heads tilted, eyes questioning. One of them said something about "mass tourism."

I smiled and held up a finger the way I'd done with the Indian woman. "Sorry. One sec."

Still hunched over, I pivoted in my seat and homed in on the baseball cap. It was moving now, but not in the direction it'd been going.

I straightened.

Maksim angled right, joining pedestrians as they crossed the main boulevard. Vehicles ground to a halt behind a red light.

I swore and raced to a crowded bus stop, doing my best to blend in. Maksim and the other pedestrians reached the other side as the traffic light splashed down to green.

The idling vehicles crawled forward.

No!

I sprinted to the crosswalk. The electronic box glowed red. *Do not cross.*

The pedestrians reached the other side and dispersed in different directions. Maksim hung a left.

"Now what?" I surveyed the situation. Cars, motorcycles, buses, and work trucks all motored through the intersection. There'd be no way to get across without inciting honks.

As I traced the baseball cap, a solution prickled my thoughts. Maksim was still going the same direction he'd been going before, just on the other side of the street. I could follow him from this side and cross over next chance I got.

I powered up the sidewalk, occasionally breaking into a run. He didn't look this way—and yet, somehow, he'd known to cross the street. How? Had he sensed me?

I shook off the worry and let my curiosity carry me up the sidewalk at a fast clip. The traffic light glowed red at an intersection. I slipped into a crowd of pedestrians and double-timed it across the boulevard.

Maksim was gone by the time I reached the other side.

"Ugh, come on." I broke into a jog, doing my best to squeeze through the foot traffic. Had he gone inside one of these businesses? Some of them were closed for the day, but the restaurants were open.

What if he was meeting that Ivy chick for dinner? They could be inside one of these restaurants now.

My attention swung to the nearest one. DoÑa Ludivina. Colorful garden lights glowed on the patio, and my stomach soured as I spied a couple sharing a meal and nuzzling each other.

Maksim could be doing that very thing with Ivy—cozying up over a candlelit meal, cuddling, kissing.

"Stop it," I muttered. "Just stop it."

I shoved the thoughts aside and paused at the next corner. This part of the city had sex shops, massage parlors, a dive bar.

Tension crept into my body. This looked like the seedy part of Barçelona, a neighborhood called El Raval. Maksim had brought me here when we first arrived in Spain. He'd left me in a dirty room in a sketchy hotel, and I'd heard everything imaginable—fights, crazy music, quite possibly a prostitution ring on the next floor.

The whole thing had left me traumatized.

He never said why he chose that place. I had assumed it was to keep a low profile, but that was also when he'd been trying to make contact with Ivy.

"She lives in El Raval," I whispered, backing myself against the nearest building.

A man and woman in Middle-Eastern robes walked past me and turned onto the next street. I swallowed and peeked around the corner. There, halfway down the block, Maksim stood on a set of steps in front of a building. He looked in my direction.

No. He was looking at the Muslim couple. He nodded to the man, saying what I imagined to be a polite greeting, while he held something attached to the building.

A door handle, I realized.

An electronic buzz cut through the quiet. Maksim pulled open the door and slipped inside.

The door was shut by the time I mustered the courage to draw closer. Grimy windows lined the front of the building. I peered up and gasped.

Maksim ascended a staircase that ran along the front of the building. I could see him through the windows. If he looked down, he'd see me, too.

I backed myself flush against the wall. His legs and feet stayed visible until he was about three stories up. Then he disappeared.

"Now what?" I took in my surroundings, trying to process, trying to think of a solution.

The Muslim couple had continued past the building. The man was on his phone while the woman carried a sack of groceries.

She peeked back at me.

Our eyes met, and her gaze traveled to the building. Worry glimmered in her eyes. Was it for me? Did she know the kinds of things that went on here?

The man called out to his wife. She faced forward and quickened her pace.

"*Permiso.*" *Excuse me.*

I whirled around to a blur of yellow jogging toward me. The voice belonged to a man carrying a cubed backpack, the kind used for food delivery, and he leaped up the cement steps Maksim had used.

He pressed something. A five-count ticked by before a garbled voice blared. *"¿Com va?"* What's up?

The delivery guy spouted off something in Catalan, and the electronic buzz followed.

He grabbed the handle and tugged, just like Maksim had, and the door swung open. This was my chance.

But what if someone saw me?

I surveyed the area. People traipsed up and down the narrow street. A car rolled past. Nobody seemed to be paying attention to me.

I sprang up the steps and thrust my hand into the opening. The door landed against my palm. My knuckles banged against the frame.

I winced, dragging the door open, and slipped through.

The delivery guy held up a receipt, checking something, and started for a set of stairs. There didn't appear to be an elevator.

I scooted past him and tiptoed up the staircase. Voices echoed from somewhere above. I rounded the third landing as the voices faded.

I ducked down and craned my neck, peering over the last few steps. A familiar form in a baseball cap disappeared into an apartment. The door snapped shut behind him.

That was Ivy's apartment. It had to be, but the voice I'd heard was male. Wasn't it? Had I misheard?

The last rays of sunlight spilled inside through grimy, front-facing windows. My pink-tinted glasses darkened everything around me, but I could still see, so I left them on.

Several doors lined the hallway on both sides. I strode past them, stopping short before I reached the one Maksim had entered. If there was a doorbell camera, I didn't want to activate it.

I slid up beside the door and listened. Techno pulsed from

inside the apartment. A laugh echoed, and it was definitely female. Could that be Ivy?

Movement drew my attention to the stairs. The delivery guy had cleared the last step and was entering the hallway. I tried to be casual, pulling my backpack around and pretending to dig through it.

He stopped in front of me, saying something in Catalan. I shook my head and shrugged that I didn't understand. He switched to Spanish and then nodded toward the door.

"You're here for *this* apartment?" I followed his stare. *"¿Comida para aquí?"* Food for here?

"Sí." He handed me the receipt, removed his cube-shaped backpack, and produced two pizza boxes. A big round logo marked each box. PIZZA MARIN.

He held the boxes and stared for a long, awkward moment. He was waiting for something. What?

"Oh, right. *Dinero?" Money?*

He nodded, and I reached into my backpack. My fingers detected the wad of euros I'd brought—emergency cash in case I lost Maksim and had to catch a taxi to Begur.

I counted out one hundred euros. That was a lot for two pizzas, but I hoped the generous tip would keep him quiet.

His eyes lit up. He asked zero questions and handed over the pizzas.

I waited until he was gone before I dared to turn toward the door. What should I do? Knock? That was what the delivery guy would have done.

A huge knot clogged my throat as I stepped forward. My heart punched out a fast rhythm, sending a burst of adrenaline into my extremities.

My legs trembled. My arms felt flimsy. I tightened my grip on the pizzas... and knocked.

6. DAMAGE CONTROL

Instant regret sloshed through me. My Spanish was terrible, and my Catalan was barely existent. What would I do when these people answered the door?

What if *Maksim* answered?

I didn't have time to process the thought before the door cracked open. A pair of suspicious brown eyes appeared.

The man said something I couldn't understand. Thankfully, the voice didn't belong to Maksim.

I angled the pizza boxes, showing him. He opened the door wider, checked both directions, and waved me in.

My pulse trilled. I couldn't believe this. I was actually going inside Ivy's apartment.

I squeezed through the door as best I could with my backpack and two large pizzas. The bottom box burned the fleshy underside of my forearm, and I winced.

He hurried to shut the door, and darkness thickened around me. I was standing inside an enclosed entryway, and I could barely see anything through these glasses.

I was about to pull them off when a sickening sound made my stomach squeeze. *Click.* I twisted around. The guy had locked the door.

He slid past me, saying something in Catalan. All I caught was *diners en efectiu*. I recognized this phrase, only because I'd heard Maksim say it so many times.

It meant cash.

"Don't panic," I whispered to myself. "He's just paying for the pizzas."

Techno pulsed somewhere off to the right. I inched forward, pulled my sunglasses down, and peeked around the corner.

The living room—what might have once been a living room—was filled with computer desks and high-definition monitors, some of them freestanding, others mounted to the wall. Thick blackout curtains covered the windows.

Blinking lights drew my attention across the room. A rack of CPUs towered in the corner.

A girl with choppy, bleached-out hair sat with her feet kicked up while she handled a game controller. Wires poked out from a cracked-open Wi-Fi router on her desk. A piercing hung from her septum, and spikes poked out from her ears.

Three monitors displayed a video game I recognized from when I'd dated Ty. It was first-person shooter, futuristic, about a criminal who'd been hired to find a missing girl.

The game played across the sleek, sharp monitors. Shouts and gunfire roared through speakers.

A huge TV hung above her and displayed several video feeds. One recorded the main entrance. Others pointed at the stairs. Yet another revealed the hallway.

I cringed. These people had every opportunity to see me *and* the real delivery guy, but they hadn't.

A familiar voice reached my ears.

My attention drifted over an array of takeout bags, chips, and soda bottles before settling on Maksim. He wore a gaming headset over his baseball cap. Six monitors—three rows, stacked in pairs—occupied the space in front of him.

I tilted my ear. He wasn't speaking in Romanian. Was that Russian?

"Hey, Yuriy!" A guy with an afro walked past the entryway.

I drew back. Had he seen me? I didn't think so, but I stayed still as he ambled into the living room.

Maksim must have been wearing noise-canceling headphones, because the guy walked right up behind him and brought a hand down on his shoulder.

Maksim jerked, whipping around.

"Come on, Yuriy. We doing this thing or not?" The guy spoke with a Slavic accent, but something about it sounded... forced. Was he faking it?

He laughed and play-punched Maksim's arm. Maksim waved him off. The guy stepped away, and I caught a glimpse of Maksim's profile. He smiled, shaking his head, while speaking into a microphone attached to the headset.

The space between my ribs clenched. If Maksim was here on business—supposedly—why was he messing around? And why was that guy calling him Yuriy?

"Bufar i fer ampolles." The guy who'd answered the door rounded the corner.

I jumped, startled. He'd said something about blowing and making bubbles—a Catalonian phrase for "easy peasy"—but I had no idea how to answer in his language.

He held a stack of cash and said something else I didn't catch. I shrugged, and confusion glimmered in his eyes. He asked a question.

No no no.

I cleared my throat and held out my hand. The guy's gaze flicked between me and the pizzas.

"Bloody 'ell, Strike. Quit faffing around, you wanker." An overhead light blinked on, and the girl who'd been playing video games appeared.

Was she Ivy?

"Where's the food?" Her eyes zeroed in on me, then on Strike's cash. "Whuz this? Pay the bloody bill."

"I ask her how much. She does not answer."

Ivy's razor-thin eyebrows converged. She aimed a suspicious look at me and said something in British-laced Catalan. She switched to Spanish.

I fumbled with the receipt, and a brand-new reason to panic made itself known. The delivery guy's name emblazoned the top of the paper.

CRISTIANO

If anyone saw that, I was done. Also, the total read 34,40€, and I could not, for the life of me, remember how to say that in Spanish.

"*Trenta y quatro y—cincuenta?* Uh... *cuarenta.*" I kept my voice low and inflected my very best accent. I even squinted, like the receipt was hard to read.

Ivy snatched the pizzas, shoved them at Strike, and pointed a look that drove like a hot spear. Her attention shifted to my yellow hair, and her pencil-thin eyebrows lifted. "Why the 'ell are you wearin' a wig?"

A jolt of panic struck. Without thinking, without using a single ounce of logic, I spun around and fumbled for the lock.

Shouts went up. Hands grabbed me.

"Thought you could get away, did ya?" Ivy stripped my backpack and tossed it to Strike. He checked the compartments while Ivy snatched the trucker hat and wig.

Sweaty, frizzy curls tumbled out.

"Who are ya? A bobbie?" She dropped the items. "Who came in wit' ya?"

"N-no one." Tears plucked my eyes. "Please. I'm by myself."

Ivy's face grew tall and wide as I spoke. "She's bloody American." Her attention swung to Strike. "The Feds."

Strike called out in Catalan.

The guy with the 'fro appeared. He took one look at me and grabbed his head. "HCF!" He cupped his mouth. "H! C! F! *Ara! Ara!*" I didn't know what HCF meant, but *ara* meant "now."

Another guy lumbered into the hall, struggling to button his pants. "Bloody hell," he said in an accent that was cleaner and posher than Ivy's. His gaze shot to me as he donned a pair of spectacles. "Who is she?" He turned to Ivy. "Are you taking the piss out of me?"

"This *ain't* a joke, you faff." Ivy grabbed his shirt and reeled him in. He stumbled forward. "Tie her up. Make bloody sure she can't scream."

"All right, all right." He raised his hands. "No need to get your knickers in a twist, mate."

Ivy dashed for the living room while Strike and the Brit dragged me through the hallway... past the dining room... past the kitchen...

I kicked. I squirmed. I yanked my arms. They held on until we reached a door. Strike pushed it open, and someone gasped.

A brunette stood at the foot of a bed, pulling her pants on. She rushed to throw on a shirt and squeezed past us.

"Wait!" I said.

She didn't look back as Strike and the Brit dragged me into the shadowy room. Bile rose in my throat. I hadn't wanted to implicate Maksim in this horribly executed plan, but there was no chance of avoiding that now. My phone was in my backpack. As soon as they found that, they'd see our message thread, all our pics and videos.

The guys angled for the bed. I screamed, louder than I'd screamed in a long time, possibly since that time I'd jumped the roof-gap in Bucharest.

"*Maksiiiiim!*" I kicked. "*Maksiiiiim!*"

The guys lifted me.

A tall form in a baseball cap appeared in the doorway

"Here!" Tears rushed. "Maksim!"

He beelined.

The Brit held him off. "We've got it, mate."

Maksim grabbed the guy's forearm. "Put her down, Tom."

"Mate—"

"Put her down! Now!"

The guys shared a look and dropped me.

Maksim helped me up and led me out of the room. We reached the kitchen when he suddenly perked up, listening. His eyes bulged. "Ivy! Ivy, no!" He broke away and raced into the living room.

Commotion stemmed from that direction—metal clanking, a drill spinning, pops and fizzles cracking.

The noises stopped.

Maksim spoke in a low, rushed voice. I couldn't hear what he said until the end. "... my girlfriend." And then "Ivy, I'm sorry."

"WHAT THE BLOODY 'ELL?"

7. NEW PLAN

Maksim stood on the sidewalk outside Ivy's apartment. I hurried down the cement steps. We'd been escorted out by the Brit, Tom, and the guy with the 'fro. Ivy watched from the windows that ran along the front of the building.

"I'm sorry," I whispered, joining Maksim. "I know this is bad—"

"It will take between sixteen and eighteen minutes to reach the car." He held me with a stony look. "You have until then to explain what the hell you're doing here and how you followed me."

He strode up the sidewalk. I managed to keep up—barely—and tried to organize my thoughts. Every explanation that came to mind sounded like a pathetic excuse.

Probably because they were. What was I thinking?

The hum of traffic greeted us outside El Raval. Heat rolled off the vehicles, forming a plume of warmth over the concrete. Fumes burned my nostrils.

Maksim checked his phone. "Twelve minutes," he said, leading me up the crowded sidewalk.

Dang it.

"I... sort of stowed away. In the trunk." I cringed. "Of the Peugeot."

Maksim's eyes went round. He hesitated, attention returning. "You rode in the *trunk*? *All the way from Begur*?"

I hugged myself and nodded.

"*Why*?"

"I thought— I-I wasn't sure if—" My gaze fell. "Guess I don't have much of an answer for you." That wasn't true. I did have an answer. Several, actually.

I thought you were hiding something.

I thought you were cheating on me.

I might be pregnant. This last thought came as a whisper that brushed across my frazzled mind. I shoved it away and hugged myself tighter.

As we walked, I noticed we were going a different way than we'd gone earlier—yet another part of Maksim's planning. He never took the same route twice. Not when driving. Not even when coming from or going to the car.

"So that's it?" He stopped at a crosswalk, and I stopped beside him. "You stowed away in the trunk for two hours, disguised yourself as a delivery person, and followed me to Ivy's because... nothing?"

My emotions swelled. I averted my gaze.

He guffawed. "Fine. Fine! Don't bother to explain, then."

"You don't explain anything to me." I met his gaze. "You set up a double VPN at the guesthouse, something that keeps me safe, but then *you* have to come to Ivy's to use *her* system. It doesn't make sense."

"That's what this is about?" His expression hardened. "You did all this because you needed to understand why I'm using Ivy's system?"

"I needed to understand what you were doing there, okay?" My voice cracked. "I'm always in the dark, and I don't like it."

"Then please. Allow me to enlighten you." He tugged on the bill of his cap, pulling it low. "Tonight I was on a call with an old associate, someone I know is being monitored by Vladimir. Ivy has her own VoIP. Do you know what that is?"

I blinked.

"Voice over Internet Protocol. She has a VoIP service running backdoor into a telecom network in Ukraine. Whenever I call Daniel—or anyone—from her system, it *looks* like I'm in Kyiv. Do you know how much I've been paying Ivy for this? Can you guess?"

I shook my head.

"Tens of thousands per hour. I am *hemorrhaging* money every time I come here. I don't do it for fun."

My mouth fell open. "Why didn't you say something? You know I have money."

"You have no access to your money—not easily—and we would have blown through the twenty grand you have. Those funds are better left as emergency cash."

"What's going to happen?"

Maksim went silent. His eyes clung to worry.

"What?" I said.

"Ivy is blackmailing me."

"*What?*"

People dining on a patio turned around. Maksim nodded politely and motioned for me to come on.

"What does Ivy want?" I asked, striding to keep up. "Money?"

"Yes. A lot."

"And if you don't pay?"

"She's going to out us to Vladimir."

A pebble wedged in my throat. "I heard y'all talking about a type of currency. You said something about transferring it from your wallet."

"It's a crypto wallet. I have to pay in cryptocurrency." He pushed out a sigh. "I promised her more than I have access to at the moment"—he let a sideways stare fall on me—"to pay for everyone's silence *and* the damages to her system."

The drilling. The popping. Ivy had started destroying her own stuff, thinking she'd been busted.

"Would the emergency cash buy us some time?"

"I doubt it. It's a fraction of what I need." Maksim wiped a hand down his face. "Do me a favor and don't try to figure this one out." His sarcasm socked me in the gut.

Traffic ground to a halt in front of us. The crosswalk changed, and everyone filtered into the white stripes.

I lagged behind, feet heavy. I'd always thought rich people had a bank account with their millions—or billions—easily accessible. That wasn't the case, apparently.

I'd spent an entire day at Kopernikus-Bank, signing papers and listening to Mr. Amsel talk about securities, stocks, bonds, commodities. Everything carried some level of risk, which was why I needed to "diversify my portfolio" to meet my financial goals.

But I didn't have financial goals. I didn't even know what that meant. So I'd given Mr. Amsel free rein to invest the funds as he saw fit. "Whatever's safest," I'd said, "with the lowest risk."

He'd been elated, assuming my goal was long-term growth. What I hadn't realized was that the money was no longer liquid and gaining access would practically require an edict.

Maksim waited for me at the next corner.

"What's the plan?" I caught up to him. "If I don't have access to my money and you don't have enough, how do we pay her?"

"We don't." Maksim yanked off his cap and raked furiously at his hair. "We're leaving. First thing in the morning."

My heart sank. "Where are we going?"

"France. Probably Nice." He said it *nees*. "I need to think this through a bit more, but Nice makes the most sense."

"Why? What's the plan?" I figured he must have a contact there, a safe deposit box. Something.

"Côte d'Azur International Airport."

I blinked. "Huh?"

"They have direct flights to the United States, and you'll be on one tomorrow."

BEGUR

8. SILENT GOODBYE

Maksim's plan sucked.

There were direct flights, just like he said, and I knew he could get me to Nice safely. But I wasn't sure if *he'd* be safe. That was the problem.

Well, it wasn't a problem anymore. Or wouldn't be soon.

"Kat. Hey." The curtain rings scraped, and my mattress sank. I wrapped myself tighter in the comforter. "Are you packed?"

"Mm-hm." I inhaled a deep breath, pretending to wake up. "What time is it?"

"Four ten. Coffee is ready, and I've packed cheese and fruit. We won't be able to stop for food."

My center tightened. He'd gassed up the car last night so we wouldn't have to stop for that, either. The only reason we hadn't left was because he needed three hours of sleep before such a long driving day.

Thankfully, it wouldn't be that long after all. He just didn't know it yet.

"Are you, um, going to shower before we leave?" My entire being tensed. I needed him to take a shower. My plan wouldn't work otherwise.

Yellow light doused me. I blinked.

Maksim straightened, pulling his hand away from the lamp. The light revealed he was still in his sleep clothes with a towel slung over one shoulder. "Going now. I won't be long."

He walked out of the room and pulled the door shut. A moment later, the shower turned on.

I launched out of bed. Maksim took a shower every morning, even if he'd taken one the night before. Thankfully, he hadn't strayed from his routine.

I was already dressed and grabbed my purse, which had been stationed by my suitcase and backpack. I tugged on the zipper and yanked out the letter I'd written a mere ten minutes ago.

My emotions swelled to bursting.

M,

> *Please don't be mad at me. I know you have your reasons for wanting me to fly out of Nice, and I'm sure your plan is the best—I know it's the best for me—but it's not practical or safe for you.*
>
> *That's why I'm doing this. I can't let you put your life at risk (again).*
>
> *I'm taking the Peugeot so you can't follow me. It'll be in the long-term parking at El Prat.*
>
> *You're welcome to go get the car and return it to Begur, but I think you should leave it there, message the owner, and tell him an emergency came up and that we had to leave right away (it's not a lie).*
>
> *I want you to stay safe and get out of Spain as fast as possible. "Don't return to a place that could be compromised." This is one of the things you've taught me, and now I'm saying it back to you.*

Leave the car at El Prat. Don't come back to Begur.

I've taken enough cash to cover the long-term parking plus a little extra for getting home. The rest is yours. I'll pay you back for everything else, including what you paid Ivy, as soon as I can.

I'm so sorry.

K

Maksim was planning to drive me to Nice, take me to the airport, and then come back here—to Begur—to return the Peugeot. That last part was critical; otherwise the vehicle would be reported as stolen.

I'd be home by then, but Maksim would still be in Europe, and he couldn't risk being wanted for grand theft auto. Understandable, right? But there was a big problem—even if he didn't stop, even if he sped and took the quickest route, he wasn't getting back here before five p.m.

The thing was, Ivy planned to contact Vladimir at the end of the business day. Right about the time Maksim would be returning.

"Can't we rent a car?" I had asked. *"Leave the Peugeot here?"*

"Too risky, and we'd have to wait until midmorning when the rental agencies open. It's better for us to leave early."

"Better for us? Or better for me?"

He hadn't answered my question, but I knew he wasn't thinking of his own safety. He was thinking of mine.

Speaking of which...

"Shoot," I whispered, reaching for my pen. I'd almost forgotten the most important part of the letter, something I hoped might give Maksim some assurance.

I scribbled a postscript.

P.S. I did everything you taught me when I booked my ticket: used the double VPN, booked the earliest flight out, and I'll be going direct from Barçelona to New York (I'll book my Atlanta flight after I get there).

Oh, and I bought the ticket right before you came in here this morning, so there's basically no risk time-wise.

I'll be okay. You don't have to worry.

I left the letter and cash on my bed, situated my purse and backpack, and then wheeled my suitcase out of the bedroom. My ears tuned in to the running water.

Maksim had been in the shower for about five minutes. Which meant I had five minutes to be gone.

Two small tumblers of coffee sat on the kitchen counter. I grabbed the one with milk and headed for the front door.

As I rolled my suitcase outside, my gaze returned to the house and lingered. I recalled the first time he'd brought me here, the times we'd cooked dinner together, that one time we'd danced in the kitchen without any music.

The memories flowed like a flash flood. My chest tightened until a sharp pain splintered my heart...

———

"Do you need help?"

Maksim's voice pulled me out of my daze. I looked up from the potatoes I'd been washing. "Hmm?"

"Would you like some help?" He nodded toward the sink. The

already-diced potatoes sat in a colander while a stream of water flowed over them. "They've been in there for a while."

"Oh." I turned off the water. "Guess I wasn't paying attention."

He ambled forward and propped himself against the counter, arms folded. Silence eased into the conversation, beckoning one of us to speak.

I took it up on the offer.

"I really liked the food we had at that little tapas place, so I looked up a few recipes. The potatoes are for, um..." I was turning toward the stove, expecting to find a pan with hot oil.

The stove was off. The oil and pan sat cool.

Maksim came alongside me.

I peered up at him. "Sooo, the patatas bravas *are going to be a little late, but the sauce is ready." I opened the fridge. "Made it this afternoon. Plus we have some of that ham and gazpacho stuff." I pulled out the sauce and soup and set everything on the counter. The glass bowls clanked. "Ugh, and I cut the potatoes before realizing I hadn't washed them, so—"*

Maksim's hand settled on mine. My cheeks warmed as he held me with a steady gaze.

"What?" I said, fighting a smile.

"Do you like this place?"

"Begur? Or you mean this house or...?"

"All of it."

"I love it." The smile shined through. "Everything's... great. Perfect, actually." It was true. We'd been here two days, and Begur had already grown on me—the hills, the beach, all the little back alleys around the old town.

Maksim's eyes turned thoughtful. He angled his head, as if listening for something. "Do you hear that?"

My smile fell away. I went rigid, listening for a siren or gunshots, an intruder breaking in. "What are we—?"

He placed a finger to his lips and then pointed up, indicating I should keep listening.

"*Is it outside?*" I brushed past him. "*I'm going to make sure the doors are locked.*"

He intercepted me and pulled me around. One of his hands slipped into mine, the other slid around my waist, and he drew me close until we were pressed together.

I pulled a soft breath, thinking he was about to kiss me—but then he lifted my hand into dance position and began to sway. I was so surprised I didn't know what to do.

Then I found myself swaying, too. He turned, and I turned with him. He twirled me around, and I let him. Eventually, we danced our way across the kitchen.

"*Do you hear music coming from somewhere?*" I tilted my head. "*Because I still don't hear anything.*"

"*Not music, no.*" His lips quirked. "*It's the distinct sound of... peace. Tranquility.*" He rocked back a step and spun me around. "*Serenity.*"

His answer came out sing-songy, and I laughed. "*Serenity. You mean, being on the run and hiding from a crime syndicate?*"

"*I mean*"—he drew me along—"*no longer having to be Ștefan's muscle. Not having to collect on the debts owed to him. Not having to manage his massage parlors and nightclubs.*"

"*Ah.*" My mouth lifted at the corners. "*I think I hear it, too, actually.*"

"*Oh?*"

"*M-hm.*" I placed a finger to one of his thick, black eyebrows and traced it. "*Does it sound like being able to talk about my dad without having an emotional breakdown?*"

His smile widened. "*It could.*"

"*Like no more freaking out that I can never afford college?*"

"*How about... no more freaking out because I'm no longer smuggling drugs and weapons across borders.*" He laughed. "*No more of that. Thank God.*"

"*No more being angry at my mom.*" I traced a line down his strong nose and along the groove of his cupid's bow. "*Mostly.*"

"*For me, ultimately, it sounds like one day being free*"—his hold *tightened—"and having a new life with those I care about most, those I..."*

I lowered my hand. "Those you what?"

He turned in a slow spin and brought me with him. "Those I care about most."

"You already said that." My brow dipped. "Were you going to say lo—?"

He crushed his mouth to mine.

My thoughts evaporated as he cupped my face. I tangled my fingers in his shirt, his hair...

THE DAM BROKE, AND THE FLOODWATERS SPILLED over. I was never coming back to this place. Worse, I might never see Maksim again.

I pulled the door shut, forcing myself to leave behind the memory, and carried my suitcase down the colorful steps one final time.

EL PRAT

9. TOOT SWEET

My eyes stung by the time I rolled my suitcase out of the parking garage at El Prat. A yellow shuttle bus idled at the end of a walkway. The door stayed open while people smoked beside the vehicle.

I passed through a cloud of smoke, and a memory from Romania surfaced. It was from the night Maksim and I had gone looking for Andrei. That club had been smoky as hell, and the memory played in vivid streams.

I'd been hurt on the way to the club, and Maksim had taken care of me. He'd been gentle, sweet, kind, even funny. I hadn't been expecting that, and as he'd gone to kiss me, I'd pulled away.

Funny how things had changed. I longed for Maksim to kiss me, to hold me, and now *he* was the one pulling away.

"Doesn't matter anymore." I rubbed out the moisture on my cheeks. All I had to do was get home, then things could go back to normal.

People boarded the shuttle, including the driver. He closed the door and said something in Catalan, then Spanish.

Everyone took their seats.

Dawn shimmered over the horizon, and the Catalonian mountains formed a rocky backdrop against the city. We cruised past palm trees and parking lots until we reached the sleek, glass airport.

Soft curves and a shiny, sloping rooftop welcomed us. Vehicles idled outside the terminal. Passengers poured out of a tour bus.

Our driver used a special lane and parked behind another shuttle. I scanned, searching for signs of anything unusual. There was no way Vladimir could reach me in time, given that I booked the flight two hours ago—less than that—but Maksim's sense of caution had been rubbing off on me.

A man rolled his suitcase through the crosswalk and headed for a revolving door.

A woman climbed out of a black and yellow car—standard taxis in Barçelona.

The tour bus drove away, revealing a crowd of tourists.

I kept scanning. Nothing appeared to be out of place.

"See? You're fine," I whispered while passengers exited the shuttle.

I stood. This was a public place—arguably the safest, most secure in the world. An international airport. So why did I feel nervous?

I rolled my suitcase to the door and stepped off. Then I made my way across the drop-off lanes, through the crosswalk, and to the revolving doors.

Suitcases skimmed the shiny floors inside El Prat. Passengers moved through the terminal—some walking, some running. Lots of people stood around, checking their phones.

Signs directed passengers to *Facturacio* and *Portes d'Embarcament*. *Check-In* and *Boarding Gates*.

Bright blue drew my attention. The passengers from my shuttle were gravitating to digital boards. I joined them, checking for my flight.

New York JFK | Departure 08.55 | ON-TIME

The sign listed kiosks 725 to 750 for check-in. I followed the arrows and quickly came upon the familiar US-based airline.

"That was easy." I'd been worried about navigating this massive airport by myself. So far, so good.

I rolled my suitcase into the roped-off section. Five minutes later, a check-in agent called me forward.

"Hello," she said through a mild accent. "Passport and boarding pass, please."

I set my passport on the counter. "Not sure about the boarding pass." I dug out my phone. "Might be in my email."

"It's okay. I will use your passport." She opened the leather document and placed it on a scanner. A green light glowed. "Flying to John F. Kennedy International in New York?"

"That's the one."

She returned my passport, and I stuffed it in my purse. I was about to do the same with my phone when I thought of Maksim.

I gnawed my lip. Surely, he'd found my note. Why hadn't he messaged? Was he angry? Sad? Maybe he was glad to be rid of me.

I shook off the thought. Even if he was, I should let him know I had arrived safely. That was the least I could—

As I woke up my phone, my stomach bottomed out. I had a bunch of notifications—texts *and* calls—and they were all from him. How had I not heard these?

"You are checking only one bag?" The woman's voice startled me.

I looked up from my phone. "Uh... sorry. Yes, that's right."

She pressed a key, and her expression turned quizzical. "There is an issue with your boarding pass." She typed a series of keystrokes. The computer beeped, and her expression fell a shade more blank.

"What's wrong?"

"I have not seen this message before." She picked up her phone. "One moment while I call my supervisor."

My stomach sank. What message had she gotten? And what could possibly be wrong with my boarding pass?

"Katherine Barrett?"

I turned and discovered three men, all in dark sunglasses, approaching. They wore a mix of slacks, khakis, and jeans, but they all had the same gun holsters. Their shirts strained against bulky arms and broad chests.

The men surrounded me.

"Are you Katherine 'Kat' Barrett?" one of them asked. He didn't sound Spanish or Catalan, and his towering frame indicated he might have been German or Nordic.

Or Russian?

10. INTELLIGENCE SERVICE

"We know it's you, Miss Barrett." The man hooked a thick hand around my elbow. His accent rang Slavic. "You need to come with us."

"N-no." I turned to the check-in agent. "Call the police. These men are human traffickers."

The woman gasped, phone still in her hand. She started dialing.

"We are Interpol." One of the men flashed credentials. "This young woman is wanted for questioning in Romania. Local police are aware of the situation." He gestured at someone standing nearby.

This fourth man wore black slacks, a matching cap, and a gray and black shirt. His sleeve read GUARDIA CIVIL. Those were the municipal police here in Barçelona. How was that possible?

It couldn't be. These men worked for Vladimir. The cop had to be dirty, or he was a criminal who'd stolen a uniform.

I focused on the check-in agent. "Please. I'm telling you. These men are trying to kidnap me. I've been hiding from them—"

"You have been hiding, Miss Barrett, but we have found you." The man dragged me away from the clerk.

"Please." I looked back at her. "I'm the heiress to a fortune. These men want to kill me and steal my money. You can't let them take me. Please!"

The cop stepped up to the counter and said something in Catalan. The woman split a horrified look between him and me—and then she lowered the receiver.

"Don't listen to him! Just call the police!"

A hush fell over the terminal. Whispers circled. Passengers, airport staff—everyone watched as the men dragged me outside.

The four of us couldn't fit inside the revolving door, so two of the men hung back while the third escorted me through. This was my chance.

I shoved the man. He hit the glass but didn't let go.

I twisted around, trying to break his hold. He twisted me the other way and wrestled my arm into submission. My shoulder strained as he shoved me forward.

The side of my face slammed against the glass. Pain bloomed in my cheekbone as the revolving door opened to the outside world.

The other men appeared. One of them ran toward a black SUV parked at the curb. The other helped restrain me.

"Help!" I made eye contact with a passenger. "They're kidnapping me! Call the police!"

The man's expression grew tall and wide. He had his cell phone out and woke up the screen.

Another Guardia Civil walked forward, saying something in Catalan.

"He's not a cop. None of these men are cops!" Tears jumped out of my eyes.

The men hauled me to the SUV and shoved me into the backseat.

One of the Russians climbed in after me, and the door snapped shut. Panic jolted me. I was in the second location.

I clamored across the backseat and popped the handle. The

door opened, but one of the other men waited on the other side. He smirked, reaching for his pistol.

"Hey!"

The man turned toward a passenger, who was rolling his suitcase this way. The guy broke into a sprint. The suitcase lifted.

"*Oof!*"

The passenger used his suitcase as a battering ram. The Russian slammed against the open door. His pistol clattered to the pavement.

The passenger swiped up the weapon and fired twice. The Russian grunted and collapsed. Shouts went up. People in the shuttle area scrambled for cover.

The passenger appeared in the open door. But it wasn't a passenger. It was Maksim.

An arm hooked me from behind. I grappled with the man as cold steel pressed against my temple.

Maksim whipped the gun toward us. "Duck."

My eyes widened. I leaned left, as far as I could, and a single shot fired. I squeezed my eyes shut.

Thump.

Warm liquid splattered my neck and ears. Dead weight slumped against me. I screamed as the man's pistol tumbled onto the floorboard.

"Grab it." Maksim nodded toward the gun. I rushed to pick it up.

I scooted across the backseat. As my feet touched pavement, a dizzy spell hit. I fell against Maksim.

He held me up. "I need you to walk. Come on."

I peered up at him. He was wearing an undershirt, his scars exposed, with wrinkled jeans and running shoes that hadn't been laced. His eyes were red and puffy. His hair was wild.

He held his attention on something behind me. The third man stood ten feet away, hands raised.

Maksim had the pistol trained on him. "On the ground. Now."

The man's jaw clenched. He reached for his holster.

Maksim fired. The round landed between the man's chest and armpit. He howled, collapsing to his knees.

Maksim fired again. The round landed in the same spot, opposite side, and blood poured. The man's arms fell limp.

Maksim walked forward, pistol steady. "You have a choice— get yourself to a hospital before you bleed out, or come after us and end up like your friends."

The man gritted his teeth, blood pouring down his arms and into his palms. Red dripped onto the pavement.

Maksim backed up, drawing me with him. Suddenly, he whipped the pistol toward someone.

One of the Guardia Civil. Maksim barked in Spanish, and the man raised both hands.

"Do you see this taxi behind me?"

I peered around Maksim. A black and yellow taxi idled at the curb. The driver's side door was open. No sign of the driver.

An unmanned motorcycle sat behind the cab. Everyone must have taken cover.

I focused on Maksim. "I see it."

"That's where we're going." He let me go. "Get in. Hurry."

I hobbled to the taxi and climbed in. My body was halfway into the passenger side when Maksim dropped into the driver's seat.

"Seatbelt." He yanked the door shut and punched the gas. The tires screeched, smoking.

He whipped the steering wheel, swerving around the SUV.

"I-I think they were Russian." I tugged on the seatbelt. "They sounded Slavic."

"They're SVR—Russian Foreign Intelligence Service." He yanked his seatbelt across him. "We don't have much time. Tell me everything that happened."

"Th-they had me—" My pulse sped up. My breathing turned ragged. "Maksim, they had me in the s-second location."

"Kat, I need you to calm down." He pressed a button on his

door panel. The window on my side lowered, and a gush of warm air swept through the car. "Breathe."

I inhaled through my nose, then pushed out through my mouth. We flew along the ring road and circled past the terminals. The buildings grew smaller as Maksim put distance between us and the airport.

He braked hard and entered a roundabout. My shoulder hit the door.

"I need to know what happened." Maksim did a head-check as we circled through the roundabout. We arrived on the other side, and he punched the gas. "Every detail."

The fresh air seemed to be helping, and I managed to recount everything in a calm manner. Mostly.

"The shuttle delivered me to the terminal before seven. The SUV wasn't there at that time. I know because I was paying attention. I didn't see anything unusual. But then the check-in agent had an issue with my boarding pass."

"What was the issue?" Maksim checked his rearview mirror.

"I'm not, um..." I followed his gaze, expecting red and blue lights.

There were none. But it was only a matter of time.

"Kat."

"Sorry." I faced forward. "The lady ran my passport, gave it back, and everything seemed fine. But as she was checking me in, she saw a message she hadn't seen before. The men showed up before we could figure it out."

"You have your passport?" He gave me a once-over.

I looked down. I was still wearing my backpack and purse, even as I sat buckled in the seat.

I unbuckled myself, peeled off my purse, and wiggled out of the backpack. My passport appeared as I unzipped the purse. "Got it. And my wallet." I moved the items aside, and sweet relief gushed. "My dad's crucifix!" A tear leaked out. "I thought it was in my suitcase."

Maksim was stressed—obviously—but he knew what the

crucifix meant to me. Dad had it when he died. "I'm glad it's in there," he said, offering a weak smile.

I kept digging through my purse, and my knuckles brushed a skinny white box.

The pregnancy test. My eyes flashed toward Maksim.

He looked at me. "What?"

"N-nothing." I stuffed the box under some receipts.

"Where's your phone?"

"My...?" Uh-oh.

I dug through my purse, searching for the device. Realization dawned. "I had it out when those men showed up. I-I think I lost it."

His jaw tightened. "Is it safe to assume my apps were on there?" When I didn't answer, his expression hardened another degree. "The double VPN? The email client?"

Regret shattered the calm that had settled on me. "Everything," I whispered, voice trembling. His frown deepened. "I-I was planning to delete them—"

"What about your location history? Searches? Did you clear anything?"

I shook my head, and he white-knuckled the steering wheel. "I'm sorry," I said, watching his face turn a deep, burning red. His arms began to shake.

He let out a growl that morphed into fury. He screamed. He punched the steering wheel. He cussed in at least three languages.

"Maksim, stop." Fear clogged my throat. "You're scaring me."

"Why didn't you take my calls? I tried to reach you!"

"I didn't know, okay? I-I didn't even pull out my phone until I got to the check-in counter."

Maksim guffawed.

"It's true! I think the phone must have been on silent." I definitely had it on silent the night before. It was possible I hadn't changed it since then. "What happened? Why were you trying to reach me?"

"Tom—the guy from Ivy's crew—SMSed after you left. Vladimir has a bounty out for you."

"A bounty?"

"Tom was letting me know Ivy's price was about to go up. Professional courtesy." Maksim sent another glance to his rearview. "Vladimir knew you were going to be at the airport."

"How? Someone in their crew?"

"I warned you he'd be monitoring databases and registries connected to the airlines. He likely had contacts ready to notify him."

"But he thought we were in Ukraine. Maksim, I bought the ticket less than two hours before—"

"You weren't cautious enough!" He muttered in Romanian, raking fingers through his hair again and again. "Tom swore it wasn't them. None of them trust Vladimir, and Ivy was hoping to get a bigger payout from me."

Something he said spurred a memory. I gasped. "Last night, you were on the phone with someone, right? You said Vladimir could have been monitoring the call?"

"I'm certain he was. Why?"

"I don't know if you heard everything that happened, but two of the guys started speaking in Catalan. One of them was shouting. If Vladimir heard—"

"He could have realized we were in this part of Spain." Maksim's expression grew thoughtful. "El Prat is the only international airport in Catalonia. It would not have been a difficult thing to deduce."

I chewed my bottom lip, watching the dusty landscape rush past my window. That blunder of mine had very likely been the culprit in this whole thing.

The next time I looked, Maksim was pulling out his phone. "Go to my messages. Open the thread with Tom." He entered his PIN, and the screen brightened.

I gawked. "My birthday is your PIN code?"

He ignored the question. "Type this exactly," he said, thrusting the phone at me. "Are you ready?"

I navigated to his messages. The thread with Tom sat at the top. "Go ahead."

"*Your location has been compromised. Ours was, too. HCF. This is not a drill.*" He paused. "Did you get all of that?"

"One sec." I kept swiping until I finished the last line. "What's HCF?"

"Halt and Catch Fire. It's computer machine code instruction that tells a CPU to self-destruct. Hackers sometimes use it for 'destroy everything.' As you may recall from last night."

His phone chimed. The message was from Tom. "WTF," I read, "with lots of question marks and exclamations." I lowered the phone. "Should I respond?"

"You should probably apologize since it's your phone that's going to compromise Ivy's place." Maksim crushed the brakes and entered another roundabout.

I nodded, shoulder bouncing against the door, and swiped an apology.

"What are you doing?" Maksim grabbed my hand. "That was sarcasm. Don't say anything else. Just nuke the phone."

"Nuke?"

"Wipe it. Factory reset. While you do that, I need to find the SAT-NAV on this car."

SAT-NAV was the European term for GPS.

"Is that anything to worry about? Could the cab company track us if the taxi has GPS?"

"Not if I disable it. Sometimes these devices are plug and play." He felt around under the steering column. "This is an older car, so I'm hoping—" He reached lower and nodded. "I may have found it."

While he worked on that, I went into his system settings. I opened up one menu after another until I located a blue button with a familiar label. ERASE AND RESET ALL DATA.

My thumb hovered—but then I thought of something.

I navigated away from the settings and went into his photos. All the pics I'd sent him were in Downloads.

I placed a hand to my mouth, trying not to sob, while I swiped through everything—photos of us at the beach, at the guesthouse, in the car.

The two of us cuddling... kissing...

I stopped on a picture from Romania, and my heart clenched. We'd been on Mt. Tâmpa, taking selfies, and they had all turned out terrible. Except for this one. We were looking at each other instead of the camera, and we were laughing.

Two streams spilled down my hand. He'd kept this pic. I hadn't realized.

"Hey."

My attention returned to Maksim. His gaze traveled between me and the phone. "Nuke it."

I wiped my face, returned to System Settings, and pressed the blue button. The phone went into Factory Reset mode.

"I need that tossed out the window as soon as it's finished. Not a second before." He grunted, pulling on something below the steering column. *Snap!* He straightened and held up a plastic device, wires protruding. "Got it."

"What's the plan? You think we can make it out of the country in this cab?"

"No. I don't." He lowered his window and tossed the device. "Which is why we're going to see Raul."

"Who's that?"

"An old associate of mine. He helped me locate Ivy when we arrived in Barçelona."

"He knows her?" I sat straight. "What if he contacts her? He could tell her where we're at."

"That would be the least of our worries." Maksim spoke slowly, the words dragging from him.

My throat tightened. "Why?"

"Because if we go to Raul, he may kill us." Maksim rubbed his forehead. "The problem is that we have no other choice."

CORBERA DE LLOBREGAT

II. OLD "FRIEND"

Burnt grass and crispy palms swept the landscape the farther we traveled. The twisty, modern buildings of Barçelona shrank while the natural landscape widened before us.

Then we were in the hills, weaving through narrow roads. Traffic grew sparse the deeper we traveled into Catalonia until only a sprinkling of cars and the occasional work truck remained.

We passed through a sleepy town called La Palma de Cervello and continued to Corbera de Llobregat. Dusty shrubs and lean, sparse trees filled the landscape.

I had my window down and caught whiffs of pine and juniper. Every so often a car cruised by, and exhaust fumes would trickle in.

We wound up a hill—to the point I was getting carsick—and finally stopped. The hills formed brown waves that rolled into the distance. To our right, a rock wall climbed twelve feet and stretched around the curve of the hilltop.

It wasn't a natural rock formation. It was manmade.

"This is it." Maksim's voice grew thin. I'd been hoping the "Raul might kill us" thing was hyperbole. Apparently not.

Maksim pulled the car up to a black gate. He waited, his attention lifting. I followed his gaze to a camera. It moved, and an electronic hum reached my ears.

The camera stopped on us.

Maksim held the steering wheel, as if expecting the gate to open. It didn't. He pulled the car a little closer, leaned out the window, and placed his thumb to a black button on a metal box.

Static crackled through a speaker. "Hummingbird," he said, annunciating each syllable.

There was no response. Maksim swore.

I peered up at the camera. It was still trained on us.

The static vanished, and Maksim leaned out the window a second time. He pressed the button again. The static returned. "Hummingbird plus one."

A loud noise shattered the stillness.

I jumped, startled. The gate was opening.

Maksim wiped a layer of sweat from his brow. I couldn't recall seeing him this nervous before.

Actually, I had. Once. We were in Romania, and he'd been worried Ştefan would find us. He knew what the crime boss was capable of, what would happen if we were caught... and he'd been right.

Ştefan's men had tortured him, focusing on the scarred side of his body and leaving him hardly able to walk. He knew they'd do that. He'd told me in advance, and that was why he'd been so nervous.

He looked equally nervous now. A chill crawled up my spine.

The dirt road carried us through a forest and up an incline. Maksim crept forward, inching us along, until I almost couldn't stand it.

I braced the dash, heart thumping. "I don't have a good feeling about this."

Maksim kept his eyes straight ahead.

We came upon a one-story wooden house with a shed-style roof that slanted at forty-five degrees. There were no windows—anywhere—and my center pinched so hard bile rose in my throat.

Maksim pulled into a driveway and killed the engine.

"What if we need to get away?" I whispered.

"There's no getting away." Maksim swiveled toward me. "I need you to know that I would not have brought you here if we had any other choice."

"Oh, God." My chin quivered. "We're not going to make it, are we?"

"I don't know, *dragă*." He brushed away the liquid fear drizzling down my cheeks. "But I care for you deeply. Always remember that." He bent forward and laced his sneakers. "No matter what happens, I do not regret our time together. Do you believe me?"

I nodded.

He finished and then leaned close. His gaze drifted to my lips. I thought he would kiss me, but he wrapped me in a hug instead.

"Maksim?" I sniffled. "I'm scared."

"I know. But I need you to be brave." He pressed a kiss to my forehead. "Wait here. Do not come in after me." He grabbed the pistols. "If Raul comes to you, do whatever you can to stay alive. Bribe him. Beg for your life. Do *not* try to run. Do you understand?"

"Yes." My vocal cords constricted. The answer scraped my throat.

Maksim unlocked the door. "Pray for me—for us—if you can." He stepped out of the car with both hands raised. The pistols went high in the air.

He used his thumbs to press a lever on each gun. The clips released and slid out. They hit the ground, and Maksim tossed the empty pistols.

They landed twenty feet away.

Maksim walked forward, hands still raised. Movement drew my attention to the house. I squinted. Had the door opened, or was I imagining—?

BOOM!

A gunshot blasted. Dirt sprayed mere feet from where Maksim stood. He jumped back, keeping his hands raised.

Clank-snap. BOOM! Dirt sprayed again, closer now.

"No!" I scrambled across the car.

Maksim motioned for me to stop. Then he turned around, giving the shooter his back, and lowered himself to his knees. His gaze wandered to me, only for a second, then he laced his fingers behind his head.

The front door opened wider. Someone shouted, and Maksim lowered himself the rest of the way to the ground. He moved slowly, methodically, and when he lay face down in the dirt, his hands returned to their last position—locked behind his head.

The shooter walked out, shotgun braced against his shoulder. He wasn't especially short or tall, not big or skinny. He was just kind of... normal, forties, with a receding hairline.

He stared down the barrel of the shotgun through a pair of polarized Aviators. His expression seemed to be caught between a smile and a snarl.

He pumped the shotgun. *Clank-snap.*

I squeezed my eyes shut and prayed—though, it was more like silent worrying directed toward the sky. "Please don't let Maksim die." Tears streamed. "Please."

The next time I opened my eyes, Maksim was in cuffs, hands behind his back. The man hauled him to standing. Dirt coated Maksim's face and clothes.

His mouth moved, forming words I couldn't make out. He sent a fleeting glance my way, and the man followed his gaze.

Terror gripped me.

The man pressed the shotgun into Maksim's back and nudged. Maksim walked forward, and they disappeared inside the house.

12. ILLUSTRIOUS GUEST

Someone rapped on the window.

My head shot up. My eyes flew open. I'd been sitting in the driver's seat, crying and muttering incoherent prayers for so long I must have passed out.

My attention lifted. Maksim stood beside my door.

"Oh my God." I fumbled for the unlock button.

Maksim held up both hands in a calming gesture. "Slowly. Don't make any sudden movements." He nodded toward the house.

Raul guarded the front door. He was still holding the shotgun, but at least it wasn't pointed at us.

"It's all right. He's going to help." Maksim eased the door open and offered his hand. "He wants to meet you."

That made me pause. "Why?"

"He didn't say, and I didn't ask." He opened the door and pulled me to my feet. "Be courteous and respectful. Answer his questions. He'll know if you're lying, so it's better to be candid or not say anything at all. Understand?"

I nodded.

"Are you ready?"

"Not really."

My answer didn't deter Maksim from drawing me along. Dirt and bits of gravel crunched under our shoes. An earthy smell—that same mix of juniper and pine from earlier—flooded my senses.

Raul watched us, head tilted. He held the shotgun at a similar angle, barrel pointed up and out. "So you're the American all this fuss has been about." His smile sweetened. "It's a pleasure to meet you, Baroness Kat. Do you mind if I call you that?" He gestured at the house. "Thank you for agreeing to join me for—well, now, I don't have any tea, but I can offer you sparkling water. You look utterly parched."

I peeked over at Maksim.

He offered Raul a polite nod. "We're grateful for your hospitality." His gaze connected with mine. "Isn't that right, Kat?"

I nodded, swallowing past the knot in my throat. "I'd love some water. Thank you."

"Then please, do come in." Raul angled himself but didn't otherwise move. Guess we were going first.

Maksim hooked my arm. We entered the house and proceeded into a dark hallway. Shivers tiptoed through me.

The door closed, cutting off the fresh air and sunlight, and I death-gripped Maksim's arm. He touched my hand and offered a reassuring squeeze.

"Den." Raul's voice pierced the darkness.

We inched toward a soft glow at the end of the hall. It took everything I had, every last bit of willpower, not to turn around and try to escape.

I squeezed my eyes shut, letting Maksim pull me toward the lamplight. We reached the end of the hall and entered the den.

"Couch," Raul said.

Maksim and I moved to the couch. I clung to him, even as we sank onto the cushions. He relaxed his hold, his arm draped casually over my shoulders.

I snuck a peek at him. He was smiling, as if we were there for dinner and a chat.

Raul angled for the kitchen. Rustling stemmed from that direction. A door opened and closed. He returned carrying a tray with two glasses and a bottle of sparkling water.

At no point did he set the shotgun down.

"You'll have to forgive me for not serving you more... properly." He slid the tray onto the side table. "I haven't decided if I'm going to kill you or not."

I reached for a glass and froze.

"Oh! Baroness, please, I'm joking." Raul's laugh rolled through his words. He circled around to a leather chair and parked himself. "Why, if I were going to kill you, I would have done it already." He offered up a saccharine-sweet smile and gestured at the water. "Please do refresh yourselves. I hear you've had a very rough day."

Tremors moved through me. My arms were flimsy, but I managed to grab the bottle of sparkling water and offer it to Maksim.

He took it and cracked the lid. I passed him a glass, hands shaking, and then grabbed mine. He filled each one.

The water fizzed. My insides felt similar, churning and threatening to bubble over.

"I hope Yuriy has expressed my utter delight in meeting you." Raul crossed one leg over the other, shotgun resting across his lap. "It seems you're all the chatter these days in my old circles."

I turned to Maksim and mouthed, "Yuriy?"

"I have a Ukrainian passport," he replied at a normal volume. "I go by the name Yuriy Petrenko."

"He speaks Ukrainian, too," Raul chimed in, "a dialect specific to the southeast region. It's sooo *interesting* how you don't know any of this"—he bounced his leg—"especially considering how *in love* you two are." His shoulders did a fluttery lift when he said that last part. His sarcasm oozed.

"I wasn't going to tell her any of this"—Maksim's tone soured—"seeing as how I planned to leave this life, and my aliases, behind."

"And yet, here you are, deeper in the game than ever before. Funny how that works." Raul's leg stopped with the bouncing. "See, I've been out for two years, and here *I* am"—he leaned forward—"*back in the game,* and not even at my own behest."

Silence descended. We had involved this man in something he didn't want to be involved in, and he wasn't happy about it. How could I set his mind at ease?

I thought of a way. Maybe. At the very least, it might convince him that I had a genuine relationship with Maksim.

"Southeast," I said, breaking the tense silence. "Did you pick that region because you're fluent in Russian?" I took a sip of water, feigning casual. "Southeast Ukraine borders Russia, doesn't it?"

Raul let out a chuckle that rolled into a laugh.

"What? He speaks, reads, and writes Russian." I sat a little straighter. "He's fluent in seven languages."

"Oh, yes, yes. I am fully aware of Yuriy's linguistic abilities, along with his many other talents." Raul's laugh settled into a grin. "But are you?"

"I don't need to know everything about his past." I pulled myself closer to Maksim. "I trust my boyfriend completely."

"Is that why you snuck into Ivy's apartment? Because you trust him 'completely'?" Raul pulled air quotes with his free hand.

My jaw slipped. He knew about Ivy's?

"Don't be so surprised, Baroness. The whole of the Dark Web knows what happened last night. You're famous!" Raul divided an amused look between Maksim and me. "Ivy is looking for you, you know. Both of you. Imagine what would happen if I turned you over to her." He snorted a laugh, wagging his finger. "Ahh, but her bounty isn't as sizable as the one Vladimir is offering— twenty million each. Fifty for delivery together, contingent that you're both alive. I suppose he wants to finish the job himself."

My insides shriveled.

Raul pushed up from the chair and angled for the kitchen. Maksim stood, gesturing for me to do the same.

I wagged my head and mouthed, "No."

He pulled me to standing and gave me a firm nudge. We made our way to Raul, who appeared totally relaxed apart from his steely grip on the shotgun.

"I'm glad you came here, Yuriy. I am. It's made me realize that I will *never* be free while that son-of-a-bitch uncle of yours is alive." Raul turned to me. "Or is he *your* uncle? There's been some debate about that online. This isn't one of those 'keep it in the family' things, is it?"

Maksim had grown up thinking Vladimir was his uncle and Ştefan was his cousin. In reality, Maksim wasn't even related to them. I was. My own uncle was trying to kill us.

"My grandfather was a wealthy man," I said. "I'm the one who inherited his estate, not Vladimir. I'll pay double what he's offering. More."

"Goodness me! I don't want your money." Raul's laugh settled into a grin that was scarily unhinged. "I want Vladimir *dead*. That's where Yuriy comes in. Isn't that right, Yuriy?"

"I'm happy to discuss those details at a later time." Maksim's expression grew cold. "In private."

"Of course, of course. When innocent ears aren't absorbing all the gory details—and I do so hope they'll be gory." Raul entered the kitchen and went through a door.

I elbowed Maksim, eyes questioning. He replied with a subtle shake of his head.

We followed Raul into the garage. Heat smothered us. A dank odor mixed with motor oil and gasoline irritated my nose.

A car alarm chirped, and a pair of headlights flashed. We were standing next to an SUV, something akin to a Land Cruiser.

"This vehicle cannot be traced to me. Make sure it stays that way." Raul faced Maksim. "Will you be proceeding with the plan we discussed?"

Maksim nodded. "It's our best option—as long as your brother agrees to assist."

I drew back. Raul's brother?

"I'll let him know you'll be in touch." Raul dangled the key fob between us. "So who's driving?"

———

THE SHAKING IN MY HANDS GREW AS WE BACKED OUT of the garage. "Um, what just happened?"

"Shh." He checked his rearview mirror, backing around the taxi. Sweat glazed his brow.

Raul exited the garage, and Maksim lowered my window.

"You'll be needing these, won't you?" Raul ducked inside the cab. When he stood, he had my purse and backpack.

"Thank you." Maksim leaned across me. "For everything."

"Don't go thanking me yet." Raul passed the items through my window. I was about to set everything on the floorboard when he dipped into his pocket and pulled out a stack of euros. "This will only go so far but may be helpful." He removed the money clip and tossed the cash.

It landed on top of my backpack.

"Don't fret, Baroness." Raul's trademark grin returned, though slightly warmer. "If anyone can keep you safe, it's 'ole Yuriy here."

I mustered up a weak smile. "Thank you."

Raul tapped the hood and then focused on the taxi. Maksim slid up the window and circled around to the dirt road we'd used earlier.

"What was all that talk about Vladimir?" I whispered. "Are you going to kill him?"

"That's something I'll have to deal with after you're gone."

"But how—?"

"Please, Kat." Maksim put up a hand. "I cannot think about that right now."

I swiveled in my seat and watched Raul. He was examining the taxi. "What's he going to do?"

"Switch out the plates, paint over the yellow, then drive it into the city."

"Into Barçelona? Why?"

"It's a stolen vehicle. It will have to be chopped." Maksim slowed to a crawl and eased through a dip in the road. "Did you steal the taxi in Begur? Is that how you got to the airport?"

"I got there by bike." Hints of guilt laced his voice. "I never told you this, but the owner of the rental house had a motorcycle."

"He did?" My shoulders stiffened. "I never saw it. Why didn't you want me to know?"

"I thought you may want to ride it. But we didn't have permission, and a sport bike would have drawn too much attention, anyway. I did, however, see it as useful—as an alternate getaway if needed—so I moved the bike to a parking lot near the town center."

Begur had tons of parking lots scattered around town—some free like the one by the grocery store, others paid. I hadn't realized Maksim was using one this whole time. He hadn't said a word about it.

"So you... what? Ran to the parking lot and rode to Barçelona?"

"Without any armor, no jacket, not even a helmet. I had no time to gather anything." His gaze met mine. "You do realize that if I had delayed, even to retrieve the helmet, I would not have made it in time.

"I'm sorry. I wouldn't have left if I'd known— Maksim, I thought—"

"I know what you thought." His voice hardened. He pushed out a slow breath. "I saw you coming out of the airport, and I knew I needed to act fast, so I parked behind that taxi and told the driver there was an active shooter. He and his passenger hid behind a shuttle. And since his car made a better getaway than the bike..." He let the thought trail off before saying, "Everything will be all right. Raul will deal with the taxi."

"Then what? Are we really meeting up with his brother?"

"That's my hope." Maksim eased through the open gate. He checked both ways, then proceeded onto the narrow road.

"I'm not sure Raul is sane." I hugged myself. "And I don't think we should accept any more favors from him."

"The favors have already been accepted, and I already know what I must do to repay him." Maksim's attention swung to the glove box. "Open that. Tell me if there's a map."

I popped the glove box, and my eyes bulged. "There's a gun."

He muttered in Romanian and shoved a hand through his hair. "We'll have to ditch that... somewhere. I don't know where yet. And I need a map to get us where we're going."

"Where's that?"

"Paris."

———

THE TERRAIN TURNED MOUNTAINOUS THE DEEPER WE ventured into Catalonia. Coastal humidity gave way to dry air, and the landscape looked more like a desert.

Maksim didn't say much, and neither did I. Our next real exchange came when I could no longer see the jagged peaks of Montserrat, a famous monastery in the region.

We were winding through the mountains and got stuck behind a tour bus. The fumes and lack of moving air prompted me to reach for the AC. European cars didn't always have air conditioning, but this SUV did, and I was going to make use of it.

Maksim intercepted my hand. "No running the air."

"Why?"

"To conserve petrol." He paced the bus. "We're two hours from the border, and that's *if* we don't get lost."

"We could stop before that. Get gas. Buy a map."

"We're not stopping anywhere in Spain."

I was about to argue when I recalled something that happened in Romania. We had stopped at a gas station, and Ștefan's contacts in the government had spotted us on CCTV cameras. That was how Ștefan and his goons had known the direction we were heading.

"You're right." I settled back. "We shouldn't stop."

The bus pulled into a vineyard, and the road opened up in front of us. Warm air swept through the vehicle, blowing my hair and delivering a whiff of flowers, spicy herb, and pine.

I breathed it all in. This place had such a wild, unpretentious beauty, and I desperately wished I had a phone so I could take pictures.

But I didn't have anything. No phone. No clothes.

No relationship.

I peeked at Maksim. We seemed to be heading for a breakup as of last night. Now I wasn't sure. I needed to talk to him, find out where he stood.

My thoughts landed on the pregnancy test. Actually, that was the first thing that needed to happen, because if Maksim did want to end things, we'd have to...

What? Figure something out? How would that even work?

My stomach soured. Yeah. I needed to take that test. I'd do it as soon as we stopped for gas.

12½. DISTRESS SIGNAL

The SUV slowed, and the feeling of going through a roundabout drew me out of sleep.

My head popped up. My eyes shot open.

Nighttime rested on the land, a dark veil broken up by highway lights and a sprinkling of stars. The clock on the dashboard glowed green.

11:49 PM

Maksim tugged on the steering wheel, bringing us through the roundabout, and turned onto a side road.

"Where are we?" I squinted into the shadows. "Please don't tell me we're out of gas."

"We're not. I stopped at a petrol station in Toulouse."

"What?" I sat up. "Why didn't you tell me?"

"I tried. You were dead asleep." He eased the SUV onto a patch of grass. "They had maps for sale, so I grabbed one." He killed the engine and flipped off the headlights.

A fresh layer of darkness closed over us.

"Is this my bathroom break? 'Cause I was hoping for a bathroom at a gas station."

"You'll need to make use of nature's toilet." He unbuckled his seatbelt. "My eyes are crossing. I need to rest."

I twisted around, observing the highway lights on the main road. There weren't any lights on this street.

"What about a motel?" I hugged myself. "Couldn't we use the cash Raul gave us?"

"It's too risky." Maksim pushed his seat back, his strong nose and square jaw illuminated by the dash clock. "I know this isn't ideal, but most hotels will ask for our passports. This is safer, and we won't be long. I only need a quick nap."

I sighed and popped the handle on my door. Light poured over us.

"Hold on." Maksim gestured for me to shut it. "I'll look for a place we can use as a toilet. Wait here." He stepped out and closed the door.

I closed mine, and shadows fell across me. The dash clock burned into the blackness.

11:52 PM

I pulled my knees in. What if a cop drove by, saw our vehicle, and decided to stop? We'd have to give our passports. Our names might show up in their system—some kind of European all-points bulletin—and we'd be arrested.

What would happen then? Could Vladimir get to us through France's judicial system?

I hugged my knees tighter.

A strange noise pricked my hearing. *Plink.* Reminded me of an acorn falling from a tree and landing on the hood of a car—except we weren't under a tree. And whatever hit us seemed to come from the side, as if someone had tossed it.

I searched the blackness beyond my window. I couldn't see past the side mirrors.

My stare returned to the clock. The time flipped to 12:01, and a chill rippled through me. I thought Maksim had been gone for two or three minutes.

He'd been gone for nearly ten.

I rocked, trying to think calm thoughts. Logical thoughts. *Think logically.* That was one of Maksim's rules.

Okay, so, if something had hit the SUV—if my brain hadn't fabricated the noise—what could it have been? And where could it have come from? I mean, we were the only ones out here.

Weren't we?

My heart fluttered. I fumbled for the lock button. *Snap.* The doors locked in unison... but then another sound followed.

Pop.

I jumped. That was the door handle. For *my* door.

I scrambled into the driver's seat. Who was that? It couldn't have been Maksim. He would've said something, announced himself.

Whoever this was hadn't said anything. They *still* weren't saying anything.

I scanned the area around the car. It was like studying a thick, black curtain. I couldn't see the nose of the SUV.

Tap tap tap.

I jumped straight up and spun around. Someone had rapped on the driver's side window. I caught a glimpse of steely knuckles carved into a thick hand.

He pressed his face to the glass. Platinum-gray eyes locked onto me. *"Bonsoir."* The glass muffled his familiar French accent.

I screamed as Émilien reared back and punched the glass.

ORLÉANS

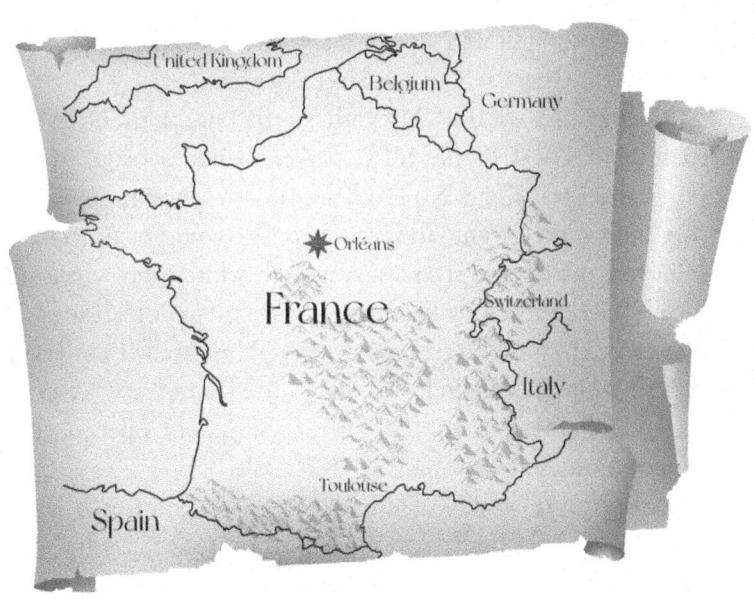

13. PATRON SAINT

I shot up straight and let out a cry. Warm, stuffy air met me head-on. Gray daylight saturated my vision.

"It was a dream." My voice startled me as I took in my surroundings. I was in the SUV, parked beside a beige stucco building, and I was alone. No Émilien. Also no Maksim.

My stare drifted right, and I gasped. The columns of a stone building sharpened into steeples. A man in white robes, the kind with bell sleeves and a long hemline, scurried over cobblestones.

He crossed himself and passed through an arched entryway that led to a gothic cathedral. Was that Notre Dame?

The car alarm chirped. The driver's side door opened, and Maksim was suddenly climbing in.

"Good. You're awake." He had a to-go coffee in each hand and two plastic bags hooked to his wrist. "I managed to find— " He caught a glimpse of me, and his expression grew serious. "Did something happen?"

"N-no. I'm fine." I pulled the lever, drawing my seat up. "You got coffee."

"I did." He handed off one of the cups. "Along with something else I think you'll appreciate."

I let the heat soak into my hands while he rifled through one of the bags. He produced two boxes the size of...

"Cell phones?" I asked, and he nodded. "Are they prepaid?"

"Like the ones we had in Spain, yes. We can use them as burners. I'll have to set them up." He tossed the other bag into my lap. A flowery design curled across the front. BOUTIQUE VANNESSA. "You may want to change into that."

Maksim had gotten me a tourism shirt with an artsy map of France. The colors of the French flag—blue, white, and red—splashed the front. Cursive scrawled the bottom.

LIBERTÉ - ÉGALITÉ - FRATERNITÉ

"That's all I could find in your size." Maksim started the SUV and reversed. "Most of the shops aren't open yet."

We pulled onto the street and eased into traffic. I rotated in my seat, admiring the arched windows of the cathedral. The other buildings on this street were plain—apartments, a tobacco shop—but the cathedral was elaborate with twin towers, a slender spire, and stained-glass windows shaped like flowers.

"I don't see any gargoyles."

My comment met with silence. I looked at Maksim. He was pacing a city bus, and his mouth was hanging open.

I traced his gaze to a perfume ad with a blonde straddling an oversized perfume bottle. She had her head tipped back, blond hair pouring over her shoulder, while one arm lay across her bare, voluptuous chest.

A slogan filled the space at the bottom.

Une rose est une rose est une rose...

"A rose is a rose is a rose?" My attention returned to Maksim.

He followed the bus onto the next street—and he didn't stop staring until the bus turned left. We kept going straight.

Finally, he reeled in his stare. His expression stayed blank until he seemed to remember me. "It's a perfume." He cleared his throat. "By a famous designer, Cheryl Breyce."

"Huh?"

"You translated the tagline correctly. It's a rose perfume, but 'a rose is a rose is a rose' is actually from a Gertrude Stein poem. In answer to your other previous question—I don't believe there are gargoyles on the cathedral." He checked his rearview. "You're likely thinking of Notre Dame in Paris. We're in Orléans." He said the city so fast I hardly caught it.

Ohr-ley-OHN? Something like that.

I didn't say anything. I just stared—kind of the way he'd been staring at that half-naked model. I'd never seen him do that before, and I couldn't help feeling grossed out.

I might be carrying his baby. The thought rattled me to the core.

"Will you hand me the map?" He tipped his chin. "It's in the glove compartment."

"W-we need to stop."

His attention flicked to me.

My hand trembled under the weight of my micro-sized coffee. I lowered the paper cup and held it with both hands. "I... have to go to the bathroom."

"Are you all right?" He glanced at my hands. "Do you need—"

"Just a bathroom. Please."

He veered left, entering a main boulevard. Modern office buildings spanned our right, followed by shops, a hotel, apartments, a parking garage...

Maksim whipped into a parallel space and pointed at a cream-colored building. A sign hung out front. KARISSA CAFÉ LITTÉRAIRE.

"Looks like a novelty café," Maksim said, "something involving books. They're open, and they'll let you use the toilet if you order something."

"I'm not hungry."

"Order another coffee, then."

I grabbed my purse and popped the door handle.

Maksim caught my arm. "When you enter—"

I jerked away, backing myself against the door. He tilted his head.

"Sorry." I made myself relax. "I really need to go."

"When you enter, greet them with *bonjour*, then ask for a *café au lait*—that's coffee with milk—and say *à emporter*. That means to-go. If you can add *s'il vous plaît* and *merci*, you'll get better service."

I recalled Dad saying something about how the French value politeness. Adding "please" and "thank you" might have seemed arbitrary, especially when I didn't know the language, but I understood what Maksim meant.

He took my coffee and set it in the cupholder. "Practice on me."

"*Bonjour. Café au lait, s'il vous plaît. À emporter. Merci.*" I didn't bother with the accent: *cah-fey oh-lay see-voo-PLAY uh ihm-por-TAY. Mehr-SEE.*

Maksim gave a nod. "Try to make it fast. And you may want to take care of that." He gestured toward my ear. "You have some on your neck, as well."

My hand flew to the spots. As I rubbed, I detected something sticky and nearly gagged.

Blood. From that man he'd shot.

Maksim handed me the bag with the tourism shirt. I took that and my purse and stumbled out of the SUV. Scaffolding covered the building's exterior. I had to go around to reach the café's entrance.

I paused at the door. That man's blood had been on me since yesterday. The thought made me want to vomit right there on the pavement.

"It's okay," I whispered to myself. "You can wash it off."

I yanked open the door and entered the restaurant. A bookcase filled the wall on my right. Customers sat around, reading paperbacks, magazines, and newspapers.

A waiter muttered in French and gestured at an open table. I repeated the phrase Maksim had taught me.

He tipped his chin toward the bar. "Talk to Jacqueline."

The waitress—Jacqueline—stood behind the bar, running an espresso machine. She hardly looked up as I approached.

I repeated the whole thing I'd said to the waiter, start to finish. As my terrible French continued, she stopped the machine and wrinkled her nose. Her expression sank into confused sadness.

"Um... *s'il vous plaît? Merci?*" Probably should've added an "I'm sorry for butchering your beautiful language" instead.

Her nose remained wrinkled as she grabbed a to-go cup. "Cash or card?"

"Cash. Also... *toaletă?*" That was Romanian for toilet. I didn't know how to say it in French, and I figured... why not butcher two languages while I was at it?

She pointed behind the bar. "Downstairs."

"Thanks. I'll be right back." I circled around to a set of stairs and followed them down to a short hallway that dead-ended with a door.

Toilettes

The word had to be plural, but when I entered, I found one urinal and one stall. Hopefully, I wasn't in the men's restroom.

I locked the door, went to the sink, and searched for paper towels. I didn't find any, so I yanked off my shirt and used it to scrub my skin.

The hot water scalded me. My skin swelled pink.

I tossed the dirty shirt, threw on my new tourism shirt, and rummaged through my purse. The pregnancy test appeared.

"So what's the plan?" I peered into the mirror. "What if you *are* pregnant? What are you going to do?"

A red-eyed, wild-haired version of myself stared back at me.

I left my purse on the sink and closed myself inside the stall—then I immediately returned to the sink, which had the only source of light.

I held up the skinny white box, squinting. A block of text scrawled the backside, and my stomach sank.

The instructions were in Spanish.

I broke open the box and shook out the test. A factory-folded sheet followed. More instructions. Surely, these would have pictures.

But they didn't.

"Whatever. It can't be that hard." I crumpled the paper and tossed it in the trash. "You pee on the stick and you wait. Easy."

Or not so easy. As I plunked myself on the toilet, five hundred questions inundated my brain...

How long was I supposed to hold this thing under the stream? A few seconds? More?

What time of day should I be doing this? American pregnancy tests were more accurate in the morning or evening—I couldn't remember which. Was the same true for European tests?

Was it okay that I hadn't showered? Could the test become contaminated if I hadn't, like, washed down there?

And what was I supposed to be looking for? A plus sign? Minus? Two minuses? Would it turn blue if I was pregnant, or if I wasn't?

I held up the stick and took a long, hard look at it. "I hate you."

The test seemed to mock me with its small size and simple design. I shouldn't need instructions for this. So then, why couldn't I bring myself to do it?

Knuckles rapped on the door. I jumped.

"Kat? Everything all right in there?" The door muffled Maksim's voice, but not his concern.

"Everything's... fine." *Dammit.* "I was, um, trying to buy my coffee before I came in here, and that took a while. Turns out I'm not very good at French."

Silence unfolded for a three-count before he said, "You're not feeling faint, are you?"

That was why he'd been worried.

I buttoned my shorts, returned the test to the box, and shoved the stupid thing in my purse. Then I cracked open the door and peered up at Maksim. "Hi."

His brow pinched. "Hi."

"Thanks for checking on me, but I'm okay. Just got in here a second ago."

"Uh-huh." His attention drifted past me. "You're certain?"

"Mm-hmm. Yep." I clamped down on my bottom lip.

He nudged the door, opening it wider. I shoved my foot against it. My purse sat on the sink, unzipped, with the pregnancy test inside. I didn't want him to walk in and see it.

Maksim narrowed his eyes. "What are you doing?"

"Nothing." I swallowed. "Just, you know, want some privacy." I forced a smile. "So... be right out." I rammed my full weight against the door.

It slammed in his face.

I twisted the lock, and a rattle followed. He was jiggling the handle.

"I haven't paid for my coffee yet." I hurried over to my purse. "Think you could go take care of that while I finish up?"

"Kat." The knob jiggled again. "Open this door."

I fished out the pregnancy test, left my purse on the sink, and hurried into the stall. A moment later, I was seated on the toilet, reopening the skinny white box.

I shook out the test, popped off the plastic cap, and stuck the litmus paper under my stream. A miniature trashcan hung beside me. I was tossing the box in there when a soft jiggle reached my ears.

Click.

The restroom door opened, and Maksim appeared at my stall —which I had neither shut nor locked.

I screamed and covered myself. As I did, the test slipped from my fingers...

Plop. It was in the toilet.

"What are you doing?" Maksim stood over me. "Are you using a mobile phone?"

"What? No!" I hugged myself. "How did you get in here?"

He grabbed my hands and pried open my fingers. The blue cap from the pregnancy test popped out and hit the floor.

He scooped it up, and his expression blanked. "What the hell is this?"

"It's... a marker cap."

He studied it. He studied me.

"Found it in my purse, and I... was going to throw away." I shimmied my shorts up and over my knees while keeping one arm crossed over my lap. "Now can you please get out?"

He circled through the restroom and paused at the sink. I heard items sifting around in a confined space.

My mouth dropped open. "Are you going through my purse?"

The noise stopped, and he returned to the stall. I glared at him.

"I know you've been wanting to talk to your friend, and I thought—" He averted his gaze. "As a reminder," he said, staring at the wall, "you cannot use normal methods to contact her. Wait until I have the new phones set up."

"I'm not contacting anyone." I folded both arms over my lap. "Even if I wanted to, how do you think I could have gotten a phone? I've been with you this whole time."

"Forgive me. I didn't mean to invade your privacy."

"Thanks," I said with an eye-roll. "Now do you mind?"

He did a one-eighty and strode out of the restroom. The door closed, and the jiggle I'd heard a moment ago returned.

Click. He had relocked the door. How? With a key? He might've picked the lock.

I waited until his footsteps disappeared, then stood and yanked my shorts up. As I turned around, my insides bottomed out.

The pregnancy test floated in yellow toilet water. My frustration boiled over. "Dammit!"

PART TWO

PARIS

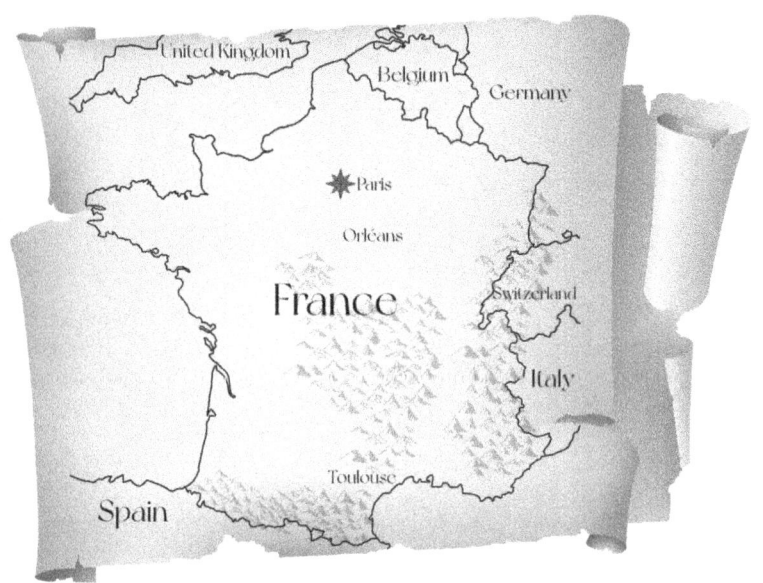

14. FINAL DESTINATION

Our two-hour trip took four-and-a-half hours. We had a map, but we couldn't use the phones, so there was no surefire way to avoid main roads and traffic cameras.

Maksim chose routes that went through villages—the smaller the better—but he didn't always get it right. On four separate occasions, we had to redirect. Two of those times required significant backtracking.

As we cruised along a rural highway, surrounded by farmland, I was convinced central France wasn't all that different from the flatlands of Georgia.

That changed as we moved closer to Paris.

The buildings grew bigger and more modern. A cluster of office buildings sprouted on our left with a name that scored the tallest one. LES BUREAUX DE TRENT. The Trent Offices.

Traffic thickened as we traveled deeper into the city. Soon, familiar sights—familiar because I'd seen them in movies—began to appear.

Wide, straight boulevards.

Pale stone buildings.

Decorative balconies—some of them wrought-iron, others made of stone.

Sloped rooftops colored in dark gray and topped with skinny, terracotta chimney pots. I marveled at the cafés, bistros, and brasseries that occupied the ground floor of each building. *Dad was here.* The realization jarred me. He'd eaten at one of these brasseries years ago. What had he called it again? Brasserie Brianna?

That was years ago, but still. Being here, seeing the things he had described, felt surreal.

Something else painted itself into the scene, something I hadn't been expecting—French flags. Blue, white, and red waved from every corner. Long banners hung between streetlights.

"Is it just me," I said, "or is France more patriotic than I imagined?"

"Tomorrow is *la Fête nationale.*" Maksim's accent rolled into the French seamlessly. "It's a national holiday. Foreigners refer to it as Bastille Day. Similar to America's Independence Day."

My attention drifted to a group of city workers hanging a banner on a decorative, vintage-looking streetlamp. They were arguing, and a white hatchback with blue lights on top stopped them.

The blue flashed, and a female cop stepped out. She was outfitted in navy—from the curve of her cap to the dark fabric of her pants. Her tactical vest, military boots, and sidearm were solid black.

POLICE NATIONALE

"Did you know about this?" I slid down in my seat. The front windows had a tint, but not much. "A national holiday doesn't seem like the best way to sneak in and out of a place, especially since we have a gun."

"We don't have the nine-millimeter anymore."

"We don't?" I blinked. "Since when?"

"Since late last night. I stashed it in a locker at the Toulouse railway station."

"You did?" My mouth hung open. "Why didn't you wake me up?"

"I tried. You were dead asleep." His words rang with familiarity, and not because I'd heard them before.

It was more like we'd had this conversation before. Under these exact same circumstances. *Déjà vu?* Possibly. Or another one of my dreams, which had an uncanny way of skewing the line between imagination and reality.

"The Fourteenth draws big crowds," Maksim said. "That will be perfect for disappearing, but it's also why I had to stash the pistol." He paused. "There are thirty thousand cops assigned to Paris at any given time. For this holiday, they bring in many more from all across the country. Look."

I traced his stare to a cluster of cops standing at the next corner. Another set of cops parked their car at a side street.

"The police presence will be a deterrent for criminal activity. Of course, we'll need to be careful, as well."

"Do you think there's any chance Vladimir could have tracked us here?"

"There's always a chance. But this vehicle is unknown to him, and I took every precaution I could." He bounced his head side to side. "Losing your phone may work to our benefit, as well."

"How?"

"My VPN is compromised, but if you did any searches for Nice—our last plan—Vladimir will direct resources there." Maksim grabbed the shifter and shoved it into the next gear. "Paris is working out better for many reasons, and it may be the only solution for you."

"What reasons?" I slanted a look. "What does that even mean?"

"Renan has a wealth of contacts here, some of whom are in the French government—politicians and the like. Raul said they may be able to get you out through diplomatic channels."

"Like, refugee status?"

"Something along those lines." He paused. "Kat, you could be escorted out of France, flown directly to the United States, and Vladimir would not be able to touch you."

"What about you?" Tears climbed into my throat. "What's going to happen?"

Maksim grew quiet. We were cruising up a tree-lined boulevard, keeping pace with the surrounding cars. Stone apartments in the Hassmannian style—a blend of modern and classical—stretched as far as I could see.

Maksim let his gaze trail over the apartments. "I'll likely face criminal charges for what happened at El Prat. But knowing Raul —knowing what he wants from me—I believe he will be calling in favors from every contact he's made in the last twenty-five years." Maksim's eyes grew distant. "As soon as you're gone, I have to find Vladimir and kill him."

"What if you can't?"

He wiped a hand down his face. "I don't know."

The hum of traffic and the occasional honk were the only sounds. We entered a wide, multi-way intersection and followed a line of traffic into a left turn.

Our silence persisted as we entered a residential neighborhood. Maksim's countenance had grown heavy Worry sank into his normally smooth features.

I reached for his hand, which rested on the shifter.

He tensed. His fingers twitched, as if torn between hoping to stay and needing to go.

Ultimately, he pulled away. Rejection crashed into me.

"I was planning to speak with you about something on the way to Nice." He swallowed. "I know you've desired more from our relationship, but that's not going to be possible. My life was complicated before, and now it's even more so." He fixed me with a serious look. "We can't be together. I need to know you understand that."

The pain in my chest radiated. My throat felt like sand had been shoveled into it.

"Do you?" he asked. "Understand?"

"Not really." My throat closed. "I know I've been messing up a lot, but—"

"It's not that."

"Maksim, I can do better. I can handle this."

"It's not you." He redoubled his grip on the steering wheel. "You could have handled these things perfectly, and we would have come to this same conclusion." His gaze wandered to me. "I'm sorry. I do care about you, but I can't be with you."

A fat tear tumbled down my face. His brows lifted, making room for his pity.

I swiped the dampness and directed my gaze out the window. He said he'd been meaning to talk to me, which meant he'd been planning this breakup. But since when? That first trip to Ivy's?

It had to be. Something had happened, something that changed his mind about us.

I watched Paris slip by as the pain inside me swirled. Fresh tears trickled. I wiped away the evidence, doing my best to keep quiet.

Maksim turned on the radio and scanned before settling on hip-hop. The lyrics ebbed and flowed—mostly in French, but English occasionally found its way into the track.

Something-something, chérie
You know I'm going cray-zee
Something-something, salut
You know I really need you

After an hour of crawling through traffic, Maksim parked on a tree-lined street. Cars crammed both sides of the road. E-bikes charged at docking stations.

Patrons scattered the patio of a *pâtisserie*. Next door to that, people came and went from a corner grocer.

Maksim killed the engine. "Bring your things."

I unbuckled my seatbelt and gathered my purse and backpack. He grabbed the bag with the phones, and we both climbed out and trekked up the sidewalk.

I sent a glance over my shoulder, then another, checking to make sure we weren't being followed.

"Let me show you something." Maksim led me over to an electronics shop. High-definition TVs filled the window, and I honed in on a news report.

Maksim must have seen it, too, because he went stark still. I clutched his arm. The report was about us.

15. LONG LOST

Maksim swore. The report showed images from El Prat, along with a shaky video of people ducking behind a shuttle.

Shots rang out. The people whimpered, shushing each other.

"Come on." Maksim guided me away from the shop.

"How did you know that report was on? Did you see it?"

"I didn't. I was going to show you something else. Try to remember this. It's important." He gestured toward a jewelry store. "See how our reflections appear in the store windows?"

I nodded.

"You don't have to look around to know if you're being tailed. Pretend you're window-shopping or fixing your hair, then check the reflection to see who's behind you." He met my gaze. "Raul saw news reports about what happened at El Prat, but the information varied between media outlets. Some called it a thwarted terror attack. Others called it a shootout, saying the perpetrators had escaped."

"You and I being the perpetrators?"

"Precisely. But our names were never mentioned, which is odd. The only reason he suspected us is because of chatter on the Dark Web and the bounties Vladimir had issued."

"What if that changes?" I hugged myself. "What if more videos surface? There were passengers everywhere. Someone must have caught us on video." I peeked up at him. "What about the airport's security footage?"

"I've considered all of this. That's why I don't want you traipsing off to Charles de Gaulle and booking a flight."

I recognized that name. Brandy and I had talked about traveling to Paris one day, and when we looked up flights, the airport code had been listed as CDG. Charles de Gaulle.

We skirted a woman pushing a baby stroller, then another walking a puffy-haired dog. A bus rumbled by, giving off a blast of heat.

We turned right at a brasserie. A stream of accented voices flowed from that direction, the patrons eating and drinking under a theater-red awning.

The narrow street passed between Haussmannian-style buildings, each five to seven stories tall. I admired the intricately carved stonework and wrought-iron balconies.

Flocks of people—tourists if I had to guess—gathered at the next corner. They were staring at something.

Maksim hung a right. I went static, my gaze lifting.

Bronze-colored beams formed a slender structure that rose above the tree line and reached into the sky. The beams soaked up the sunlight, giving the metal a glossy look.

The Eiffel Tower. Those tourists were snapping photos and capturing video.

Maksim hooked my arm and pulled me away. *"Flics."*

"Huh?"

"Flics. Cops. To our seven."

My brain had to do all kinds of translating. Apparently, he'd seen the police—that much I understood—but I racked my brain, trying to remember what "seven" meant.

On a clock, with twelve o'clock being in front of us, he was saying the cops were behind us and to the left. To our "seven," or seven o'clock.

I turned and caught a glimpse of the same type of cop I'd seen earlier—navy blue everything, funny curved cap, and a uniform that would have been too warm for a mid-winter's day.

"Don't look." Maksim slung an arm over my shoulders, making me face forward.

I recoiled.

He hesitated and then lowered his arm. "Forgive me. I was only—"

"I get it." I hugged myself. "But this is all really confusing"—my throat felt dry, crispy, and my voice broke—"and I'd appreciate if you didn't send mixed signals."

"Fair enough." He put six more inches of space between us, and awkward silence followed us up the sidewalk.

We stopped in front of a pristine white-stone building with stepping balconies and flower boxes. "This was Dom's place." Maksim skimmed the apartment numbers listed on an intercom. He pressed one. "Hopefully, he still lives here."

"Who's Dom?"

"A friend of mine."

"You mean, like Raul?" I frowned. "That kind of friend?"

"An actual friend. Vladimir knows nothing of him, which makes this the perfect place to lie low." He scanned the street. "If we can avoid the *flics.*"

Seconds ticked by. A minute. No one answered the intercom.

A man in a business suit squeezed past us. *"Excusez-moi."*

I stepped aside as he reached out with a magnetic key card. He placed it against an electronic pad, and the light switched from red to green.

The man tugged on the glass door and slipped inside.

Maksim caught the door. We waited, but the man didn't give us a second glance.

"Well?" Maksim pulled the door wider. "After you."

The entrance opened up to a foyer with a parquet floor. Two chandeliers doused the area in light.

I followed Maksim through a set of French doors and into a

stairwell. "Dom lives in the penthouse." Maksim lowered his voice. "There's an elevator, but the stairs will be more private."

"We're walking up?" My feet dragged to a stop. "When there's a perfectly good elevator?"

"You never know when you'll encounter a nosy neighbor, a watchful landlord, or—for any reason—the police. We need to stay out of public view as much as possible."

I groaned.

Our shoes shuffled up the sleek steps, our movements echoing around us. It was a nice stairwell, all things considered, with a solid-wood banister and artwork on the walls. The space was enclosed, no natural light, but LEDs radiated a soft yellow-gold, adding to the ambiance.

We were halfway up when I asked, "How certain are you?"

"About?"

"You said Vladimir doesn't know anything about this friend of yours. How can you know for sure?"

"I guarded these friendships vigilantly, more so than any others I've ever had. Ștefan knew nothing about them, so Vladimir shouldn't, either."

"But... how? Why?"

"I thought I was coming here, to Paris, if Ștefan ever agreed to release me from my obligations." We rounded another floor and continued up toward the next. "These were going to be the relationships I would have as a free man. I needed to ensure they stayed separate from that life. The only way to do that was to keep them a secret. From everyone."

Something he said—the way he said it—made the hairs on my neck prickle. I searched my memory, trying to figure out why, but I couldn't put my finger on it.

"Is something wrong?" He settled a serious look on me.

"No." I averted my gaze. "Just tired."

We arrived at the top floor and stepped onto the landing. An elevator waited on our left. A door stood to our right.

Maksim headed for the door. A raised voice came from the

other side. There was a pause, and then the guy exclaimed, *"Bah non! Non!"* The door muffled his thickly accented voice.

"Doesn't sound like we came at a good time," I said.

Maksim gave a quick double-knock. When the shouts continued, Maksim knocked again, louder.

Footsteps treaded our way. The door swung open.

Dom was six feet of lean body, silky hair, and flawless skin under a perfectly coiffed five o'clock shadow. Platinum chains hung at various lengths around his neck. Rings accented his fingers. His eyebrows were dark like Maksim's, though not as thick, and his eyelashes were long enough for a mascara commercial.

He held a phone to his ear and locked eyes with Maksim. The phone slipped and clattered to the floor. *"C'est pas vrai!"* He grabbed his head. *"Je ne te crois pas!"*

I was no French expert, but I thought he said something like "this can't be true" and "I don't believe it."

We all stood there, staring at each other. Maksim broke the silence. "Can we come in?"

Dom snapped up his dangling jaw, scooped up his phone, and ushered us inside.

The apartment opened up to a spacious den littered with moving boxes. A chessboard, pieces midplay, sat on the mantle of a faux fireplace.

"Un moment," Dom said. *"S'il vous plaît."* A moment. Please.

He placed the phone to his ear. Whatever he said next went over my head.

I gravitated toward the windows overlooking his balcony. The Eiffel Tower stood guard over the neighborhood, the bronze beams weaving into metal latticework. We stood one story higher than the other buildings, so there was nothing to obstruct the view.

I brought my hand to the glass. If I walked outside, if I could put myself on the other side of this window, the Eiffel Tower would be within arm's reach.

That was how I felt. The tower was that close.

"*Allô? Allô?*" The urgency in Dom's voice gave way to a growl. I turned as he lowered the phone and rattled off something in French.

"Can we keep it to English?" Maksim let a fleeting glance sweep over me. "For Kat's sake?"

Dom pulled a soft breath. "Ohh," he said, covering his mouth. Either he realized I wasn't French or he felt sorry for me. Possibly both. "How goes?" He focused on Maksim. "You look..." Dom studied him. "Exhausted."

"Because I am. But it's a long story, and I only have a moment." Maksim's attention drifted to Dom's phone. "Do you mind if I ask who that was?"

"Mm?" Dom's attention swiveled to his phone. His features tightened. "*Bah non.* It was my bank. They have lost eight thousand euros!"

Worry carved lines into Maksim's features. "What do you mean they lost it?"

"I do not know, but it is happening to many people. *C'est pas ouf.*" *Sey pah oof. It's not great.*

He tossed his phone on an oval coffee table and plunked himself on the couch.

His explanation seemed bizarre, and something about it set Maksim on high alert. "Who do you bank with? Where are they based?"

"BEC—Banque et Commerce." Dom peered up at Maksim. "They are based here. Why?"

"Do they have any branches in Germany?"

I finally understood why Maksim was asking, and my stomach lurched.

"This is a French bank." Dom split a quizzical look between us. "As far as I know— Ahh, but wait." He glanced at his phone. "Their cybersecurity is located in Germany. This is what they say to me."

I felt the color drain from my face. "It's Vladimir," I whispered. "Isn't it?"

"Who is Vladimir? Does he have my money?" Dom's smooth forehead creased. "Maksim, *mon ami,* what is happening?"

I interjected before Maksim had a chance to answer. "Could I borrow your phone?"

Dom reached for the device.

"No." Maksim stepped in front of me. "Not yet."

"I have to call Mr. Amsel."

"Vladimir could be monitoring calls to the bank. He could be betting you would hear about this... whatever it is." Maksim turned to Dom. "You say this incident was not limited to your account?"

"Bahhh non." Dom swept his hair to the side. The silky locks lifted off his forehead and settled into perfection. "The *banque* says it is global."

Maksim led me toward the door. "This incident may or may not be a coincidence. You can call Mr. Amsel when I have the phones ready. Your friend, as well."

He kept referring to Brandy as my "friend" rather than using her name. Like she was a total stranger to him. Like we both were.

"Stay here." Maksim opened the door. "Don't go anywhere without Dom. Don't call anyone."

"Where are you going? To meet Raul's brother?"

"To accomplish the first step in doing that, yes." He said one more thing to Dom—in French—and his mouth fell into a straight, serious line.

Dom's gaze flicked to me.

I wanted to know what Maksim had said, why he'd said it in French, but he left before I could form the question.

16. LONG LAST

My dreams were patchy, incoherent. In one, I was running from Vladimir. In another, from a lion.

Why a lion? Somehow, it seemed familiar.

As the dream progressed, I found myself running through the streets. I couldn't figure out who was chasing me. Each time I turned around, there was nobody there.

Still, I kept running, and all the while, Brandy's voice echoed around me. *I tried to warn you about Maksim.*

The lion roared as a motorcycle thundered past. My eyes shot open. I was lying on a couch with a cashmere blanket on top of me. My head rested on a throw pillow.

I sat up, and the biggest, brightest nightlight greeted me through uncovered apartment windows.

The Eiffel Tower.

A spotlight swung from the top, rotating in a full circle. The tower's golden glow streamed.

"Maksim?" I dragged my stare from the view. The rest of the apartment was pitch dark. "Hello?"

Silence filled my ears, leaving behind a soft ring.

I stood, intending to search for a lamp or light switch. My foot found something solid instead.

I toppled forward. "Ouch!" I belly-flopped onto the floor as keys rattled. The jangle twisted, and the door opened.

A six-foot-tall silhouette with amazing hair and a moderate build appeared in the doorway.

Dom made his way inside. Paper rustled, and when the kitchen light blinked on, I spied him carrying a sack of groceries. A simple, elegant logo stamped the side. BONPRIX CHRISTINE. A baguette stuck out from the top.

He was unpacking the food when he noticed me. "*Bonsoir.* How are you?" His hair, still perfectly swept to the side, gave a slight bounce as he looked up from the groceries.

"Fine." *Sort of.* "How long have I been asleep?"

"Since many hours." He held up a round block of cheese. "Maksim said you would be hungry."

"Is he still gone or...?"

"Still gone, *oui.*" Dom slid a bottle of white wine out of the fridge. "We could both use this, no?"

"I don't drink." I limped around the box that tripped me. "Are you moving?"

"I wait to hear about a job." He braced the counter and glanced at a moving box next to him. "It would require a move."

"That's a shame." I joined him in the kitchen. "Pretty sure you have the best view in Paris."

"You have not seen the best part." His smile warmed. "Nice shirt. It is appropriate in advance of our holiday tomorrow."

I peeked down at the tourism shirt. Wrinkles marred the blue, white, and red map. "Maksim got it for me. My other shirt was, um, dirty." I wasn't about to tell him *why* it'd been dirty—a.k.a. with someone else's blood.

He threw together a charcuterie tray—cheeses, olives, deli meats—and handed me two wine glasses. He had not one but *two* bottles of wine.

I followed him past the guest bathroom, the spare bedroom, and finally into the master bedroom. A set of French doors led to a classic balcony on our right. A modern, minimalist bathroom in various shades of cream sat to our left.

Dom went to the right, and my heart came alive. "Are we eating on the balcony?" I asked.

"*Bah non.* Tonight we dine at the best table in Paris." He said it *pah-RREE.*

He made his way to a set of stairs that led to a loft area with a large window. The pane was already open, and Dom climbed straight through. I trailed him.

As my head broke the surface, I gasped.

The rooftops of Paris stretched around me. City lights glowed, and there, right in the middle of it all, was the Eiffel Tower. The spotlight swung around, completing another turn.

Dom edged past a row of terracotta chimney pots. "Your table, *mademoiselle.*"

There wasn't a real table—just a blanket on a flat section of roof—but I would have taken this over a restaurant any day.

"You weren't kidding about the view." I made my way over to the blanket. "This is incredible."

"It is the one thing I will miss after my move." He took the wine glasses. "The baguette warms in the oven with the brie. I must not forget them." He set the glasses down. "Many French are pairing charcuterie with the red wine, but I like to begin with the white. Mm? It's okay?"

"Okay, but... I'm not twenty-one." *And I might be pregnant.*

I let that last thought evaporate. I hadn't been nauseated since the other day, and I definitely felt like I was about to start my cycle. I'd still take the test, but I didn't think I was pregnant. *Probably.*

"Your age is not a problem here. Please, if you do not enjoy the wine... *bahhh.*" He waved me off. "You will enjoy it. Live. Love. It is not as if you have to drink the sea."

That made me chuckle.

He plucked out the cork and tipped the bottle toward my glass. Yellow liquid flowed.

He poured himself a glass and then swirled the wine. "This is a *viognier.*" He said it *vee-yohn-YAY.* "You may detect notes of stone fruit and ambrosia. I am eager to know if you will like it, mm?"

I copied him—tried to—and ended up splashing myself. Go figure.

"Okay, so..." I wiped my leg. "What's the deal with all this? We could've eaten on your couch or the patio. Why bring me up here?"

"I knew you were hungry, and I suspected you may enjoy the beautiful view." As he lifted his glass, a twinkle entered his eyes. "And..."

I swallowed my first sip. Huh. This stuff was pretty good. Tasted like liquid candy, but without all the extra sugar.

"And?" I said, taking another sip.

"I am curious what brings you to Paris." He nibbled a bite of cheese. "Maksim has not been here in more than one year. Then *poof*"—Dom gestured with his free hand, fingers breaking apart—"here he is, and he has you, and you both look..."

I took my first bite of cheese. It was aged cheddar, and it was delicious. Hadn't realized how hungry I was.

I shoved the entire slice in my mouth. "We both look what?" I mumbled. "Homeless?"

Dom chuckled. "It is not a bad description."

"You wouldn't be wrong. I guess we are kind of homeless. Maksim definitely is." I collected a wedge of blue cheese, another slice of cheddar, and took a bite of each. Then I took another sip of wine—except this sip was more of a gulp. "Really, it's a vacation gone awry," I said between bites.

"Are you two together?" His eyebrows flew high. He leaned forward, chomping on the cheese. When I looked away, he took a swig of his wine. "Nooo. You are his girlfriend?"

I shook my head.

"His wife?" Dom grabbed his head. *"Mon Dieu."* My God.

"No, no. I *was* his girlfriend. But now..." My emotions

swelled. I snatched up several pieces of salami and shoveled them into my mouth. "We were together," I mumbled, chewing, "but then he broke up with me." I gulped everything down with the rest of my wine, trying hard not to cry.

Dom's expression grew tall and wide by the time I lowered my glass and held it out to him.

He rushed to fill it. "So you are not together now?"

"Apparently not." I retracted my hand, and the glass went straight to my lips.

"I do not understand." Dom topped off his own glass. "If you are not together, then why did you arrive together? And why do you look like this? Like something terrible has happened."

Maybe it was the wine. Maybe it was the simplicity of Dom's kindness. Whatever the case, I spilled the entire story—my trip to Romania, the scavenger hunt, how I'd met Maksim.

How we'd learned who he really was, who *I* really was. Who my dad and grandfather were. All of it.

Correction: most of it. I left out certain details—like being wanted by the authorities. I did explain that I'd nearly been kidnapped at the airport. I did *not* mention the shootout.

The wine flowed. For the most part, the tears did not, even when I talked about my relationship with Maksim. Normally, I would've been crying my eyes out, but a wonderfully numb sensation settled over me.

"*Pardonne-moi.*" Dom pushed up. "I want to hear more, but please. I need one moment." He skirted the chimney pots.

"*No problema.* Oh! Um..." I grimaced. "Sorry. I'm not sure how to say that in French."

Dom grinned and shook his head. Then he disappeared through the open window.

Paris kept me company while he was gone—the whir of traffic, the honks, the shouts. A police siren was the only thing that set me on edge, but with the Eiffel Tower right there—close enough for me to soak in the golden glow—I didn't feel afraid.

A splash of wine sat in the bottom of my glass. I swirled it, watching it glide around. As I did, I had the distinct impression *I* was the one being swirled tonight, even though I was the one holding the glass.

Dom returned with brie on a charcuterie board and a baguette wrapped in cloth.

"Yum." I reached for the baguette, then hesitated. "Is it okay to, like, touch it?"

"But of course! See?" He broke off the end and passed the baguette to me. The brie had an X cut into the top, revealing gooey, creamy cheese. Dom gestured toward it.

I grabbed a spoon and slathered the cheese onto my baguette. One bite, and my entire mood brightened.

"Oh my gosh." I covered my mouth, chewing. "This is incredible."

"Our food is very good here." Dom took my glass, dumped out the droplet, and proceeded to fill it with red wine. "Now please." He returned the glass. "Try it with this."

I swirled the wine and took a whiff the way Dom had. A fragrant bouquet of fruits and florals overwhelmed me. I took a sip... then another... then another. My eyes grew bigger each time.

"*C'est bon?*" *It's good?*

"Really good." I returned to the brie and baguette. "How have I never tasted food like this before?"

"I suppose we are both having a new experience, mm? I did not know Maksim grew up in a crime family." Dom gulped the last of his wine. "He said he was in shipping—imports, exports."

"He sort of was. Just a different kind." I noticed a hint of reticence in Dom's eyes, and regret flooded through me. "He doesn't do that stuff anymore. Just so you know."

"Oh?" Dom noshed on the baguette. "And why are you so sure?"

I told him about Maksim's motorcycle accident, how he'd met Daniel and Madă, how they'd taken care of him. "That whole thing changed him, and that's when he decided to leave his life of crime."

No sooner had I spoken the words than I wanted to take them back. Because I *didn't* know if that was what happened. I'd thought so based on everything Maksim had told me, but after hearing him talk this afternoon, it seemed like he'd been thinking of getting out before his accident.

Had I misunderstood?

"That must have been the last time I spoke with him." Dom's expression turned thoughtful. "His accident was last year?"

I nodded. "Early summer."

"*Bah ouais.* I did speak with him. I remember it perfectly." Dom sat with one leg bent. He rested an arm over his knee and looked out over the city. "I never knew what to think."

"About the way he disappeared?" I dipped a piece of baguette into the melty brie.

Dom sighed, attention drifting.

"What's wrong?" I sat straight. "Is it something I should know?"

"No, no. It is nothing, actually." He responded with a weak smile. "Only a little memory I have."

"Is it something to do with his e—"

Dom gasped, catching a glimpse of his watch. "*Oh là là.* It is almost the time."

I'd been planning to ask about Maksim's ex. Maksim had learned she'd been unfaithful thanks to a so-called "mutual friend." I'd been wondering if that friend was Dom.

I let myself forget about it as he scooted closer and held his watch toward me. "*Cinq. Quatre. Trois.*" He was counting down in French: Five. Four. Three.

The hour changed, and he gestured toward the Eiffel Tower. "*Mademoiselle,* I present to you... *la tour Eiffel.*"

Tiny bits of white light erupted all over the tower. The flashes moved and danced until the slender structure looked like a sparkler on the Fourth of July.

I crawled to the edge of the roof. "Is this something related to Bastille Day?"

"This is normal—every hour for five minutes. Tomorrow there will be a special presentation." He tilted his head. "Will you be here tomorrow?"

"I'm not sure." The plan was to get me out of Europe as soon as possible, but what if Raul's brother couldn't help? What if his contacts fell through or something else went wrong?

How was I going to get home?

17. BASTILLE DAY

I heaved a gush of pink—the third so far—into the toilet. My throat burned. I rested my chin on the toilet and moaned.

Dom and I finished both bottles of wine last night, and we'd been working on an after-dinner drink—Cognac? Armagnac?—by the time Maksim had shown up.

We'd been lying on the blanket, watching the Eiffel Tower's spotlight swing around, while Dom taught me La Marseillaise—the French national anthem.

"Again. This time with more... something, I don't know what." He flung his hand. "Pretend that you are French. You must believe these lyrics unto the depths of your soul."

"I can't. When I remember the words, I forget the rhythm. And when I remember the rhythm, I forget the words."

"*Bah non.* Impossible is not French." He rolled onto his side and propped himself on his elbow. "Again... *un, deux, trois, quatre.*"

All of Paris seemed to glow behind him, and something about the way his eyes sparkled in that golden light inspired me to try again.

So I did. With all my heart.

"*Allons enfant de la patriiiie! Le jour de gloireee est arriiiive!*"

Dom flitted his hand to the beat. I flitted mine, and as we started into the next verse, Maksim was suddenly standing over us. He. Was. *Furious.*

"What the hell is this?" He shouted the question, his beautiful, black eyebrows converging.

Dom scrambled to his feet. "You asked me to feed her and keep her occupied. So..." He rubbed his neck, glancing at the spent charcuterie boards and wine glasses.

"I didn't say to get her drunk!" Maksim helped me up and led me to the window. He might have carried me at one point. Everything was a bit hazy; though, I did recall telling him how amazing he smelled. He must have taken a shower.

The memories blurred as I flushed the toilet. *Do not throw up. Do not throw up.* I silently repeated the mantra.

Dom was in the kitchen by the time I lumbered in there. He looked up from an espresso machine and smiled. *"Bonjour."*

"Bon—"

The machine rumbled to life. I flinched.

"Un expresso?" He nodded toward the machine as hot, black liquid dispensed. The most wonderful earthy aroma filled the air.

Nausea twisted through me.

"Just water for now."

He pulled a glass from one of the moving boxes, which sat on his dining room table. "I am out of the sparkling water, but the water from the sink is good."

"Do you have any ice?"

"Ice?" Confusion splintered his expression.

I sighed. Europeans weren't into ice. Or air-conditioning. It was morning, and I could already feel the summer heat seeping into Dom's apartment.

"Maksim has left us a note." Dom swiped a piece of paper off the counter. "You can read it?"

I shook my head. "It's in French."

"Ahhh, but your rendition of La Marseillaise was so good." He grinned. "Are you sure you cannot read it?"

I rolled my eyes. "Ha."

He chuckled. "Maksim tries to contact someone today. A friend? It is the person who will help you fly to the United States." Dom set the note on the counter. "He asks me to take you shopping so that you have clean clothes for your journey. *Mais attends,* this is a problem because many shops are closed today."

"How come?"

Dom pointed overhead as a distant, high-pitched whir grew louder. The sound morphed into a rumble that buzzed the building before growing faint. Shouts and applause followed.

My mouth tumbled open. "Was that a plane?"

"Jets. From our air force." He led me over to the windows. The building across the street was full of people standing on their balconies. Everyone clapped and pointed skyward.

Dom opened his balcony door. As we stepped outside, my attention lifted to blue, white, and red smoke trails.

The colors of the French flag.

"A big parade happens now at the Champs-Elysees and the Arc de Triomphe."

"Really?" I perked up. "Arc de Triomphe?"

"Mm-hmm." He sipped his espresso. "We could go, but I have another plan in mind, if you may be interested?"

I gnawed my lip. Maksim and I had seen that news report less than twenty four hours ago. What if more video footage had surfaced? There might be an APB out for me.

Dom's eyebrows flew higher than the fighter jets. "Something is wrong?"

"I'm not feeling the greatest, but also—remember what I told you last night? I-I don't think it's a good idea for me to go out. Maksim doesn't want me to."

"He said you mustn't go without me. *Non?*"

That was true. Maksim did say that before he left yesterday.

"It is my understanding," Dom continued, "you are here because it is the safest place to hide from that man, Vladimir. If you are safe, then who are you afraid of?"

Should I tell him about the shootout?

Dread twisted through me at the thought. Maksim had been protecting me—he'd rescued me from a near-kidnapping—but I didn't know if Dom would understand. What if he reported us to the cops? Even if he didn't, he might tell us to buzz off, that he didn't need any trouble.

"The situation is messy," I said slowly, "and it's risky to be out in public."

"Yes, but you could wear a hat or change your hair." Before I could argue, he said, "My plan involves *la tour Eiffel*."

I perked up. "The Eiffel Tower? Really?"

"*Bah oui*. And so, we will be very close to the apartment—in case you must leave." He turned me around and guided me inside. "Have a shower. Relax. I will search for an open boutique."

"But Dom—"

"No, no. Please. Do not make your decision yet." He paused outside the guest bathroom. "By the time you are finished, I will have a plan, and *then* you can decide."

DOM DISCOVERED A HANDFUL OF BOUTIQUES THAT were open, but he also had a neighbor who was about my size.

"She is pregnant," Dom said, "and she cannot wear many of her clothes."

My throat dried at the mention of "pregnant."

I didn't have time to process the thought before he began sifting through a selection of clothes. "These linen pants are light and fresh, and I think they will be perfect with this." He held up a white tank top. "I may have something to cover your head."

He entered his closet and returned with a navy headscarf wide enough to cover my bulky black hair. Mostly.

"Ahh, *ça alors*." He turned me around and inspected the outfit. "*Magnifique*. And the pants help to hide the shoes." He was referring to my running shoes, which he thought were hideous, but they'd have to do.

I tied the scarf at my chin and checked myself in a full-length mirror. The tank top hugged me. The linen pants flowed.

"You don't have any sunglasses, do you?"

"I may." Dom had opted for chino shorts and a fitted white polo. He came alongside me, and I watched a grin creep up his face.

"What?"

He nodded toward the mirror. Took me a full five seconds before I realized what was funny.

"Twinsies!" I said with a laugh.

He chuckled and retrieved a neckerchief—navy, like my head-scarf—along with two pairs of sunglasses.

He handed one pair to me and slid the other onto his face. Then he fastened the neckerchief, tucked a hand into his pocket, and expertly struck a pose. With his tan loafers and designer watch, he looked like he'd stepped off the cover of *Men's Vogue*.

I slid on the sunglasses. They were big and round and hid my face. Perfect.

"We look alike." Dom gestured at our matching clothes. *"Qui se ressemble s'assemble."*

"What's that mean?"

"Those who resemble assemble. Something like that."

"Okay, but how did you end up with all these accessories?" I lifted the sunglasses. "That's what I want to know."

"I wish I could say it is from my many dates." He swiped his wallet off the bedside table. *"Mais attends,* I am not interested in casual dating, and I am far too busy for a serious relationship."

"What do you do?"

"Bahhh, it is nothing important—and yet it requires much dedication and time."

"Zookeeper?"

"Close! A model and actor." He chuckled and offered his arm. "Shall we?"

I nodded, and he led me through the hall. Colorful abstract paintings hung on either side of us. "So. Have you been in anything I would have seen? I used to work at a movie theater."

"My projects extend only to France. But that may change very soon." He flashed a grin. "My last audition was for an American TV show."

"Really?" I perked up. "Which one?"

"It is a new comedy-drama. The pilot has not aired, but it is filled with an all-star cast and is expected to do well." His mouth hitched. "I auditioned for the part of the 'swoon-worthy' French teacher, who becomes the object of affection for the other teachers." He waggled his eyebrows. "And also many of the parents."

"Oooo!" I nudged him. "That's exciting."

"*C'est vrai.*" It's true. "And the show will be filmed in Hollywood. I cannot believe it." His brown eyes sparkled. "Many of the cast receive luxury sponsorships. That could be me."

"You'll have to let me know what happens. I live on the East Coast, but I could fly out and see you."

"Ahh, *formidable.*" Terrific. "It would be a comfort to know someone, and I would treasure seeing you again, *mon amie.*" *Mohn ah-MEE. My friend.*

I couldn't help but smile. He had such a way with words.

Afternoon heat greeted us outside, and throngs of people swarmed the neighborhood. Everyone seemed to be headed toward the Eiffel Tower.

We walked alongside Dom's apartment building, hung a right, and crossed over the street. Two blocks later, the neighborhood funneled into a park.

Dom was talking about different traditions—parties at the fire stations, the light show we were about to see—when I noticed a familiar form in the crowd.

I craned my neck. Raven hair and a sharp nose came into view. My pulse jumped.

"Dom." I grabbed his arm. "Do you see that guy?"

"Mmm?" He traced my line of sight. "Which one? Him?" He gestured toward a man with kids.

"No, the one with black hair, stocky build. He was by himself." *I think.* "He was wearing pants and a dark shirt."

Dom and I stepped behind a tree, waiting for the crowds to thin. They finally did, but...

I used my hand as a visor and scanned. Everyone in the vicinity wore light, summery clothes. Émilien—or the person I'd thought was Émilien—had been wearing dark clothes.

But I didn't him anywhere.

"Sorry, I must have, um..." I changed course. "I'm getting a headache. Might be affecting my vision."

"Ohh, *la migraine.*" He pronounced it *mee-GREYN.* "You will feel better after we arrive, mm? You can relax, and we will have the best view in all of Paris. You will see."

Dom pulled me through the crowds. Police officers in equestrian-style uniforms patrolled on horseback. One of them looked at me.

I turned away, and Dom tilted his head.

"Thanks for bringing me here." I hooked his arm and gestured at the Eiffel Tower. "It's gorgeous, and it's *right here.*"

"She is spectacular, *non?*" Dom's attention trailed up the tower. "The French, especially the Parisians, have a love-hate relationship with her. Many express disdain, yet we gather here for our national holiday." He shrugged. "It is a paradox."

A stage stood at the far end of the park, and a crew set up lights and speakers. We weaved between people seated on the grass until a female voice called out, *"Dominique!"*

Dom waved. *"Bonjour, Sabrina. Ça va?"*

"Ça va, merci." A girl—college age, dark skin—pushed up from a blanket. She and a guy had a spread of food and drinks similar to what Dom had prepared last night.

My stomach sloshed.

Dom and the woman greeted each other with a kiss on the

cheek. The guys did the same thing, and it seemed just as friendly and natural.

The woman began to chat away in French.

Dom interrupted. "I would like to introduce you to Kat. She is American."

"Oh!" The girl brightened. "I am Québécoise." *Keh-beh-KWUAHS.*

Her accent tripped me up. It wasn't the same as Dom's, but it wasn't exactly dissimilar, either.

After a moment of smiling and nodding, I blurted "Canadian! Sorry." I shook my head. "From Quebec, right?"

The guy smirked. "That would be the meaning of Québécoise." It wasn't a sarcastic remark, per se. Actually, it sounded kind of playful. Even so, awkward silence wriggled into the conversation.

Dom came to the rescue. "Kat, please allow me to introduce Sabrina"—he gestured at the girl—"and Timothée." He pronounced the guy's name *tee-moh-TEH.* "Kat is visiting for one or two days only. She is the friend of Maksim."

"Maksim?" Sabrina's smile grew. "We just saw him at Mar—"

"You were feeling ill, *non?*" Dom stepped in front of me. I could have sworn he waved off Sabrina. "Please," he said, ushering me onto the blanket. "You should take a seat."

I removed my sunglasses and peered around him. "Sorry, you saw Maksim where?"

"At Marie's."

My gaze traveled to Timothée and then to Dom. Timothée's mouth hung open. Dom looked worried.

"I don't know what that is," I finally said. "Is it a restaurant?"

Timothée was the next to speak. He directed his question to Dom—in French—and I had the distinct impression he was talking about me.

Dom replied, and Sabrina's expression went from lighthearted to horrified.

"What am I missing?" I stepped closer to Dom. "What's Marie's?"

"It's not 'what,'" Timothée said, "it's 'who.'"

"Okay, then *who* is Marie?"

Nobody answered. And nobody looked at me. My heart tumbled down into my ribcage. No.

Dom met my gaze. Pity overflowed from his expression.

No! I wanted to take the question back. I didn't want to know who Marie was, because I already knew. The puzzle piece had clicked into place.

She was Maksim's ex. That was where he'd been since we'd arrived.

18. SECRET MESSAGE

I pushed through the crowd, stumbling past picnickers and park-goers. The migraine bloomed into a *thump thump thump* in my right temple. The edge of my vision blurred.

"Kat!" A series of *oof*s and *uff*s followed me. Dom pulled me to a stop.

I jerked away. "You knew."

"I did."

"Why didn't you tell me?"

"I am sorry. He asked me not to." Dom lifted his sunglasses, revealing his earnestness. "He did not say why, and I had no time to ask. When I learned that you and he had been together, I assumed he did not want to upset you."

I hugged myself. "So they're back together."

"I do not know, and I did not realize Sabrina and Timothée have seen him." We loitered by a raised platform where a camera crew was setting up. Dom lowered his voice. "Before Maksim left yesterday, he asked if Marie lived in the same apartment. Prior to last week, I would not have known the answer. Now I do. By chance."

"Right." I guffawed. "By chance."

"I am telling you the truth. She was not speaking to us—me,

Sabrina, Timothée—for many months. We all knew about her affair, and after Maksim disappeared, she blamed us. *Pffft.* Obviously."

Maksim had broken up with his ex after she cheated. After he learned the truth from that "mutual friend" of theirs.

"It was you, wasn't it?" I asked. "You were the mutual friend who told him."

Dom nodded. "Marie did not know which of us told Maksim. But I believe now she does. Sabrina and Timothée have never implicated me during this time. Then, one week ago—after these many months—Marie knows I am to blame."

"How? What happened a week ago?"

"Sabrina received a call from Marie, who wanted to reconcile. I did not receive such a phone call—I assumed because Marie has let herself go. She is not working, she has gained weight—this is according to Timothée and Sabrina—but then I discovered scratches like this"—he swiped his hand back and forth—"all over my car."

"Someone keyed your car last week?" My mouth fell open. "You think it was her?"

"It must be. She has learned the truth—that *I* was the one who told Maksim about her affair—and she has enacted her revenge."

"But who could have told her the truth? Sabrina?"

"*Bah ouais,* it must be Maksim. There is no other."

"But that's impossible. Maksim was with me last w—" My mouth locked up. "Last week," I finished in a whisper. Maksim had gone to Ivy's last week. Could he have contacted Marie? Told her the truth and ratted out Dom in the process?

Dom huffed a sigh. "We are always betrayed by our own, *non? Mince.*" Damn

Tears sprang to my eyes. Why would Maksim do that out of nowhere? And if he did—if that's what really happened—why would he implicate a friend who had trusted him?

Something else occurred to me.

"Oh, crap."

"What?" Dom touched my arm. "What is it? Please, I must know."

"I think Maksim has been in contact with Marie for a while. He started acting weird a few weeks ago, and—I don't know for sure, but I'm willing to bet we're not here by accident."

Dom took a quick breath, ready with more questions, when his phone chimed a long, melodic ring. He checked the caller, and his brow dipped.

"Is it Maksim?"

He shook his head and took the call. *"Allô?"* A pause. *"Oui?"*

I could vaguely hear the other person. It was a man, and he was speaking in French.

Dom gestured, silently excusing himself, and ambled toward a line of trees at the park's edge. He kept the phone pressed to one ear and used his finger to plug the other.

He stopped under one of the trees.

I stayed by the platform, pinching my forehead. The blur of light spread, moving up the side of my eye until half my vision turned fuzzy. Conversations unfolded at a moderate volume, but my ears processed them with a sharp edge.

I winced and threw on my sunglasses. The camera crew didn't seem to be recording yet, but I felt safer hidden behind the glasses. They helped with the light sensitivity, too.

"The heck is taking so long?" My attention returned to the tree. A group of girls stood there. Dom was gone.

I left the platform.

"Excuse me?" I smiled at the girls. "Did you happen to see where that man went?" I pointed toward the tree. "The one who was on his phone?"

The girls giggled. "No English," one said.

"Sorry. Uh, *je suis désolée." Jeh-SWEE dez-oh-LEHY. I'm sorry.*

They giggled again and returned to their conversation.

I continued to the tree. Its thick foliage had a cooling effect —a welcome change after being in the blistering sun. If I couldn't find Dom, I'd wait here. But where could he have gone?

I circled around the trunk. Part of me expected to find his phone on the ground, as if he'd dropped it. But why would he do that?

He might've been kidnapped.

I shook off the thought. Now I was being paranoid.

"Kat."

I jumped. Dom stood behind me, phone in hand.

"Forgive me." He glanced at the phone. "I was not expecting the call."

"Who was it?"

"A journalist. He was asking for..." Dom pocketed his phone. His Adam's apple dipped.

"Asking for what?" I came alongside him. "A statement or something?"

"*Bah oui.* A statement." That was all he said.

"Listen, I'd love to hear more"—I pressed on my temple—"but this headache is getting worse. I need to lie down."

Dom snapped out of his stupor. "Of course." He took my arm. "We will go to a pharmacy and find medicine for you."

"I didn't bring my purse."

"It's okay. I will buy it, and I may need some, too. Perhaps I have *la gueule de bois.*" When I sent a questioning look, he said, "Hangover."

"Pretty sure that's what's wrong with me."

"Then we will suffer together. Mm?" He smiled. "It sounds good?"

I chuckled, but my insides had gone numb. Maksim acted like he couldn't be with me because of his ties to the crime world. But that wasn't true, was it? This had to do with Marie.

He must still be in love with her.

The closest pharmacy wasn't nearly as close as I would have hoped. Dom swore it was a thousand meters, but in the heat, with this migraine, the walk felt more like a couple of miles.

Stone apartments towered over us. The pharmacy occupied the ground floor.

"Do you mind if I wait here?" I gestured at a bus stop. Trees dotted the sidewalk, and the bench sat in a shady section. "I'm betting the pharmacy doesn't have AC, and I'm afraid I'll be sick."

"AC?"

"Air conditioning."

"Ahh, it is okay by me." He nodded toward the bench. "Wait here. I will return." He disappeared inside the packed pharmacy while I ambled over to the bus stop.

Traffic stacked the street. Fumes burned my nose, and the nausea pressed harder. Maybe waiting outside wasn't the best idea.

I reached the bus stop as a passerby rammed into me. I spun away from the bench, nausea swelling, and nearly threw up on the sidewalk.

"*Pardon,*" the man called.

I moaned. This must have been a really bad hangover. *Or you really are pregnant.*

Shut up, I told myself.

"*Mademoiselle?*" Another man approached, saying something in French.

"I'm American."

"My English is not good, but please, may I help?" He took my arm and helped me to the bench.

As I sat down, something poked me in the hip. My hand moved to the spot, and a crinkle reached my ears. Was that a piece of paper in my pocket?

"You are very warm," the man said. "Do you need water?"

I nodded, and he disappeared into the restaurant next door.

When he was gone, I dipped into my pocket and discovered a folded-up piece of paper. I felt sure it hadn't been there earlier.

I unfolded the paper, which was a cross between notebook and grid, and discovered two lines of cursive.

18½. LIGHT SHOW

I lay on my side, watching Paris' golden glow radiate. Unfortunately, that glow didn't include the Eiffel Tower.

Dom's guest room was on the other side of the apartment, so my view consisted of gray, slanted rooftops and that was about it. I could hear traffic on Avenue de Suffren, but I couldn't see it because of the mature trees that lined the sidewalk.

I rolled over and re-read the mysterious note for the nine-hundredth time. *Your trust is misplaced.* It was talking about Maksim. It had to be.

Unless it was talking about Dom.

But... no. Maksim was the one who'd been less than forthright. He might have been flat-out lying. He'd definitely been covering his tracks.

Then there was the matter of who wrote the note. The man who'd bumped into me? The one who'd helped me onto the bench? Someone else?

The man who'd helped me had never returned. I hadn't waited long—only until Dom came out—but still. How long could it take to get a water?

"Kat?" Knuckles rapped on the door. "May I enter?"

I slipped the note under my pillow. "Come in."

The lever turned, and the door opened. Classical music drifted into the room from somewhere outside the apartment.

I tugged on the sheets, wrapping myself tighter. I didn't have sleepwear, so I'd stripped down to my undies with the tank top I'd been wearing.

Dom leaned against the doorframe. "I thought you may want to know... I have heard from Maksim."

I sat up. "What'd he say?"

"That he will be here tomorrow." Dom scratched at his five o'clock shadow. "He has a mobile phone for you."

"Has he made contact with that person he's been trying to reach?"

Dom shook his head, and my mood sank.

I had a theory that Raul's brother, Renan, may have decided he didn't trust Maksim, either. I could only imagine why.

"Should I confront him?" Dom asked. "About Marie or anything else?"

I pushed out a breath. The air vibrated my lips. "I'm not good at stuff like this, but... I'd say not right now. Not until we're sure about him one way or the other."

Dom played with his hair, combing it with his fingers and sweeping it to the side. "My trust for Maksim has vanished. I have no confidence left for him."

"I understand." My thoughts landed on the note. I hadn't shown it to Dom because, well—I didn't *think* the message was about him, but I couldn't say for sure.

"The light show is beginning." He thumbed behind him. "I'm going up to the roof if you wish to join me. If you are feeling better, of course."

"I am. A bit."

"Then we should hurry." Dom checked his watch. "It started at twenty-three, and it is twenty-three-oh-two."

Translation: 11:02 PM.

I waited until he was gone, then snatched up the linen pants and threw them on. Then I hurried after him.

Nighttime hovered over the city, and Paris' golden glow pushed back against the darkness. Dom and I settled onto the rooftop picnic blanket.

The Eiffel Tower rose up from Champs-de-Mars, and I could see the crowds packed onto the green.

The colors of the French flag lit up the tower while the French national anthem played. Dom sang along softly. I hummed, recalling what he'd taught me the night before.

As the song concluded, the red and white dissolved, leaving the entire structure coated in deep, sapphire blue.

A shrill whistle pierced the air. Shouts followed, claps, as the white light returned and washed over the tower before dropping all the way to the legs.

The bright white burst. *Pop!* Fireworks exploded into spirals. I gasped as dozens of them shot out from the structure and sparkled along the sides.

The bursts continued—down the tower, back up—until the fiery explosions formed a crown around the top. Classical music thundered.

Tiny bits of white light glittered. *Pop! Pop-pop-pop!* The fireworks continued, the explosions building, mounting.

Boom! A gold ring of fire and light exploded above the tower. *Boom-boom! Boom!* The percussions rattled me.

I was reminded of the landmines in Romania, of that secret village Maksim and I had found, and dread poured into me. I'd set off a mine—completely by accident—and Maksim had been knocked unconscious. Later on, I had set off more mines, and I had very nearly died.

My heart palpitated. Sweat slicked my hands.

"It's amazing, is it not?" Dom cast a grin my way. He didn't seem to notice my nervousness.

A pink glow cascaded over the tower. The light morphed into purple...then yellow... then orange. Balls of light shot out from the skinny section, going forth as a spray synched with classical music.

The explosions fizzled out, the music tapered off, and the tower settled into a burning, bleeding red.

Smoke poured off the structure—an aftereffect of the fireworks—and the stench of gunpowder laced with carbon stung my nostrils.

The smell grew stronger as the smoke looped up, climbing into the air. I pushed myself onto my knees.

The smoke thickened, reflecting the array of colors splashed across the tower. I could hardly see the sparkles now.

The veil spread, curling up and over one building and stretching toward us. "What is that?" I whispered.

Dom said something. He might have been speaking in French.

Fireworks erupted in new and more elaborate sequences, but I couldn't break my gaze from the smoke. I thought I must be imagining things until the first wisp seeped over the edge of our roof.

My eyes widened.

"Something is wrong?" A gentle touch connected with my arm. "Kat?"

My attention shot to Dom.

"Mon Dieu." He snapped to attention. "You are bleeding."

"Where?" My hand flew to my face. I didn't detect anything unusual until my fingers brushed beneath my nose.

Warm, slippery liquid coated my fingers. I stared at the bright red smear. Nosebleed. I never got those.

Dom yanked off his neckerchief. "Here. Use this."

"N-no." I put a hand up. "That's too nice."

"It is nothing. I never wear it." He scooted closer. "Please."

I let him wipe the blood and press the scarf beneath my nose. "Thanks."

He answered with a gentle smile.

Green, blue, and pink exploded in bright circles. The glitter effect rolled through the tower. I scanned, searching for the smoke, but didn't find it.

Am I dreaming? I pinched my leg just to be sure. I was definitely awake, and the nosebleed was definitely happening.

And that smoke? It had been there a second ago, but now it was definitely gone.

19. UNVEILED SECRET

We waited all morning for Maksim.

"Have you tried texting him?" I entered the living room.

Dom stood by the faux fireplace, checking his phone. He was holding his head.

"Is that him?" I hurried across the room. "Dom?"

"Mm?" His attention wandered to me.

I stopped beside the couch. "Was that Maksim?"

"*Non.*" He pushed out a breath, cheeks puffing. "Family drama—my brother, my mother." He pocketed his phone. "It never ends."

"Oh. Sorry." Disappointment slinked through me, but I forced a smile. "I know all about family drama."

Dom parked himself on the couch.

I settled beside him. My attention moved to his spent espresso on the coffee table. "Have you been up long?"

He nodded absently. "I have other problems. Bigger than my family for once." He hesitated. "I heard from the journalist."

"Again? Is he writing a story about you or...?"

"Yes, but I do not understand why." Dom massaged his eyes.

"The man asks me about an accident. *Mais attends,* I was not in an accident."

The hairs on my neck stood at attention. "Are you sure he's a journalist?"

"Yes, of course. He identified himself and his newspaper. He is one of their senior staff."

Okay. A bit unusual, but nothing to be alarmed about. Yet.

"He must have the wrong person." I touched Dom's arm, and his gaze entwined with mine. "You seem really worried."

"My career causes me to be... how do you say it? High profile? I cannot risk being confused with someone else."

"But if he prints a story that isn't true, you can make him print a retraction. You might have to get a lawyer, but there's a process. Journalists can't just say whatever they want about people."

He nodded but didn't relax. I wasn't feeling too relaxed, either. The last thing I needed was a reporter snooping around.

"Did he say when the story would run?" I asked.

"He gave no timeline. Why?"

"Nothing, really." I propped my elbow on the couch arm and used my fist as a headrest. "Just trying to figure out how to lie low."

"Your situation, yes." Dom leaned back. "I was too worried about my problems. I forgot about yours."

"I don't want to end up with my picture in the paper. A retraction would help you, but it wouldn't help me."

"Because of that man, Vladimir?"

"Yep. He has contacts all over Europe, and the—" I was about to say the cops were looking for me, too, but I stopped myself.

Dom didn't know about the shootout. He didn't know Maksim and I had been on the run from the authorities.

"The crime boss," I said, changing course, "likely hasn't tracked us here. Maksim took extra precautions, but a picture of me in a news story could alert Vladimir to my whereabouts."

"*Mon Dieu.*" Dom's eyes overflowed with concern. "Can you continue to wear a scarf and sunglasses? Would that be safer?"

"It would, but the weather is really hot, and it would be nice to look different without all the extra layers." As soon as I said it, an invisible lightbulb blinked on above my head. "Wait a second."

"Yes?" Dom scooted forward. "You have thought of something?"

My head gave a slight up-and-down.

"Tell me, please, what is it?"

Normally, I wore my hair in a bun or ponytail. Today, it was down. I grabbed a section of black curls and examined them. "Do you know of any good salons?"

———

I SAT IN A LEATHER CHAIR, SIPPING ON A GLASS OF sparkling water. Dom sat across from me, flipping through a magazine. We were in a *salon de coiffure*—hair salon—but it looked more like a club.

Textured wallpaper shaped like crystals covered the walls. A shiny silver chandelier hung in the center of the room, while pendant lights on glittery chains dangled above each hair station, brightening the space where the stylists worked.

There were eight stations, and they were all full. But Dom knew the owners, and as soon as he called, they offered to squeeze me in. They even brought in an extra stylist.

"What about this?" Dom flipped the magazine round, showing me a blonde with stick-straight, chin-length hair.

"My hair shrinks up as soon as it's curly. I'll look like Shirley What's-Her-Name. Cochran. Temple. That child actress."

Dom shrugged.

A lanky man sashayed into the waiting area. Dom stood and greeted him with a kiss on each cheek. They had an exchange before the man turned to me and extended a hand.

"This is my very good friend, Robert." Dom said it *roh-BEHR*. "He and his partner, Georges, own the salon."

"Such a pleasure to meet you." Robert's accent curled across his words. He took my hand and gave it a kiss. "I will be overseeing your transformation today, *mademoiselle*."

"Transformation?" I looked at Dom.

"It will be drastic," he said. "Will it not?"

"Here at Salon Robert, we use the most advanced products and techniques." He adjusted his black-rimmed glasses and studied my hair. "It is virgin?" he asked, plucking at my curls.

"It's never been dyed, if that's what you mean."

"You are certainly a level one, but I believe we can take you to a level seven today without compromising the hair's integrity." He released the curls. "Should you wish to go even lighter, you will need to return after a little time."

"What's level seven?"

"Medium blond."

"That should be light enough." My attention returned to Dom. "You think?"

Dom nodded.

Robert called out to a woman. She was tying her apron and waltzed over to us. They had an exchange.

"We must see how the hair responds," Robert said, "but it is possible we can use a special relaxer after."

"To straighten it?" I asked.

"Straightening would do too much damage. No, this product will relax the curls enough to make them more manageable. This would be the most we could do in one sitting."

Robert excused himself and disappeared behind a shiny curtain in the back.

"Hey, Dom?" I fidgeted with my purse. "I have plenty of money, but I don't have access to it right now. Would you maybe be willing to, um—"

"*Mon amie*, please. Do not worry about any of this."

"Are you sure? I feel really bad."

"Don't." He brushed his thumb over my chin. It was a friendly gesture, not romantic, but it felt kind of... intimate.

My cheeks warmed. I looked down.

"You have been through a lot. I want to help." He took my hand and gave a tender squeeze. "I hope you will let me."

I met his gaze. "Thanks."

He smiled and then peered past me. "You are being summoned."

I followed his gaze to Robert, who had the curtain pulled aside. He was waving me over.

"I am going to call my agent." Dom held up his phone. "To speak with him about the journalist."

I smiled. "I'll be here."

Robert held the curtain, ushering me toward a hair-wash station. "*Merci*," I said, squeezing past him.

I paused and looked back. He was already gone. Hopefully, his agent would have a solution. And I *really* hoped that journalist wouldn't do any more digging until I was gone.

My stylist only spoke French, but Robert was there to translate. "You have a lot of hair," he explained. "The timing is very important, so I am going to assist."

The two of them parted, sectioned, and foiled my hair until I looked like the chandelier out front. Creamy bleach coated every inch.

A styling station opened up within the hour. Large windows spanned the salon, and I noticed Dom pacing the sidewalk out front. He was still on his call.

The foil started coming off, and the stylist had to rinse my hair. When she finished, I scanned the windows. Pedestrians hustled up and down the sidewalk, but Dom wasn't among them.

Robert was whipping up a mixture of toner when Dom returned. Our eyes met in the mirror, and I waved. He didn't wave back. He didn't even smile.

He cut between the styling stations.

"Not quite a seven." I combed at my hair. "And it's really brassy, but they started with the ends and finished with the roots, which somehow made it even."

Dom didn't respond. His expression had become unreadable.

"This lady is about to add the toner"—I gestured at the woman—"then Robert wants to talk to me about a cut. We're thinking long layers that will look natural, straight or curly."

Dom remained silent.

I rotated in my seat. "Is something wrong?"

"I need to know the truth." His matter-of-factness clamped down on my midsection. He spoke to the stylist in French, and the woman stepped away.

I watched her disappear through the shiny curtain.

Dom rubbed a hand over his stubbled cheeks and down around his chin. "Are you and Maksim in trouble with the police? Is that the true reason for all this?" He motioned at my hair.

My stomach bottomed out. I swallowed past the rock in my throat and nodded. His frown deepened.

"I'm sorry," I whispered, peeking over at the next styling station. The stylist didn't seem to notice us, but the guy who was getting his hair cut glanced our way.

I stood and pulled Dom over to the waiting area. "Maksim and I didn't do anything wrong. But..."

Dom rolled his eyes. "There is a 'but'?"

"Those men who tried to kidnap me had guns. They had me in their vehicle and were about to take off. Then Maksim showed up, and—"

Dom waited. "And?"

"He disarmed one of the men and shot him. Then he shot the guy who was holding me hostage."

Dom grabbed his head.

"Maksim didn't kill the third guy. Just wounded him." I lowered my voice. "Barçelona municipal police were there. They could have been fake cops, but Maksim thinks they were dirty."

His anger dissolved into confusion. "I don't understand what this means. Dirty?"

"Real cops but corrupt. That's why we haven't gone to the police. If I'm extradited to Spain, those same cops might very well turn me over to Vladimir."

"How could you keep this from me? I cannot be involved in this. It will ruin my career!"

"I'm sorry. I didn't mean to—" A pause. "This isn't why the journalist keeps contacting you, is it?"

Dom's expression blanked. His stare circled the salon. "No."

I exhaled a long breath and plunked myself in a leather chair. "Maksim and I needed someplace to stay for a day or two, and it didn't seem like a big deal to exclude certain details. I see now that it was." I slipped my hand into his. "Dom, I'm sorry. Will you forgive me?"

He started to pull away. His attention fell to my hand, and he plunked himself in the chair next to mine. We sat there—hand in hand, quiet—until my stylist waved.

"I think she needs me."

Dom didn't respond. I was about to repeat myself when I noticed he was looking at the receptionist. Actually, he might've been looking at something on her desk.

"Hey." I stood, and his hand slipped from mine. "They still have a lot to do with my hair, so."

He nodded absently.

"This will stay between us, right? The stuff I just told you?"

He hesitated. His eyes flashed toward me, but then he looked away.

The woman cupped her mouth. *"Mademoiselle?"* She waved again.

I focused on Dom, pleading with my eyes.

He sighed and waved me away. I smiled, giving his shoulder a grateful squeeze, and returned to the styling station.

The woman fussed over my hair, fingering the brassy locks

and showing me the bowl of toner. As my attention shifted, I noticed Dom was no longer in the waiting area.

I scanned the windows. He wasn't out front, either, and heaviness sank to the pit of my stomach.

Please don't let him go to the cops. Please please please. But I had a feeling that was exactly what he was doing.

20. DRESS REHEARSAL

"Are you looking for your friend?" The receptionist smiled from behind her desk. "The very handsome man who was here earlier?"

"I am. Do you happen to know where he went?"

"He had a meeting with his agent. He said he would return when he is finished." She gave her counter a once-over. "I apologize. I was going to write the message, but I cannot locate my notepad."

"How long ago did he leave?"

The girl touched a pen to her chin, eyes thoughtful. "He spoke to me, saying you are—" She hesitated, brow lifting. "You are his friend, *non*? Not his girlfriend?"

"No, no. Just a friend."

Relief washed through her features, but the expression was soon marred by disappointed. "I thought he would ask for my telephone number. I suppose he was very busy. He left and then returned ten minutes later, saying I should give you the message about his meeting." She passed me a piece of scratch paper. "Please, would you give him my telephone number? He is a very handsome man, and I see him in here sometimes."

"Sure." I slipped the number in my purse. "I'll let him know."

Robert's voice startled me. *"Et voilà! Très magnifique!"*

"Oh." My cheeks warmed. "You think so?"

"I know so. You look beautiful, darling." He took my hands and kissed them both, one after the other. "It is the perfect cut, and with the additional treatment, you will find the curls easier to flatten." He led me over to the styling tools and grabbed a circular hair dryer, then a really expensive-looking flat iron.

"About that." I cleared my throat. "Dom had a meeting with his agent, and... The thing is, he was supposed to pay for everything."

"This is not a problem." Robert placed the styling tools in a basket and swiped an array of products from the next shelf. "Take this to Heather. Have her calculate the total and add it to the account of Dominique." Robert smiled. "You are welcome to wait as long as you wish, but you have been here many hours. Perhaps you would like to enjoy lunch or have a drink somewhere."

The mere thought of alcohol churned my stomach. "I'm good. But I really need to do some shopping. Are we in a good area for that?"

"Mademoiselle." His smile brightened. "We are in Saint-Germain-des-Prés. Have you heard of it?"

I shook my head.

"This neighborhood is famous for its shopping. I can recommend many fabulous places."

"Okay, but I specifically need, um, underwear?"

"Lingerie?" His eyebrows gave a bounce.

"Nooo." I wagged my head. "I lost my belongings, and I don't have any underwear. *Normal* underwear. I need clothes, too, but from someplace budget friendly, if you know what I mean. Since I'm having to replace everything."

"I know of an excellent secondhand shop where you can purchase quality clothing at affordable prices. I can likewise direct you to a shop for undergarments."

I exhaled the breath I'd been holding, already feeling lighter. "That would be perfect."

THE UNDERWEAR SHOP WAS ON THE SAME STREET AS the salon. I normally wore stretchy, sporty underwear, the kind that didn't ride up while running or lifting weights, but this place had nothing like that.

I settled for three pairs of the softest, stretchiest undies I could find. They weren't all that soft, actually, and they didn't fully cover my tush—which was beyond annoying. I also couldn't find a bra without wire, padding, or lace.

The secondhand shop required a short walk. As I passed beside a men's clothing store, I paused to check my reflection.

Long, smooth layers framed my face. I held up a chunk and examined the color. We hadn't reached the level we were aiming for, and my hair hung on to the warm tones more than expected.

The result? Brandy's shade of hair but bronzier.

The thought of my best friend sent a wave of sadness crashing into me. She was probably so worried, but I couldn't do anything about that until Maksim finished setting up my new—

I caught a glimpse of someone's reflection in the storefront window, and my thoughts came to a screeching halt. It was a man, and he was across the street.

I started to turn, but Maksim's voice rushed in. *"Pretend you're window-shopping or fixing your hair. That will let you see who's behind you."*

The man seemed to be on a call, and every so often, he glanced my way. I could have sworn he looked familiar.

Rule Seven lit up my thoughts: *Assume you're being tailed.*

I played with my hair, flipping it, fingering different sections. I watched that man the entire time.

Several seconds ticked by before he pocketed his phone and

continued on his way. He didn't pause or look back, and I wondered if I had imagined the whole thing.

But what about yesterday? Someone had slipped me a note, and I was convinced it'd been Raul's brother. Was that why I recognized this man? Had I encountered him yesterday?

I turned, about to cross the street and follow him, but I didn't see him anymore. Either he'd gone into one of the stores or he'd turned a corner.

The secondhand shop was a five-minute walk, and I didn't see that man—or anyone else suspicious—on the way there. I even waited and watched from inside the shop, thinking the man might pass by.

"*Bonjour.*" A woman's voice startled me.

I wheeled around and came face-to-face with the store clerk.

"S-sorry." I placed a hand to my chest. "I was, um—"

"You are American?"

I nodded.

"I speak a little English." She gestured to a set of curtained alcoves. "Those are the fitting rooms. You can try on the clothes before you buy, but we do not accept returns."

"Thanks. I'm basically replacing my wardrobe, so I might be a while."

She shrugged and ventured behind the counter.

I grabbed any- and everything that might fit—skirts, shirts, dresses, shorts—and hauled the clothes into the first fitting room.

DOM HADN'T RETURNED TO THE SALON BY THE TIME I finished shopping. I considered waiting for him, but I didn't want to draw attention to the fact that I'd been ditched.

His apartment wasn't far. I decided to go there and hope he was upstairs making calls. I hoped *really* hard he wasn't sitting in a police station, signing an affidavit about what I'd told him.

I passed between a row of parked cars and Dom's apartment

building. I was loaded down with shopping bags—shoes, scarves, sunglasses, and several new outfits. Plus the underwear. Plus the stuff from Salon Robert. Plus...

Something from the pharmacy. My mind wandered to the little white box. Another pregnancy test. I hadn't started my cycle yet, so I did some calculating.

I was officially one to three days late, thereabouts.

This wasn't something I could put off any longer. Maksim was going to show up with my phone sooner or later, and I needed to be prepared with whatever I was going to tell him.

A family approached the entrance to Dom's building. I didn't have a way inside, so I decided to follow them in.

My new leather wedges padded over the pavement. My new dress, which was much shorter than I normally wore, rode up. I tugged on the thin material—best I could with all the shopping bags—and hurried toward the entrance.

The man had a baby strapped to his chest and a thin, summer beanie on his head. He unlatched the harness and did a handoff to the mom, saying something as he did.

His baritone voice jarred me. I froze.

The woman strapped on the harness and secured the baby. She was tall, blond, and voluptuous up top. A bit around her hips, too. Other than that, she was rather slender.

I pulled my sunglasses down. Her lips were plump, stained in rosy pink, and her eyes reflected the color of periwinkles.

I replaced my sunglasses. Why did she look so familiar?

She sent a fleeting look and said something to the guy. He stepped to the side, gesturing for me to pass. I recognized his smile, and my heart tumbled into a free-fall.

Maksim.

He said something in French. When I didn't answer, the smile slid right off his face. He walked forward, expression tentative, and reached out.

I didn't budge—couldn't—as he removed my sunglasses. His eyes went round and wide.

My attention shifted to the woman, and an epiphany rolled across my thoughts. She was the half-naked model I'd seen in that perfume ad, the one Maksim had been staring at when we were in Orléans.

All the puzzle pieces snapped into place—the model, the baby, Maksim's weird behavior.

"Oh my God." I dropped every single shopping bag and covered my mouth. Warm streams spilled down my hand as I turned around and ran up the sidewalk.

21. UNEXPECTED DETOUR

I didn't make it far in my new shoes. A pebble rolled beneath the wedge, and my knee buckled. I collapsed with a cry.

Jeans and black motorcycle boots stopped beside me. Maksim tried to help me up.

Hot pavement cooked my bare legs, but I didn't care. I yanked my arm out of his grasp. "Don't touch me."

He squatted, bringing himself eye-level. "Kat, I'm sorry. I was going to tell you."

"Oh, really?" Fury burned in my chest. "Because it sure as hell doesn't seem like you were."

"I was working on it." He offered his hand again. "We've been able to stay below the radar here. Let's not make a scene."

I peered past him.

The blonde craned her neck, staring while she and the baby crossed to the opposite sidewalk. She didn't seem happy that I had interrupted her family outing.

Maksim took my arm and lifted. I tugged at the new dress, desperately wishing it were longer. Bits of dirt smeared my thigh. Maksim reached to wipe it.

I swatted his hand.

"Forgive me." He raised both hands in surrender. "Habit."

"How long have you known about...?" I couldn't speak past the rock in my throat.

"The child?" Maksim finished, and I nodded. "There's an old number I used to have. I hadn't checked it since the bike accident, but I decided to do so after I had access to Ivy's system. I thought, perhaps, old contacts may have reached out and that they could prove useful for keeping tabs on Vladimir." His gaze wandered. "It was then that I realized my ex had been trying to contact me—to let me know she was pregnant and that she was going to have the baby."

"Marie," I whispered.

He focused on me. "Dom told you."

"It was his friends, Timothée and Sabrina." I snatched my sunglasses. "Dom never said a word before that, and *nobody* has said anything about a baby."

"They don't know." Maksim raked his teeth over his bottom lip, which was notably chapped. I could only imagine why. "I didn't mean for you to find out this way. I was planning to explain everything after—"

"After what? You get married? Have more kids?"

"After I take a paternity test." He fixed his beanie. "That's where we're going."

"You have to take a—" My mouth tumbled open. "That's right. Because she cheated on you."

"She didn't, actually. She claims she didn't."

"And you believe her?"

"I don't know what to believe." He rubbed his forehead. "Marie has blue eyes, but Julien has brown eyes like me."

"Julien?" My chin quivered. "That's the baby's name?"

Maksim nodded. "He's six months old."

My mind spun. This whole thing felt surreal, like I'd been dropped into a bad dream. But hearing his son's name grounded everything in reality.

"Are you in love with her?" Tears choked me. "Is that why you broke up with me? Because... Because..." Too many emotions collided at once—anger, regret, sadness. I couldn't form a cohesive thought, let alone express one.

"I've desired a family for many years," he began slowly. "Since I was a teenager. Younger. I dreamed of having a wife and children even as a boy."

My stomach flipped. He'd always wanted a family, and now he had one.

But what about me? What if *I* was pregnant?

"I have your phone." He pulled a smartphone from his pocket and handed it over. "I've set up another double VPN, as well as a VoIP." He placed a folded-up piece of paper in my hand. "Instructions for how to use them are here. Do not give any indication of where we are. Assume Vladimir is monitoring anyone you speak to. Understand?"

I stared at the instructions. This was the same kind of paper as the note from yesterday.

"Kat." Maksim gripped my shoulders. "Are you listening?"

My gaze connected with his. His brown eyes caught the light the way they always did on a sunny day, and the earthy layers of a desert landscape shined through.

He said Julien had his eyes. What if our baby ended up with—?

Stop it. You don't even know if you're pregnant.

Marie called out from across the street. Her voice strained, matching her pinched expression. She had officially migrated into "pissed off" territory.

Maksim lifted a hand, telling her know to wait. "I have to go. But I can't leave the phone with you unless you—"

"Read the instructions. Assume I'm being monitored at all times." I sniffled, nodding. "Got it."

"You need to call Mr. Amsel first. Make sure that security breach didn't affect any of your accounts. Do *not* book any flights."

"'Kay."

"Promise me." He stooped, once again bringing himself eye-level. "I need to hear it."

"I promise." The answer was barely audible, but I managed to get the words out.

He straightened. "Do you have your passport?"

I dug it out of my purse.

"I haven't been able to make contact with Renan." He took the passport from me.

My shoulders twitched. Should I tell him about the note? I decided to probe instead. "Is that unusual?"

"It is considering Raul was involved." Maksim tucked my passport in his pocket. "I'm working on a contingency plan. It's a last resort, but it could work." He cleared his throat. "I've, um, spoken to Daniel. He's been checking on Émilien daily. He's still in prison."

An invisible weight lifted off me. At least Émilien was locked away.

"Madă has a cousin in the Romanian government," Maksim continued. "She's reaching out to him, checking to see if he can put pressure on EU officials. Perhaps they can extradite Émilien to Brussels."

"Brussels?" The heaviness returned with a crushing blow. "That's near here, isn't it? Close to France?"

"Just north of here."

"You think Émilien should be *closer*?" My voice pitched.

"Putting him in EU custody would ensure the most secure detainment."

The idea of Émilien being in a neighboring country made me shudder.

"Hey." Maksim touched my arm. "I know this isn't easy, but I hope you'll continue to—"

"Trust you?" I pulled myself out of his grasp. "You keep saying that"—my attention flicked to Marie—"but trust is in short supply."

"Kat, I never intended to hurt you."

"Of course you didn't." I hugged myself. "You just used me— first as a summer fling, now as justification for coming here."

His jaw tightened. "None of that is true."

"It's not?" My emotions swelled, pressing against my heart, my chest, my throat. I turned away, unable to stop the flow.

I threw on my sunglasses. Tears leaked behind the lenses.

"Dom's telephone number is programmed into your phone." Maksim's voice fell low. "My new number is in there, as well, in case you need anything."

"Which I hopefully won't." I wanted my words to hurt him. Instead, they sliced and diced me until my insides felt shredded.

The tears poured harder.

Maksim turned to go but then faced me. "I know I don't tell you this often, but you did well." He gestured at my hair. "I didn't recognize you at all. That will be helpful if we resort to the contingency plan."

He left me there and crossed the street. Marie waited for him.

As he reached the opposite curb, she tangled her arms around him and raised up on her tiptoes. She was going to kiss him, and she was going to make sure I saw.

The pain inside me deepened, spreading, until everything ached.

Maksim dodged the kiss—barely—and led Marie up the sidewalk. They each sent a fleeting glance my way, though Marie's was more of a glare.

22. FRENCH COP

"Kat?" Dom stepped off the elevator and hurried across the hall. "*Oh là là!* Why are you crying?"

I sat next to Dom's door, leaning against the wall. "He has a baby."

"Who does?" Dom's expression went tall and wide. "What do you speak of?"

"Maksim and Marie. They have a baby. *Together.*" I cried into my hands.

"*Oh là là. Oh, mon Dieu.*" Dom helped me up. Then he gathered my shopping bags and opened his door. "Shh, everything will be okay."

"Did you tell the police?"

Confusion glimmered in his eyes. "About a baby?"

"About me." I wiped the slosh from my face. "Is that where you went? Are they coming for me?"

"*Non, mon amie.*" No, my friend. "Nobody is coming for you."

Relief gushed, swirling with my other emotions.

Dom ushered me inside the apartment and helped me onto the couch. As he set the bags down, the pregnancy test fell out. He didn't notice, but I did.

I didn't bother to pick it up. Hell, I might not even take it.

Dom ventured into the kitchen and returned with a glass of water. I sipped on it while filling him in about Maksim and Marie.

His expression grew more and more troubled. "*Oh, mince.* I cannot believe it."

"Sabrina and Timothée went over there. How did they not realize she had a *baby*?"

"Perhaps they did but preferred not to say more." Dom paced the living room. "I must—" He hesitated.

"What?" I waited, but he didn't go on. Also, he looked kind of... startled. "Dom?"

He pressed a finger to his lips, silencing me. Then he went to my purse and unzipped it.

"What are you—"

He jammed the finger to his lips again. After sifting through my purse, he pulled out a pen. He then whipped something out of his pocket.

A notepad?

It was. The kind with a carbon-copy layer. Seemed like an odd thing to carry around—and yet, I had a vague recollection of someone talking about missing their notepad.

He scribbled something.

Don't say anything.

My eyes bulged. I mouthed "Why?"

He scratched through that note and scribbled something else.

~~Don't say anything.~~
Where is the mobile Maksim gave to you?

I pulled out the phone.

He snatched it and hurried into the kitchen. I followed him.

By the time I arrived, he was setting two phones—mine and his—in the fridge.

I gaped. "What in the world—"

"*Bah ouiaaas.* This is bad." He shut the door and dragged me out of the kitchen. I stumbled after him. "When we were at the salon," he began, "after I went outside to make calls—"

Knock knock knock.

Dom fell silent.

"Are you expecting someone?" I whispered.

He shook his head.

The knock repeated, louder. *"Monsieur Dubois?"* Mih-SHUR doo-BWAH.

"Your last name is Dubois?" I whispered.

Dom peeled his stare away from the door. *"Oui."* He swallowed. "Dominique Dubois."

The man said something else, and Dom hustled to the door. The man on the other side was in his late thirties or early forties. His dark hair was short. His mustache blended with a trimmed goatee.

"Bonjour. Excusez-moi." The man nodded in my direction and then continued speaking to Dom, who grew tenser by the second.

I walked forward. "What's going on?"

"The building is being evacuated," Dom said.

"What? Why?" I focused on the man and noticed an orange band on his sleeve. He wore jeans and a black polo, but the message across the band was clear.

POLICE

My center pinched. Dom said he hadn't called the police. Had he been lying?

"For what reason are we being evacuated?" Dom asked. "Is there a fire?" He looked and sounded genuinely confused.

The man was about to answer when an earsplitting alarm

pierced the stillness. He jolted, glancing around inside the hallway.

"It *is* a fire." Dom patted his pockets and returned to the kitchen.

I called after him. "Are you getting your phone?"

"*Oui.*"

"Grab mine, too." I exhaled, waiting—but when he returned, he didn't have either phone. "Where are they?"

"We go without them."

"Are you serious?" I gestured at the fridge. "They're right there."

He plucked his keys off the bar, ignoring me.

I rolled my eyes and marched into the kitchen. "Fine. Do whatever you want. I'm taking mine." I snatched my phone out of the fridge.

Dom looked poised to object. He took one look at my phone and shut his mouth. What was his deal?

The cop waited inside the doorway. "You are American?" he asked, accent dripping.

"Um, yeah."

"You will need to bring your passport." The cop lifted an eyebrow. "If you have one?"

"'Course." I grabbed my purse. The passport wasn't in there, but he'd never know that. Hopefully.

The cop walked out and headed straight for the elevator. Dom ushered me out and locked the apartment.

"We shouldn't go that way," I said to the cop.

He slanted a look. "*Pardon?*"

"We could get stuck in the elevator. Because of the fire."

"It's true." Dom headed for the stairwell. "This way is better."

The cop—if he really was one—gestured for me to go ahead. I slipped inside the stairwell and shuffled down the steps.

I didn't slow down until I caught up to Dom.

We merged with foot traffic flowing from the apartments on the next floor. Panicked voices competed with the *whoop* of the fire alarm. I kept expecting to smell smoke, but a volatile mix of colognes and perfumes filled the enclosed space instead.

The sea of people grew as we descended. A woman waddled down the stairs in her robe. Several people carried dogs and cats.

I threw a glance over my shoulder. The cop was helping an old lady. He made eye contact with me and offered a smile and nod.

I focused forward. "We need to disappear."

"Now?" Dom said. "Why?"

"That guy's asking for my passport."

"You do not have your passport." He lowered his volume. "You said you gave it to Maksim."

"But if that man really is a cop, he'll be able to search my name with or without an ID. Dom, there might be an APB out for me." We rounded the next floor. "What were you trying to tell me before he showed up?"

Dom's stare flicked behind us. Surprise crisscrossed his face as he glanced to and fro.

The cop was gone. But... he'd just been there.

"You have your phone," Dom said. "*Non?*"

I focused on him. "It's in my purse."

He grimaced and kept glancing around. Finally, he shook his head.

"What's wrong?"

"There is a café," he whispered, leaning in. "They have tables in the back. Very private. Ask to be seated in this area and wait for me. I will deal with the *flic.*"

"What will you say if he asks about me?"

"*Bah ouais.* I will say I do not know you."

"Dom." I pulled him to a stop. "The man found us in your apartment."

"I will say I met you only today and brought you there for sex." He shrugged. "*Ça marche?*" *It works?*

Words evaded me.

Residents packed the ground floor. We pushed through the crowd until summertime heat greeted us.

"Café Laurent on the Avenue de Suffren." He pointed me in the direction. "Go."

Cop cars idled with their lights on. A fire truck rumbled, blipping its siren. I did my best to blend in with the residents.

When I felt sure no one was watching, I turned the corner and bolted for Avenue de Suffren.

23. SECRET ADMIRER

Buses chugged up the two-lane street. Pedestrians roamed the sidewalk. I hustled past couples and families, people walking their dogs, shoppers going in and out of stores.

Off-white stone buildings occupied the space on my left. Modern stucco apartments towered on my right.

I kept going... one block, two.

There. People dined around an outdoor patio covered by a dark red awning. CAFÉ LAURENT.

The patio took up half the sidewalk, while another section of tables and chairs extended onto the street, filling the space where cars would have parallel parked.

A maître d' greeted me.

"Uh, *parlez-vous anglais*? I-I need a table in the back."

"Zis way, *mademoiselle*." He led me past the patio and through the busy dining room. The bar was packed. So was the dining room.

Silverware clinked under a hum of conversations. Clangs rattled from the kitchen, while a rich aroma of garlic, onion, and roasted meat filtered into my senses.

The sounds softened as we rounded a corner.

"Voilà." He gestured at a table. There were others but no customers. Just me.

The man left a two-sided menu in English and returned to the main part of the restaurant. Five minutes went by. Ten.

A waitress appeared. *"Bonjour, je m'appelle Elize."* Hello, my name is Elize.

The lady continued in French. I stopped her.

"Can I just get a *café au lait,* please? And some water?" I felt bad for not speaking what little French I knew, but I had bigger fish to fry.

Where was Dom?

The waitress left a cloth napkin and silverware and then disappeared. I unzipped my purse, planning to pull out my phone, then remembered what Dom had said. *"I will deal with the* flic.*"*

I closed the zipper. Better not text. He could be midconversation with that cop.

I propped my elbow on the table, using my palm as a chin rest, and let my thoughts wander to the other oddity—that paper Maksim had written the instructions on. Same kind yesterday's note had been written on.

But Maksim couldn't have written the note yesterday. That didn't even make sense... unless the paper had come from the same source.

Marie. She had keyed Dom's car out of spite. What if she slipped me the note—also out of spite—to keep me away from Maksim?

The waitress returned with my coffee. After she set everything on the table, a single glass of red wine remained on her tray. She set that down, too.

"I didn't order wine."

"It is from another customer." Her mouth curled up. "He saw you enter and said to deliver it to you." She placed a folded napkin in front of me. "And he gave me this. I think he likes you."

I picked up the napkin, jaw saggy. "Is this a customer you know? Have you seen him before?"

She touched her chin, expression thoughtful. "I'm not sure. I don't think so."

"Can you show me? But I don't want him to know I'm looking."

She beckoned me. I followed her to the end of this back section and watched her peer around the corner.

She straightened. "He is not there."

"He's not?" I poked my head out. "Could he have moved?"

"He is wearing a hat. Uh..." She motioned with her hand.

"Like a baseball cap? A beanie?"

She shook her head. "The word in my language *le chapeau*. Here, I will show." She did a quick search on her phone.

I stared at the image. "A fedora?"

"*Oui*. It was black."

I scanned the dining room, the bar area. I didn't see anyone in a fedora until...

There. Outside the restaurant. I spied him through the large windows. He was crossing the street.

I threw everything into my purse, making doubly sure the napkin was in there. "I'll be back to pay for the coffee."

The waitress replied, but I was already weaving between tables.

I barreled out of the restaurant as the fedora disappeared into the backseat of a town car. The windows were tinted, but I could make out the driver's chauffeur hat.

He merged into traffic before I could step off the sidewalk.

"Dang it." The driver wasn't speeding. Could have caught up to him if I'd been in a car.

"Taxi?" someone said. I barely heard the accented voice as I angled for the brasserie's main entrance. The person repeated himself. "Taxi?"

I peeked over and found a rotund man, medium height, standing beside a blue sedan. The sign on his roof glowed yellow.

Taxi Parisian

"What's this?" The familiar voice pulled me around. Dom strode up the sidewalk. "I told you to wait inside."

My attention traveled from him to the taxi and then back again. "Get in the cab."

"Why? What are we doing?"

"Just get in." I hauled him toward the taxi. "Excuse me?" I paused in front of the cabbie. "Did you see that man just now? The one in the hat?"

"Gustave sees everything, *mademoiselle*." He bowed. "Whether friend or foe, I saw the man of whom you speak."

"Did you see the town car he got into?"

"*Assurément.*" Most assuredly.

I opened the back door and shoved Dom inside. "Then follow that car."

"*Oui, mademoiselle!*" The cabbie did a French salute—palm flat and facing outward; elbow pointed to the side. Then he dropped into the driver's seat.

I didn't have my door shut before he whipped the car onto the road. He cut off the next wave of traffic, including a bus, and an array of honks went up.

The cabbie—Gustave?—didn't seem to notice, blasting his horn while giving us a thumbs-up. Miniature French flags hung from his rearview mirror. An actual French flag, the kind you'd put on a flagpole, draped the passenger seat.

He barreled into a multiway intersection that had no clear right-of-way and without any regard for the other cars. Dom scrambled for his seatbelt.

Stone apartment buildings loomed at every corner, and fancy restaurants and cafés took up the ground floor of each one. The town car turned right at one such restaurant.

I pointed "There!"

"I see him." The cabbie's attention returned to the rearview mirror. "Gustave sees all, *mademoi—*"

Dom shouted, clutching the seat in front of him. Gustave crunched his brakes, and the cab skidded into a crosswalk.

A lady carrying a tall yellow TOUR GUIDE flag jumped out of the way. Her tour group scattered.

Gustave lambasted them with his horn. He didn't stop until the very last tourist had cleared out. Dom and I shared a worried look.

"Um, Gustave?" I leaned forward. "We want to be discreet—"

He punched the gas. His tires squealed. Smoke and the essence of melted rubber filtered into the air.

He zoomed forward, careening onto the side street. I slammed into my door. Dom slammed into me.

We zipped past eateries, boutiques, offices... and all the while, Maksim's rules blazed through my mind. *Be discreet. Avoid unwanted attention.*

I cringed as we sped past pedestrians. They stared, looking horrified or offended. A mix of both. Then I spotted the one person I absolutely could not risk encountering.

"Gustave! Cop!"

"Flic!" Dom translated.

Gustave crushed the brakes. The car ground to a crawl.

The cop had parked in a parallel space. A navy polo hugged her lean form, though I could barely see her under the heavy-duty tactical gear.

She noticed us, and her eyes narrowed.

"Gustave is like the ninja," the cabbie whispered. "Do not worry, *mademoiselle.* The police will not know we are here." He flattened his hand and karate-chopped the air.

Dom's expression ballooned. He looked like he wanted to safety-roll out of the car.

The cop had to know something was up—she was staring like she knew—so I whipped out my new phone and pretended to snap pictures of our surroundings. I even made a "wow" face and grabbed Dom's shoulder excitedly.

He stared at me like I'd lost my ever-lovin' mind.

Gustave inched along, and I managed to sneak a peek at the cop.

She was still staring at us.

Gustave picked up speed at the next block. When we didn't immediately catch up to the town car, he revved the engine.

"This is good! Hey!" I tapped his shoulder, intervening before he hauled ass. "We need to be discreet, remember? Like the ninja?"

"Oui, mademoiselle." He did another French salute and focused on the road.

"Who is that?" Dom's attention flashed ahead of us. The town car was three vehicles away. "Why do we follow them?"

"The waitress delivered a note to me. She said it was from a man wearing a fedora. I saw him get into *that* town car."

"And we are chasing him?" Dom's mouth flew open. "Kat—"

"I know, I know. But I'm pretty sure that's Raul's brother, Renan." When Dom's stare blanked, I added "You know. The person Maksim has been trying to make contact with?"

"Are you certain?" A troubled look overshadowed his shock. "What did the note say?"

I sifted through my purse. The napkin lay crumpled beneath my wallet.

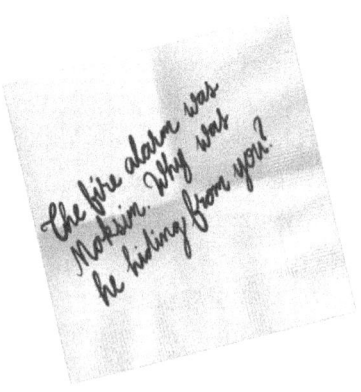

I read the note and gasped.

"This does not make sense." Dom rubbed his chin. "You said Maksim was taking a paternity test."

"I thought he was."

Gustave hung a sharp left. I flew across the backseat and slammed into Dom, smashing him against the door. He grunted, then screamed, as a car barreled toward us.

The driver blasted his horn and whipped to the side. Tires squealed. The next car skidded to a stop.

Gustave checked his mirrors and gave us another thumbs-up. Dom fumbled with the lock button. We were back up to speed before he could get the door open.

The town car cruised ahead of us.

"Gustave?" I leaned forward. "It's better if you—"

I was going to say "hang back" when the town car catapulted forward.

Gustave gunned it. The momentum sucked me backward. The back of my head hit the headrest.

Dom braced the seat in front of him. "I am jumping out. I no longer care about the consequences."

The town car ground to a stop.

Gustave crushed the brakes and skidded... and kept skidding. Dom and I screamed.

Tap. Gustave's front bumper nudged the town car. The chauffeur climbed out. This was my chance.

I unlocked my door and pushed it open. The chauffeur froze when he saw me running toward him. "Who's in there?" I pointed at the car. "Is that Renan?"

The chauffeur replied in French.

Gustave shouted revolutionary cries. *"Vive la Republique! Vive la France!"* I glanced that way and found him waving the French flag.

I focused forward. The chauffeur held up both hands in a calming gesture.

I brushed past him and marched to the town car. The driver's side door was open. I pressed the unlock button, yanked open the back door, and...

My shoulders fell. The man in the hat was gone.

24. NEW ROUTE

I stared at my phone, trying to process what I was reading.

> **ME:**
> Did you go back to Dom's today?

> **MAKSIM**
> Yes.

> **ME:**
> Did you pull the fire alarm?

His silence filled the gap with a resounding "yes." He *had* pulled the alarm. But why?

> **ME:**
> Mind if I ask why you came back?

The messages hung there, unanswered, looking pathetic. Like a poor soul who'd been stood up.

Maksim was ghosting me.

The phone vibrated. A familiar number with a 404 area code appeared. Brandy.

"Hello?" I said, answering the call.

"Kat?" A pause. "Kat, is that you? Can you hear me?" Her husky voice warbled under an electronic buzz.

"I can hear you. Can you hear me?"

A pause, longer this time. "Barely."

Great. We were having a connection issue.

"Are you in Russia?" Brandy asked. "I heard a woman's voice, and she sounded Russian."

I had heard the same voice. It was a pre-recorded message that was probably saying something like "please hold" or "wait while we connect your call." Maksim's VoIP was set up through Ukraine, and their language was pretty close to Russian.

"I can't tell you where I am. I'm sorry."

"Huh?" Brandy's voice pitched. "Babe. You're gonna have to..." As she said "to," the warble took hold and drew out the word. *Toooooo.*

I pulled the phone away from my ear. Ugh.

The noise ceased, and mumbling followed. There were two voices now, and one of them was deeper.

"Is that Dave?" I asked.

"Hang on, babe. Dave's saying something."

I rolled my eyes. This same thing happened when I had called Mr. Amsel. I ended up sending him a secure email instead.

Should I do the same for Brandy? Or a text?

I disconnected the call and browsed my apps. When Maksim and I were in Spain, he'd let me use a messaging app to talk to Brandy. That app wasn't on here, but I saw another I recognized.

This particular app had end-to-end encryption, and Brandy's family used it for a group chat. Had he known that when he downloaded it?

I made sure I was logged into the VPN.

ME:
Hey. Message me here.

BEE:
Babe! WTH?!

ME:
Sorry. Not enough bandwidth for a call I guess.

BEE:
Where are you? I've been trying to reach you on that dumb app Maksi-Pad made us use.
Keep getting a weird message.

"Maksi-Pad" was Brandy's name for Maksim. She'd never thought very highly of him, and she made that clear when we were in Romania.

Just wait 'til I tell her about the Marie thing.

My composure cracked. I inhaled a shaky breath and swiped a reply. There was a real temptation to tell her about Maksim's ex, their baby, and everything else going on.

I resisted. There'd be plenty of time for that later. For now, I had to be vague so that I didn't give away our location.

ME:
Don't use Maksim's app anymore. Uninstall it.
Do a factory reset.

BEE:
Why?

ME:
The app's been compromised. Someone could use it as a backdoor to get into your phone.

> **BEE:**
> WHAT?! KAT, WTH IS GOING ON?!

I clamped down on my bottom lip, debating how much to share. By the time she sent a follow up ??? I still hadn't decided.

Dad used to have a saying. *A wise person uses few words, and a person with understanding is even-tempered.* Maybe less was more in this instance.

> **ME:**
> Sorry. Can't talk about it now. I'll tell you everything when I'm home.

> **BEE:**
> This is such bullshit! Where are you? You better tell me or I'm calling the cops on Maksi-Pad.

> **ME:**
> Do NOT call the cops.

> **BEE:**
> That settles it. I'm calling them.

> **ME:**
> I'm serious, Bee. You have no idea what kind of trouble that would bring.

> **BEE:**
> Which is exactly the point. I'm bringing all the trouble to that dude.

> **ME:**
> NOT TO HIM. TO ME (and other innocent people). I'm serious. Do NOT involve the police.

"Other innocent people" was a reference to Dom. I had to be vague in case someone was monitoring Brandy's phone.

Dom's voice reached me from down the hall. He was making calls, still dealing with that journalist, and sounded more frantic tonight.

> **ME:**
> Anyway, just wanted you to know I'm okay and that I'll be home soon.

> **BEE:**
> How soon?

I was about to type *I don't know* when an idea occurred to me.

> It's going to take us a few days to get where we're going, but then I'll be on the first flight out.

That was my attempt at 4D chess. If Vladimir assumed he had a few days to track me down, he might make plans around that intel, which could give us an advantage. Maybe.

> **BEE:**
> I don't trust any of this, Kat. Not one bit.

> **ME:**
> I know. I'm sorry.

> **BEE:**
> If I have ONE iota of a bad feeling, you can guarantee I'm getting the FBI involved. I'm not messing around. I better see you in a few days.

> **ME:**
> You will. Miss your face.

> **BEE:**
> Miss yours more. Dave says hi. He's legit
> worried about you, too. We all are.

Raul's final reassurance rushed in. *"If anyone can keep you safe, it's 'ole Yuriy here."* Maksim was part of the craziness, admittedly, but he was the only one who could help me.

Wasn't he?

Brandy and I said our goodbyes with lots of hearts and emojis. Then I pushed off the bed and tiptoed out of the guest room.

Dom's voice grew louder as I entered the hallway. I didn't know many cuss words in French, but he shouted the few I knew.

I knocked. "Dom?"

The door opened, and he waved me in. He had a call on speakerphone while he navigated an automated menu. His hair hung disheveled, unkempt, a little greasy. "Forgive me. I did not mean to disturb you."

"You're fine." I sat cross-legged on his bed while he followed the prompts. "Who are you calling?"

"The newspaper. I want to know if the story will run tomorrow."

"Why? Is that what the reporter told you?"

"Bah oui, but he did not say more." Dom tossed his phone on the bed and flopped back. "What did he write? Will my name be mentioned? I want to know, so I can prepare."

"Could you call them from the roof? I'm hungry, and it's supposed to be a clear night."

"Perhaps." He rubbed his eyes. "Today was crazy, *non? Oh là là.* What to think about the note?" He slanted a look. "And what about the man in *le chapeau?* He was gone. *Poof!"*

Poof was right. I had seen Renan—or whoever he was—climb into the town car, and none of us had seen him climb out. The chauffeur hadn't been much help, claiming he'd never picked anyone up.

"I must ask," Dom said, "are you *certain* the man in the hat is not this uncle of yours, Vladimir?"

Maksim had shown me rare photos of Vladimir. The crime boss was tall and well-built—nothing like the man in the hat.

"I'm one-hundred-percent sure. They're not even the same height." A sigh escaped. "The man in the hat was probably Raul's brother, Renan. It's the only thing that makes sense."

"But why does he leave notes instead of answering Maksim? This does not worry you?"

"It does." I picked at a cuticle. "A little."

"I worry, too. Maksim has lied many times. Perhaps this man knows something we do not."

"He hasn't lied, per se. Just, you know, withheld information." My shoulders slumped. "He wasn't sure if the baby was his, which was why he never told me. He was planning to after the paternity test."

Dom stared at his phone. Worry glimmered in his eyes as he grabbed the device and shoved it under his pillow. "I was curious, actually"—he lowered his voice—"because I noticed something from the pharmacy when we returned." His eyebrows flew high. "This item was on the floor."

My mood sank. The pregnancy test.

I scooted across the bed and grabbed a pillow. Dom positioned himself opposite me.

"I... might be pregnant."

"Nooo. It cannot be!" Dom glanced around dramatically. "Is this how it works in your country? We lay down like this and... *voilà!*"

I laughed, and a tear broke loose.

He reached over and brushed it away. "I am sorry, *mon amie.* Maksim is not who I thought he was."

"He doesn't know."

Dom went rigid. "No?"

I shook my head.

"Will you tell him?"

"I have to take the test first. So far, I've been too scared." I hugged the pillow. "I was scared before, and now that I know he has a family, a baby, the things he's always wanted—" I sniffled. "This is going to sound stupid, but no matter what he's done... Dom, I love him, and I don't want to ruin his life."

"What about your life? It means nothing?"

My bottom lip quivered. I burst into tears.

Dom wrapped me in a hug. I buried my face in his shirt. "Shh." He rubbed my back. "This is a big problem, and it is the fault of Maksim alone. *C'est juste un ducon.*" He's just a jerk.

We stayed like that for a while. It was nice. Strangely natural. But as the crying subsided, he asked me the oddest question. "Did you stop somewhere?"

My face rested against his chest. I lifted my head and peeked up at him. "Huh?"

"When you and Maksim drove here, to Paris, did you stop during your journey?"

"We had to stop a bunch of times when we were going the wrong way. But if you mean actual stops—"

"Oui. Actual."

"Then, yeah. We stopped twice."

The corners of his mouth sank. "Where?"

"Toulouse and Orléans. Why?"

His expression grew distant.

"Dom?"

"It is nothing, *mon amie.* Only a little thought I had." He kissed his first two fingers and touched them to my nose. "I will go prepare the roof. You are hungry?"

I nodded.

"Good." He winked. "Wait here. Rest." He slid off the bed, headed up the stairs, and disappeared through the window.

My mood improved at the prospect of another rooftop picnic —but something about our conversation bugged me.

No. Not the conversation. That question he'd asked about the places Maksim and I had stopped. I couldn't put my finger on why, but a sense of foreboding settled on me.

24½. TORN APART

I sat on a bed, knees pulled in, and buried my face. Sorrow dripped down my cheeks and chin.

"Kat?" The baritone voice stemmed from across the room.

I looked up and found Maksim striding toward me. Sheer curtains surrounded the bed, making him look fuzzy at first glance.

Wait, sheer bed-curtains? Were we in Begur? We had to be, but I thought we'd left Spain.

Maksim pushed the curtains aside and climbed onto the bed. "What happened?" He reached for me and then hesitated, glancing around. "How did we get here?"

"I have no idea."

His gaze circled the room before landing on me. He tilted his head. "What's happened to your hair?"

I reached up, tugging on an elastic band. My hair was piled into a towering bun, and as the elastic came off, a smooth, bronze cascade spilled down.

Maksim took a lock between his fingers. It was practically the color of Brandy's hair. Slightly less red.

Understanding lit his face. "You changed it. In Paris."

He was right. I remembered now. Dom had taken me to a salon.

Confusion prickled my thoughts. "None of this makes sense. We were in Paris. Now we're here? I don't know. Something about it feels…"

"Wrong?" Maksim's gaze trailed over me. "Like we're not supposed to be here?"

"Yeah." I met his gaze. "Why is that?"

"I tend to get this same feeling—something of a premonition —when danger is afoot." He stood, pushing the curtains aside, and stepped over to the windows.

"Do you see anything unusual?"

"A lot of fog." He returned and stationed himself beside me. "Begur was never foggy."

"Okay, but why? And how did we get here?"

"I'm not entirely certain we *are* here." He pinched at his throat, expression thoughtful. "This may be a dream. But it doesn't feel like one." His hand settled on mine.

My pulse trilled.

He slid closer. His jeans brushed my leg, and I lost the ability to think. We sat side by side, shoulder to shoulder, and as he turned toward me, my breath hitched.

"This feels real," he whispered, caressing my face. "Does it feel real for you?"

I caught his hand and glided my fingers over the callouses. His knuckles were dry. His pads and fingertips were rough.

This did feel real. *He* felt real.

"What's the matter?" He brushed his thumb over my chin, and warmth shivered through me. "Why were you crying?"

My thoughts collided. Why was I…?

Oh. I remembered, and pain penetrated my chest.

He leaned in, head tilted, and angled his mouth toward mine. Our lips brushed.

I pulled away. "You're not supposed to do that."

"I'm not?" His mouth tipped up. "*Dragă*…"

"Don't call me that." A tear leaked out. "Y-you can't do that anymore."

"Do what? I always call you that." He said it like he genuinely didn't know.

"You broke up with me." My voice quavered. "Three days ago."

"Why would I do that? Kat, I'm—" He froze, and I could see the glint of understanding in his eyes, the remembrance. "Julien."

I nodded, hugging myself, trying not to fall apart.

Maksim flickered before my eyes, a lightbulb running on its last watt. He said something, but his voice grew distant, staticky.

I reached for him. My hand found air.

An empty feeling bloomed inside me before sinking to the bottom of my being. How emptiness could have a weight, I wasn't sure, but it did. And it was incredibly heavy.

As I watched Maksim flicker and fade, I realized how badly I wanted him to stay. But he couldn't. Neither of us could.

25. NEWS REPORT

My eyes peeled open to a sheen of morning light. My attention moved to a cashmere blanket on me, and my thoughts rewound to the night before.

Dom and I were supposed to have another rooftop picnic, but I had no recollection of it. Must have fallen asleep.

I rolled over. The other side of the bed had been slept in—comforter pulled back, sheets wrinkled.

"Dom?" I sat up.

There was no response.

After checking the roof, the balcony, and both bathrooms, I still hadn't found him. Finally, I gave up and went to the kitchen. Might as well make coffee.

The espresso machine, so shiny and advanced, mocked me from the counter. I tugged on the black handle but couldn't get it to slide out the way Dom had.

"Café it is," I said, heading for the guest room.

I was dressed and had my purse before I remembered—I didn't have much cash. I also didn't have a key to the apartment, so I wouldn't have any way to lock up.

But I did have a phone. Maybe I could search online for a video tutorial.

I retrieved the phone and flipped on the light in the kitchen. I'd already logged in to the double VPN, but that was yesterday. Was it still logged in?

With most apps, that would have been easy to figure out. But this was a janky app Maksim had rigged—either with someone else's code, his own, or some combination of the two.

As I scanned the app tray, searching for additional instructions, I found a folder named READ ME. I pressed the icon, and the folder opened to a bunch of saved documents.

VPN NOTES

VoIP NOTES

VoIP TROUBLESHOOTING + NUANCES

REMINDERS: THINGS TO SAY / NOT SAY

My breath caught as I came across another document. HOW TO USE DOM'S ESPRESSO MAKER (STANDARD EUROPEAN ESPRESSO MACHINE).

"This has to be a joke," I said. But it wasn't. Maksim had listed the steps, provided video links, and even noted that Dom didn't take milk in his espresso, so he didn't usually keep milk in the house.

I rolled my eyes, which had gone moist. Why did he have to be so thoughtful?

My attention landed on an app shaped like a music note. I pressed it, and a music player launched. The program was janky, but it had all the songs that had been on my old phone. He'd even recreated my Summer Mix and Workout playlists.

Emotion clogged my throat.

I closed the music app, and my eyes shifted toward an unnamed text file. I opened it and read the note.

My hand flew to my mouth. A thin stream leaked down my hand.

"Is everything okay?" Dom's voice startled me. I whirled around to face him.

He stood at the entrance to the kitchen, looking fresh and

clean, his beard trimmed, his hair bouncy. He wore white chino pants with a fitted navy polo.

He walked forward. "Something has happened?"

"N-no." I rubbed out the dampness. "Sorry, I—need coffee."

"That is all?" Relief rinsed away his concern. "*Mon Dieu*. I thought there has been some tragedy."

He put himself between me and the espresso machine and proceeded to brew a shot. "I thought of something while I was out."

"Oh, yeah?" I slept the phone. "Where'd you go?"

"To buy a newspaper. There was a story, actually, but my name was not included. I think my agent handled the miscommunication."

"Dom, that's great."

"*Bah oui*. I am feeling much better." He punched up a playful eyebrow. "And I want to take you someplace special to celebrate."

"Would it require going out?" Tension wound through my stomach. "Yesterday was pretty risky. I wasn't thinking clearly, and—I feel like we should stay in."

"But you look so different now. I am shocked to see this beautiful redhead in my kitchen. But then I understand it is only my friend, Kat."

My cheeks warmed. I chuckled. "Whatever."

"It is true. You look different *and* beautiful." He eased into a smile. "Come with me, please, to *one* boutique. If by tonight you are not excited for my adventure—a very low-risk adventure— then we do not have to go."

DOM AND I STROLLED UP AVENUE DE SUFFREN. TRAFFIC stacked the street, and exhaust fumes burned my nostrils.

"So what's this 'low-risk' adventure you have in mind?"

"I will explain soon," he said with a grin. "For now, all you must know is that we visit a boutique."

We walked alongside a row of parked cars. As we passed a work van, I noticed the electronics store Maksim and I had seen our first day. A cooking show played on a TV. Professional cyclists played on another.

The TVs flickered and switched to a live news broadcast. A man and woman sat behind a news desk, looking straight into the camera.

I gravitated to the window as a WANTED photo appeared on the screen. "Dom. That's him."

"Mm?" He followed me. "Who?"

"Vladimir." Short waves of silver topped his head. Pale blue eyes peered out from beneath his dense eyebrows and tanned, leathery skin. The photo must have been taken during the winter, because he was wearing a suit and tie under a long wool coat.

Dom touched my shoulder and gestured toward the store. "We should hear the report, *non*?"

I nodded.

A clerk greeted us as soon as we walked in. Dom addressed him in French, and the man circled around the counter and met us at the front.

After rotating one of the TVs toward us, the man grabbed a remote, and the volume began to climb.

"...exclusive coverage of this standoff happening in London," the female news anchor said. Her blond hair fell in layers to her chin. Her voice held an edge of authority through her British accent.

"The Răzvan crime family are well known to law enforcement across Europe," the man chimed in. He was British, too. "We are just learning that Vladimir Răzvan—head of the Răzvan crime family—may have been responsible for the shootout that happened at El Prat International Airport late last week."

"What network is this?" I asked. "Do you recognize them?"

"*Chépa.*" That was slang for *I don't know.* "But their logo looks familiar, *non*?" Dom gestured at a massive TV mounted behind the two anchors.

A semitransparent globe filled half the screen. IB-TV NEWS took up the rest.

He was right. The logo did look familiar. It was probably a major news network in the UK.

Aerial video footage showed police with tactical gear swarming a townhome in a posh neighborhood.

"That's right, John," the female anchor said, "and now an armed response unit have surrounded the summer home of Vladimir Răzvan here in London and have been attempting to gain entry for—" She cut herself off and pressed a finger to her earpiece. "This is an update..." She paused, then focused on the camera. "I have just received word that the police have breached the barricade. Authorities are *in* the home of Vladimir Răzvan."

"We may have footage of that, Jonna." The man pressed his earpiece and nodded. "I'm being told we do."

A video appeared on the gigantic TV behind them. The scene showed a SWAT team crushing their battering ram against the townhome's front door.

"If Vladimir goes down, I wouldn't have to jump through all these hoops to get home." I fidgeted. "Could probably just book a flight."

Dom wrapped an arm around me. "It is very good news, *mon amie*."

He was about to say more when the clerk interrupted us. Totally forgot he was there.

He and Dom had a back-and-forth, and Dom's cheeriness ebbed.

The clerk punched a button on the remote, which muted the broadcast, then rotated the TV until it faced the outside world.

"Unless we are going to buy something"—Dom hooked my arm—"he wants us to leave."

"What about the report? We need to know—"

"I will find it." He held up his phone. "Don't worry."

26. EVENING WEAR

My tension uncoiled as we left the electronics shop. The authorities were closing in on Vladimir. They even realized he was behind the incident at El Prat.

It's almost over. I wanted to say the words out loud, but I didn't dare. Not yet. Not until I knew for sure.

Dom and I strolled up Avenue de Suffren and cut over to a narrow one-way called Avenue de Champaubert. A seven-story building resembled the Hassmannian style, except these windows were tall and rectangular and each had a stepping balcony. The absence of arches gave it a modern flair.

Movement drew my attention to the right. A work van cruised by, and it looked strikingly similar to the one we'd seen on Avenue de Suffren.

LES PEINTRES
TÉL: 07 77 00 77 00

"What does *les peintres* mean?" I butchered the pronunciation.

"*Bah non.*" Confusion spread through Dom's features. "Do

you mean *les peintres?*" He said it *lay PAHNT* and added a guttural *rh* at the end. "It means the painters. Why?"

That explained the ladder mounted on the roof.

"I noticed that work van on Avenue de Suffren." I pointed. "Before we went into the electronics shop."

Dom craned his neck, trying to catch a glimpse. "Avenue de Suffren is a busy street. I am sure it is nothing." He shrugged— but heaviness had sunken into his features.

He looked worried now. That made me worried.

"Is there something you're not telling me?" I grabbed his arm. "Dom?"

"Noooo. Oh, I am sorry." He pushed up a smile. "Please. Ignore me. I am thinking a lot these days. How do you say it in America?"

"You have a lot on your mind?"

"Yes, exactly." He wrapped an arm around me. "We arrive soon to the boutique. So much the better, mm? And I know of a salon that is very close."

"Hang on, a salon?" I ran a hand down my brassy hair. Waves were already forming as humidity set in. "I was planning to use the styling products Robert gave me."

"This salon has makeup artists, as well." Dom bounced his eyebrows. "I have heard many good things."

"Hang on a second—"

"No, no. You promised *not* to decide until we arrived at the boutique."

"Yeah, but—"

"It is my wish that your time here is special. It has been special for me, *mon amie.* Today may be your last day." His brown eyes lost their glimmer. "I hope you will let my wish come true."

My chest swelled. He was right. Today could be my last day— and night—in Paris. Would I ever come back? Would I ever see Dom again? He was moving to L.A., so it was possible.

But not certain.

"Could we check on that standoff? See what's going on?" I

wrung my hands. "London is a little too close for comfort, and I'd rest a lot easier knowing Vladimir is behind bars." *Or dead.*

That was a morbid thought, admittedly, but the man had shot and killed his own mother—my grandmother—when he found out she had a mixed bloodline. The man was capable of anything.

"I will check on the situation." Dom guided me. "*You* will try on the dresses, and *I* will provide the updates. It's a deal?"

"Deal." I stuck out my hand, and we shook on it. "No promises on the makeup, but I can always buy makeup and do it myself if it's really necessary."

We reached the boutique, and Dom handed me off to the clerk. They had a lengthy exchange, and the woman's smile grew bigger by the second.

She guided me to a rack of designer dresses. Accent lights cast a shimmery glow over...

"Evening gowns?" I slanted a look at Dom.

His mouth tipped up.

The dresses were organized shortest to longest. The woman sized me up and then focused on the longer ones.

Dom headed for the entrance. "I will visit the salon and discover if they have availability."

Before I could stop him, he pushed through the door. An electronic chime ushered him out.

"Your boyfriend said you will attend *l'opéra*." The woman held a dress up to me. "Will this be your first time visiting Opéra Bastille?"

"Uh, yeah, but he's not my boyfriend. Just a friend."

"But of course." Her lips quirked, eyes filling with glee. I had a feeling she already believed what she wanted to believe about us. "Do you know *La forza del destino*?" She replaced the dress and walked me across the store. "*The Force of Destiny?*"

"Is that a clothing brand or...?"

She giggled. "It is the opera you will see tonight. The story is about love, vengeance, destiny." She lowered her voice. "Many strange events surround the creation of this work. Some say the opera is cursed."

I resisted an eye-roll. "Oh, good. Definitely don't have enough of that in my life."

"This is a big event, very important, and your attire *must* be appropriate." She gave me a thorough once-over. "I think you may be a thirty-six." She sifted through a rack of floor-length gowns. "A four or six in US sizes, *non*?"

"That's right."

She selected a sparkly, rose-gold dress. The train flowed, and the neckline plunged.

"It's gorgeous." I held it against me. "But the front is a little too low."

She tilted her head. "Do you think?"

My mouth twisted. The neckline stopped at my belly button. "Uh, yeah. For sure."

She replaced the dress and selected a sparkly one with thread-like spaghetti straps and no back.

"How about something with more coverage?" I said.

We settled on a gold-sequined dress with a slouchy neckline, a satin off-the-shoulder in red, a sparkly sapphire dress—also off-the-shoulder—and a teal one-shouldered.

"Would you like to wait for your... friend?" Her shiny smile returned. "I think he would love to see you in these."

"He is paying for it, but..." My attention swung to the entrance. "I'm not sure how long he'll be."

"It's okay. I will prepare your room." She angled for a row of curtained alcoves. "Have a seat, please, and I will call you when the space is ready. Perhaps your friend will return by then."

She disappeared behind one of the curtains. Fabric rustled. Hangers clinked.

She emerged empty-handed. "Would you like something to drink? Water? Espresso?"

"I'm okay. Think I'll get started."

I didn't have enough up top for the slouchy neckline, and the red number made me look like I was starring in a musical about the Moulin Rouge.

We were down to the sapphire and teal dresses.

"I like them both." The woman touched her chin, eyes pensive, and studied me in the sapphire gown. "This off-the-shoulder style has a classic look." She rotated me toward the mirror. "What is your opinion?"

"Classic works." I tugged at the top, which curved around my upper half in a soft heart shape. "It's a little loose."

"I think the next size down will be perfect." She crossed the store and disappeared into the back.

I raised up on my tiptoes. The dress hugged my legs, all the way to my knees, before falling in a bell shape to the floor. The woman had called it a trumpet style.

The off-shoulder sleeves added to the classic vibe, and the sapphire-blue fabric matched my eyes. Hopefully, she had the next size down.

I padded barefoot into the dressing room, planning to de-robe, when an idea sparked. I grabbed my phone and shuffled over to the mirrors.

My hair fell in long, bronzy layers. I piled it to one side—mimicking Dom's hair—and slid one hand to my hip.

Shoulder hitched, head tilted, I snapped pics of myself doing various poses with all kinds of puckered lips. Modeling 101.

I turned to the side, arched my body, and tipped my head back. My hair cascaded the way Marie's had in that perfume ad. My hand moved to my forehead, and I ramped up the sexy faces.

My camera roll filled up.

I swiped through the pics and doubled over, cracking up. "Dom is going to *die* when he sees these," I said, choosing the best ones. Then I used the share feature and hit send.

My attention fell to the last pic, the one where I was mocking Marie. I sent it with a message attached.

> **ME:**
> Marie who??

I snorted a laugh and re-entered the dressing room. I had my zipper down and one arm free when my phone buzzed from atop my purse.

I snatched the device, biting down on another laugh, and opened the message. My smile did a U-turn.

"A question mark? That's it?" Figured I'd get a laugh emoji. At the very least, an lol.

And then I realized *why* he'd sent a question mark. Because the message wasn't from Dom.

> **MAKSIM**
> ?

My heart skidded into my stomach. *Crap. Crap crap crap!* I had sent every single one of those pics to Maksim.

Heat scorched my face.

The door chime rang. I pulled on my dress, rezipped, and ducked out of the fitting room. A glance toward the mirror revealed that, yes, my face was indeed fire-engine red.

"Cannot believe I did that." I death-gripped my phone and readied myself to show Dom.

But I didn't see him. Or anyone.

"Hello?" I padded across the boutique. "Dom?"

Dresses lined the walls. Mannequins stood in the windows. Had I imagined the chime?

I turned as someone came through a door. It was the clerk who'd been helping me. I jumped. She jumped.

"Oh là là là là." She clutched her chest, panting.

I echoed the sentiment. "Sorry. I thought I heard someone come in."

She lowered her hand. "Your boyfriend?"

I didn't bother correcting her. "That's what I thought. But he's not here."

"I'm sure he will return soon." She handed me the same dress in a smaller size, draping the long trumpet skirt over my arm. "I think it will fit. I hope. The style is too perfect for you."

I returned to the fitting room. The smaller dress was snug, but I managed to wriggle into it by the time the door chimed again.

Dom's voice floated to me.

I grabbed my phone and shuffled out of the dressing room. He was talking to the clerk, and his gaze flicked to me.

His upbeat expression morphed into serious. *"Waouh. Je n'en reviens pas."*

The woman beamed. "It means 'I am not coming back from this.'" She winked, and my cheeks reheated. "It fits, *non?*"

"Maybe?" I twirled, showing her. "What do you think?"

That was directed to her, but Dom's head did a slow affirmative.

He cleared his throat. "The salon has availability. Are you interested to have your makeup done? They can do your hair, as well."

"I'm game, but... Dom, I messed up." My attention fell to the phone. Maksim hadn't texted again—not yet—but he'd been reacting to every single pic.

Some of his reactions were hilarious—the *contemplative* emoji, the cat *wow* face, the monkey covering its eyes, the emoji with the bent eyebrow.

The last two were much more somber—a red heart wrapped in a white bandage, which he'd placed on the pic mocking Marie, and a broken heart on the MARIE WHO?? text.

An ache penetrated my chest.

"I don't understand." Dom walked forward. "How did you mess up? In what way?"

"It's... nothing." I tucked the phone behind my back.

He tilted his head. "Are you certain?"

"Mm-hmm. Yep." I forced a smile. "I was wondering,

though... Could you check on that standoff while I'm getting dressed? It would put my mind at ease."

"Of course." The biggest, shiniest smile broke across his face. "After that, we go to the salon."

27. YIELD SIGN

Hot wind rushed over my face, threatening to mess up my hair, as we cruised up Avenue de Suffren. Fumes assaulted my senses, but I caught a whiff of Dom's cologne.

It was nice. Muskier than I normally liked. Muskier than Maksim's cologne.

The thought of Maksim made me cringe. He hadn't responded since the text-messaging debacle. Just the emoji reactions. What had he meant by those last two hearts? Was he brokenhearted that I'd been making fun of his girlfriend? Or that I had noticed the perfume ad in Orléans?

Dom accelerated, following a line of cars into a left turn. The smell of mud and water hung in the air.

"You look beautiful." Dom peeled his attention from the road and gave me a once-over. *Très magnifique.*"

A blush hit my cheeks. "Thanks," I said, shifting in my seat. "You look great, too, and your car is amazing. How much did it cost to fix?"

"Fix?"

"It got keyed a week ago, right? Paint job looks great. Wouldn't have guessed there was any damage."

"It may have been two weeks ago. And they charged a lot." Dom tugged on his collar, which was buttoned to the top and secured with a bowtie. He glanced at me. "How goes for you? Will you survive the *celofan*?" He meant cellophane.

The clerk had sworn a smaller size was best for my gown. It kept everything from falling out—her main concern—but I could hardly breathe. Or move. Dom and I had been joking that I was wrapped in sapphire-blue cellophane.

We reached a bridge and turned right. Pedestrians ambled on the sidewalk. Traffic slowed to a crawl, and cyclists zipped past us.

Movement drew my attention to the right. I gasped, seeing the reason for the mud smell. "The Seine River!"

I'd said it "sign," and Dom whipped a startled look at me. "*Sehn*," he corrected. "The River *Sehn*. *Mon Dieu*." He gave his head a swift shake. "You may mispronounce anything else: croissant, Paris"—he inflected an overly dramatic American accent—"but I draw the line at *la Seine.*"

"Okay, okay." I raised my hands in surrender. "But I get points for trying, right?"

"None! Never!" His smile slipped through. "Ah, but for you, perhaps one or two points. Only because you are my friend."

I chuckled.

Several pedestrians snapped photos of the Eiffel Tower. The bronze beams stretched into the sky, reaching for the last bits of deep gold sunset.

"Before the opera, I want to show you something." Dom craned his neck, observing the cars in front of us. "*Bahhh*. If we can survive the traffic."

Twenty minutes later, we hung a left and cruised alongside the river. We were on the narrowest road I'd seen yet, and the cobblestones rattled us.

We entered a residential neighborhood and wound through the streets. I was about to ask which *arrondissement*—district— we were in when a blue roadway sign appeared.

Av. Victor Hugo

"Oh!" I popped up in my seat. "Victor Hugo wrote *Les Mis*."

"*Bah ouaiiis*. You know so much. You are practically French!" A hint of friendly sarcasm twanged, and I couldn't help but laugh.

"I don't know many French writers, but I know *Les Mis*. Brandy's sister helped design the set for our school's production."

"Who?" Dom divided his attention between me and the road. "Brandy is a person or a drink?"

Oh. Right. He didn't know about Brandy. Or Brandy's family. Or Dave. I hadn't told him anything about my life back home. Maksim, on the other hand, knew everything. We used to stay up all night, talking, sharing stories.

Tension coiled in my rib cage as I recalled those sweet moments. If I had known they'd be so fleeting...

"Brandy and I have been best friends since junior high." I swiped at a stray tear. "Her family let me move in with them after my dad— After he—" I fidgeted, suddenly feeling awkward.

Dom waited. "After he died?"

I nodded, gripping my new clutch. It was made of satin and matched my dress. "Brandy is one of the reasons I need to get home. She's so worried about me. The thing is"—more fidgeting —"I kind of don't want to go home. I mean, I *do*. I want to see her. But I feel like I don't belong there anymore, like my old life is a million miles away. A billion. But then I also don't belong here, so..."

"You are in the painful in-between. This is what my agent calls it. I understand this feeling well." He pushed out a breath. "Speaking of my agent, I have heard from him." Dom's brown eyes sparkled. "I got the part."

"For the TV show?" I twisted toward him. "The one in LA?"

"Yes, but there was some confusion about the details." His eyes kept on glittering. "You live in Atlanta, *non?*"

I nodded.

"I thought the TV show was being filmed in Los Angeles. But, according to my agent, it is being filmed in your hometown."

"You're moving to Atlanta?" I shrieked and grabbed his arm. "This is so crazy! I can't believe it!"

"*Ouiii.* I am very excited." He reached over and touched my knee with a tenderness that didn't match his quirky, upbeat mood. His expression softened, and my entire face went up in flames. "I want to speak with you about something else."

"What is it?"

"I know the heartache that befalls a child when their father has abandoned them. I have experienced this, and—" He took a deep breath. "I am no expert, but I am willing."

My brain buzzed, trying to piece together what he meant. "Willing to do what?"

"Be a father to your child—a father figure—since Maksim has abandoned his responsibilities."

My eyes widened. "Oh. Dom—"

"We do not know each other well, but I am a very driven man, and I do not expect some additional commitment. I am offering instead to— How do you say it? Co-parent?" He shrugged. "As I said, a father figure."

My mouth hung open. I wasn't sure what to say.

"You do not like the idea?" Dom sat straight. Regret exploded through his features.

"It's not that. Not at all. Just—"

His brow creased.

"I appreciate the offer. Really. I just wasn't expecting it. Plus..." I slipped my hand around his arm, above his elbow, and his biceps flexed. He wasn't as muscular as Maksim, but he wasn't frail, either.

He shifted into the next gear. "Yes?"

"I haven't made any decisions. I haven't even taken the test." My voice blended with the whir of traffic. I upped my volume. "I'll let you know as soon as I do. Then we can talk through the options. Deal?"

"I was getting ahead of myself, I suppose." He exhaled a laugh. Pink dusted his cheeks. "It is because I want to help."

"I know. I'm grateful."

"I hate that Maksim is the source of your troubles." Dom's jaw tightened. "It is not fair that you and your child must suffer because of his negligence."

Maksim was in the dark about all this, and I was about to express that—but Dom already knew. I'd told him multiple times.

He had his reasons for being upset with Maksim, and they had nothing to do with me. The fact was, Maksim may have told Marie—very likely *had*—that Dom was the one who'd snitched on her. Now Dom was channeling that hurt and betrayal into anger.

That was understandable. And anyway, this wasn't the time to go correcting him. Not after he'd been so kind and considerate. I'd re-explain about Maksim later. For now, I was going to let him enjoy the evening.

I was determined to enjoy it, too.

Our tires rumbled over the cobblestone. We neared a major road, and Dom pointed. "That is what I want to show you."

I craned my neck. "What?"

The cars in front of us entered a roundabout—the biggest I'd ever seen—and a huge stone structure stood at the center.

"Oh my gosh!" I pushed myself up, trying to peer over the windshield.

Dom gripped the steering wheel, and we catapulted into the roundabout. My seatbelt grabbed me. I bounced off the seat, grinning and totally in shock.

Trees dotted the sidewalk on our right. Tourists stood around, snapping photos of the world-famous monument.

Arc de Triomphe.

Stone carvings decorated the exterior, highlighting an array of angels, soldiers, and philosopher types. Traffic flowed through the circle.

"Do you have your phone?"

My neck strained as I stared at the arch. I lowered my gaze to Dom. "Huh?"

"Your phone." The whir of traffic nearly drowned out his voice. "You do not want to take photos?"

I gasped and fumbled with my clutch. Photos. Of course. Why hadn't I thought of that?

We circled around to the back of the arch, and I was afraid he might exit off. Instead, he kept cruising along until we circled around to the front.

I activated my camera and snapped photo after photo before switching to video. A work van obstructed my view, but I had a clear shot after the vehicle sped up.

Being so close to the monument—with the structure being so immense—I couldn't capture it all. I zoomed out, putting the lens in fisheye, and the whole roundabout entered the shot.

Cars and motorcycles breezed past. Someone honked. Dom waved them around, and a Maserati zipped past us before exiting off.

"We need to take this next exit." Dom turned on his blinker. "Did you capture enough video?"

"Not yet." I pointed the camera at him. "Ladies and gentlemen, I give you Dominique Dubois, actor and tour guide extraordinaire."

I figured Dom would laugh, but he actually wrinkled his nose. "What? Too corny?"

He swallowed, tugging on his collar again. *"Bah non.* I... am very camera shy." His mouth tipped up. "I am new to this."

"Whatever, Monsieur Golden Globe. I'm going to start calling you Oscar." I flipped the camera's lens, putting it in selfie mode, and then leaned in. "Say cheese."

"Cheese?" He pronounced it *sheez* while blinking out a perplexed look. "What does it mean?"

"That you're supposed to smile. It's what we say in America." The phone was still in video mode. I pressed an icon next to the Record button.

Dom pulled his gaze from the road and pointed it at the phone. *Snap.* The camera grabbed a still image and showed us a preview.

"Wow." I stopped recording and pulled up the still image. I'd never gotten a selfie right on the first try, but I had this time.

Dom held a sultry expression on the camera—lips slightly parted, one eyebrow playfully arched. My expression wasn't anything to write home about—just a smile—but the makeup made my eyes and lips pop.

Between that and my bronzy updo, I barely recognized myself.

"It's good?" Dom weaved through the traffic and exited the roundabout. "How do we look?"

I showed him the pic. *"Magnifique. Parfait."* Magnificent. Perfect.

"Ahh, yes. We are like Bridgette Bardot and Jacques Charrier."

I lowered the phone. "Who?"

He chuckled. "I will show you photos of this famous couple when we arrive to the Opéra Bastille."

28. UNEXPECTED DETOUR

We navigated a torrent of traffic on our way to Place de la Bastille. This was where the infamous Bastille prison had stood—hence the holiday of the same name, Bastille Day.

An oxidized-green column towered over the plaza. A gold angel held a torch atop the monument.

Dom drove past a curved glass building several stories high. "That is the opera house."

Flat-screen TVs played a promo video at the entrance. People were already flocking that direction.

We idled in traffic outside a parking garage. Dom looked at me, about to say something, when his phone chimed.

He checked the message. His excitement ebbed.

"Something wrong?"

"*Oui.*" He glanced at the traffic behind us before re-reading the text. "We are in the wrong place."

"The parking garage?"

"The opera house." He tried to smile, but his tone fell flat. "Forgive me. I was mistaken somehow."

"It's fine. I bet y'all have a lot of opera houses here."

He didn't acknowledge the comment as he shifted into

reverse. The driver behind us honked. Dom backed up as much as he could, yanked on the steering wheel, and whipped onto the road.

We backtracked, cruising along the street we'd used earlier. After twenty minutes of dense traffic, we finally entered a multi-way intersection.

People swarmed the area, hustling over sidewalks and meandering around a gorgeous stone building. Columns lined the façade, while gold angels stood guard on top.

Académie Nationale De Musique

"Is that where we're going?" I pointed. Dom remained silent, reading another text. Uneasiness crept into my being. "Hey, Dom? Dom."

He looked at me.

"What's going on?" My eyes flashed toward his phone. "Who are you talking to?"

"No one." He slept the screen. "It is a friend."

"Is this friend meeting us or something?"

"Actually... yes. He will be there. He is the reason we have the tickets." Dom tucked away his phone. "They were a gift from him."

"You could tell him we hit traffic. You definitely don't have to mention that we went to the wrong place. I won't say anything."

He bit down on a smile that didn't quite land. "I have already explained the situation. It's okay."

He wasn't acting like it was okay. Maybe this opera house had rules about arrival time. I would have asked, but I didn't want to stress him out more.

We bypassed the building and turned onto an itty-bitty street called L'Olympia. High-end shops and boutiques lined both sides of the road. Motorcycles and scooters filled the sidewalk on our right.

We stopped behind a line of traffic, while more traffic piled in behind us. Car fumes overwhelmed me—to the point where I began to feel queasy. Wished I'd brought a bottle of water or...

My stomach convulsed. I covered my mouth, abs tensing. *Don't throw up. Don't throw up.* But I was going to if I didn't get out of these fumes.

I tapped Dom's arm and lowered my hand enough to speak. "I need to get out."

His gaze trailed over me. "Your dress and shoes. Of course. Those will be difficult for walking." He pressed the unlock button. *Snap.* "Wait for me at that street." He pointed. "I will park."

He hadn't gleaned the exact reason I wanted out, but he wasn't wrong, either. Walking would be difficult, even without feeling queasy.

I grabbed my new clutch, pushed open the door, and stepped out. My stilettos touched pavement, but I struggled to pry myself out the rest of the way.

Dom slipped a hand under my butt. I clenched as he lifted and gave me a boost. I stumbled forward. The dress squeezed my torso and hips, and I struggled to steady myself.

Dom stretched across the front seat and pulled my door shut. "Wait at the corner. I will be there soon." With that, he continued into the garage.

I shuffled down the sidewalk, stilettos clacking. The thin straps bit into my foot. The sole was so thin I may as well have been barefoot, walking on the pavement.

I took a deep breath—in through my nose, out through my mouth. The tightness in my stomach eased.

Another breath, deeper. The rest of my body relaxed. Well, as much as it could in this dress. Should've gone with the larger—

The thought vanished as my stiletto slipped into a crack in the sidewalk. My knee buckled. I toppled sideways, my heel still caught, and collapsed against a scooter... which then fell into a motorcycle... which then hit the next two, three, four motorcycles... then another scooter.

People grumbled in French. Someone yelled. I tried to turn, but I was lying on the first scooter with my hands smashed against the tire.

A black mess transferred to my palms. Great.

Someone hauled me to my feet. My dress snagged on the scooter, and a sickening *rip* followed.

"Oh, no." I reached for my leg. My fingers discovered fabric, then skin. "No! Shoot."

The man who had helped me proceeded to shout and gesture at the bikes. Other people stood by, shaking their heads with disdain.

"I am so sorry. *Vraiment désolée.*" I put up both hands in a calming gesture. "Please. *S'il vous plaît.*"

A familiar form in a tuxedo approached. He stepped in front of me, putting himself in the line of fire.

The man turned his anger on Dom. They went back and forth. Pretty sure they were dropping insults and F-bombs.

Dom drew me away. He and the guy kept arguing, but their shouts trickled off.a

"*Putain,*" Dom muttered, shaking his head. "Kat, what happened? Are you hurt?"

"I'm not. But my dress is." I fingered the rip. "And look this. I'm filthy." I went to show him my hands and then gasped. "My clutch!"

Dom brought us to a standstill. "Where is it? In the car?"

"I had it with me. When I fell."

"*Oh là là.*" Dom grabbed his head. "What was in it?"

"My phone." I felt the color drain from my face. "The one Maksim gave me."

Dom swore, glancing around. "Wait here."

He backtracked and scoured the sidewalk. People were picking up their bikes and scooters and, to Dom's credit, he inquired with each one. He even approached the man he'd been arguing with.

The man glared, arms folded, and shook his head.

Dom slouched, turning toward me. We made eye contact, and every muscle in my body tensed.

"Come." Dom hooked my waist and pulled me away. "We must go."

I resisted. "But we have to find my phone."

"*Bah non.* We must arrive to the Palais Garnier." *PAH-ley gahr-NEEyey.* "My friend waits."

"Dom, you don't understand. If the wrong person gets that phone—" My insides sank as I thought about it. Maksim's VPN, his apps—everything would be compromised. Again. "We have to find it."

"*Bah non.* Do you not understand? Someone has taken it. It is gone." He straightened his tux jacket. "I am sorry, but please. We cannot delay."

Tears plucked my eyes. I gathered my train, giving my feet space to walk, and did my best to keep up with Dom, who hurried ahead.

Traffic rumbled on the main road. As we angled for the stone building I'd seen earlier, Dom slowed his pace and mustered up a weak smile. "I am truly sorry about the phone. But I think you do not need to worry."

I guffawed, and a tear slipped out. Stupid. How could I be so stupid?

"The likely scenario," he continued, "is that the thief will wipe the phone and then sell it. They will not care about personal information or photos."

"You don't understand. Maksim's apps are on that phone. He's given me access to a secret double VPN and a Voice-over IP he set up. He's going to kill me."

"He will not touch you." Dom wrapped an arm around me. "You don't have to worry about Maksim anymore."

The way he said it made the hairs on my neck prickle.

People in evening wear flocked to the stone building. Gold trim ran along the roof, while stone columns lined the façade. The music academy, or whatever it was, fill the far end of a plaza.

Place de l'Opera

"We made it." Dom's smile warmed. "I thought we may not." The opera-goers climbed cement steps that led to a black and gold gate. We followed them.

I was deeply concerned about the phone, but I couldn't help marveling at this amazing building with its intricate stonework—the pillars, the steps. "Even the balconies are made of stone," I said.

Dom dragged his stare from his phone and swept a hand over his hair. His attention roamed. "This way," he said, drawing me up the stairs.

We went through the gate and stationed ourselves at the end of a line. Five minutes later, we stood in front of a ticket window.

Dom addressed the worker in French. She typed something into her computer.

"*Excusez-moi? Madame?*"

I pivoted toward the sweet voice and came face-to-face with a teen girl. I pointed at myself. "Me?"

"*Oui.* The man said you speak English. My English isn't very good. I'm sorry." She tried to hand me something. "He said this belongs to you."

My jaw sagged. The girl had my clutch.

I rushed to open it and gasped. My phone was inside. "Where did you find this?" I looked past her. "What man?"

"There." She turned toward the cobblestone plaza and pointed at a decorative streetlamp. Sunset was nearly over, and a soft, golden glow radiated from the lamppost.

The girl lowered her hand, brow furrowing. "He is not there."

"Who? Did you know him?"

She shook her head. "My friends and I are here to see a school-mate. She has a part in the ballet. This man stopped us when we crossed *la place*"—she said it *lah plahs*—"and asked if we speak English. He gave me fifty euros to return your sack."

She meant "purse," but I wasn't concerned about that part. "Did you say this is a ballet?"

"Oui, madame."

"You're sure? It's not an opera?"

"Most operas are hosted by l'Opéra Bastille." She shrugged. "Only so often does the Palais Garnier host them."

A boy called out to her. He stood with a group of teens at the end of the line.

"Those are my friends. Please, excuse me." She started to turn.

I touched her arm. "One last thing. Could you tell me what the man looked like?"

"He was not very memorable to me." Her eyes turned thoughtful. "Oh, but I do remember he wore *un chapeau*. How do you call it in English?" She gestured at her head.

My stomach sank. "Hat?"

She nodded as the boy walked forward and dragged her back to their group. The other kids whispered. Two of them giggled.

My heart thudded as I tapped Dom on the shoulder. He was still talking to the woman in the window, and she seemed irritated. "Dom." I tapped again. "Hey."

He waved me off.

"Dom, we're in the wrong place." I wedged myself in front of him. "This is the ballet, not the opera."

"It is... what?" He expression blanked. "The ballet?"

"Yes. Opera Bastille was the right place after all."

"Alors, I am mistaken about the performance, because I know we are in the correct location."

The people behind us addressed Dom. He held up a hand and continued speaking to the worker. She barked in French and gestured for the next couple to come forward.

They pushed past us with a huff.

Dom muttered, exhaling his frustration. "They do not have our tickets. Can you believe it?"

"Dom." I gripped his shoulders. "We're in the wrong place."

"I understand why you may—"

"Look." I showed him the clutch.

He did a double-take. "You found it?"

"Someone brought it to me." I thumbed at the kids. "That girl said a man in a *chapeau* gave her fifty euros to deliver it."

I watched the gears crank behind Dom's eyes. He glanced around the plaza.

"The man's already gone." I opened the clutch, revealing my phone. "But everything's in here."

"Perhaps it was someone else, not the brother of Raul. Perhaps a stranger who happened to be—"

"Wearing a fedora on a hot summer evening?"

Dom slid a finger along the collar of his tux. He tugged, expression grim. "We need to leave."

"I agree."

"We go to l'Opéra Bastille." He turned on his heel and marched through the black and gold gates.

"Go... what? Where?" I shuffled after him. "Dom, wait! Can't we go back to your place? My dress is messed up and..." My gaze fell to the clutch. The flap was open, and something white snagged my attention.

I reached past my phone and pulled out a piece of paper. It was another note written on the same grid-style paper as the first one.

I unfolded it.

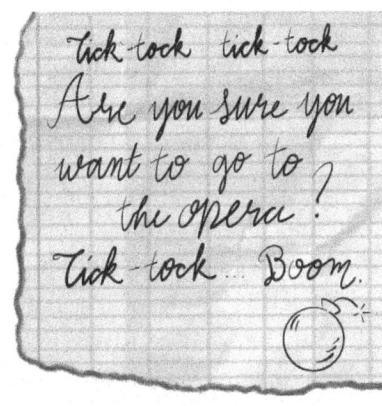

29. RENEWED HOPE

My insides folded in on themselves. Suddenly, I felt very exposed standing there by myself.

Well, mostly by myself. There were people standing in line and many more milling about the plaza. But I felt naked without Dom.

An atonal siren shattered the quiet. Blue lights raced past.

Another set of blues chased the first. Then another. Their sirens left behind an eerie echo.

Everyone in the plaza muttered to each other. Dom stood at the corner, staring after the cop cars.

I peeled off my stilettos, planning to run—or waddle—to him, but a gentle hand gripped my arm. *"Madame?"*

I peeked over my shoulder and found the young girl behind me. "I don't have time to talk, sweetie."

"But I heard your friend mention of l'Opéra Bastille. And you mentioned the opera, too." She held her phone toward me. "This is happening now. I don't think you should go."

I squinted at a video of a curved glass building. A reporter was saying something in French.

"There is a... I don't know how to say it exactly." The girl tapped her chin. *"Terrorisme? Explosion?"*

"Terror attack? Explosion?"

"There is no *explosion* yet, but it is possible."

"Like, a threat?"

Her eyes lit up. *"Exactement.* The threat of *une bombe."* She pronounced it *boomb.*

"You mean a bomb threat?"

She nodded.

My thoughts landed on the note. *Are you sure you want to go to the opera?* Renan had known. He'd even drawn a bomb.

I thanked the girl and hopped down the steps. "Dom!"

He turned.

I waved until he ambled in my direction. Pavement scraped my bare feet as I shuffled across the plaza. We met on the sidewalk. "Dom, look." I shoved the note into his hands.

He read the message, and his eyes bulged. "Where did this come from?"

"It was in my purse." I lowered my voice. "It was Renan. He was warning us about the bomb threat."

"What bomb threat?"

I repeated what the girl had told me. Dom was able to pull up news articles with a quick search.

"I think that's where those cop cars were heading," I said. "We can't go to Opera Bastille."

"We can't?" Dom pinched at his throat. "May I ask why not?"

"Dom. It's a bomb threat. The place will be crawling with cops, not to mention news crews." I grabbed his arm. "We have to go to your apartment. Now."

He didn't argue. He didn't say much at all, actually—not by the time we reached the car, not even when we pulled onto the road.

Paris' golden glow burned into the thickening darkness. Dom's phone buzzed from his pocket—again and again and again —until he silenced it.

"Is he mad?"

Dom's attention flicked to me. "Who?"

"Your friend who bought us the tickets. Is he mad that we're bailing?"

"I am not sure. Maybe." He rubbed his chin, expression tense. "Actually..." He hesitated.

"What?"

His mouth was poised to speak whatever was on his mind. Instead, he swallowed and shook his head. "I need to speak to my agent."

"About?"

"Everything. These notes you are receiving. These strange occurrences." He huffed a sigh. "I do not think Renan is trustworthy."

"The notes are creepy. I get that. But if you had met his brother, you'd see he's a bit unhinged, too. Unhinged, but willing to help."

"And how do you know this Renan isn't the one who threatened the opera? Hmm?" Dom gripped the steering wheel. "Perhaps he wants to *appear* like he is helping when truly he is harming."

"Dom, where is this coming from? You didn't say anything about this when I showed you the other notes."

"I have had more time to think." He rubbed his neck. "We should be careful until we are certain of this man's motives."

There was no way to be certain about anyone's motives. But I wasn't going to argue.

Dom rolled to a stop beside his apartment building. Parked cars stacked the curb, and his street was extra quiet.

"I am going to call my agent." He disconnected a keyring from his fob. "Take this. I will join you soon."

The keyring held the key to his apartment and the magnetic card for accessing the building. "Are you sure? I don't mind waiting."

"Please don't. I must park, and it will take time. See?" He gestured at the parked cars on either side of the street. "It is very crowded here."

I gathered my things and pushed open the door. My hands were full, but I dragged myself out of the car and shut the door.

Dom pulled away. I watched his taillights shrink to tiny red embers. He turned at the next corner and disappeared.

I tucked the clutch under my arm and stepped onto the sidewalk. Dom's house key and keycard were in my left hand; the stilettos hung from my right.

I took the card and tapped the door. A red light flipped green. *Click.* I gripped the handle.

Footsteps quickened nearby. I turned.

Streetlamps illuminated the parked cars. Shadows encased a section of sidewalk, but most of the neighborhood was well-lit. The Eiffel Tower stood nearby, warming the darkness.

I held my breath, listening. My ears detected traffic from Avenue de Suffren while a stream of voices echoed from the park. I didn't hear anything else.

I yanked open the door and stepped inside. Smooth tile greeted my bare feet. The elevator must have been on the ground floor, because the doors opened as soon as I pushed the button.

The moment I stepped inside, someone caught the door to the apartment building.

I watched a man with ginger hair slip inside the foyer. Reminded me of the way I'd snuck into Ivy's building, and a heavy dose of anxiety spilled through me.

The man beelined for the elevator, catching the doors. The sensor activated, and the elevator opened.

He smiled and nodded. *"Bonsoir."*

I offered a polite smile.

Next thing I knew, he was asking me a question. At least, it sounded like a question.

I clenched up, averting my gaze. Normally, the language barrier didn't bother me, but right now I felt vulnerable.

Awkward silence unfolded. He repeated himself and gestured at the panel containing the floor numbers.

Oh. He was asking which floor I needed.

I reached past him and pressed the button for Dom's floor. Then I stationed myself as far away from the man as I could. The elevator wasn't as small as the ones in Romania, but it wasn't very big, either, and I found myself wishing for more space.

The man's attention drifted to my feet as the elevator ascended. He spoke again, smile widening, and gave me a thorough once-over. I replied with a shrug.

He must have caught the social cues, because he stopped talking and pulled out his phone.

The digital number above the door climbed. My gaze returned to the door panel where a single, solitary number glowed.

Top floor. Dom's apartment.

6

The man hadn't selected a number. Why? Dom's place was the penthouse, and there were no other apartments on that floor.

My stomach sank.

I tried to tell myself it was fine, that the guy was busy with his phone. And anyway, what could he do to me in a public elevator in a fancy apartment building? The moment I screamed, people would come running.

Wouldn't they?

My mind raced. Maksim and I had gone over this scenario, but I was drawing a blank. Should I pull out my phone? Call Dom? Pretend I was getting a call from Dom?

The elevator ground to a stop. The doors opened. I looked at the man and abruptly noticed his size—tall, broad shoulders, thick arms.

This was not your average Frenchman.

He leaned a shoulder against the interior wall, phone in hand, and swiped a message. He glanced over his shoulder, and his pale blue gaze landed on me.

I squeezed past him, death-gripping Dom's apartment key

while readying my stilettos. These heels were my best chance for a weapon.

I shuffled to the apartment. As I opened my fist, readying myself to unlock the door, I fumbled the keyring.

The brass key and magnetic card clattered to the floor.

My hands trembled as I scooped them up—and that was when it dawned on me that I hadn't heard the elevator doors shut.

The man was still there. We were all by ourselves on this top floor.

30. ENEMY FRIEND

The door to Dom's apartment opened. Maksim stood in the doorway.

I let out a cry and flung myself at him.

"Oof." He rocked back a step.

My heart pounded out a drum solo. "Hi."

"Hi." His baritone voice boomed against my cheek. As I peered up, checking to see why he'd gone quiet, I noticed his thick eyebrows drawing together.

I traced his stare.

The ginger guy held a hand to the elevator doors, keeping them open. He backed up and pushed one of the buttons.

The doors closed, cutting off our view.

"Who was that?" Maksim's expression turned a shade more serious. "Why was he up here?"

"I'm not sure." I let go and entered the apartment. "He— Maybe he thought I would invite him in for sex." I wasn't sure why I said that, especially after being so freaked out—I was *still* freaked out—but the cheeky comment forged ahead without permission.

I tossed my clutch on the coffee table and peeked at Maksim. His mouth was hanging open.

I resisted the urge to snicker. "How'd you get in?"

He pushed the door shut. "Key."

"Dom gave you a key? Or you stole one?"

He snapped the lock in place. "Marie had a spare."

That made me roll my eyes. "A spare she never returned after she got busted cheating on you?" I tossed the brass key and Dom's keycard on the bar and waited for Maksim's response. *"She didn't cheat,"* I imagined him saying. *"Don't talk about her like that."*

Silence unfolded instead.

I risked another glance. A strange look twisted through his features. Confusion? Sorrow? Something else?

He ambled into the kitchen. "Where were you?"

Should I tell him about the opera? Renan's note? I didn't want him to know I had lost the clutch—along with my phone—so I started with the bare minimum.

"We were supposed to go to the opera." I dropped my stilettos on the floor. "There was a bomb threat."

"That sort of thing is common, unfortunately. A lot of terror cells in Europe." Maksim dug through one of Dom's moving boxes and pulled out a glass. "And your dress?" He held the glass under the faucet, filling it with water. "I assume those pics weren't for me."

"That was a joke." My throat closed. "Meant for Dom."

Maksim took a drink. His eyes judged me from behind the glass.

"I'm going to pay him back for the dress," I blurted. "And for my hair. Anything he's paid for."

Maksim swallowed and lowered the glass. His attention traveled to the door. "Where is he?"

"Parking the car." *And making a call.*

There was so much I'd left out of this conversation—about tonight, about the things that'd been happening—but something inside me held that information in a death grip.

"Have you made contact with Renan?" I watched Maksim's reaction.

He rubbed a hand over his cheeks, across his chin. He was hiding something, and he was debating how to filter it out of his response.

"You haven't," I said. "I know you haven't."

"Do you?" He settled against the opposite counter. "And what do you know about it, exactly?"

I could have told him about the notes—probably should have —but the explanation refused to come out.

He folded his arms, crossing one foot in front of the other.

I pointed at myself. "*I'm* the one who should be asking the questions around here."

"All right." He gestured for me to go ahead.

"First of all, why did you need my passport? Where is it?"

"Presently, it's in your room. A black-market dealer wanted to see it."

"A black market... what?" My jaw slipped. "Are you serious?"

"I was going to have a fake one made. Or purchase a real one that contained someone else's identity and a clean record, but those come with challenges."

I couldn't believe what I was hearing. "Why are we resorting to this? What happened with Renan?"

"Vladimir has been apprehended." Maksim took another drink of water. When he finished, he brought the glass down with a bang. It hit the counter so hard I thought the bottom might break.

"So they did catch him," I whispered.

"You knew about this?" Maksim's attention returned. "Why didn't you tell me?"

"I-I only found out today. There was a standoff." I gnawed on my bottom lip. "But this is good news, right? Now I can leave?"

"There may yet be complications. Because of El Prat. Renan's contacts would have been helpful for mitigating those."

"I don't understand. Why won't he—"

"Because he was only going to help us for Raul's sake. And Raul was only helping because he wanted *me* to take out his enemy. Now that his enemy has been dealt with—for the moment —I have nothing to offer." He raked a hand through his hair. "That's why."

That explained why Renan wasn't being cooperative. But what was with the notes? I really thought he'd been watching out for me. Unless—

"I didn't know you liked the opera."

Maksim's voice reeled me out of my thoughts. I looked at him in time to see his Adam's apple dip.

He offered up a weak smile. "I would have taken you. Had I known."

A wave of sadness crashed into me. "Why would you say that?" My vocal cords constricted, pinching off most of the question.

Even so, I knew he'd heard me, and yet he didn't answer. And he averted his gaze.

Jerk.

I turned away and padded across the living room. The Eiffel Tower rose above Paris' golden glow—a slender nightlight for the city.

When I was a kid, Dad had put nightlights all over the house. That was when Mom's addiction had peaked, and I was having problems sleeping.

"Light extinguishes the darkness. That's why lights keep bad dreams away." Dad's voice streamed through my conscience. He was right. Somehow, the nightlights had helped, and they became a tool for battling my fear of the dark.

Maybe that's why the Eiffel Tower made me feel better. Like having my own personal nightlight during the darkest time of my life. One of the darkest.

Maksim's boots—a brand-new pair—scraped the floor. He stopped beside me and gazed out the huge windows. "You look like her."

"Excuse me?" I whipped a look at him. "Like who?"

"La tour Eiffel."

"Oh." I thought he was going to say Marie. "I'm not sure what you mean. The Eiffel Tower looks golden. I'm wearing blue."

"There was a light show the night of the Fourteenth. Perhaps you saw it. During an interlude, the tower was lit in deep blue. About the same color as your dress." He gestured. "The way it fits you—how the train falls to the floor—reminds me of that night."

I gawked. This guy had the audacity to say these things— these sweet, sweet things—after dumping me?

But he hadn't wanted to dump me. Not according to the note he'd left in my phone.

```
You have to know I didn't want this, that I'm
only doing what I believe is right. Not for
my ex's sake, but for the sake of my son. I
can't let him grow up thinking his father
doesn't love him.
```

```
He needs that. He needs me. So I have to give
up the thing I want most… you. I'm sorry. -M
```

Maksim touched my arm.

I pulled away. Tears soaked my face, and I knew he could see them. There was no hiding anything under the glow of my nightlight.

"I'm sorry," he whispered.

"Yeah. You've said that." I rubbed out the dampness. "You don't need to apologize anymore, okay? I get it. My dad would've said you're doing what's good and noble, and you know what?" My voice fractured. "He would've been right. You're doing the right thing."

"Am I?"

I rolled my eyes, and another tear slid out. "You know you are."

"And what if *you* were pregnant? What would be the right thing to do in that instance?"

If I'd been sitting down, my jaw would have fallen into my lap. I shut my mouth and tried to play it off. "Good thing I'm not."

"Oh, you're not? Are you sure?" He reached into his back pocket and pulled something out.

I recognized the skinny white box. My center pinched.

"Are you saying there's no chance you could be pregnant?" He took a step. "Not the slightest?"

"Th-that's not mine." I looked down, hiding my horror. "Must belong to one of Dom's girlfriends."

"Daniel and Mădă are having dreams that you're pregnant. Daniel just shared that with me tonight, and then I come here and find this in the bathroom."

My heart clenched.

"When exactly were you planning to say something?" His voice hardened. "*Were you* planning to say something? Or were you going to run away before you had to tell me a goddamn thing?"

"I was going to, I swear, I just— I didn't know when, and I've been scared to take the test, and—" I clamped down on my bottom lip, fighting my emotions.

"Were you going to kill it?" Maksim's voice fell low, gravelly. He grabbed my arm.

"Maksim, stop."

"Tell me the truth. Is that why you didn't want to tell me? Because you were going to kill our child?" His anger dissolved into the look I'd seen earlier—confusion, sorrow, and something else.

Pain. That was the unfamiliar expression. I'd never seen Maksim so hurt.

He released my arm. But his eyes held on to the question.

I pushed him away and shuffle-ran across the living room. My hip bounced off Dom's couch and propelled me into the barstool.

Maksim caught me and pulled me around.

I struggled to break his grasp, knowing I couldn't... and realizing I didn't want to. My emotions poured freely as he reeled me in.

His lips connected with mine.

Passion ignited, and something else, too. Regret. The kiss was full of regret—mine and his. All of it melted away the moment I stopped fighting him, stopped resisting.

Our mouths became one, moving with each other, dancing in time. I tangled my fingers in his hair. His arms cocooned me, pulling me so close there was only one way to be closer.

"I love you," he mumbled without breaking away. "Kat, I love you."

It's not true! That voice inside me, the thing that always held me back, shouted. I recognized it.

Fear of rejection.

Fear of failure.

Fear of disappointment.

I came up for air, lips swelling. "We can't do this. You're with Marie."

"I'm not with Marie."

"Wh-what about Julien? I thought—"

"Julien may not be my son."

My shoulders sagged. "What?"

"It's possible, of course, but Marie has been acting out of character, and I've begun to have doubts."

"But... you took the paternity test."

"There was no test." He pushed his sleeves up. Pink scored his cheeks, and he was out of breath. "Marie never scheduled one."

"Why not? I mean—" The answer hit me. "Oh. Right. Because if she cheated—"

"I don't know anything for certain, but Daniel has encouraged me to pursue the suspicion. He's been right about everything else thus far."

"So that's why you're here"—I hugged myself—"saying these sweet things. Now it makes sense."

"Kat, I've professed my love for you many times, in every language I know—except for English." He raked at his hair, attention drifting. "This is the first time I've said it in your language." His gaze returned, and his brown eyes lit on my hair.

"What?"

"Nothing. I love you." He took a bronzy tendril between his fingers and tucked it behind my ear. "I'm in love with you."

Shivers rippled through me.

"You shouldn't say that." I shut my eyes and clenched a fist, trying to rid myself of this horribly wonderful feeling. "Don't say things you don't mean."

"And if I do mean them?"

"You don't." I opened my eyes. "You can't."

"I do, and I'll prove it to you." He pulled out his wallet and opened it.

I lost my breath as he produced a sapphire ring. It looked like the one Princess Kate wore, the one that had belonged to Princess Diana once upon a time, with a halo of diamonds set around a deep blue solitaire.

"This ring belonged to Mada's grandmother. When the communists arrived in Romania, after the king was forced to abdicate, she buried it in her garden. Mada and Daniel found it five years ago when the courts restored the property to their family. Mada brought it to Sibiu when you were in the hospital. I was going to give it to you—I had plans—but then I discovered the voice messages from Marie, and I began to question everything. I was confused."

My eyes flashed to his. "You're still confused."

"I'm thinking much more clearly." His attention traveled to the Eiffel Tower. The turn-of-the-hour sparkles flashed, dancing and glittering over the beams.

Maksim focused on me. "I would have asked your father first if I could have."

I took a measured step back. "Asked him what?"

His expression settled into a look of resolve—then he got down on one knee, and my hands flew to my mouth. "Katherine Elizabeth Barrett, I love you with all that I have, and all that I am, as a man."

"Wait." I tried to pull him to his feet. "You don't know what you're doing."

"I know exactly what I'm doing." He gazed up at me. "I want you to be my wife, and I'll do whatever I must in order to make this right."

Fresh tears streamed. "You're doing this here? *Now*?" I gestured at Dom's apartment, then at myself—my ripped dress, my dirty feet. *"While I look like this?"*

"Yes." He pushed up and gathered me in his arms. I pulled away and slapped him. A welt formed on his cheek, but all he said was "I love you. Marry me."

I buried my face in his shirt and cried.

He held me, rubbing my back while whispering in Romanian. Was he saying he loved me? Had he really been saying it all along?

He cupped my face, drawing my gaze to his. Then he leaned in and planted a tender kiss to each cheek. Another to my forehead. To my nose.

My lips.

I let myself get lost in the kiss—in him—and I barely noticed as he scooped me up and carried me to the guest room.

He closed us inside and locked the door. And then I let him put the ring on.

31. FRIEND ENEMY

Daylight seeped beneath my eyelids. An earthy aroma filtered into my senses, rousing me a bit more.

I opened my eyes and found myself tangled in sheets. For a split second, I thought I must be in the rental house in Begur.

But I was in Paris. In Dom's guest room. With Maksim.

The night came back to me, and heat plumed in my face. I gazed at the sapphire ring on my left hand. The halo of diamonds winked at me in the morning light.

I rolled over, expecting to bump into Maksim. He wasn't there, but his clothes lay folded and stacked on the dresser. My evening gown lay in a heap beside the bed.

I tucked the sheet under my arms and sat up. "Maksim?"

The bedroom door opened, and Maksim walked in. He was wearing a white dress shirt—not unusual for him—but instead of rolling the sleeves at his elbows, he had them fastened at his wrists.

His gaze discovered mine, and his eyes lit up. He crossed the room in two strides.

"Good morn—"

He stooped and planted a passionate kiss, cutting off my greeting.

I tangled my arms around him, and the kiss deepened. He tasted like coffee and spearmint, and I breathed in the aftershave rolling off his smooth cheeks.

He pulled away, grinning. "I hate to break this up, but I have an appointment."

"Oh?" I rolled onto my side. "Paternity test?"

"That's later today." He snatched a blue necktie off the side table and slid it under his collar. "This morning, I'm meeting with a team of attorneys at a law firm."

"I didn't realize you have an interest in law."

"It's a recent development." He folded the two ends of the tie until they formed a knot. "I need a quality legal team to help me get immunity."

"You're wanted in Spain. This legal team can help with that?"

He met my gaze in the mirror. "I'm wanted in more countries than that, and for many more crimes."

A boulder formed in my rib cage.

"That said, I have a wealth of information that would be extremely valuable to EU authorities." He threaded the tie one last time and slid the knot up to his collar. "If they agree, I could receive immunity everywhere in the EU."

"What if they *don't* agree?" I sat up, keeping the sheet wrapped around me. "What's the worst-case scenario?"

"Life." His answer socked me in the gut.

"Life... in prison?" My jaw slipped. "*That's* your worst-case scenario?"

"Actually, I could be extradited to Russia and end up in a Siberian prison." His expression turned thoughtful. "That would be exponentially worse."

His answer landed like ice water. Every part of me froze up.

He caught a glimpse and returned to the bed. "But with everything I can give them—names, places, intricate knowledge of criminal operations—there's a very good chance the police will want to work with me." He lowered himself to the mattress and caressed the side of my face. "If not for total immunity, then for a type of plea deal."

"Plea deal, meaning—you'd still serve time, just less?"

He nodded, and my gaze shifted to the pregnancy test. I'd been planning to take it last night, but the instructions said it would be more accurate first thing in the morning.

"I'm late. Possibly by five days." I drove a fingernail into my cuticle. "What if I'm pregnant and you end up going to prison and—?"

"Let's see what the attorneys say before we run through those scenarios." He stood. "We have to hope for the best. This is the only way."

"But it's not." I climbed off the bed. "Use one of your fake passports and let's go to America. We'll keep a low profile and—"

"What? Never return to Romania? Never return here? Julien may be my son, and I would never be able to see him again."

"It's better than ending up in prison!"

"This *is* a prison, Kat—hiding, being on the run." He looked away. "I love you, and I desperately want to be with you, but I cannot live like this anymore. I must be free of this life, whatever that may look like."

"When did you decide this?"

His phone vibrated from the bedside table. He scooped it up... but not before I saw the name.

I pulled the sheet tighter. "You're still talking to Marie?"

"I'm taking the paternity test this afternoon." He swiped a text. "I need Julien to come, and Marie is being difficult."

I bit down on my thumbnail. What if Maksim went to prison? I'd have to live here, in France, if I wanted to see him. I'd be raising our baby all by myself. I might have to deal with Marie and—

Maksim was putting on a suit jacket when the front door to Dom's apartment opened and closed.

His attention shifted. So did mine. Dom hadn't come home

last night—or not that I'd heard. Then again, a tornado could have blown through Paris and I probably wouldn't have heard.

Maksim crossed the bedroom.

"Hang on." I slipped in beside him and eased the door shut.

His eyebrows converged. "What are you doing?"

"Shh." I placed a finger to my lips.

"It's Dom. I know his gait."

I made a chopping motion at my neck, telling him to cut it out.

He tilted his head—then his eyes narrowed. They kept narrowing. "You don't want him to know I'm here."

"I—"

"Have you *slept* with him?"

My head jerked. "What?"

"Have. You. Slept with him?"

I folded my arms. "Have you slept with Marie?"

"Don't sidestep." His stare burned into mine like fire through paper. "Did something happen?"

"No. Not at all." Except that one teensy thing I wasn't planning to tell Maksim.

He studied my expression. "You're lying."

"I'm not. I just—"

Footsteps paused somewhere down the hall. Maksim reached for the door handle.

"Please." I grabbed his hand. "I promise. Nothing happened, but..."

His stare hardened, and I suddenly realized the awfulness of what I was about to say. I'd thought it was sweet in the moment, but saying it out loud—repeating it to Maksim—made me grimace.

"Dom's been upset with you. He feels like you've mistreated me, so—" This was the awful part. "He sort of offered to co-parent with me, to be a father figure to the baby, if I really am... you know."

A vein throbbed in Maksim's forehead. "You told Dom you were pregnant before you told me?"

"This has all been hypothetical. I haven't even taken the test yet." I touched Maksim's arm. "He was under a wrong impression, and I didn't know how to correct him. And I feel really bad about it, but that's why I don't want him to see you. I need to talk to him first."

Footsteps rolled down the hall.

Dom stopped outside the guest room and knocked. I sent a pleading look to Maksim. His expression softened, and for a split second, I thought I was in the clear.

"Kat? Are you in there?" The handle turned, and Maksim's eyes exploded into a bonfire.

He yanked the door partway. I couldn't see Dom, but I heard the surprise in his voice. "Maksim. I-I was not—"

"Expecting me? I gathered that when you tried to walk in here." He pushed the door open the rest of the way. "Did you consider she may not be dressed? Or was that the hope?"

Dom stood in the doorway, still wearing his tux pants and dress shoes. He'd removed his jacket, opened his top buttons, and rolled up his sleeves.

His stare traveled to me. I'd been behind the door, and as I came into view, shock crisscrossed his face. I was wearing nothing but a sheet, my hair was chaos, and my makeup was very likely smudged.

His attention fell to the gown—the beautiful designer gown *he'd* bought for me, which I had flung onto the floor as if it meant nothing. As if *he* meant nothing.

Seeing his gift rumpled and tossed aside seemed to knock the wind out of him. The light in his eyes dulled.

Guilt veered into me.

Maksim interrogated him in French. Dom's expression sank until I couldn't stand it.

"Stop." I put myself between them, facing Maksim. "He hasn't done anything wrong."

"He didn't pay for your hair? Your clothes? A dress for the opera?" Maksim narrowed another look. "You don't find inappropriate?"

"I was going to pay him back."

"I warned him you were off-limits."

"You and I weren't together!" I caught myself and lowered my voice. "We didn't do anything. *He* didn't do anything. He was only being nice."

Maksim guffawed. "Without any ulterior motives, I'm sure."

Dom said something. Whatever it was brought Maksim barreling toward him.

I threw myself between them. "Stop!"

Maksim pushed Dom into the hallway and slammed him against the wall. A painting crashed to the floor. Dom shouted. Fists flew. Knuckle connected with bone.

Dom hit the floor, moaning. A speck of red colored his lip.

"Stay away from her." Maksim shook out his fist. "That's my final warning."

"Or what? Hm? You will kill me as you killed those men at the airport?" Dom leaned forward and spit.

Maksim jumped back.

I dragged him into the guest room and slammed the door. "How could you do this? Dom has been nothing but kind to me. He's been letting me stay here!"

"That doesn't give him the right to seduce you."

"He wasn't— We weren't—" I wrapped two fists and held them at my sides. "You are *such* a hypocrite."

"Am I?" He folded his arms. "And why is that?"

"You come in here, waving your holier-than-thou banner, while you've been sleeping with your *ex* for the last three days." My voice cracked. "I haven't been doing that. *You* have been doing that."

"You have no idea what I've been doing." He snatched his wallet and passport and opened the door.

He was halfway down the hall when, to my surprise, he made a U-turn and offered a hand to Dom.

Dom looked like he wanted to spit again.

"Just go." Emotion climbed into my voice. "Please."

Maksim's icy gaze melted. He stepped over the painting and trekked down the hall. The front door shut a moment later.

"Are you okay?" I reached for Dom.

"I am fine." He waved me off. "Maksim is the asshole. Not me."

"He isn't normally like this," I whispered.

"I have always known him to be possessive. It's one of the reasons I believe Marie was unfaithful. He smothered her, and she did not like it at that time. I don't know why she so freely returned to the behavior she despises." Dom rubbed his jaw. "Perhaps... she did not."

"What do you mean?"

"I'm only suggesting a theory for why he returned. He says he broke up with her?"

I nodded.

"What if she broke up with him?" Dom flipped his hair to the side. It didn't have its usual luster this morning, or its usual bounce. "Perhaps you are his second choice, the one he comes to when he does not get what he wants."

I hesitated, then shook my head. "I don't think so. She was watching us like a hawk the other day. She even tried to kiss him in front of me."

"Did you understand what was said in our conflict? Why Maksim lost his temper?"

"N-not exactly."

"It was not about you. It was about Marie." Dom sighed. "I spoke the truth—that his possessiveness drove her away—and he did not like it."

"Why would he care what you say about Marie if...?"

Dom's eyebrows flew high.

"Oh." I leaned against the wall. "He wouldn't care if he didn't still have feelings for her."

"*Exactement.*" Dom tipped his chin toward my hand. "I see he has given you something."

My stare fell to the ring. My insides tumbled into a free-fall.

"I assume it is from him," Dom said. "But I do not trust his motives for giving it to you."

I sank to the floor. My mind spun. Everything had been so clear last night. Problems seemed fixable. Life with Maksim felt feasible. Now everything was a mess again.

Dom held out his hand. I took it, and he pulled me up. As he did, my mind replayed the night—but instead of hopefulness and excitement, intense sorrow came crashing down.

This wasn't going to work. No matter how we went about it.

"Where'd you go last night?" I clutched the sheet tighter. "You never came home."

"That, yes." He scratched at his five o'clock shadow, which was looking more like a beard. "I, um, slept at my agent's apartment."

"I thought you were going to call him."

"We agreed that meeting was better. The hour grew late, and... I drank a lot." He walked me into the guest room. "I am sorry for not sending a message."

"I'm sorry, too. For what Maksim did."

Dom guffawed. "It would not be the first time, *mon amie.*"

I gasped. "He's hit you before?"

"In the metaphoric sense, yes, because he betrayed me. What he did today hurt less." Dom's lip swelled. He dabbed the spot, wincing. "I came to tell you something. Do you remember the friend I mentioned last night?"

"The one who got us the tickets?"

Dom nodded. "He is the lawyer of a politician, actually. He and his boss want to meet with you."

That was ironic. Maksim was meeting with lawyers today, too. "Why would they want to meet with me?"

"The lawyer has been reviewing your circumstances and searching for loopholes. He has found one." Dom's tone brightened. "Kat, you can go home."

32. TOUTE SUITE

I didn't have an appropriate outfit for meeting with a lawyer. The floral button-front dress was the nicest thing I'd bought, but it was too short for an office setting.

I opted for stretchy black shorts, which were a level up from denim, and a black-and-white-striped top.

After a quick version of my morning routine, I grabbed my passport and phone and crossed the bedroom.

Halfway to the door, I paused. My attention drifted to the bedside table. The white box with the pregnancy test glared at me.

I glared back. "The feeling's mutual."

My gaze fell to the sapphire ring, and alarm bells sounded in my head. What was I thinking? That I could marry Maksim and all our problems would vanish?

Not only would those problems *not* go away, they were bound to get worse. Exponentially. I pictured Maksim in prison while I had to deal with Marie.

And her baby. And my baby.

But I might not be pregnant. Maybe I'm not.

My heart clenched as I twisted off the engagement ring and set it on the dresser. Then I walked out of the guest room.

Anxiety followed me down the hall. Rings never fit me, but

the engagement ring had fit perfectly. The diamond halo had even sparkled like the Eiffel Tower.

It took every last drop of willpower not to run into the room and put the ring on. I couldn't make that decision right now. There were too many what-ifs, and I wasn't in the right headspace.

Dom waited for me by the front door. *"Allez. On y va."* Ah-LEY. Oh-nee-VAH. Come on. Let's go.

I held up my passport. "You're sure this is all I need?"

"That is all the attorney said to bring. I have mine, too."

The fight with Maksim played in my mind—a bad movie on repeat—and my heart dredged up feelings of grief, fear, regret. Everything coagulated, forming a boulder in my stomach.

Dom seemed nervous. I waited by the elevator while he returned to the apartment three different times, retrieving something he'd left behind. He didn't say what, and he never emerged with anything.

Several excruciating minutes later, we were exiting his building. A black sedan idled out front. Dom held the back door.

I climbed in, and he climbed in after me.

As soon as he had the door shut, the driver pulled onto the road and routed us to Avenue de Suffren. Silence filled the car as we cruised up the busy street. The Eiffel Tower peeked out from behind the apartment buildings.

We hung a left, and I finally caught the full scope of the bronze beams rising from Champ-de-Mars. The tower was as beautiful as the day I'd first seen her, but something dampened the glimmer I would have normally felt.

I gazed out my window, watching the city stream past us. We reached the Seine and crossed over the murky waters. Paris was lovely but foreign. What if I had to live here? Could I manage on my own with Maksim in prison?

"I need to tell you something." Dom's voice pinched in a way I hadn't heard before.

We were turned, heading north, and as I pivoted in my seat, I caught the driver's gaze in the rearview mirror.

He broke eye contact and focused on the road.

"I was in French Polynesia for *vacances*," Dom began. "Vacation. It was last October. I visited the touristic islands, of course—Bora Bora, Tahiti—and it was magical. The most amazing adventures of my life." Everything about him had dulled, despite the context of what he was saying, as if life itself had been sucked out of him.

Dom talked about the friends he'd made during his trip, and how they'd ended up in the capital, Papeete, and I could detect where brightness and joy should have been found in the story.

Should have. But wasn't. He was describing an amazing place that he'd experienced with amazing people—yet his voice rang sad, his mood slipping.

My phone vibrated. The screen brightened.

MAKSIM
Where are you?

I rolled my eyes and slept the phone. Dom fell silent.

"Sorry." I laid the device face down. "That was—" I shook my head. "Never mind. Go on."

"Papeete has a vibrant nightlife, and my new group of friends—"

The phone vibrated.

"I'll put it on silent." I pressed the side button—once, twice. The phone didn't vibrate again.

My attention returned to the rearview mirror. The cabbie's gaze shifted in the reflection, moving from me to Dom—and that was when I noticed that he wasn't using GPS.

Normally, cabbies had their phones mounted on the dash with the GPS up and running. Same for ride-sharing drivers. This guy didn't.

I was about to ask Dom about it when he continued with his

story. "It was the end of my trip. I was to come home in three days. The same held true for most of my friends. So we went out and had a good time. The best. I drank so much... and then I drove."

"Oh." So that was why his mood didn't match the story. "This doesn't sound like it's heading in a good direction."

He forced a smile that never reached his eyes. "After the others returned to their hotels, my friend and I decided to hit one more club. It was a place we had visited before, and we had not been able to return even though we had wanted to. Now we had the chance, and my friend said I should drive. I refused, of course, but he insisted. And someone..." Dom rubbed the back of his neck. "Someone died."

I gasped.

"She was a young girl—only thirteen—and a local. I don't know why she was out so late, and in the road, but the truth is that..." He inhaled a shaky breath. "The truth is that I blacked out, and I did not awake until the police arrived."

"Oh my God. That's—" What? Horrible? He already knew that. "I'm sorry. I mean, I'm sorry for her and for the end result and—"

"It wasn't my fault!" Dom's voice boomed. The eruption seemed to come from nowhere, but I knew better than that.

Mom had hurt a lot of people with her addiction, especially Dad and me, but nothing was ever her fault. Dom was doing the same thing, telling himself—probably for a very long time—this girl's death wasn't his fault.

"Polynesia is not like the mainland France. They are supposed to follow regulations, anticorruption laws, but they have some of the highest levels of corruption. Many French are knowing this, as did I, and so... I bribed the police."

My mouth hung open. I snapped it shut.

When I was in Romania, I bribed a ride-sharing driver to dump his pickup and take me instead. That was the first time I'd found myself running away from Émilien, and I'd been desperate to get away.

Dad used to talk about this very thing. "*Desperate times make for desperate people, and desperate people are capable of anything.*" His voice resonated deep inside my conscience.

Dom must have been pretty desperate that night. Strangely, he seemed kind of desperate now.

"Afterward," Dom continued, "I returned home and never heard anything. I had given the police my birth name, Dominique Dubois, even though my name had already been legally changed to my stage name—Dom de La Fontaine. I thought perhaps this was why, or simply that the bribe had worked."

"Your stage name is Dom de La Fontaine?" A red flag waved in the breeze. "The cop who came to your apartment called you Dominique Dubois."

He took a breath and let it out. "*Oui.*"

I grabbed his arm. "What if he was investigating you?"

"He may have been." Dom stared out his window for a long time. He didn't seem as troubled by this as me. Unless he was in shock.

"What about your friend, the one who was with you that night? Could he have reported the accident or...?"

"He was not discovered at the scene. We crashed nearby to the seafront, and the police said that, due to drunkenness and being disoriented, he may have fallen into the water and drowned."

"But what if he didn't? What if he survived, went home, and reported the accident? He might've had a guilty conscious. He could have done it weeks or months later."

"It is possible. His flight was the following day. Perhaps he fled the scene and returned to America, therefore escaping any consequences."

His friend was the passenger, not the driver, so I wasn't sure what kind of "consequences" he could have meant. I kept the comment to myself.

"As for my name," Dom continued, "he knew me only as Dominique. This is why it must not be him."

"But if the cops know... Oh, Dom. This is bad. You could go to prison." I grabbed my head. "You and Maksim will both be in prison."

Dom's head whipped around. "Maksim goes to prison? Today?"

"No, but he might end up there. Eventually."

Dom scowled. "No one deserves it more."

"I can't believe this. It's like something out of a—" I froze when the epiphany struck. I grabbed Dom's arm. Hard, to the point where his muscles tensed. "The journalist. He found out about the accident. *That* was the story he was going to run, wasn't it?"

A muscle jumped in Dom's jaw. His head did a slow up and down.

"Who told him?"

"*Bah oui.* I know who."

33. JUDAS ISCARIOT

"So who was it?" I hung on to his arm. "How did the cops find out?"

The driver said something from the front. Dom replied, and they went back and forth. They both seemed irritated.

"What's he saying?" I leaned closer. "He isn't acting like an Uber driver," I whispered.

"This is not a taxi. It is the personal car of the lawyer." He nodded toward the man. "He is the chauffeur."

"Are you sure? How well do you know these people?"

Dom didn't respond immediately, and I reached for his hand. His head rotated slowly until a blank stare landed on me.

"How do you know the lawyer?"

"Through the politician."

"And how do you know the politician? Maksim always says that unless you know—"

"I do not care what Maksim says!"

I drew back.

Dom held up an angry finger. "Do not speak of him in my presence." Anger singed the edge of his voice. "You do not believe what kind of man he is despite your own experiences. That is why you need this help."

My brow pinched. What was that supposed to mean? What kind of help? I wanted to know, but I found myself afraid to ask.

Afraid, and wishing Maksim was here.

I reached for my phone. It lay tucked beneath my left leg, face down on the seat.

"They knew about the accident." A pained expression spread through Dom's features. "All of them."

I froze. "Who did?"

"The lawyer. The politician who oversees the operation. His agents."

"Wait, what operation? Dom, what are you talking about?"

"Maksim is wanted in many countries. Government agents have been following him. He has stolen a hard drive with classified material, and they need it returned. It is a matter of national security."

"What?" I could no longer hold on to my composure. "Is that who we're going to see? Government agents?"

"And the lawyer. This is to ensure you are protected under French law." Dom turned toward me. "If you cooperate and answer their questions, they can ensure your safe return to the United States. Otherwise, you are going to have big problems here."

Panic plucked at my insides.

My attention returned to my window, and my chest caved in. The buildings had begun to look smaller, grimier. There were a few Hassmannians—not many—and they were sprinkled between apartment blocks that ranged in decay level.

Public housing.

Arabic scrawled signs—Middle-Eastern restaurants, shops, grocers—and I was reminded of the couple I'd seen in El Raval. This neighborhood looked similar, down to the graffiti that wall-papered the ground floor of every building.

My attention drifted to a caged-in basketball court, the kind

I'd seen in New York City, with a Metro line that rumbled over-head. The guys loitering on the court weren't dressed for a pickup game. Actually, they looked like the people Mom used to hang out with, especially the dealers she would buy from. Several of the guys stumbled around like they were high.

The driver's eyes flashed to the rearview mirror, and I searched for all the lessons Maksim had taught me.

My mind blanked.

I craned my neck as we crossed a bridge. Down below, several rows of train tracks ran side by side and crisscrossed each other. I forced my brain into overdrive, hoping for a solution.

One came to me. I could jump out of the car and run for the nearest Metro stop. That might work. If the guy would slow down enough.

"You will cooperate with these agents," Dom said. *"Non?"*

"No. I-I mean... yes. Of course." I cobbled together an upbeat demeanor. "I'll definitely do my best."

"C'est génial." That's great. "It will be the best for all of us. We have nothing to lose and all to gain." That logic sounded suspiciously like a slogan, and not one he'd concocted on his own.

These guys could be Russian agents faking French accents and credentials. They could be Ivy's crew, come to track us down. Hackers could pull off something like this, couldn't they? They'd definitely know how to dig into Dom's past.

Then there was the worst-case scenario. What if I was being delivered to Vladimir or Émilien?

But Vladimir had been apprehended. And Daniel said Émilien was in jail. That left one other possibility—these people really were who they said they were, and this was why Maksim was talking about going to prison. He knew the authorities were on to him.

But even if that were true, this whole thing was sketchy as hell. So... shouldn't I let Maksim know where I was? Just in case?

I peered across the backseat. As I did, I lifted my leg the tiniest bit and slid my phone beneath me. I was now sitting on—

Realization came in for a rough-and-tumble landing. "Is *this* why you put our phones in the fridge?"

Dom looked at me.

"The government agents. Have they been listening to us? Is that why you put our phones in the fridge the other day?" I watched his unsettled expression morph into a cringe. "It is."

"They have been listening because of Maksim."

"Dom."

"What was I supposed to do? Hm?" He shoved his hair back so hard it stayed in place. "They approached me the day we visited Salon Robert. They have been conducting an operation. Something black, black something."

"Black ops?"

"*Exactement.*" Dom snapped his fingers. "They are conducting these black ops involving the hard drive Maksim stole, and the politician is overseeing the mission."

"And he's French?"

Dom paused. "The politician? Of course."

"And the agents?" A quick glance to the rearview mirror. The driver held his attention on the road. "They all work for the French government?"

"*Oui.*"

"How do you know?"

Dom talked about the credentials they'd shown him, the equipment he'd seen—all kinds of things that honestly could have been staged. While he talked, I used my right hand to dig the phone out from under me.

"You should have seen their surveillance equipment. *Pffft.* There is nothing like this available to normal people. It was like the films I have seen about the FBI and the CIA."

I resisted an eye-roll. Ivy's crew had that and more. Crap. It really could be them.

The phone lay flush against the seat. I had to wake it up, enter the code, and open Maksim's last message all without looking down or otherwise drawing attention to myself.

After I had the message thread open, I used the tip of my finger to swipe a text. *Rough neighborhood. Train tracks. Middle eastern businesses.* I had no idea if autocorrect was working for or against me, and I couldn't risk checking.

I paused, searching for a road sign or Metro stop. As I did, Dom's voice landed on a question mark. Silence followed.

I pushed the phone under my leg. "Sorry, what?"

"I asked about Toulouse. This is where they believe the hard drive is hidden."

My hand rested on the edge of the phone, my fingers itching to swipe the rest of my message. I went stark still. Dom had asked about Toulouse before. I hadn't known why.

"Maksim didn't hide a hard drive there," I began slowly. "He hid a gun—not his, someone else's. He didn't want to risk bringing it into Paris with the Bastille Day festivities."

"They said you would think that." Dom sighed. "Kat, you must understand... Maksim does many things without your knowing. They have been watching him. They know his secrets, as they knew mine."

"But—"

"Did you see him hide the gun and only the gun?"

"Well, no. But I can tell you where he hid it. It's in a locker at the Toulouse train station. I'm sure they could figure out which one by reviewing the security footage."

Dom slanted a look. "Are you certain there were cameras? Did you see them?"

The spark of hope inside me fizzled. "I-I was asleep in the car. But I know all the train stations have video cameras."

He propped his elbow on the door panel and held his head. "Let them ask their questions. And please, be cooperative."

"I'm telling you. I don't know anything else. All the questions in the world won't help if I don't have the information. So then what's the point—"

"I will not be held responsible for this!" He rubbed a hand across his face, mumbling in French. "Everything I care about, everything I have worked for, is at stake. I will not allow Maksim to destroy it."

Why would he say that? Maksim and I were the ones who were in trouble here. Not him.

Except he was in trouble. I hadn't even realized...

"They're the ones who leaked that story to the journalist." My mouth hung open. "They leaked it and then held it over your head. To get you to cooperate."

"*Arrête.*" Dom held up a hand. *Stop it.*

"That's how the situation got resolved—not because your agent figured it out, but because you agreed to work with them. And they're the ones who got the journalist to kill the story, too." I went numb as the epiphanies pinged. "Is that why an initial story ran, one that didn't include your name? So you'd know they were serious?"

"*Arrête!*" His eyes ignited. "I do not know how the journalist became aware of my accident. I know only that these agents had the power to stop the story, and they did."

I rolled my eyes. "Don't be naïve. They have that guy in their pocket."

"You do not know that, nor do I." He shoved a finger in my direction. "You do not understand. My career would have been destroyed before it ever began. The TV show? *Poof.* Sponsorships? *Poof.* I did not have a choice!"

"My mom used to pull this bullcrap, Dom. Let me tell you— the night of the accident was a multiple-choice test, and you picked the wrong answer. You could have: A. chosen to walk, B. taken a cab, C. hitchhiked."

He glared.

"You're my friend, and I care about you. But please. Stop acting like you're the victim." I shoved my hand toward the driver. "You don't know who this is. He could work for Vladimir for all you know."

The driver didn't remove his eyes from the road—but he did twitch ever so slightly when I said Vladimir.

My thoughts returned to the phone. I had to let Maksim know where we were.

"This is Maksim's fault." Dom's voice jarred me.

I tensed up.

"Le con." Dom squeezed a fist. "Maksim is the one who stole the hard drive. He has placed both of us in danger."

I swallowed my hesitation and woke up the phone. The screen brightened in my lower peripheral. What should I do? Finish the text? I considered calling but as soon as Maksim picked up, his voice would boom through the phone.

Unless I sent the text first. Then he'd realize something was wrong.

Without looking, I pressed the screen somewhere in the general vicinity of the Send icon. Five seconds ticked by. Ten.

Dom peered out his window—and that was when I finally looked at my phone. The message had sent, but the text had been autocorrected to hell.

> **ME:**
> Right neighborhood twin table Joe of Middle Warren businesses

Son of a—

The car slowed, drawing my attention to massive apartment blocks. We cruised past a white sign outlined by a red border.

Saint-Denis

Dom muttered in French. The driver slowed, letting pedestrians cross the street.

A flash of white permeated my lower periphery. My phone was silently ringing. It was Maksim.

34. WOLF'S LAIR

I touched the green Answer icon and fumbled with the side buttons. That was the only way to turn down the call volume without going into the settings. It wouldn't turn the volume off completely, though, so if Maksim said anything, Dom and the driver would hear.

The call was live. So far, Maksim hadn't spoken.

"Where are we?" I boosted my voice. "Are we taking a train from"—I recalled the sign—"Saint Denise?"

Dom blinked out a confused look. The driver was once again eyeing me through the mirror.

"I... thought you said something about a train." I focused on Dom. "Am I misremembering?"

"I do not think we are taking a train." Dom leaned forward, saying something to the driver. The man didn't utter a word. *"Meeerde."* Dom settled back. "He does not tell me."

"I'm pretty hungry. You think we could stop at this, um—" I pointed at a restaurant. The sign was in Arabic, and I didn't see a translation in English or French.

Crap!

People loitered on the sidewalk. One of them stepped off the curb, and the driver slammed on his breaks. Dom's seatbelt caught him. I launched into the passenger seat in front of me. My phone toppled onto the floorboard.

The driver blasted his horn. The young guy gave us the middle finger. It was now or never.

I grabbed my phone. "Making a run for it." That was intended for Maksim.

Dom's blank stare turned to realization as I plucked the lock and tugged on the handle. The door wouldn't budge.

I tried again, grunting. Panic exploded through me. I looked at the driver in time to find him swiveling around. He lunged for my phone.

I pulled it out of reach. "We're by a Middle-Eastern restaurant," I shouted to Maksim. "There's—" I glanced around. "There's public housing everywhere—"

The driver lunged again. He had his seatbelt unhooked and snatched the device. I screamed.

He jammed a finger to the red icon, ending the call. Maksim's name disappeared.

"No!" I pushed off my seat, lunging for the phone. Almost had it.

Dom unhooked his seatbelt and put himself between us.

"What are you doing?" I grabbed Dom by the shirt and shook him. "Don't you see? He's taking me to Vladimir!"

"*Mon Dieu.* Vladimir has been captured. I have seen the most recent report."

"But he might—"

"Nooo, *mon amie.* Your heart has blinded you." He forced me into my seat. "Why is it impossible to believe that Maksim has done these things? Hm? You don't want to believe me."

"Why can't you believe *me* that something's wrong?" A cold sweat broke out over my body. My pulse thudded. "The government wouldn't do all this."

"You do not understand the importance of the hard drive." The driver spoke for the very first time.

Dom and I snapped to attention.

"Your friend is right," the man said. "Vladimir Răzvan and his immediate associates have been apprehended by UK police—because of *our* surveillance. We've been investigating the Răzvan crime family for a long time." He rotated in his seat, facing me. "I could hurt you. I have a gun, and I could shoot you both now. The people in this neighborhood"—he gestured at the guys gathered along the curb—"they would consider it entertainment."

A chill shivered through me. "P-please. Don't hurt us."

"I don't plan to hurt you." He faced forward and proceeded up the road. "I am not even going to arrest you. That's not what this is about." He held up my phone and gave it a jiggle. "But I am keeping this for now. So that you don't tip off your boyfriend." He tucked the device inside his suit jacket. "Do you remember what day you were in Toulouse?"

I nodded.

"Time?"

"It was the middle of the night. I-I don't know exactly."

"You can give us a range, perhaps. That will be helpful—for us and for you." His accent was light, unrecognizable. "The more information you provide, which then leads to the recovery of the hard drive, the more leverage the politician will have for assisting you. His legal counsel has the paperwork drawn up."

"And me?" Dom leaned forward. "He has my paperwork, too?"

The man gave a curt nod. "Sit back, please. We are arriving soon."

We zigzagged through side streets, burrowing deeper into the neighborhood. All I could think about was Maksim. He was probably so worried.

We pulled up beside a one-story building with a flat roof and roll-up industrial doors. Partially renovated apartment blocks loomed from across the street.

Two cars and a black SUV waited in a parking lot. Our driver pulled up beside one of the cars, and I gasped. It was the town car we'd been following the other day.

Or... it looked like the same town car. Wasn't the same driver. Light tint colored the front window, doing a poor job of hiding the man. His chauffeur's hat swiveled as he looked over at us.

Our driver let Dom out, then came around to my side. I debated shoving the man, making a run for it, but the fear I felt and the logic of what I knew clashed.

A politician was supposed to be here. Maksim had said *Renan* knew a politician. Actually, he might have said "contact in the government." Whatever the case, if Renan was here, he was obviously involved in this. And if Maksim really had stolen a hard drive—from Ivy's, maybe?—that could be why Renan didn't trust him.

Thoughts of Maksim came tumbling down. I caught up to our driver as he led us toward the building. "Sir? I was wondering..."

He let an annoyed look fall on me.

I cleared my throat. "I was wondering if Maksim will get in trouble for the hard drive."

The man unlocked a door and pulled it open. Dom entered. I stayed where I was, glancing all around, and the man's annoyance redoubled.

"Maksim Răzvan will be facing charges for the hard drive. We already know he took it, and we will be presenting it to the court whether you cooperate or not. You could be listed as an anonymous source if you so wish, but understand—you're not informing on him. You're simply helping us retrieve the hard drive more swiftly than we would have otherwise. It is a matter of national security for multiple countries across the EU."

"And you're sure it was him who took it?"

"I'm not at liberty to discuss his known associates. I'm sorry, but please." The man ushered me through.

The inside of this building wasn't as bad as the outside. We passed an office with a desk, phone, chair, computer. Another office with a desk and phone.

The next room was much bigger with a long table pushed

against the wall and a stack of chairs standing in the corner. Conference room? I would have thought so, except that a superthin flat-screen TV—biggest I'd ever seen—filled the back wall.

My attention moved to a solid desk stationed in front of the flatscreen. My eyes gravitated toward a logo.

IB-TV

My heart skidded into the pit of my stomach. Why did that seem familiar? Where—?

We reached a door, and the man opened it. I hesitated.

He shoved me, and I stumbled into a warehouse. Two men stood at the far end, shaking hands beside a cluster of wooden crates.

They glanced our way. One of them wore a black fedora.

I pulled a sharp breath. "Renan!"

He picked up a leather duffel and angled for a side exit.

"Wait!" I broke into a sprint.

He pushed through the door and vanished into the sunlight. I reached the exit. I had one foot outside when two sets of hands jerked me to a stop.

The chauffeur waited beside the town car, door open. Renan dropped into the backseat, and seconds later they were pulling out of the parking lot and onto the craggy street.

I lost sight as they passed beneath a bridge and disappeared behind a row of brown apartment blocks.

The hands tugged, trying to reel me inside, when movement plucked at my vision. My head swung that direction.

The next-nearest apartment block towered over the street, and a tall, well-built form in a gray suit approached from that direction. A smaller form with wavy blond hair walked beside him.

I recognized the blond, and my heart leapt. "Andrei?"

It was. I'd met him in Romania where he helped me break

into the university to find Dad's records—something I thought I needed for the scavenger hunt.

I had considered Andrei more than an acquaintance. He'd been a friend, and I had shed many-a-tear thinking he was dead— another of Ştefan's loose ends tied up.

But he wasn't dead. Clearly.

I honed in on the tall man. He certainly looked the part of a politician with his tailored suit and gray hair. My stomach squeezed so hard I thought my organs might rupture.

"No." I spun around, surprising the men who'd grabbed me, and sprinted straight between them.

That so-called politician was Vladimir.

35. OPERATION VALKYRIE

I sprinted past Dom and angled for the door we'd come through. This was a setup. All of it. That news report we'd seen had been filmed here. The articles we'd found must have been fake.

Unless Vladimir really had been apprehended... and then released. I wasn't sure, but I didn't have time to think it through before hands grabbed me.

I screamed.

The driver hauled me around and crashed a fist into the side of my face. Pain exploded and spread through my head. Darkness seeped into my vision. Stars pulsed.

I felt myself being dragged across smooth cement. Shouts rang out. Scuffles ensued, and the sound of something hard connected with something soft, fleshy.

"*Oof!*"

I forced my eyes open and discovered Dom crumpled over, clutching his stomach.

The driver released me. I collapsed in a heap, and the urge to cry swelled to uncontrollable levels.

I had let myself, almost entirely of my own free will, be delivered to the second location.

Several sets of footsteps approached. I pushed up, shaking my head, blinking. The footsteps stopped. My vision cleared, and pairs of legs came into view.

I lifted my gaze. Vladimir, Andrei, and a host of men—secret-service types in suits, ties, and sunglasses—surrounded us. I crawled away from Vladimir, and one of the suits grabbed me.

He hauled me to my feet and spun me around.

Vladimir stalked forward, his icy blue stare penetrating mine. He stood taller and broader than Ștefan—what I remembered of Ștefan—but they had the same dead eyes, same stony expression.

Every part of me froze over with fear.

He stopped. His complexion had an olive hue, similar to Dad's, with wrinkles that enhanced his scowl. His thick gray eyebrows formed a sharp V.

He glared for a long moment. I cowered against the security guy, squirming. Vladimir leaned in—closer, closer, until the whites of his eyes came into view. Then he grabbed my face and squeezed so hard it brought me to my knees.

I whimpered.

He yanked me around, still holding my face, and shoved me to the floor. My shoulder hit, then the side of my head. Pain bloomed in both spots.

Vladimir gripped my arms and hauled me around.

"Uncle!"

He tilted his head.

"Uncle, no." I shielded my face. "Please."

"How dare you call me that!" His voice drove low, menacing, with a heavy Romanian accent. "Filth." He spat on me.

Saliva landed on my hands and forehead.

"Wretched sewer rat. That is what you are. Nothing more." He grabbed my face again and squeezed.

My lips pinched.

"I would torture you—a slow, excruciating road to death—if not for the word of my son, who promised you to another."

Vladimir yanked my head around, forcing me to look across the warehouse.

Raven hair and a stocky build swaggered toward us. The closer he drew, the clearer his features became—sharp nose, gray eyes.

Terror shredded my insides. Tears poured until I had nothing left but incoherent mumblings.

Émilien.

Vladimir redoubled his grip, crushing my cheeks, and shoved. The back of my head hit the cement floor. My vision crossed.

Dom rushed to my side. I reached for him.

He scooped a hand under my head and lifted me to sitting. He was saying something. I couldn't understand him.

My ears tuned in, and I realized he was speaking in French. He was ranting, shouting. He wrapped an arm around me, and relief swelled. He hadn't known what he was getting himself into. He'd been blind... just like I had.

But I wasn't alone. That was my only consolation.

Émilien stopped between Andrei and one of the secret service types. Andrei stuffed his hands in his pockets, refusing to look at me.

"Bonjour, ma petite belle." Émilien's voice, the throaty way he spoke, made my skin crawl. His expression heightened to amused as his attention shifted.

Dom held a wide-eyed stare—wider than I'd ever seen—on Émilien *"C'est toi,"* he whispered. *It's you.*

"Mais oui," Émilien replied. *But of course.*

"Wait, what?" I pointed at Émilien. "You know him?"

Dom's head gave a slow up and down.

"How?"

Émilien bent an eyebrow. "Are you going to tell her? Or should I?"

Dom gulped. "He's the *flic.* The one I bribed in Tahiti."

My eyes bulged. "Dom, he's not a cop."

I hadn't finished the sentence—hadn't gotten the last word

out—when Émilien yanked a pistol from his waistband and fired twice.

Bang bang! The shots rang out. Two bullets landed in Dom's chest.

Dom staggered backward and hit the floor. Blood bubbled up from the wounds. Thick, red liquid pooled beneath his body, and a blood-chilling scream pealed out of me.

Everything turned fuzzy. My hearing grew distant.

Suddenly, I found myself leaning over him, saying something. What? I couldn't hear myself. I couldn't think.

My vision came into focus. My hearing followed. "It's okay. You're okay." I pressed a palm to each gunshot wound.

The blood bubbled up, rushing over my palms.

"Oh, God. Dom, hang on."

Hang on for what? The question ricocheted through my mind, bouncing around, spinning. I wasn't sure why I said that. Nobody knew we were here. There wasn't an ambulance coming. Vladimir wasn't going to take him to the hospital.

Even so, I said it. "Just hang on, okay? Stay with me."

His eyes grew distant. His face turned pale. I watched a tear leak from his eye and slide along his temple. Another took the same path.

He was looking up, but his gaze never really connected with mine. It was almost like he couldn't see me. "Kat?"

"I'm here." Tears blurred my vision. Red covered my hands. "Dom, I'm here. It's going to be okay."

He lifted his hand and placed it on mine. The gesture sent a fresh wave of tears pouring down my face. *"Je suis navré."* His pale lips barely moved. His eyes glassed over. *"Je t'adore, mon amie..."* His last words drifted off before a whispery breath escaped him.

"Dom?" I pressed harder, hoping to plug the wounds, hoping there might be a chance. His hand rested on mine, limp. "Dom?"

I took his face in my hands. Blood transferred into his beard as I tried to get him to look at me. His eyes held a blank stare.

"Nooo! Nooo!" Rivers rushed down my face.

Someone hooked my waist and dragged me away. I kicked and screamed, desperate to break the hold. "Let me go! Dooom!" I sobbed his name.

Laughs circled the room. Émilien said something in French, and it sounded an awful lot like he was taunting someone.

I settled myself enough to catch my breath and take in my surroundings. Andrei was the one who'd grabbed me. The security agents grinned while Émilien held up a phone.

He was recording me. With *my* phone.

"Bastard." I choked on the insult, unable to contain my grief. Dom was dead. There was no coming back from that, no second chances. He'd made a mistake—a horrible mistake—and now he was gone.

"Are you speaking to me?" Émilien peered out from behind the phone. "Or your boyfriend?"

I froze.

Émilien smirked as he pressed a button and flipped the phone around. Maksim's face, with a look stretched wide in horror, filled the screen.

"Maksim!" I scrambled to get up.

Andrei held me in place. I spun around and slapped him. Blood smeared his cheek. Dom's blood. My hands were covered in it.

Andrei's head snapped to the side. His eyes lit with shock before settling into guilt.

"You helped them." I gritted my teeth. "You helped them kill Dom. He didn't know any better, Andrei. He didn't understand any of this."

Andrei set his jaw. The guilt never left, but a look of resolve overshadowed his features. He glanced at Vladimir, then Émilien, and shoved me to the ground. "Shut up."

"Kat!" Maksim shouted through the phone. By the time I managed to look up, Émilien had the phone flipped around and was saying something smug.

Maksim screamed an expletive. "I'm going kill y—!" His voice vanished.

Émilien tossed my phone behind the crates while Vladimir barked orders in French.

The security guys headed for the offices, peeling off their suit jackets as they went. Émilien rolled his sleeves and joined them. With Bastille Day—and cops crawling all over Paris—they must've needed a makeshift headquarters, something outside the touristy areas. Now they'd have to dismantle the space, make it look like no one was here.

Two men grabbed me and hauled me toward the side exit.

I threw a look over my shoulder. Dom's body lay in a pool of red, and a fresh wave of panic struck. "Wait. Please. We can't leave him here." I struggled. "Please!"

They kept dragging me.

Two security guys walked the perimeter. A third inspected the area by the crates and boxes.

"Monsieur Răzvan." The third guy reached down and picked up a briefcase.

Vladimir and Andrei were ahead of us. Andrei pushed open the door as Vladimir turned. My henchmen jerked me to a stop, waiting to see what their boss would do.

The security guy held up the briefcase and started toward us. Vladimir waved his hand in a dismissive motion, which prompted the security guy to give the briefcase a puzzled look. I didn't understand everything the man said, but I caught *nom*—name— while he studied the top of the briefcase.

"Vladimir Răzvan," he read, accent dripping.

A flash of orange exploded. A shockwave barreled into us.

35½. HOUR GLASS

My eyes peeled open. Smoke billowed. Flames licked at the air, fueled by a lump of black.

Nausea swept through me. That lump was the man who'd been holding the briefcase, and it was only half of him. His other half lay thirty feet away.

I rolled onto my stomach and crawled toward the open door. Andrei blocked my path. I couldn't tell if he was dead or just unconscious. Vladimir lay beside him.

I pushed myself to standing. I needed to run, now, before the men woke up. I stepped over Andrei and stumbled into the open doorway.

Something hooked my attention and dragged it to the spot where I'd woken up. One of the security guys lay in a distorted heap—legs and arms bent at odd angles—with his glasses blown off and a horrified expression seared onto his face. His partner, the one who'd been helping to restrain me, lay nearby.

A girl with long, bronze hair was lying between them.

Wait... that was *me* lying between them. But if I was there, then how could I be standing here by the door?

"Oh, no." My mouth slipped open. "This can't be happening."

But it was.

I patted myself. Everything seemed normal until I discovered my hair was no longer bronze. It was black, my natural color.

The me on the floor had bronze hair.

"What the...?" My gaze circled the warehouse as I searched for something, anything, that might explain what was going on.

Movement blurred by the crates. I turned and caught a flash of golden mane. A lion?

It was, but not just any lion. The same lion that had been showing up in my dreams since Romania.

I ran toward it.

Dom's body came into view, and my legs went static. Grief rushed in, and I fell to my knees. What he'd done—the lies, the selfishness—should have infuriated me. But he'd been swept up in a chess match he had no business playing.

I had no business playing it, either. If I had warned him, if I had been upfront about the dangers...

"Dom." I crawled alongside him. Half his body had been blackened by the explosion. His eyes were still open. "I'm sorry," I whispered. "I'm so sorry."

Let the dead bury their dead. The voice that rang through my thoughts belonged to Dad, and I didn't understand what he meant. Was he saying all these people were dead? That I was, too? I didn't feel dead.

A growl drew my attention to the right.

The lion stalked behind the crates, moving methodically and swatting its tail. That was when I understood—I couldn't mourn Dom. There would be a time for that, but that time wasn't now.

You have to focus, Kat.

I pushed up and hurried toward the crates. The lion was gone, but I discovered something lying on the floor.

My phone.

I stooped, intending to grab the device. My fingers went straight through it. I stared at my hand. It didn't appear transparent or ghost-like. Still, I couldn't pick up the phone. So then, how...?

The epiphany rocked me.

I did a one-eighty and sprinted through the smoke. Vladimir stirred. Andrei moaned.

I knelt beside myself—beside the me on the floor—and shook her. Red covered her hands. Her face was pale.

"Wake up." I shook harder. "Kat, you have to wake up. Now. Wake up!"

PART THREE

36. MISSION FAILED

A low ring resonated in my ears. Smoke carried a charred smell into my nostrils and down my throat.

I rolled over, coughing, and pushed myself up. Everyone and everything lay as they'd been in the dream.

My attention shifted to Andrei and Vladimir, both of whom had begun to stir. Andrei lay across the doorway.

Frantic voices reached me from across the warehouse. They stemmed from the office area, and they were coming this way. I had to go. Now.

I pushed up and stumbled to the open door. ***Note every possible exit.*** The rule pinged from somewhere deep in my psyche.

Apart from this side door, what other exits were available? I didn't see any across the warehouse, but there was the main entrance inside the building, the one we'd used to access those offices.

I spun on my heel and crossed the warehouse as fast as I could. The phone. I needed the phone, and it was over by the crates. There'd be no way to retrieve it and then cross the warehouse a second time to use the side door.

Émilien and the security goons were going to show up any second. I needed another exit.

The ringing in my ears subsided as I reached the crates. My phone lay on the floor, just like it had in the dream—or whatever that'd been—and I scooped up the device. A long crack marked the screen, but the phone was otherwise fine.

Footsteps drew closer, slowly at first, then more rapidly. Shock permeated the voices.

More security guys rushed into the warehouse.

I peered out from behind a stack of crates. One of the men held a fire extinguisher, and a plume of white dust covered the flames. The others checked for survivors.

My attention traveled across the warehouse. I needed to sneak into the office area while the men were preoccupied.

Or I could wait, see if the men disperse, then make a run for it out the side exit. That was another possibility... unless they thought to look over here. Then I'd be busted.

Listen to your instinct. Maksim's rule rose above my doubt. I looked at the side exit and then the offices.

Offices.

I edged alongside the crates, ducking down and keeping behind each stack. *Be discreet.*

At the end of the clutter, I peered around the corner. I was about halfway across the warehouse, and the men were still preoccupied at the far end. Two of them helped Vladimir up. Émilien stood over Andrei, pointing and glancing around.

"Where did she go?" Émilien shouted the question. Andrei shook his head, blinking.

I sprinted to the door and slipped through. That office with the phone, desk, and chair had been cleared out. So had the conference room. All that remained were the wall mounts that had been holding up the flat-screen.

I was right. Vladimir *had* been using this place as a type of headquarters, and they'd been trying to clear out.

"Assholes," I whispered. Their ruse had been enough to fool

everyone, even Maksim. He really thought Vladimir had been apprehended *and* that Émilien was in jail.

IB-TV had been a phony news network. I understood that much. But what about the legitimate networks that had been reporting on the standoff? Dom had pulled up articles straight from their websites. He'd shown me.

How had these guys pulled that off?

I tiptoed up the hall and peeked around the corner. The windows around the entrance had been boarded up. I eased closer and peeked through a thin crack between the boards. I didn't see any more men, but there was a white work van parked out front.

Les Peintres
Tél: 07 77 00 77 00

I blinked so hard my eyes crossed. That was the van I'd seen outside the electronics store. No way that was a coincidence.

Vladimir's men must have... what? Tampered with the TVs? Maybe they screencast the phony news segment. The van had been close enough for that.

A male voice broke the silence.

I whipped around and found Émilien striding up the hallway. He held a phone to his ear while speaking in rushed French. His hair crisscrossed every which way. His eyes reflected worry.

His attention landed on me. Shock exploded through his features.

I fumbled with the lock and rammed myself against the door. It flew open, and I stumbled outside.

My legs carried me toward the nearest apartment block. A crowd had formed, and several people trickled this way.

"Help!" I waved frantically.

The people froze.

Émilien growled, bearing down on me. I lengthened my stride the way I had in soccer, whenever I'd found an open stretch of field.

I was angling toward the apartment block when shots rang out. The crowd scattered. Émilien shouted.

I threw a quick glance.

One of the security guys must have been chasing after us, and now he had the gun trained on me. Émilien doubled back, screaming in French.

Another shot rang out.

The round whizzed past my ear. I ducked, following the stampede to the apartment building. A woman stood at the entrance, holding the door.

The people piled inside the entryway. I was the last one there, but I didn't make it.

The woman slammed the door in my face and twisted a lock. My eyes bulged. I yanked on the handle. She shook her head.

Bang! Another shot.

The security guy lay motionless on the sidewalk. Émilien, now holding a pistol, climbed into a black SUV. The driver gunned it.

Dust circled the tires. The SUV launched forward.

A burst of panic drained the strength from my knees. I banged on the door. "Please!" I said to the woman. "You have to call the police."

"*You* call the police." The glass door muted her thickly accented voice. She glanced at something in my hand.

My phone. I'd been holding it in a death-grip.

I woke up the screen and pressed Maksim's name. "Where should I go?" I asked the woman.

She crossed her arms and glared. Teenagers, small children, women all huddled around her. So many frightened eyes, so many people trembling.

Émilien and his men would kill any one of them to get to me. The woman was right not to let me in.

I sprinted alongside the building while the SUV closed in. I hung a left and found myself on a grassy path behind the apartments. Graffiti wallpapered the ground floor. Laundry lay draped across balcony railings.

I followed the path in a dead sprint until I started to encounter more and more dirty diapers, beer bottles, food wrappings. Bits of orange plastic tugged at my vision, and my feet lagged to a stop.

Syringes. Everywhere. I'd been running through them. The urge to vomit swelled. My vision blurred.

Brakes screeched. Shouts followed.

"Kat?" Maksim's distant voice shook me out of the daze.

I turned and spied Émilien jumping out of the SUV. One of the security guys trailed him. The man was tall, bulky, with pale skin and reddish hair—the ginger from the night before, the one who'd slipped into the elevator.

The epiphany stunned me. Had that been yet another kidnapping attempt?

I swore and broke into a sprint. Plastic cracked and rolled under my shoes. My stomach churned. I kept going.

"Kat!" Maksim's shout vibrated the phone.

"I'm here." I pressed Speaker. "I'm behind an apartment building. Émilien and one of his men are chasing me."

"Don't lose the phone."

"I'm not sure what to do." I reached the end of the building. That building with the warehouse sat to the left. Another apartment block sat to the right.

I went right, sprinting beside a parking lot with stripped, broken-down cars. "I'm trying to figure out where I am—"

"Don't lose the phone! Can you hear me? Whatever you do, do *not*..." An electronic tone drowned out his voice. Chatter hummed. He was somewhere public and crowded. Metro station?

The electronic tone faded. "—hear me? I said I'm almost there."

My heart trilled. Almost here? "You know where I am?"

"I'm tracking you." A pause. "Are you someplace safe?"

"Not exactly." I glanced over my shoulder. Émilien was ahead of the security guy, who limped along, shaking out his foot. Something thin and orange hung from his shoe.

Gross. A needle.

I turned my attention to the upcoming apartment block. A green metal fence with sharp points on top cordoned off the property. Trash littered the courtyard.

I raced alongside the fence until I reached a rusty, janky gate hanging by a single hinge. I turned in, sprinted up the walkway, and ducked inside the building. The ceiling was charred black, and a burnt smell filled my nostrils.

Note every possible exit.

Mailboxes lined the walls, and several of them hung open, as if they weren't being used anymore. I followed them to the right, searching for an exit. I didn't find one.

I pressed a light switch on the wall. Nothing. This was an abandoned building.

I started toward a staircase and paused. The entrance hung open, and I could see Émilien sprinting through the gate.

I took the phone off speaker and raced up the stairs. "How close are you?" I whispered.

"Six stops."

Tears plucked my eyes. He wasn't going to make it in time.

Think logically.

An idea sparked. I didn't have time to run through every scenario, but I felt sure the idea could work. Maybe. If I played my cards right.

"Hey, Maksim? I-I'm going to put the phone away and hope Émilien doesn't see it. We should be in a black SUV, something like a Suburban."

"Can't you run? Hide?"

"No." My ears tuned in to footsteps. "Dom got duped," I whispered, continuing toward the second floor. The shadows thickened. "He's dead. Émilien killed him."

Silence filled my ear.

"Renan was there." I wiped a loose tear. "He tried to assassinate Vladimir with a briefcase bomb. There were dead bodies, a fire—but Vladimir survived."

The footsteps drew closer and morphed into a shuffle. Émilien was in the stairwell.

"I'm hanging up. Don't call." Another tear leaked as I whispered, "Maksim, I'm sorry."

I hung up before he could reply.

37. MEGA LOMANIAC

Maksim was tracking me—somehow—and he was using the phone to do it. Which meant I couldn't let anything happen to this phone.

But where could I hide it? My bra?

If I'd been wearing a sports bra, then maybe. But I was wearing a normal bra, and it wouldn't hold an entire phone.

I could tuck it into my shorts. But what would stop him from checking there?

My foot came down on the top step and slipped. I snapped forward, catching myself with my free hand, and I very nearly vomited right then and there. I had slipped in an oily substance.

Light trickled into the stairwell from down below. As I stared at my hand, stomach lurching, an idea buzzed through my thoughts.

I steeled myself and swiped my hand through the grease—or whatever it was—and smeared it across my shirt, shorts, leg. Then I slid out my passport and tossed it into the last sliver of light.

I stuffed the phone deep into the back of my shorts, underwear and all, then straightened my shirt and plunked myself on the top step.

The oily substance soaked into my shorts. Bile rose in my throat and spilled into my mouth.

I forced a swallow and leaned back, trying to make it look like I was getting up. As soon as Émilien came into view, I moaned and gave my head a hard shake. He rushed up the last steps and yanked me to my feet.

I screamed, backing myself against the wall, and raised my red-and-black-streaked hands. He looked like he was about to slap me when he noticed the grease all over the right side of me.

His attention fell to his hands, which were now a mix of red and oily black. He wrinkled his nose.

I sidestepped to the next stair down. I was already nervous, being so close to Émilien, but I made extra-sure I was trembling.

He snatched my wrist and hauled me away from the wall. "Don't hurt me!" I turned myself around, doing my best to stay facing him—and to keep the bulge in my shorts hidden.

"Where is the phone?" He swatted at my front pockets.

I squeezed my eyes shut. "There," I squeaked, pointing into the shadows. "I-I fell." I hunched my shoulders, cowering a bit more. "P-please. Don't hurt me."

Émilien pulled out his phone and activated the flashlight. Trash carpeted the floor all the way into the hallway.

Someone entered the building and called out in French. Émilien answered, and the footsteps raced our way.

Émilien barked orders, and when the man arrived, he grabbed me. I kept my back pressed against the wall while Émilien walked forward, shining his light over the trash.

His left shoe came down on my passport. The security guy noticed and snatched up the document. I kept my mouth shut.

Émilien pocketed his phone and my passport and treaded down the stairs. I dragged my feet, forcing the security guy to pull me along.

The black SUV idled out front. Émilien climbed into the backseat, and the security guy hauled me that direction. I twisted and turned, pretending to struggle. In reality, I was trying to keep the bulge in the back of my shorts hidden.

Émilien hauled me into the backseat. The phone jostled. I sat straight, pressing my lower back against the seat.

The security guy shoved me aside and then jerked the door shut behind us. Two more security guys were in the front. One of them locked the doors, and the driver punched the gas.

We zoomed past the building with the warehouse. The work van was gone, as were the other cars, and bright orange flames engulfed the entrance. More flames exploded from the roof.

Émilien leaned forward, cutting off my view. "There will be nothing left soon. The fire will burn so hot, officials may not be able to identify your friend's body." His mouth tipped up. "All the better for us."

My bottom lip trembled. I set my jaw. "Where are you taking me?"

"Listen. Do you hear it?" Émilien held up a finger.

A siren echoed in the distance. My ears tuned in, and I detected an atonal wail. *Wee-oo-wee-oo-wee-oo.* Police siren? If so, we were moving toward it, not away.

We left the residential neighborhood behind and entered one with shops and eateries. They were all very small, and most were rundown.

"I know you will blame me for your friend." Émilien examined his manicured nails. "But Maksim is the reason he is dead."

"*You* shot Dom. That's why he's dead."

Émilien's hand flew. His palm crashed into my cheek, leaving a plume of shock amid the fiery sting. Memories from Romania flooded in—the club, the first time I'd met Émilien. He and Maksim had gotten into a confrontation, and when Maksim left, Émilien had punched me in the face.

Same spot. Left cheek.

Before I could finish the thought, he slapped me again. And again. Then he gripped my throat and squeezed. I clutched his wrist, squirming. He gritted his teeth and squeezed harder, crushing my vocal cords. "You *will* learn to respect me."

I gurgled, clawing at his forearm.

He shoved me into the security guy. "Maksim learned to employ methods, even technology, that gave the appearance he was in one location while in truth he was in another. *Du coup,* when his allegiance came into question, I was tasked with learning his true whereabouts. I tracked him here and discovered this network of companions."

I hunched over, holding my throat, gasping. My brain barely registered what he said.

"I found many delicious morsels about his girlfriend," Émilien purred, "some of which have been very useful. But this friend, Dominique, proved more difficult—some speeding tickets, one disgruntled ex-girlfriend. Nothing spectacular." Émilien sat back. "And so, I orchestrated the spectacular, something we could use if the need ever arose. And of course, it did"—he settled his arrogant gaze on me—"when you arrived in Paris."

The gears in my brain turned, rolling over the information, processing it. Dom had told me about his vacation in Tahiti. He'd driven drunk at the insistence of a friend, someone he'd met during his trip, and had hit and killed a local girl. Then he bribed the cops to let him go.

Our last moments in the warehouse rushed back to me. Dom had recognized Émilien. *"He's the flic. The one I bribed in Tahiti."*

"It was a setup." The realization escaped as a whisper—mostly because I couldn't believe what I was hearing, but also because I could hardly talk. "You... orchestrated that whole thing?" I croaked. "In Tahiti?"

"Down to his companion who, 'strangely'"—he inserted sarcasm—"disappeared after the incident." Émilien's thin lips curled up at the corners. "This man was one of our people, of course—in case you are not so clever as Domnule Răzvan believes you to be." He reached over and pinched my chin. "But I think you are, *ma petite belle.* I think you understand me perfectly."

I jerked away. There'd been something odd and unsettling about Dom's story. I hadn't been able to put my finger on it, but now, hearing Émilien explain what happened, shed more than enough light.

What police officer would be so dismissive about a missing person? To say, oh, your friend must have been in a drunken stupor and fallen into the water, so we're just not going to look for him...

That hadn't made sense because Dom hadn't been dealing with real cops. He'd been dealing with criminals posing as cops, and all because they—Émilien and Vladimir—had wanted dirt on Maksim's circle of friends.

Traffic thickened as we continued through the neighborhood. We went through a traffic circle and came to a crawl. There were fewer apartment blocks and more businesses in this area. I noticed the Middle-Eastern restaurants and shops again, along with a few that advertised themselves as Senegalese with red, green, and yellow flags waving out front.

I stared at everything, brain buzzing with Émilien's explanation.

"Why?" I whispered.

Émilien craned his neck, checking the line of traffic ahead of us. He slanted an annoyed look. "Why what?"

"Why did you need Dom—or anyone—to get to Maksim? If y'all felt like Maksim was a threat, why not just kill him? Why go through all the trouble?"

Émilien rolled his eyes. "Perhaps you are not as clever as I had hoped."

I glared. "Sorry I don't think like a criminal."

That probably wasn't the wisest of remarks, and when the security guy stiffened beside me, my regret levels shot through the roof, out of the car, and into the atmosphere.

I waited for Émilien to slap me. Instead, he chuckled. "I like this about you. It is a type of spark, a fire, that burns within you."

He leaned in. "I am going to enjoy both stoking *and* extinguishing this fire, *ma chérie*."

Fear tore through me.

"Tell me, how did you know I like the redheads? Mm? It's like you *want* my wildest fantasies to come true." He twisted a lock of my bronze hair around his finger.

I shoved him. He grabbed my wrists and laughed as I tried to punch him. I yanked and pushed, desperate to reclaim my hands.

"Oh, yes. Yes!" He laughed harder. *"Le feu, le feu."* The fire, the fire.

Movement whizzed past. A motorcyclist was lane-splitting the two lines of traffic. I caught a glimpse and then reeled in my attention. All thoughts of the phone, of Maksim finding me, went out the window as I grappled with Émilien.

The security guy shouted. I couldn't understand him, but I suddenly felt a hand dip down into my shorts.

I whipped around. The guy had my phone.

Émilien hauled me around and crashed his fist into my face. My head whipped back. Pain exploded in my nose. Darkness streaked my vision, and I slumped against the security guy.

38. GET AWAY

My vision sparkled like the Eiffel Tower. The flashes moved across a veil of blackness draped over my eyes. I blinked away the lights. Lifted my head.

The security guy and Émilien were inspecting the phone like their lives depended on it. They kept flipping the device, checking apps. Even the two guys in the front seemed concerned, turning around and asking questions.

Émilien had disclosed a lot of information. Maybe they thought someone had been listening on the phone that entire time.

Movement drew my attention to the window. Someone paced between the two lanes of traffic. At first, I thought it was a homeless guy, but as my vision cleared, I recognized the tall form and broad shoulders.

Maksim checked his phone and then looked up. His attention landed on our vehicle, and he marched over and pressed his face to the back window.

I gasped. "In here!" I shoved the security guy forward and crawled behind him, slapping the window.

Maksim raced to the next vehicle. He hadn't heard me.

I slammed my hand down on the power-window button

when Émilien yanked me back. I pulled my legs around, thinking I could kick out the window. The security guy grabbed my torso and held me in place.

I screamed.

Traffic moved forward. The driver followed the line of cars through the traffic light. The guy in the passenger seat pulled out his gun.

I wrestled and kicked and managed to free my right leg. I twisted around and slammed my foot into the man's arm, his shoulder. I kicked the driver next.

He pulled away, saying something in French. As he looked back at me, Maksim appeared and ran alongside the car. He had something in his hand.

Émilien pointed, shouting.

The driver focused forward as Maksim held the object—something long and skinny—against the windshield. He pulled one side back, as far as he could. When the tension reached its peak, he let go.

The object snapped forward, and a huge spiderweb spread across the driver's side of the windshield. The glass didn't fully break, but the crack was big enough to disrupt the driver's vision.

The man leaned to the side, peering around the spiderweb, and followed traffic through a roundabout. Maksim launched into a sprint, crossing straight through the circle.

Drivers hit their brakes. Honks went up. Men rushed out of the shops and restaurants.

Maksim readied the object, which looked like an old-style car antenna. Brandy's family had one on their nineties minivan, and I remembered Dave messing around with it one day, unscrewing the antenna and joking that Brandy wouldn't be able to get the AM radio stations anymore. Maksim must have pulled it from a car in traffic.

Émilien's driver sped up and turned, aiming the SUV at Maksim. I reared back and kicked his arm. His hand jerked, and the SUV cut right.

Maksim ran alongside the vehicle. In one swift motion, he held the antenna against my side window, pulled back, and let go. The glass ruptured. He punched through the pane and grabbed the security guy who was holding me.

I watched the man's face go wide as Maksim hauled him through the broken window. Everyone drew their pistols. The guy in the passenger seat crawled into the back.

Traffic suddenly cleared in front of us. *"Allez allez,"* I screamed. *"Flic!"* I hadn't really seen a *flic*—cop—but my idea worked.

The driver gunned it, and the security guy flew face-first into the backseat. I rammed my foot against his head, crushing his sunglasses. *Crack!* His skull hit the door, and the man slumped.

Émilien hooked an arm around my throat. I tugged, pulled, clawed. His hold tightened, and blackness seeped into my vision.

We sped up the road. As the driver twisted around, assessing the damage in the backseat, he didn't notice the garbage truck pulling out from a side street. Neither did Émilien, who was more concerned with choking me out.

I pointed, trying to yell.

The driver focused forward. He saw the truck and yanked the steering wheel. We whipped left—but not in time.

The right side of the SUV slammed into the garbage truck. Émilien's arm came loose as we went up on two wheels. My vision returned, blood thumping in my head, and I had enough awareness to throw my hands up the moment Émilien tumbled onto me.

We collided with the unconscious security guy, and all three of us bounced around as the SUV rolled onto its side and then onto its roof before finally coming to a rest.

We were upside down.

I stilled myself, glancing around, listening. The security guy lay beneath me. Émilien lay on top, eyes closed, mouth ajar.

Commotion stirred outside the car.

I twisted around and discovered several sets of legs gathering outside the busted window. A dark face with thick, black hair appeared. The man said something in broken French and an Arabic accent.

A familiar baritone voice stretched from farther down the block. Footsteps pounded, and the bystanders made room.

Relief gushed as the footsteps stopped outside the SUV. I recognized his boots, but it took me a second to process the slacks.

Maksim knelt, surveying the situation. "How many are armed?"

"All of them," I whispered. "Maksim, I'm stuck."

"Take my hand." He reached through the window. I took it, and some of the oily substance transferred.

That hand was the greasiest, so he gripped the other and hauled me out—little by little by little. My arms and shoulders cleared the car. My torso came free of the human sandwich, then my hips.

I was halfway through the window.

Something jostled inside the vehicle. Metal clanked, and a hand hooked my shorts. I screamed.

Maksim bent forward, wrapping me in a hug, and kept pulling. I braced the ground, planning to kick my way free, but as my hand touched the pavement, metal connected with my wrist and wrapped around it.

Clickclickclick. The metal tightened. It was a handcuff. One of the men had slapped a cuff on me.

The barrel of a nine-millimeter appeared in the broken window. The gun was pointed straight at Maksim. I scrambled to move him. "Watch out!"

A round exploded from the chamber. The crowd scattered. Maksim dodged but refused to let me go.

Another round fired off. Another.

A group of men grabbed Maksim and dragged him away from me. "No!" I lunged.

He fought through them, but one of the men was built like a rugby player, and he managed to hold on to Maksim.

Two other men raced over to me. They pulled hard, trying to haul me to my feet. My entire arm, wrist to shoulder, ached. My elbow popped, and I screamed.

"Stop it! *Arrête!*" I was cuffed to something inside the SUV.

Another pistol fired off multiple times in succession. The driver had managed to crawl out of the SUV and was firing into the air.

The two men ducked away. Maksim kept wrestling with the other three men until the driver grabbed me and pressed the pistol to my head.

The tension on my right arm slacked off. Émilien crawled through the broken window, holding his pistol left-handed. The other end of the cuff was secured to his right wrist.

No wonder these people hadn't been able to pry me away. I'd been cuffed to *him*.

Émilien hooked his cuffed hand around me and pressed his pistol to my head. The driver then pointed his gun at Maksim and the three men. All of them raised their hands except Maksim.

The police sirens grew louder. Blue lights flashed off to the right, but the cop couldn't get through. Some drivers moved to the side, but too many had gotten out of their cars, and those people had since taken cover because of the gunshots.

Traffic stacked both sides of the street.

A double honk drew everyone's attention the other direction. A man in a gray suit and dark sunglasses stood on the hood of a car, waving.

The security guy Maksim had pulled out of the SUV.

Honks went up around him, then more, until they had nearly drowned out the sirens.

Émilien nodded in that direction. *"Allez."* Let's go.

I planted my feet, fighting him, inching the other direction. If I could hold out long enough for the cop to get here—

He yanked our cuffed hands and hauled me forward. As I stumbled into him, he crashed the butt of his gun into the side of my head.

My vision faded. I heard Émilien grunt, then I was hanging upside down. Felt like I was floating. I blinked. Shook my head. Forced my eyes open.

Émilien had tossed me over his shoulder and was carrying me up the street. The driver walked beside us, keeping his pistol trained on the only three people who hadn't taken cover. They were the men who'd been wrestling with Maksim.

But... Maksim was gone.

39. VANISHING ACT

Émilien leaned forward. I slid off his shoulder and landed against something warm.

A car. The security guy hopped down from the hood and dropped into the driver's seat. The other security guy climbed into the passenger seat. Émilien shoved me into the backseat and climbed in after me.

Be aware. Maksim's rule jarred me. My vision wobbled, but I forced myself to focus and assessed my surroundings.

The car sat parked at a corner, pointing in the direction of a one-way street without traffic. Because he'd been blocking that traffic, I realized. That was why the other drivers had been honking.

As soon as Émilien had the back door shut, the driver gunned it, and we were speeding up the narrow street.

Émilien held the pistol in his left hand—directly by my head —while his right hand remained cuffed to me. But I was cuffed on my right hand, too, which meant anytime he moved his hand, I ended up reaching across him. And if I moved, he would end up reaching across himself.

He leaned forward, tucked the pistol into his waistband, and then reached into his pocket. He was saying something in French to the guys up front.

They had an exchange. The driver was explaining something while Émilien pulled out a tiny object and stuck it into the cuff lock. He twisted, and the cuff disengaged.

He re-cuffed himself on the left wrist—I was still cuffed on the right—and returned the key to his pocket. If only I could get that key, then I could—

Wait a second. I *could* get the key. It was right there.

I reached toward his pocket, then stopped myself. Even if I could slip that key out of his pocket, what would I do after that?

Nothing. I was in a moving car, going way too fast to jump out. And even if the driver slowed down, I would have three armed men to contend with.

Avoid unwanted attention.

Yeah. A dramatic getaway wasn't going to work. I needed to bide my time, wait for the right opportunity. But when? And where was Maksim?

Assume you're being tailed.

I peered out the back window. Cars trickled onto the one-way street, but none of them appeared to be in a hurry—drivers looking for a way around that accident if I had to guess. Definitely no cop cars, and nothing that could have been Maksim in pursuit.

Émilien did a head-check, following my line of sight.

"It's only a matter of time, you know."

Émilien settled a glare on me. "Oh?"

"Everyone in that traffic jam saw us. Cops are going to be canvassing this whole neighborhood soon."

"They will. You are right." Émilien's mouth tipped up. "And they will be searching for *this* car."

I wasn't sure what he meant, but then the driver took a call. He went back and forth with the caller while turning down side streets and even making a U-turn.

Five minutes later, he parked inside an alley. We all climbed out—Émilien dragged me out—and headed for...

My stomach twisted into a knot. We were heading for the

304 DAWN TO DUSK

work van I'd been seeing. The inside had been stripped of whatever equipment and seats had been in there, and there weren't any other security guys. Just the driver.

Émilien wrestled me into the van while the police sirens grew louder. There were several now, but any hope I had fizzled out. The cops didn't know about this van. They would be searching for the silver car.

The van door slid shut, and we pulled onto the street at a totally normal, not-running-from-the-cops speed.

Please let Maksim find me. Please, God.

We wove through the streets of Saint-Denis. The men spoke only in French, but I caught a handful of words—*l'aéroport, les appartements, l'hélicoptère.*

The airport.

The apartments.

The helicopter.

Now, I would have thought we were going the airport to board a helicopter, except there were several negations surrounding that part—words like *non* and *ne pas.*

From what I gathered, we were *not* going to the airport—but Vladimir was. I picked up on that when Émilien said "Domnule Răzvan." He also mentioned Andrei.

They were going to the airport, but we weren't? And what was the deal with the helicopter?

We approached a set of brown tower blocks—similar to what I'd seen earlier, down to the graffiti and laundry hanging outside, but these were taller.

As we circled through a roundabout, I noticed a taxi behind us. I was sitting on the floorboard, so I didn't get a good look, but I wondered if it could have been Maksim.

The taxi exited the roundabout before we did, and I slumped. Not Maksim.

Our van pulled into a parking lot stationed alongside a courtyard. Graffiti stained park benches and even a tree. People came and went from the apartments—twenty-somethings with back-packs, moms with small children, people carrying groceries. Several teens loitered outside, smoking cigarettes and staring at their phones.

We parked, and the driver killed the engine. He was saying something while glancing all around, and the security guys shared a look.

The guy was nervous about something. The location? All the people around? Those were my best guesses, but why? What were we doing here?

Another layer of their plan peeled back as a dark object in the sky drew closer. A helicopter?

My attention traveled up the building, and my heart skidded down into my stomach. Unlike the buildings in Dom's neighbor-hood, with their gray sloped rooftops and chimney pots galore, these block-style apartments had flat roofs. Perfect for landing a helicopter.

That was how they were planning to make their getaway. The helicopter was the second location. The knot in my stomach tightened.

"The police have helicopters," I blurted. "There's no way you're getting out of France like this."

"No?" Émilien knelt on the floor beside me. He leaned in, placed his mouth by my ear, and whispered, "Watch me." His hot breath mixed with his body odor nearly knocked me out.

I pulled away.

He pulled me back and licked the side of my face, jawline to cheek and even up to my temple. His saliva felt like slime on my skin, and my stomach roiled.

The inside of the van grew shadowy while this was happen-ing. Come to find out, the security guys were covering the back windows with cardboard while the driver unfolded a sunshade and placed it across the windshield.

The men zipped themselves into matching coveralls, each

donning a commercial-painter-style hat, and grabbed paint buckets, rollers, brushes.

As they piled out, Émilien stopped one of the security guys. The two of them had an exchange, their attention on something in the courtyard, and when Émilien finished, the man walked over to a little boy who was playing nearby.

I opened my mouth to scream.

Émilien grabbed my face the way Vladimir had and yanked me around. "Do it," he growled, "and I will kill him."

I went static.

The boy raced over to us. Émilien let me go, and a smug look spread across his face.

He dipped into his pocket, pulled out his wallet, and handed the boy a fifty-euro banknote, all the while explaining something.

The boy nodded. *"Oui, monsieur."*

Émilien patted the boy's head and rustled his hair. *"C'est très bien ce que tu fais."* It's very good what you're doing.

The boy's attention fell to our cuffs. He asked a question, and Émilien's response—whatever it might've been—was cool and composed.

The boy shrugged and pocketed the cash.

"What'd you tell him?" I held up my cuffed hand, indicating what I meant.

Émilien chuckled. "That you have been a very bad girl, but that if he helps me, I have more of those fifties for him. Buuut"— he tipped his head side to side—"maybe I would rather kill him than pay him. I will see how I feel in that moment, mm?"

Nausea swirled through me. He wasn't joking. He really would kill that little boy if he felt like it.

Émilien untucked his shirt, hiding his firearm, and closed up the van. Then the three of us angled for the apartment building. I scanned the area, searching for a way out of this.

Two young guys—eighteenish—leaned against the building. I hoped they might notice the cuffs, but they held their undivided attention on their phones.

Émilien cleared his throat. My gaze shifted to him, and he gave a warning shake of his head. "Don't do it," he mouthed, nodding toward the little boy. The Frenchman placed a thumb to his neck and made a silent, slitting motion across his throat.

That was what he'd do to the boy if I made a scene.

The boy bounced along, leading us. He had no idea what he was getting himself into, no idea what these men were capable of. *Just like Dom.* The epiphany hit rock bottom within me. My feet lagged. Émilien gripped my arm and dragged me.

The other three guys waited inside the entryway. The boy motioned for everyone to follow him.

Instead of leading us to the main stairs where people came and went, he led us off to the side. We passed residential mailboxes, turned a corner, and went through a door that put us in a second, smaller stairwell. A musty odor mixed with concrete and dust overwhelmed my senses.

The little boy went first, followed by the security guys, then Émilien and me, and finally the van driver. This building had to be fifteen stories tall—twice the height of Dom's apartment—and we were climbing the entire way.

My throat tightened. I would've given anything to take those stairs with Maksim again. I had walked them with Dom, too, but going the other way. *The day of the fire alarm.*

The incident came back to me. Whatever happened to that cop, the one who'd come to Dom's apartment? Dom had waited for him after I'd left for the café, but he said the cop never showed up.

How? We'd all been in the stairwell, along with the other residents of the building, and everyone had ended up in the foyer on the ground floor.

Except maybe not everyone had. Maybe there'd been a secondary stairwell—something like we were in now—that branched off from another floor. That was possible. But then, why would the cop take a side stairwell? Why not meet Dom in the foyer?

As we rounded the second level, one of the security guards turned and said something. He hesitated, peering past us. I followed his line of sight to who I assumed was the driver...

But the driver wasn't behind us.

Émilien reached back and dipped into his waistband, drawing his pistol. The security guys unzipped their coveralls partway and reached into their holsters.

They brushed past us. I took a step in that direction.

Émilien jerked the cuff, tugging me the other way. "No, no." He pointed the gun up the staircase. "Go."

We followed the little boy at a steady jog. I dragged my feet, panting, pretending to be more tired than I was. Émilien yanked his cuffed hand. I bumped into him.

"Do *not* toy with me," he said through gritted teeth.

The little boy stopped and turned around. As Émilien switched to French, I realized my hand was by his pocket.

The cuff key.

Émilien faced me forward, gave a shove, and we were once again jogging up the stairs. ***Always be ready.*** This rule was the reason Maksim never relaxed or let up. I hadn't been ready a second ago, but I should have been.

I would be.

We were halfway up the stairwell when something clattered down below. I hadn't heard the men in a while, and I'd assumed they might have been doing a perimeter sweep.

Émilien called down. There was no response, and he picked up speed. I double-timed it, trying to keep pace with him. My attention drifted to his pocket... again... again.

The same clatter echoed from down below. The door, I realized. Someone had opened and shut it. This time, a deep voice drifted up the center shaft. A surprised shout followed.

Émilien hesitated. I pumped my arms, attention locked onto his pocket, and rammed straight into him from behind. He snapped forward, bracing the staircase.

My right hand was cuffed, but I'd fallen against him in such a way that my left hand was free to roam. And it did. I swore, letting my full weight come down on him—and knowing I was going to pay for that—as I dipped into his pocket.

40. BICYCLE KICK

"*Putain!*" Émilien pushed up.

I reclaimed my hand and made a fist so tight I couldn't feel anything. Had I actually grabbed the key?

Émilien's free hand flew toward my face. His palm connected. *Smack!* Fire lit up my cheek. He landed three more slaps, each one connecting with greater power.

The last one sent me staggering. I crashed to my knees, fist still curled. *Don't open your hand. Keep it closed.* My knuckles pressed the smooth floor.

Émilien grabbed my hair and hauled me to my feet. He probably would have slapped me again, but tussles and punches from below distracted him. He peered down the center shaft.

I followed his line of sight. The security guy's grunts and shouts became evident. The other person didn't utter a peep while the sound of knuckles connecting with flesh and bone drifted up the stairwell.

Maksim.

Émilien shoved me up the stairs. The little boy ran ahead of us. We circled around to the tenth floor. Eleventh. Twelfth. Each time we hit a landing, I hoped we would go through the metal door that likely led to a hallway with apartments. With people.

We didn't, and I knew why. The helicopter was picking us up on the roof.

Never, ever reach the second location. Maksim's top rule, the one he'd been training me for, the most critical of them all, blazed through my thoughts.

I'd let myself get taken to all kinds of second locations today. I could *not* let myself get taken to the ultimate one now.

Émilien dragged me along. I was behind him and opened my hand the tiniest bit. A hint of silver peeked out.

Émilien glanced back. I closed my fist and pumped my arm, pretending to do my best to keep up. All the while, my mind raced.

Hypothetically speaking, let's say I could uncuff myself. There'd be nothing to stop Émilien from chasing me down and re-cuffing me... unless I could lock him in a room somewhere. Or an apartment?

No. I might be able to lock myself in an apartment, but not him.

Okay, so then what about that option—locking myself in an apartment? That should be enough to evade a kidnapping— maybe—and the people might be willing to call the police.

There were too many "mights" and "maybes" in that idea. The truth was, I had no guarantees that anyone would let me in their apartment. And even if they did, there was no guarantee Émilien wouldn't—or couldn't—bust down the door.

We reached the thirteenth floor. Only two levels left, then the roof. *Think, Kat.* I racked my brain for every source of wisdom, knowledge, advice I'd ever received. Movies. Podcasts. Literally anything.

My thoughts shifted to the lion. It had shown me the phone in that dream—I thought because I was supposed to call Maksim, but it must've been because Maksim was tracking the phone.

I didn't understand how the lion would have known that—I certainly hadn't—but I'd always felt like Dad was still watching out for me, still helping me out. So... even though I didn't have a solution, maybe he did.

Dad? I might be able to get out of this cuff, but I don't know how to get away. What do I do?

We reached the fourteenth floor and rounded the landing. The boy was a full level ahead of us now. Émilien managed the same, steady pace, while my pace continued to slow.

My thighs and calves burned. My side ached. I grabbed the banister and used it to pull myself up.

Used it to... wait, what?

My attention landed on the banister. It was old, made of metal, and a couple of the vertical bars were loose. But the railing was sturdy overall.

The gears in my head began to crank. An idea took shape— unlock my cuff and then latch it to the railing. Then Émilien couldn't come after me.

He turned the corner, heading for the next level. Grunts and punches reached us from down below, but they were growing more distant. Maksim wasn't making any progress up the stairwell. Was he fighting both security guys? Why hadn't there been any gunshots?

I wasn't sure, and there was no way to find out. I had to act now.

"Wait." I hunched forward, hands bracing my knees, and gulped air. That greasy stuff was still on my hands, and I found it near-impossible to hold myself up. "Need... a second."

He yanked our cuffed hands. I stumbled forward, and he shoved me to the floor. "You think you can delay the inevitable, but you cannot. I will not allow it."

I struggled for a breath, inhaling dirt and whatever other disgusting substances had accumulated on this floor. I knew what I needed to do, but a jolt of fear drained my resolve.

What was I thinking? There was no way I could do this. Not without Émilien realizing. And what would he do when he realized I was removing the cuff? Punch me? Knock me out? Then I'd never get out of this situation.

But how could I get the cuff off before he realized what was happening? It seemed impossible with our wrists locked together. I moved, he moved.

My thoughts wandered to a distant memory, something I'd practically forgotten. Suddenly, Dad's voice cascaded over me. *"Don't give up now."*

The stairwell melted away. I was no longer face down on the floor but lying face up on a patch of grass. Émilien was gone. I looked behind me and discovered a soccer goal.

"My thumb!" That was my voice. *"I think I jammed it."*

The memory scooped me up and swallowed me whole.

"You don't need your thumb to do a bicycle kick." Dad retrieved the ball. His athletic pants hugged the bulge around his midsection and fell loose around his sneakers.

"I'm not trying it again, okay? It's too hard." I tugged on my thumb and winced as two sections of joint pulled apart. Gross. That part of my hand was already swelling.

That wasn't the only injury I'd sustained. My wrist, arm, elbow, ribs, back—everything hurt, all because I had insisted on learning how to do a bicycle kick.

Bicycle kicks are required in soccer when the ball comes into play at head-level or higher—out of reach for a normal kick. The player jumps up, hikes one leg, and then brings the other leg up and around to connect with the ball.

The move requires skill, agility, and power. It also requires pain because of the landing—on the player's back or side.

I cringed, ribs aching. Should have known this would be impossible. I was only fifteen, but Dad thought I was ready. I had thought so, too, until about forty-five minutes ago.

Dad strolled up to me, ball in hand. "Pain causes us to ask

ourselves, 'Is this worth it?' But when tomorrow comes, you will ask yourself a different question: 'Do I regret giving up?' Physical pain comes and goes, but regret will haunt you forever. Most of that regret, in my experience, comes from giving up before we truly needed to. So then, what is the solution?" He flicked the ball to his other hand, mouth poised in a grin. "Any ideas?"

I shook my head.

"It's simple. A very simple concept." He offered me his free hand. "All you have to do is never give up."

DAD'S WISDOM ECHOED ALL AROUND ME—BUT HE WAS no longer there. I was in the stairwell, on the fifteenth floor, and Émilien was about to take me onto the roof.

No.

He hauled me to standing. The memory played—the abject failures, the ultimate victory when I finally executed the move. I had done it that day, and I'd done it many times since.

And now I was going to do it again. With Émilien's head.

I gathered every bit of strength I had, every bit of resolve. I bent my knees, stooped, and flung myself up and back. I hitched one leg. I brought the other around.

Keeping your eye on the ball was the key to a successful bicycle kick. No matter what was happening or who else was around, it was critical that the striker focused on that one thing.

I kept my eye on the ball—or the head—I was aiming for. Émilien's face widened as I leaned into the motion, refusing to think about anything else. Not the pain I was about to experience in my back. Not the possibility of landing on my wrist.

Absolutely nothing else.

I angled myself, bringing my left leg around. I let out a grunt that morphed into a growl that unfurled into a scream.

Wham! My foot connected with Émilien's forehead, and his

head whipped back. I crashed to the floor, partway on my side, while the Frenchman dropped.

Pain exploded through my ribs, my back, my elbow, my hand... but Émilien was dazed.

I forced myself to sit up and then opened my fist. Silver winked up from the mess of black and red inside my hand. I pinched the key between my fingers, shoved it into the keyhole, and twisted.

The cuff disengaged.

Émilien moaned, blinking. I leaned over and latched my side of the cuff to the nearest vertical bar fixed to the railing.

The Frenchman shook his head and pulled himself up. His eyes were open now, and he took a long, hard look at his hand, which was now cuffed to the bar.

Confusion splintered his features. He looked at me.

I backpedaled out of reach, tossed the key down the center shaft, and darted through the door behind me. It opened into a hallway lined with apartments.

I took off in that direction but then paused. Maksim was in the stairwell. I had to go help him.

But if I did that, I'd risk being nabbed by Émilien. Whether he was cuffed to the railing or not, he was still strong, and he was fully capable of taking me down with one hand. I couldn't risk that.

I could, however, use the main stairwell and then cut over on the next floor. I wasn't sure how I'd help Maksim once I got there, but I had to try.

I raced through the hallway. "Help! Call the police!" I cupped my mouth. *"Police! Flics!"*

Doors cracked open, but they shut again as I sprinted past. The main stairwell appeared on my left. I angled that way and flew down the first flight.

I skidded to a stop. The little boy, the one we'd been following earlier, stood on the steps. He recognized me and pointed, saying something in French.

Footsteps shuffled up the stairs. The second security guard appeared.

I sprinted up the stairs and darted into the hall. Footsteps bore down on me. I was reaching for the door to the smaller stairwell when a hand came down on my shoulder.

The man spun me around and barreled his fist toward my face. I ducked, and his hand collided with the door. He wailed.

I shoved him. He grabbed me and flung me against the wall. The back of my head hit. Red dots pricked my vision.

He yanked open the door and pushed me through. I collapsed next to Émilien, who sat on the floor. I rolled away and crawled toward the steps.

He caught my shorts and dragged me back. "You are going to pay for that."

I screamed.

"Kat!" Maksim's voice floated up the center shaft. Footsteps ascended, followed quickly by more grappling and grunts. "Kat, hang on."

Émilien said something in French. The security guy produced a cuff key. Presumably not the one I'd tossed down the center shaft.

He unlatched the cuff from the railing and closed it over my wrist. I was once again cuffed to Émilien.

Despair flooded me.

All you have to do is never give up. Dad's wisdom came back to me. I couldn't let myself give up. Not now. Not yet.

The security guy asked a question. Émilien said Maksim's name and made a dismissive motion. The security guy nodded and pulled out his pistol.

"No!" I grabbed the railing and kicked. If I'd been on the grass, it would have been a sliding tackle, but instead of striking a ball, my foot connected with the man's hand.

His pistol flew. It hit the railing on the level below us and then tumbled down the center shaft.

"Guuun!" I leaned over the railing. "Maksim!"

Maksim's head appeared several stories down. He reached out. Another set of hands grappled with his.

Émilien dragged me away. "I will deal with you later." He shoved his greasy hair into place. "We have no time for it now."

The security guy grabbed my legs, and the two of them hauled me up the stairs. I squirmed, kicking, punching. The men had my upper and bottom halves locked, so I had no range of motion.

They managed to carry me that way all the way to a skinny set of stairs and then through a door. Warm sunlight poured over me. They'd found the roof access.

The helicopter's propellers beat the air. The wind kicked up. I peered past Émilien. The chopper was already landing on the roof, pushing up a cloud of dirt.

Gunshots rang out from inside the building. I twisted around, legs and arms still bound, and aimed my mouth in the direction of the door. "Maksiiim!"

There was no response.

"Maksim, they're taking me! The helicopter— It's—" Heaviness filled me. My emotions swelled, pushing up a fresh batch of tears. "The helicopter's here," I whispered as the men hauled me toward it.

41. DIG DEEP

I was tired... of running, hiding, fighting. Émilien had me now. I no longer had to concern myself with being found.

The chopper's blades pumped, whipping my hair around, and a strange sense of relief swelled. But how? How could I be experiencing *relief* while in the middle of being kidnapped?

But I did. It was over. I didn't have to worry about this anymore.

Wavy strands of bronze hair crisscrossed my face. Every time I'd seen myself with this new hair color, it didn't feel real, like I was seeing someone else. That may have been another reason I didn't feel panicked—because, in a way, I was detached. Like I was watching everything unfold through an action camera strapped to someone else's forehead.

But this wasn't a glimpse of someone else's reality. It was a glimpse of mine, and the will to fight—to keep fighting—warred against my willingness to give up.

The latter was winning. Maybe it had already won.

I let a dazed stare fall to my arms and hands, which were still stained with Dom's blood and that greasy black goop, whatever it was. My attention drifted to the roof access. The door oscillated under the chopper's wind, but no one was coming through it.

A tear spilled out. Maksim wasn't coming, because he'd been shot. That had to be why he wasn't up here yet. He was dead, and it was my fault, and I was going to be dead soon, too. We'd lost the battle *and* the war.

The engines roared. Everyone was strapped in, and Émilien put on a headset. The pilot was saying something as he shifted gears. The helicopter lifted.

Movement blurred in my peripheral.

I turned and every tear that had been rising, every emotion that had been swelling spilled over. Maksim—held back by the security guy—was fighting his way through the roof access.

He grabbed the guy and swung him around. The man's back hit the door. Maksim launched forward, but the man grabbed him again.

He needs help. This was the first thing that sped through my thoughts, but I couldn't help Maksim. I was in this helicopter, and we were taking off.

I stared at my hands. My wrist swelled pink where I was cuffed to Émilien, and I still had that oily substance all over me. How could I help Maksim when I hadn't even been able to—

My heart leapt. The oily substance. Would that be enough to get out of the cuff?

Maybe, but... no. I couldn't. We were already taking off.

And then another thought—one that was altogether different from my usual train of thought—washed over me. *It's your decision alone, but you must decide now.*

The security guy caught a glimpse of what was going on down below and pointed. The pilot hesitated, saying something into his headset. Émilien answered.

I had to decide now. Right now.

The front of my shirt and shorts held on to some of the oily substance. I rubbed my wrist in it—underside and top. A lot of it got on the cuff, and I did what I could to smear it around.

I found more on the back of my thigh, my shorts. I did what I could and then discreetly unbuckled my seatbelt.

Émilien finished speaking into the headset. The pilot nodded, and we began to ascend again. Had they considered staying for the other security guy? Maybe they were hoping to take out Maksim.

We angled right, starting to move away from the building. I had to do this—now or never.

I ducked out of the seatbelt while yanking at the cuff. The metal band slid around, but I couldn't get the cuff over the widest part of my hand.

Émilien whipped a look as I slid out of the open door. The wind blew my hair around. My feet found the skid along the bottom of the aircraft.

With my right arm above me, I hopped off, hoping gravity would aid my attempts. Émilien was strapped in, and his arm stretched while I dangled there.

I struggled, kicking and twisting. My elbow strained. My shoulder popped out of its socket. But the stupid cuff would not come off.

The pilot shouted, hovering. The security guy leaned over and tried to grab me. I swatted his hands at first. But when he nearly caught me, I opted for a different strategy.

I gripped his jacket and yanked—as hard as I could. I was stuck hanging there, so there was no risk to me, but there was for him.

He lost balance, his momentum carrying him forward. He screamed as he toppled head-first out of the helicopter—and he kept screaming.

My attention fell, and I watched as he plummeted alongside the fifteen-story building. His legs hit a balcony, and his cries devolved into a wail eventually drowned out by the roar of the chopper.

He hit the ground far below, and I winced. We'd been over the roof a second ago. We must have drifted off to the side.

"Kaaaat!"

I craned my neck and found Maksim waving. The security guy he'd been fighting was gone. But where?

Maksim raised his arm, grabbed his hand, and pinched. What was he doing?

He twisted his arm, showing me his...

"Thumb," I whispered.

Suddenly, I was being pulled up. Émilien must have been retracting his arm. He was reeling me in like a fish.

I gripped my cuffed hand—not an easy thing to do while hanging there—and pressed on the joint at the base of my thumb. While I did that, I made my hand as small as I possibly could, drawing my fingers together.

The helicopter started forward. We were crossing over the roof, about to fly past it. I had to do this *now*.

I shoved hard on the joint—same joint I'd injured when Dad taught me to do that bicycle kick. I'd dislocated it plenty of times since then. Nothing too serious, but enough so that whenever pressure was applied, my body remembered, and the joint tended to slip out of its—

Pop.

—socket.

My heart climbed into my throat. My stomach lurched as air rushed up around me. I was out of the cuff, and I was falling.

I looked down. We had reached the roof's edge, and the only thing available to me was the ledge. Needed to land there—on the ledge—and do a modified safety roll onto the roof. That might be tricky, though, because I was facing the wrong way.

I turned midair, forcing myself to twist into position. By the time I was ready, my foot missed the ledge. I had misjudged.

"Heeeere!" Maksim sprinted toward me. He hadn't reached the edge by the time I did... and so he dove. There was nothing for him to grab onto, no way to catch himself.

He just dove head-first off the roof, reaching for me, stretching, while I did the only thing I could do. I grabbed his hand.

42. LAST CHANCE

Maksim and I screamed as we free-fell alongside the building.

We jerked to a stop. My head whipped back, yanking on the cords in my neck. The joints in my arm and shoulder popped.

I winced and peered up.

Maksim had grabbed onto a balcony one story down from the top. He had me by the wrist and was holding me so tight my bones felt like they were being crushed.

Tears sprang to my eyes. A pathetic whimper escaped, but I did not, under any circumstances, want him to let me go.

"Next balcony down." Maksim grunted. "Look."

I peeked down. The visual gave me vertigo. I looked away.

"Kat. Next balcony down." That was all Maksim managed to get out before I saw red liquid leaking down his arm. Same arm he was holding me with.

A thin drizzle of blood slid closer to our hands. I gasped.

"Balcony." He grunted again. "On three. One..."

I shook my head. We were hanging off the side of this balcony, which put the next-lower balcony off to the side, as well. I'd have to swing over and try to land inside the microsized space.

"... two..."

I had misjudged the roof. What if I misjudged this, too?

"... three." Maksim angled me in that right direction. I kicked my legs, hoping for the best.

I caught air and pulled a sharp breath. My feet landed on concrete—or whatever the balcony was made of, and I realized... I'd made it.

Two sets of wide eyes peered through a window-style door. A preteen girl stood on the other side, holding a toddler. They both looked terrified.

Multiple gunshots rang out. We all three jumped—the girl, the baby, and I.

"Nancy!" The accented voice called out, pleading in French.

The girl snapped the window lock and hurried across the apartment. A woman waited by the front door. When the girl and toddler arrived, the woman—their mother from the looks of it—ushered them out of the apartment.

They all disappeared into the hallway.

I directed my attention north. Émilien stood on the ledge, greasy black hair whipping in the wind. The helicopter settled onto the roof several feet behind him.

The Frenchman trained his pistol on Maksim, who hung from the banister above mine.

"Stop!"

Émilien's stare shifted. His eyes discovered me, and although he looked like he wanted nothing more than to pull the trigger, he didn't. Why?

Maksim lowered himself to the underside of that balcony. He let go and dropped into mine.

I grabbed onto him. He wrapped me in a hug, and I cried into his shirt the way I had last night. More. Because today I had a million other reasons to cry. Dom had been with me one minute and dead the next.

He'd been foolish—so had I—and now he was gone forever.

My hand rested on Maksim's arm, and warm liquid pooled

beneath my palm. I gasped. Bright red covered my dirty fingers. "You're hurt."

He grimaced, twisting the arm for a look. A slit in his sleeve revealed a gash.

"Were you stabbed?"

"I think I was shot." He pressed on the wound. "I don't feel a round. Hopefully it's just a graze."

Hopefully?

Movement rustled overhead. Grunting. Maksim swore and reached for the glass door.

"It's locked," I said the moment he tugged. The door didn't budge. "The cops are almost here. I can hear their sirens. Why isn't Émilien trying to get away? Why's he coming after us?"

"He sees you as his property." Maksim's answer came swiftly and simply. I didn't understand it, but I didn't have time to ask for clarification. "Come on." Maksim hoisted himself onto the railing. "We have to find an open apartment."

I swung one leg over the railing and then the other. He lowered himself to the next balcony down. I didn't have the arm strength for that, but I could dangle.

Or I thought I could.

As I hung there, arms stretched above my head, hands gripping the vertical bars, the tendons in my right arm stretched. I gritted my teeth and bit down on a scream.

Maksim guided me down, keeping both hands on my feet, legs, hips, waist. Finally, I let go. His strong arms enveloped me, and I ached for them to hold me longer—all day, into the night— but Émilien was directly above us.

We tried the glass door on this floor. Locked.

Maksim swung a leg over this railing, ready to drop to the next level down.

"Wait!" I grabbed him. "I can't. My arm—" I held my right shoulder. "Maksim, I can't."

He glanced around and pulled himself back in. "You're going over there." He faced me toward the balcony directly on our right.

The glass door to the apartment was propped open... but the balcony was at least six feet away, maybe more.

"Are you crazy?" I leaned over the railing. The drop sent a wave of vertigo spinning through me. "I-I'll try the next level instead."

Émilien's grunts grew closer, and a look of panic blasted through Maksim's calm. "This is faster," he said, hoisting me up. "Can you stand?"

"No." My legs quaked, and the railing—the whole balcony—shook. "Maksim, please."

"I'll help you. On three. Ready?"

"No!"

"One. Two..."

Émilien growled. I looked up in time to see him lowering himself to our balcony. His boots dangled beside my head.

"... Three." Maksim gave a boost the very moment I jumped.

I sailed toward the other balcony. My shoe caught the rail, and I tumbled forward—but I was tumbling *into* the balcony, not outside of it.

My hands landed first. Then my face.

I scrambled to get up at the sickening sound of knuckle connecting with bone. Émilien and Maksim had taken up fighting stances on the other balcony and were entering hand-to-hand combat.

Émilien threw a jab. Maksim blocked it.

Émilien tried an uppercut, a right hook. Maksim bobbed and weaved, his fists raised and ready. But he hadn't taken a shot yet.

Émilien whipped out his pistol. Maksim grabbed the barrel, twisted around, and bent Émilien's wrist back. The Frenchman howled, and the gun fired.

The round whizzed past my head.

I ducked as another gunshot rang out. Another. Glass shattered, and a blood-curdling scream peeled out of someone. Shouts echoed from neighboring apartments. A baby cried.

Click click click.

I peeked over the banister. Émilien was pulling the trigger, but no more rounds fired. He was out of ammo.

Maksim disarmed him and tossed the pistol over the side. The black object free-fell alongside the building.

Émilien dropped down and then powered forward, lifting Maksim off his feet.

I screamed as Maksim went over the railing. He tumbled head over feet, trying to grab the next railing. His hand connected, but his momentum carried him right past it.

I watched him reach for the next one. "Maksim!"

Émilien climbed onto the railing. He was about to jump over here.

I darted inside the apartment. The place was small, with the kitchen practically in the living room, and I didn't see anyone. I raced for the door, unlocked it, and sprinted into the hallway.

Which way?

First thing that came to mind was the small stairwell, the one I'd ascended earlier. But if the police came—if they would freaking get here already—they'd likely come charging up the main staircase used by the residents.

I angled that direction. People peeked through their doors, but no one offered to help me. I didn't expect them to after gunfire. Sounded like someone had been shot.

I leapt down the first set of stairs. The landing jarred my body. My ankles and knees throbbed, but I kept going.

Grunts trailed me. As I reached the next floor, Émilien's footsteps pounded to a stop. "Surrender now, or you will pay heavily for this."

His threat—the way he uttered it—made me freeze. I turned on my heel, facing him.

He walked forward, eyes narrowed, hands curled at his sides. "I *will* catch you, and when we are alone, when there's no one else to help you, I will make you suffer for what you're doing now. Or..." He held up a finger. "You can come with me, and I will be merciful to you. And I will leave Maksim alone—I will let him live

—*if* he survived that fall." Émilien bobbed his head. "Anyone else would have no chance at all, but for Maksim? I say fifty-fifty."

"Try one hundred." The baritone voice stemmed from behind and below.

I whirled around and found Maksim limping up the stairs. He held his ribs, favoring one leg. But he was alive.

I raced down the stairs and flew into his arms. He swayed, still holding his ribs, and caught me.

"You're surrounded." Maksim held a stone-cold look on the Frenchman. "The police are here. There's nowhere to run."

Voices drifted up the staircase. Footsteps shuffled.

Émilien's fists began to shake. He gritted his teeth, turned around, and sprinted up the stairs. I listened as his footstep grew distant—one story, two stories... all the way to the top.

All signs of him disappeared. He must have been on the roof. I could hear the helicopter... and then I could have sworn I heard another one.

"He's getting away," I whispered.

"Not this time." Maksim limped to the nearest landing. "I called in a police report, saying their chopper was the terror group responsible for an explosion in Saint-Denis." He pointed up. "That's likely the Gendarmerie."

I held on to him as he lowered himself to the floor. Blood leaked down his arm. His face was pale. "I need you to do something. A few things, actually. They're important."

"Maksim, you're hurt." I stationed myself beside him. "We need to get you to a hospital."

"The police are going to arrest me." He tipped his head back until it rested against the wall. "Daniel and Madă's telephone numbers are in my phone. Call them. Tell them there's been an emergency and that they need to fly out here. Do *not* tell them what happened over the phone. Don't even tell them I'm in jail."

"Why?"

"They've seen a van outside their home, and Daniel has been tailed multiple times."

I gasped.

"Likely Vladimir's men. Less is more—in case their calls are being monitored." He dug out his phone and handed it over. "You'll need to contact my attorney, Jérôme Charles, after that. Say you're calling on behalf of his client and that he needs to send someone to whatever police station or hospital you've been taken to. Tell Maître Charles it's better that you speak in person and that his client has already paid the retainer. He'll send someone. Do *not* talk to the police before that person arrives. Everything you say will be used against you and also against me. Wait for that member of the legal team." Maksim cupped my chin and gently drew my head around.

Our eyes met.

"Do you understand?"

I nodded. I'd been dreading this scenario, hoping I could avoid it, wondering if I would. Now here we were.

Maksim's gaze shifted, and a pained look—the same one I'd seen last night—spread through his features. "You lost the ring."

"Huh? Oh, no, I—took it off. Earlier."

"Earlier." His gaze entwined with mine. "As in, after our fight?"

I wanted to say that had nothing to do with it, that I'd left the ring behind to keep it safe. But that wouldn't have been true.

I'd been confused, worried, unsure of myself. Unsure about him. But how could I say any of that after what he'd done to save me?

I scooted closer and rested my head against his shoulder. He wrapped me in a hug.

"How were you tracking me?" I asked. "On the phone."

"I installed a hidden tracking app. I wasn't sure if I would ever use it—I hadn't thus far—but I received an anonymous SMS this morning. I believe it was from Renan."

"About me?"

Maksim nodded. "Have you been in possession of your phone this entire time?"

My throat closed. "Mostly."

An annoyed glint reflected in his tired eyes. "Right. Well, at whatever point Renan came into possession of it, he discovered my tracking app. This is the SMS." Maksim reclaimed the phone and opened a message thread. "I received it while I was at the law firm."

> I planned to put a tracker in your girlfriend's phone, but it seems you've already done that. Do you know where she is now? -R

"I don't get it." I peeked over at Maksim. "Why would he want to track me?"

"He surely realized something was amiss. Perhaps he had suspicions about you, or perhaps about Dom." Maksim closed his eyes. "He may have been surveilling all of us from the moment we arrived."

"But the briefcase bomb—"

"I know." Maksim rubbed his eyes. "I've been asking myself the same questions ever since you told me. How long had they been planning the attack? Before we saw Raul? After? Were they using us?"

"Renan was shaking hands with one of the security guys when I walked in. It looked like they'd come to an agreement, a deal, but I feel sure Renan left the briefcase."

Maksim returned the phone to me. "And you're certain Dom is..." His jaw flexed. "There's no possibility he could have survived? Because if there is—"

"He's dead." My emotion swelled to choking. "Émilien shot him twice in the chest, and he bled—God, he bled—until he slipped away. Then there was the explosion, and"—I sniffled—"afterward, they set the entire place on fire. I think the bomb messed up their plans. They had to get rid of all the evidence quickly, no time to keep cleaning up."

"Do you know any more?" Maksim's eyes flashed to mine. "How did Dom get involved with them?"

"It was more that they got involved with him." I highlighted the whole horrible story—how Dom had been set up in Tahiti, how Émilien had posed as a cop, how Vladimir had been using that staged crime scene to manipulate Dom. "They knew about him, Marie, everything you'd been planning here." I hesitated. I'd been wondering about that myself, about the discrepancies in Maksim's story.

He looked at me.

I fidgeted, unable—unwilling?—to ask for clarification. "Dom thought they worked for the French government, some kind of black ops team overseen by a politician. He was convinced government agents were the only people who could have known about his so-called accident. That's why he helped them."

"Vladimir couldn't find any dirt, so he manufactured it." Maksim stared off into space. "Because of me. Because they had become suspicious of me."

"But why did they have to kill him? All he wanted was to salvage his career. That's it. He wasn't a threat."

"In their eyes, he was. Vladimir doesn't leave loose ends." Maksim touched my hand. "I'm sorry it happened." His voice thinned. "I'm even sorrier you witnessed it."

A quiver shook my bottom lip. I bowed my head.

Footsteps pounded up the stairs. An authoritative voice called out. Maksim called back, and the person answered with what sounded like a command.

"I was going to ask what happened to you"—he gave me a quick once-over—"but I'm out of time."

"Hopefully, I can tell you soon. It's a long story." I glanced at his arm. "You might want to get that cleaned ASAP. I'm a walking biohazard, and I accidentally touched your wound."

He replied with a single nod.

The stampede drew closer. Maksim was about to be arrested, jailed. What if this turned into a worst-case scenario? What if this was our last moment together with him as a free man?

"Maksim, I... I haven't taken the pregnancy test."

A phantom smile touched his lips. He leaned in and kissed my forehead. "Stay here. Don't resist. Don't answer their questions."

A flood of emotions trickled down my cheeks. "I'm scared."

"I know, *dragă*. But you're also very brave." He brushed away the streams, planted a tender kiss on my nose, and pushed himself onto his knees.

Dark uniforms turned the corner. Shouts went up, rifles and pistols angling toward us. Maksim lowered himself to the floor, grimacing, and laced his fingers behind his head.

Men in solid black uniforms, kevlar helmets, and face shields charged forward. They continued up the stairs while blue uniforms grabbed Maksim.

He gritted his teeth.

"Don't hurt him!" I pushed myself up. "He's injured."

A female cop pulled me away.

"The people you're looking for are on the roof." I pointed up. "Roof."

"We know." The cop's accent dripped. She held up a pair of cuffs. "Hands, please."

I recoiled, picturing Émilien and all the things I had to do to get out of those cuffs.

Don't resist. I swallowed my anxiety and placed my hands behind my back.

The woman must have realized I was a victim, because she turned me around and cuffed me in the front, rather than from behind.

That wasn't the case for Maksim. He was on his feet, hands cuffed behind his back, while two large cops hauled him down the stairs.

As they rounded the corner, heading for the next flight, Maksim looked over at me. A soft smile warmed his eyes as he mouthed "I love you."

The words tumbled through me, wanting to come out in any form, even a whisper, even a silent gesture like he'd done.

He was gone before I could get my mouth to cooperate.

43. HAPPEN STANCE

12 HOURS LATER

Maître Jérôme Charles waited until the detectives—a male-female pair—were on their way out before he let himself relax. His paralegal, Béthanie—a brunette with dark hair that cascaded down her back—escorted the detectives out of my hospital room.

This was a shared room, but I didn't think the other patient minded the foot traffic. At least, I hope she didn't. She hadn't stirred since we'd been here. She might've been in a coma.

"I think that went well." Maître Charles pointed at a messenger bag on the floor. A younger lawyer—his name was Patrice—scooped up the leather strap and handed the bag to his boss. "And how do you feel, Miss Barrett?"

"Is that a pleasantry?" I asked. "Or you want to know the truth?"

He chuckled.

Béthanie returned and asked a question in French.

Maître Charles checked his watch and nodded. "We should be going. The police will register your statement along with the physical evidence of your abduction, and then the local prosecutor will be notified, and then he or she will order the police to investigate Monsieur Lefebvre." He was referring to Émilien.

"And you're sure he's in jail?" I fidgeted with the thin blanket lying across me. "He was supposed to be in jail in Romania, too, but he got out."

"He is being detained, and the police have enough evidence and witnesses, including your own eyewitness testimony, to keep him there during their investigation. This process is called *la rétention de sûreté*. Secure detention. It is for dangerous and violent offenders who are at high risk of offending again."

I pulled the blanket up. "He's definitely at risk of doing that."

"You needn't worry. Not about that." He shouldered the messenger bag. "Your boyfriend, on the contrary, leaves us much to be concerned for. But we will do our best to liberate him."

A knock interrupted us.

Béthanie crossed the room, heels clicking, and returned to the door. When she reappeared, she was followed by a uniformed police officer. He greeted us, saying something in French, and then excused himself.

"I am happy to see the authorities take this case seriously." Patrice glanced toward the officer, who I could no longer see because of the faux wall in the room. "There are two *flics* stationed here and two more at the entrance to *l'hosto*."

I'd been hearing *l'hosto* since I'd been here. It was short for *hospital*.

"Rest assured, Miss Barrett, you are safe." Maître Charles extended his hand. I accepted, and he gave a firm shake.

He turned to go, and his employees followed him. Silence folded itself around me, sinking and settling with the weight of everything that had happened.

I lowered my bed and rolled onto my side. Maksim and I had been in a hospital bed like this. In Romania.

My thoughts wandered into the memory—waking up in the oxygen chamber, seeing Maksim and Madă across the room.

Daniel and Levi had been there, too. So had Brandy, Dave, Brandy's dad, her little brother.

Tonight, though, it was just me. Daniel and Mădă were on their way—supposedly—but for the moment I was alone.

I gazed out the window. Soft yellow light burned into the darkness all the way down the street. A handful of cars motored past.

Strange voices plucked at my attention.

I leaned forward in the bed, trying to see past the faux wall, and fiery pain poured into the right side of my body—neck, shoulder, elbow, wrist. That was the side I'd been cuffed on.

I pulled a sharp breath and peered around the wall, which extended the length of my bed. The police officer who'd introduced himself to us stood outside the doorway, talking to someone, while his partner sipped from a paper coffee cup.

The officers checked credentials and motioned for the person to go in. The man entered, and I pulled a sharp breath. It was the cop, the one who'd come to Dom's apartment. The same orange police band encircled his left arm.

Panic fluttered through my rib cage.

I grabbed Maksim's phone and pressed Call to the last number I'd dialed. Daniel's voicemail came on. I swore under my breath.

"Good evening." The man stepped past the faux wall. "May I come in?"

"No." I pulled my blanket up. He must have thought I was self-conscious in my hospital gown, because he averted his gaze.

"I'm a detective with the national police. Do you remember me?"

Assess every possible threat. The rule barreled into my thoughts, and I wasn't sure why. I decided to be extra careful. Just in case.

"I will not need too much of your time, Mademoiselle Barrett," the man continued. "Perhaps five minutes."

"My lawyer is Jérôme Charles. I'll give you his number. You can talk to him."

"Ahh, Maître Charles. An excellent criminal defense attorney." The detective nodded, hands resting on his hips. "It is usually the criminals who need such attorneys. *Non?*"

"I wouldn't know, but I'm sure he'd love to discuss that with you." I scrolled to Maître Charles's number. "Here, let me call him."

The detective shot a startled look. "I am not here to discuss your case, *mademoiselle*, nor the case against your boyfriend." He reached into his pocket. "Or is he your fiancé?"

I hesitated.

The detective pulled out a shiny object, pinching it between his thumb and index finger. The sapphire ring. It'd been at Dom's apartment—which meant *he* had been in Dom's apartment.

He walked forward and set the ring on the rolling bedside table. "I came to ensure that was returned to you. Your other belongings are in the possession of the antiterrorism unit. They are investigating Monsieur Dubois' involvement with the men who kidnapped you."

"Dom wasn't involved with them. They tricked him. He thought they were with the government."

"He did not know Émilien Lefebvre prior to today?"

Dom hadn't known Émilien, per se, but he *had* met him before. Once. Explaining that, however, might implicate Maksim, since he'd been the reason behind Vladimir's scheme.

The detective rocked back on his heels, eyebrows raised. "That bad, hm?"

"Are you allowed to question me like this? When I've already told you to call my attorney?"

"This is informal—primarily to return the ring. I also want you to know why I approached you both at Monsieur Dubois' apartment."

"You mean, 'to evacuate the building'?" I pulled air quotes.

"Is that even legal? Are cops in France allowed to just make stuff up?"

"One of our undercover officers witnessed Monsieur Dubois entering and exiting a vehicle linked to Émilien Lefebvre. That is how I became involved. I have been investigating Monsieur Lefebvre for a very long time. I needed to understand who this new player was, but the situation was... complex."

I folded my arms. "So you did make up the evacuation thing."

"The undercover officer made it clear what the risks were. My goal was to bring Monsieur Dubois to the station—a place that would be safe for questioning. The lie was to protect the officer and his undercover status. I hope you can understand." He pushed up an apologetic smile. "May I ask, *mademoiselle*... What was Monsieur Dubois' involvement with Marie Blanchet?"

"I don't know a M—" My mouth froze on the name. "Oh, um, is Marie Blanchet...?"

"The woman your fiancé has been with for these last days? Yes. That is her. She is being detained and questioned in this case. Did you know?"

"No." My jaw sank. "Why is she being detained?"

"We've discovered phone calls between her and an associate of Monsieur Lefebvre." The detective sent a quick glance over his shoulder. "That is all I can say, unfortunately, but the detectives investigating your case should—"

Voices carried into the room. I couldn't see past the faux wall, but I could hear the cops talking to someone. I heard a man's voice. Then a woman's.

I sat up. "Madă!"

Footsteps hurried into the room, and Madă appeared from behind the wall. "Kat? Oh my goodness." She squeezed past the detective. "Daniel!"

Daniel appeared. He and Madă went back and forth in Romanian while Madă fussed over me.

She switched to English. "What has happened to you?" She inspected my wrist, the one that had been cuffed to Émilien, and gasped. The skin swelled pink, while shades of black and blue formed. Her attention moved to my hair, and her surprise heightened.

I was about to explain myself, but the detective was still standing there. My eyes flashed toward him.

He nodded goodbye, did an about-face, and walked out. I heard an exchange of *au revoirs* outside the room, and then his footsteps disappeared.

"Um, so... my hair." I plucked a piece of bronze and held it up. "I had to change how I look. Not that it helped."

"How is Maksim?" Daniel grabbed a chair and dragged it across the floor. He ushered Mădă to sit down. "We became concerned when you wouldn't answer our questions over the phone."

"He is safe, isn't he?" Mădă lowered herself to the chair. "Please, where is our Maksim?"

I cringed. "He's sort of in jail."

Mădă placed a hand to her chest. Daniel grabbed his head.

"I'll explain everything," I said. "But I want you to know—" Emotion rose in my voice, and my vocal cords constricted. "I want you to know how relieved I am that you're here. How grateful. I'd be alone without you."

Mădă took my hand and gave it a squeeze. Daniel reached toward me, about to grab my other hand, but his attention swiveled to the rolling table.

Correction: to the sapphire sitting on the table.

He picked up the ring and held it up to the light. His smile sparkled more than the diamonds. "Does this mean what I think it means?"

THE NEXT DAY

I sat on the toilet, staring at the latest pregnancy test. This entire time, whenever I'd gone to take the test, I'd been afraid I might be pregnant. But after everything that happened—the kidnapping, the car accident, trying to get away from Émilien—I was suddenly afraid of the exact opposite.

I inhaled deeply, pushed out the breath, and made myself relax. As soon as I started peeing, I held the test under my stream and counted to ten. I was counting fast and decided to start over.

After washing my hands, I padded out of the bathroom and joined Mad on the bed. She and Daniel had found an apartment in a quiet neighborhood in the south of Paris—a town called Gentilly—and the owner let them lease it for a month. We didn't know if we'd need that long, but it was still cheaper than a hotel, and I felt a semblance of normalcy.

I crossed my legs and showed Mad the pregnancy test. The litmus paper revealed the first signs of a pink line.

She re-read the instruction. "One line is a negative test. Two lines means positive."

I nodded, thinking. Processing. As she skimmed the information, my thoughts drifted to something that had happened in Romania. "Hey, Mad? I've been wondering..."

"Yes?" She kept her attention on the paper.

"It's hard to explain, but—basically, when I was in Romania—"

She looked at me.

"I guess I was wondering if there's any reason I would have healed faster there than I'm healing here." I folded my arms, holding my right elbow. "Seems like that was the case."

"You were in an oxygen chamber. That is why you healed faster." She smiled. "The doctor explained everything."

"But there was another time, too. Before that. I had an injury, and it healed overnight."

Realization dawned across her features. She lowered the test.

"Romania has a long tradition of the Călușari—dancers believed to be endowed with healing powers. They would travel around, going from home to home while promising good health and prosperity to the villagers, and many people claimed to be recipients of miraculous healings. It is my personal belief that God is the author of such miracles, but"—she nudged me—"perhaps the Călușari have paid you a visit, mm?" She winked.

I frowned. "Right."

"Forgive my teasing. I know you are worried." Her attention fell, and the brightness in her mood dimmed. "Where is your engagement ring?"

"It's safe. I just—"

She scooted to the edge of the bed. "Yes?"

"The truth is... I don't exactly know what to do. About, you know, getting married." I met her gaze. "I love Maksim, and I know he loves me—he's proven it so many times—but I'm not sure how a marriage would work between us. What if he goes to jail for a long time? Or... what if he falls out of love with me and regrets all this time and energy he's wasted? What if *I* fall out of love with *him*? We could end up hating each other the way my mom and dad did." I shivered. "That would be horrible. It *feels* horrible just thinking about it."

Madă's smile softened. "All marriages are surrounded by uncertainty. Two lives, which have existed independently, are now being fused together in permanent ways. When one person moves in a direction, the other feels it. There's an effect that cannot be denied or avoided. Even very small things can feel very big."

I slouched. "That sounds terrifying."

"It can be. But it can also be wonderful." She slid a piece of my hair aside and stroked it. "It is difficult *and* rewarding, painful *and* beautiful. It is many things—good and bad. I hope you won't let the bad keep you from experiencing the good. Don't let fear rob you of true love and immense joy."

My last moments with Maksim rushed in. *"I'm scared."* That's what I had told him. And what had he said in response?

"I know, dragă. *But you're also very brave."*

"May I ask...?" Madă took my hand. "What is the one thing you can take comfort in when you are married? Do you know?"

I shrugged.

"That the one you love—who also loves you—is with you. So you are both facing these fears together."

"Kind of like how Maksim and I faced those men together?"

She squeezed my hand. "Now you are understanding."

Yeah. I guess I did understand. So then, why did the idea of being pregnant and marrying Maksim feel so much scarier than being kidnapped by ruthless criminals?

Maybe it didn't, actually.

"Well?" I craned my neck. "Is there a second line?"

Madă focused on the pregnancy test. A fresh smile spilled across her lips.

44. BLIND JUSTICE

TWO DAYS LATER

Forty-eight hours. That was how long the police had been allowed to detain Maksim. By the end of that time, the prosecutor had petitioned for some kind of special hearing.

The alleged "crimes" Maksim was being charged with fell into a gray area. He'd committed destruction of property, caused bodily harm, and even killed one of those security guys—but only because he'd been trying to stop a kidnapping.

In light of the complexities, five magistrates—no jury—had been called to decide if Maksim should be detained or if he could safely be released while the police continued their investigation.

Maître Charles's driver dropped us off outside a multiplex of stone buildings guarded by a huge iron gate. Bright gold fleur-de-lis topped the fence while an elaborate royal crest—also gold—crowned the entrance.

Stone columns and a dome roof accentuated the main building, while the French Republic's motto emblazoned the façade.

LIBERTÉ · ÉGALITÉ · FRATERNITÉ

I was reminded of the tourism shirt Maksim had given me. I'd seen the motto somewhere else, too. Gustave's cab, maybe? Whatever the case, I had looked up the translation at some point. *Freedom. Equality. Brotherhood.* Hopefully, the judicial system valued these concepts in a practical way. If so, I felt sure they'd see the truth—that Maksim had been helping, rendering aid, not causing harm like Vladimir's men.

Maître Charles led us through an arched entryway where ornate decor and more stone columns awaited. A marble floor stretched around us, and Béthanie's heels *click click click*ed the entire way.

Maître Charles and Patrice wore black robes with white, frilly collars that spilled down the front. Their matching black dress shoes clacked.

We passed through a long, arched corridor and headed for the courtroom known as the Voltaire room. A pair of French cops guarded the entrance.

Maître Charles showed his credentials, and they waved us through a set of oak doors big enough to belong in a castle.

We went through two normal-sized doors and entered what had to be the most gorgeous, elaborate courtroom I had ever seen in my life.

"Holy crap," I whispered. "The hearing is going to be in here?"

"It is." The open room caught Béthanie's soft voice and bounced it around. "Isn't it beautiful?"

"Very." Golden chandeliers outfitted in large globe lights hung from the ceiling. A painting that had to be bigger than Brandy's whole house filled the wall on our right.

Tall, skinny windows covered by oak panels lined the wall on our left, letting in a cloudy gray sky and hints of a cool breeze. Well, coo*ler* than what we'd been experiencing.

Several photographers stationed themselves along a waist-high wood partition. A sketch artist sat at the far end, already penciling the scene.

I scanned for Daniel and Madă. So far, I didn't see them, but they promised they'd be here.

Maître Charles showed his credentials once more, this time to a lady, then we passed through a gate in the partition and entered an area with tables and microphones.

"Here we are." Maître Charles gestured at a long table situated below a massive glass box on the right side of the room. I wasn't sure what the glass box was for and, oddly, instead of facing the front of the courtroom, we actually faced the opposite side, sitting across from a table that looked exactly like ours on the other side of the room.

A team of people in black robes took their places at that table. Two flat-screen TVs and a long row of speakers mounted the wall.

Twenty minutes ticked by. Thirty. Suddenly, commotion stirred. I assumed someone had entered the courtroom, but when I glanced left, I found everyone looking at us.

Rather, behind us. I twisted around, following their stares.

Maksim stood in the glass box. He wore a navy suit jacket and tie over a white dress shirt. His handcuffs linked to a waist chain, and every time he moved, the chain restricted him.

I lifted a hand, hoping to get his attention.

"Not now." Patrice pulled my hand down. "Do not show emotion, whether good or bad, toward him."

"But—"

"You will have an opportunity to speak on his behalf, but even then, you must not express anything too romantic or senti-mental. Stick to the facts. Explain clearly why he's not a danger to society."

"Wait... I have to speak on his behalf?"

"You are not required to." He faced forward and motioned for me to do the same. "But it could help him."

Sweat broke across my neck and forehead. A podium with a microphone stood at the center of the room. Was that where I'd be speaking from? What would I say?

A feeling, like a magnet, tugged on me. I started to turn but hesitated. I glanced left, then right. Nobody seemed to be paying attention.

I sent a glance up and over my shoulder. Maksim held me with a gentle smile. His eyes shifted, checking our surroundings, and then he winked.

Heat flooded my body. I focused forward.

I could still feel the magnet, and my pulse thrummed under the draw. It took every bit of willpower I had to resist looking—but I did do something else.

I'd worn my hair in a low bun with a few loose strands framing my face. Without looking at Maksim, I lifted my hand and smoothed my hair into the bun a bit more. Then I tucked the loose strands behind my hair.

I did it all with my left hand... and I made sure he was able to see the sapphire.

The magnet pulled hard until I could almost feel his heart racing with mine. The sensation persisted until a set of five magistrates in judges' robes entered the courtroom. One of them wore red while the others wore black.

Everyone in the courtroom stood. I pushed back from the table, following suit with Maître Charles and his associates. When they sat, I sat.

The magistrate in red offered for the trial to take place in English or French. "We do not have the ability to hold the hearing in Romanian, but we do have a Romanian interpreter if you should need it, Monsieur Răzvan."

Maksim answered in his usual flawless-sounding French. All the magistrates shared a look, eyebrows raised, and nodded as if impressed.

The woman in red gave no such indication.

I didn't understand the rest of the hearing. Various people walked forward, giving testimony—or whatever they were doing—and I could tell some of it was bad.

Patrice whispered translations when he could. "This is the family member of someone who died in their apartment due to a

stray bullet. They claim Monsieur Răzvan pulled the trigger."
And then ten minutes later. "This person witnessed the same
shooting, but they say it was Monsieur Lefebvre who fired."

Even police officers came forward, testifying to Maksim's
behavior. From those who arrested him to those who processed
him at a station, they all said the same thing—he displayed exem-
plary behavior.

Béthanie reached behind Patrice and touched my arm. "This
is very good," she mouthed with a smile.

Everyone was heard, and the evidence was reviewed. Finally, it
was my turn.

"They will ask you questions." Maître Charles patted my
hand. "You've done well with all the questioning thus far. You'll
do well now."

I hoped so. For Maksim's sake.

Maître Charles led me out from behind the table and
stationed me at the center podium. The mic was a bit high after
those cops, so I pulled it down. Feedback droned.

"I'm sorry. Uh... *pardonnez-moi. Merci beaucoup.*" My voice
penetrated the speakers and filled the courtroom. "*Je m'appelle*
Katherine Barrett—"

"Mademoiselle Barrett, you should continue in English.
Please." The lady in the red robes offered a friendly gesture, indicating I should go ahead, but her eyes narrowed at me through her
spectacles.

"Yes, ma'am. I mean, Your Honor."

"You will address me as Madame le président." She gestured
toward the other judges. "And you will refer to each of these as
Madame or Monsieur le juge. Are you ready to answer our
questions?"

Maître Charles gave a reassuring nod.

"Yes, Madame le président," I said into the mic. "I'm ready."

A lot of their questions had nothing to do with what
happened during the kidnapping. Instead, the magistrates—especially the one who called herself the president—focused on my

relationship with Maksim. The more this woman drilled down into that, the more she was making it sound like...

Well, I wasn't sure exactly, but I had the feeling she was trying to discredit my eyewitness account before I could give it.

"So you have been romantically involved with Monsieur Răzvan." Her thin eyebrows lifted above her spectacles. "I thought you said Vladimir Răzvan is your uncle. Is the shared name a coincidence?"

The other judges exchanged quizzical looks. Several of them looked appalled.

There was a logical explanation, one I was fully able to articulate since I knew the story. But I didn't know if I had permission to share it, because it wasn't *my* story. It was Maksim's.

I glanced at him. His expression had gone stoic, but I detected an annoyed glint aimed at the woman.

"Mademoiselle Barrett, I must ask that you not look to Monsieur Răzvan for guidance." That same woman jotted a note. "It shows you have coordinated your answers."

I sat straight. "That's not why—"

"There are perhaps certain *cultural* practices in Romania that are not acceptable here in France. Having a romantic relationship with someone's relative is one of them."

My eyes widened. "That's not a cultural practice in—"

"Please. Do not interrupt the court." The woman held up her hand. "I think we have heard enough from this witness. Mademoiselle Barrett, you may go. We do have one more witness who wishes to testify..." The woman continued, elaborating on the idea of fairness and how it was a big part of the judicial system in France.

I watched the hope disappear from Maksim's eyes. This woman had already made her decision, and she was going to influence the other magistrates.

He knew it. I knew it.

"I'm a victim, and I won't be silenced." My voice through the overhead speakers surprised me. I shook off any lingering hesitation and placed my mouth to the microphone. "Thank you for your time. I'll be available to all media outlets where I'll be discussing in detail how this court silences victims."

Murmurs circled through the courtroom. The woman fumbled for her gavel and banged it. "This is not a show!"

"I will also be available to discuss the court's racial prejudice against ethnic Romanians... or were you referring to my Roma Gypsy ethnicity, Madame le président?"

The murmurs amplified. Cameras clicked and flashed. The woman banged her gavel, shouting in French this time.

"My grandmother, Zora Brațiu, was silenced because of her ethnicity," I continued. "She was forced to hide her Roma lineage so that she could go to college, and then she was silenced forever by her own son—my uncle, Vladimir Răzvan—when he discovered the truth about her. He murdered his own mother because she was Roma."

The woman in red banged her gavel until the other magistrates intervened. Several of them had an exchange. The woman pursed her lips while another magistrate leaned forward and spoke into her mic.

"In our republic," she began, "under the leadership of a past administration, the government committed crimes against people of Gypsy—Roma—descent. Let the record show that this court has no bias against the Roma or Sinti peoples, and we do not silence anyone on such a basis."

"Then...as a display of the court's fairness, would you allow me to finish?" Again, my own voice surprised me.

The magistrate—a younger woman with brown hair to her shoulders—gestured for me to go ahead.

"My dad's brother, Vladimir, was a member of the Securitate —Romania's version of the Nazi SS or East German Stasi. They were a ruthless group, and after the fall of the Ceaușescu regime, Vladimir changed his name to avoid facing charges for his crimes, and also so he could profit off the post-communism reconstruction efforts." I glanced over at the glass box.

Maksim held me with a watchful gaze.

"Maksim Răzvan *isn't* related to my family. His parents, like my grandmother, were killed by Vladimir. Maksim was only three years old when it happened, and he was kidnapped."

Gasps went up. Whispers.

The woman in red slammed the gavel down. Based on her fiery expression, she might have preferred to slam it over someone's head. Namely mine.

"Maksim's father was an investigative journalist known for exposing government corruption. He died trying to expose the Răzvan crime family for their involvement in human trafficking. His wife lost her life, too, and Maksim was taken. There are public reports and plenty of newspapers articles if you don't believe me.

"So it's true... Maksim *was* raised in the Răzvan crime family. But it's also true that he's a hero—because of the way he rescued me *and* because of the way he allowed himself to be rescued. He could have continued in the footsteps of Vladimir Răzvan. He could have chosen what was easy and familiar, not asking any questions, but he saw another way and took it. He's not perfect, but he's good and kind, and he does what's right even when it's to his own peril. Just like his father, Petar Ćosić, the Croatian journalist who was brutally murdered because of his work."

The name circulated through the court in surprised whispers —Petar Ćosić. Some spoke it as a question. A few, clearly, knew who he was. I could only imagine what the headlines would look like tomorrow.

They needed to be in Maksim's favor. I had to make sure of that.

"In conclusion, I hope the judicial system—" I hesitated. "I hope *this court* will not allow Vladimir Răzvan to commit yet another heinous crime—the murder of Maksim's reputation and selfless works. Please don't let evil prevail again. Please do what's right."

Flashes brightened the room. This time, most of the

murmuring came from the judges—everyone except the woman in red, who looked the other way.

"Thank you, Mademoiselle Barrett." One of the male magistrates spoke into his microphone. "I have no further questions."

"Nor do I," the nice female magistrate said.

They all took turns saying the same thing. I was told to step away from the podium.

Maître Charles patted my hand as I dropped into the seat beside him. "You did well."

"You think so?" I pulled my chair closer. "I wasn't sure how else to make them listen."

"I may need you to repeat that speech during the trial." He pushed up a grin. "This hearing is to determine Monsieur Răzvan's status during the investigation—whether he be free or remain in detention. The trial will be even more important."

A blush hit my cheeks. "Sorry. Guess I got carried away."

"No need to apologize." His smile widened. "I think it will help him. We can—"

The lead magistrate interrupted. At first, I thought she was admonishing Maître Charles. Then I heard two phrases I recognized.

La victime. The victim.

La salle d'audience. The courtroom.

Maître Charles flipped a switch on the table, turning on his microphone, and said something. His features exuded surprise.

The woman replied and pointed across the courtroom.

I leaned over to Patrice. "What's going on?"

"They're making you leave," he whispered.

My speech wasn't received well. The judges are insulted. This was the first thing I'd thought. The *actual* reason I was being asked to leave never, in a thousand years, would have occurred to me.

"Émilien Lefebvre is going to testify," Patrice continued. "He is requesting that Maksim remain detained for the duration of the investigation—the same punishment he himself is receiving."

"He's being brought here?" I pointed. "Into *this* courtroom?"

Patrice nodded, and all that courage I'd mustered drained out of my body. "That is why you're being asked to leave," Patrice said. "So that you do not see your attacker."

"But he's a criminal. There's no question about what he did to me."

"Of course. But even criminals have rights, and the court has decided he has the right to testify about his dealings with Monsieur Răzvan. They say such knowledge could have a bearing on the court's decision."

I twisted around to make eye contact with Maksim. He death-gripped the rosary, his full attention turned toward the entrance.

"Béthanie? Would you...?" Maître Charles gestured for his paralegal to take me.

She pushed back from the table. I matched the movement but could hardly get the chair to budge. My hands and arms shook. So did my legs.

Patrice helped me, and I finally managed to stand. I glanced at Maksim once more while Béthanie led me past the glass box.

His gaze connected. He looked like he wanted to mouth something to me—another "I love you" like yesterday?—but he glanced toward the magistrates and then lowered his gaze.

Béthanie and I passed through the small gate in the partition, moving past the cameras and the sketch artist. Two familiar faces sat in a pew on the left.

Daniel and Madă.

Madă offered a reassuring smile. Daniel's attention drifted past me. He might have been looking at Maksim.

A short hallway stretched between the two doors of the entry-way. Béthanie went through the first door and then stopped.

I stopped behind her—and that was when I saw the two police officers coming through the next door. They were leading someone in cuffs.

That someone was Émilien.

45. SAVING GRACE

My attention shifted to Émilien the very moment he noticed me. I pulled a sharp breath, hands flying to my mouth.

He smirked until his eyes flashed to my hand. To the ring. His mouth drilled down into a scowl.

He shook off the cops and shoved Béthanie. She bounced off the wall. One of the cops lunged. The other reached for his pistol.

I staggered backward.

Émilien tackled me in the courtroom, and shouts went up. The people nearest us scattered.

"*Whore.* You think you can marry him?" He spun me around and dropped to the floor, dragging me with him, then wrapped his legs around my waist. "You belong to *me*," he growled in my ear.

I was lying face up, my back and shoulders pressed against him, as he brought his hands over my head. The short chain between the cuffs landed on my throat.

Pain ignited. My scream turned into a gurgle.

I clawed at the cuff chain. Béthanie did the same. Neither of us could get our fingers between my skin and the metal links. Why wasn't he wearing a belly chain like Maksim? Or ankle cuffs? This asshole should have been in shackles, but he wasn't. Why? My thoughts faded. Darkness seeped into my vision.

Béthanie screamed at the cops. They aimed their pistols, trying different angles, but he was using me as a human shield. His legs wrapped tighter, and my thoughts shifted. I'd finally taken the pregnancy test. Madă had held my hand while we waited for the results.

Émilien's shoes dug into that delicate spot on my body. I shoved a hand beneath his heel, protecting my lower abdomen.

Daniel knelt beside us and grabbed Émilien's pinky. Pretty sure he was trying to break it.

Émilien clenched his hands, balling them into fists. Daniel tried again. He couldn't pry the pinky loose.

Dark clouds spread across my eyes. My throat stung.

Béthanie and one of the cops stood over Émilien and grabbed his wrists. They pulled. Hard. The chain loosened—enough to let me breathe—but the relief didn't last.

Émilien curled his biceps. The chain re-settled across my throat.

Someone dropped to the floor and slid in beside us. I slanted a look and found Maksim at the edge of my periphery. He took one of his own cuffed hands and slipped it through the space that existed between Émilien's arm and shoulder.

I could see Maksim's hand. I felt it brush the side of my head.

He pushed up with a grunt. The short chain between his cuffs caught the chain between Émilien's. Maksim pushed up—like doing a weird, lopsided pushup—and the hold on my throat loosened.

He screamed at someone. That person dropped beside Émilien, taking up position on the other side, and gripped the chain from underneath.

It was Daniel. He lay flat on his back and pushed up in time with Maksim. Émilien growled, fighting them... but his wrists slowly lifted, and so did the cuff chain.

Air washed down my throat.

Émilien still had my lower half immobilized. Suddenly, he howled in pain—from what, I wasn't sure, but his legs loosened.

Béthanie hauled me to standing.

Maksim and Daniel rolled away as the cops tackled Émilien. I thought they would tackle Maksim, too, until a third cop helped him up. The man was holding a belly chain and fastened it around Maksim's waist.

Maksim glanced side to side, as if checking for onlookers.

That was the last thing I saw before several cops escorted me out of the courtroom.

———

THE JUDGES WERE RELEASING MAKSIM. THEY DIDN'T have much of a choice after that debacle.

Two guardian police drove us to the police station where Maksim was being processed. It was across the city, but I was happy to get as far away from that courthouse as possible.

Everyone kept saying how the police should have done a better job of restraining Émilien. That was true, but why was he being allowed to testify, anyway? And what was the deal with that one magistrate?

The whole thing was sketchy.

The police station took up most of the block and was squeezed in by apartments on all sides. The apartment buildings varied in style—Haussmannian, Art Déco, stone, brick—but the police station was a modern glass building with metal trim and sharp, square edges.

HOTEL DE POLICE DU 17E

Two cops stood guard out front, each armed with a heavy-duty rifle. Our guardian cops parked out front, and we all headed inside.

Stairs stretched around to the upper stories on our left; a glass wall filled the space on our right. Cops answered phones behind the glass. I wondered if it was bulletproof.

Our guardian cops directed us to a row of red plastic chairs. Daniel plunked himself beside me. Madă sat on the other side, clasping her hands and murmuring in Romanian. Probably praying.

My heart sprinted so hard I felt like I was running through Saint-Denis again, but as her whispers continued, my thoughts settled into a soft hum.

"It's a miracle."

Daniel's voice drew my attention. "What is?" The words scratched my throat.

"That they are releasing Maksim until the trial. Something was entirely wrong with that situation in the courtroom." He pursed his lips. "They could have set up a virtual meeting or even denied Émilien's motion to speak. But I believe they brought him there on purpose."

"Why would they do that?"

"There's no way to prove it, but... if Maksim had reacted more forcefully or emotionally, he would have displayed to the court that he cannot restrain himself."

"Restrain himself?" I sat straight. "Even though I was being attacked?"

Daniel's head gave a sure up and down. "The court would have undoubtedly denied his request for release—but that may have been the plan. Perhaps the judges needed a way to justify some decision they had already made."

Or a decision one of them made. Could the head judge have orchestrated that whole thing? Done things to provoke Maksim into overreacting?

Daniel was right. There'd be no way to prove that. But it did make sense.

"They were not counting on our Maksim's quick thinking."

Madă smiled and rested a hand on my knee. "We are thankful to God for this outcome."

"Agreed." Daniel settled back. "Thank God Maksim kept his cool. He used his brain instead of his brawn."

I was about to ask a follow-up question when one of our guardian cops returned. He spoke in French, and Daniel beamed a shiny smile. "Maksim is ready. He'll be down in a moment."

My heartbeat double-timed.

I pushed up from the chair and stepped out of the alcove. Maksim's voice drifted down to me. I straightened the blouse Madă had loaned me and dusted off the black trousers. Hadn't even checked a mirror. Probably should have in light of everything that happened.

I patted my hair and detected several loose strands. I hurried to smooth them as a tall form and broad shoulders appeared at the top of the stairs.

Navy blue uniforms escorted him—one on each side—yet he looked strangely at ease. All of them did. They were smiling, chatting.

Maksim locked onto me, and the conversation grew quiet. The cops shared a look.

They took turns shaking his hands, and then Maksim treaded down the steps. He had his suit jacket in one hand and the sleeves of his dress shirt rolled at his elbows.

He paused on the second-to-last step. "Hi."

"Hi," I croaked, peering in the direction the cops had gone. I cleared my throat and tried again. "Making friends?"

"Something like that." His voice bounced with playfulness, but his lighthearted expression frayed around the edges.

He stepped down to the last stair, attention moving to my throat. There was no covering up the marks.

I tucked my chin. "You're okay?"

"As far as I can tell." Another step. We stood toe to toe, and my pulse trilled. "And you? How are you feeling?"

Truthfully, I didn't feel well at all. We were alive, but I was shaken. My body ached, especially my right arm, and my trachea hurt every time I swallowed.

But I didn't want him to worry. So I just smiled.

He placed a finger under my chin and lifted, inspecting my throat. His thumb grazed a section of swollen skin, and a sting ignited.

I winced.

Maksim flexed his jaw. "Have you seen a doc—"

I lifted up on my toes and crushed my mouth to his. He rocked back, catching me, and melted into the kiss. I melted with him.

He worked our lips together. My hands moved over his chest, his shoulders, down his arms, around his waist. Rock-hard muscle flexed beneath my fingers.

He caught my left hand and reeled it in. "Is this a yes?" he whispered, kissing my knuckles.

He stopped on my ring finger. The sapphire glistened under the lights.

I nodded, lips aching—the only good ache in my poor, injured body.

His mouth tipped up. He tugged on my hips, pulling me close, but his playfulness ebbed. "What about... the other thing?" His voice fell low and gravelly, full of emotion. "Have you—"

"Yes," I whispered.

He studied my expression. "You took the test?"

I nodded, and his arms engulfed me.

A sweet voice cascaded over us. Maksim removed one arm and put it around Madă. Daniel joined us on the other side.

We all ended up in a big group hug, and I found myself wishing Dad were here. He would have adored these people. He would have loved Maksim.

"So." Daniel let go and knuckled a stray tear. "When is the wedding?"

GENTILLY

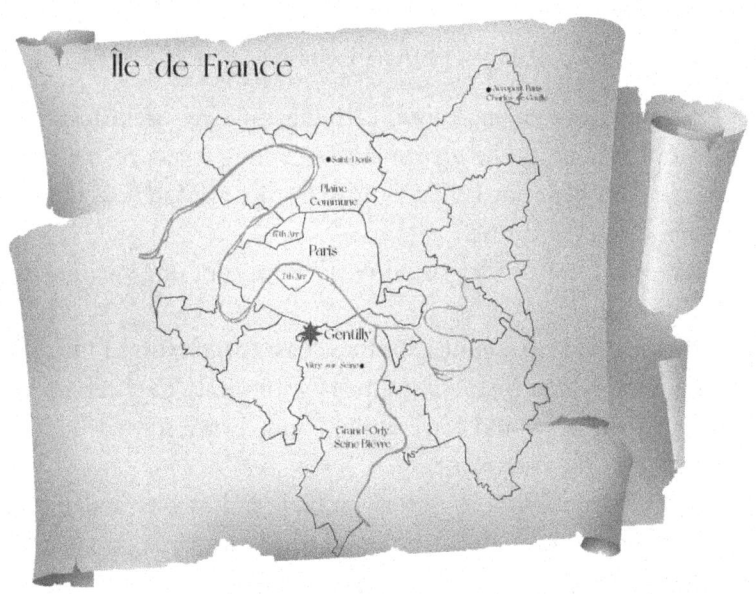

EPILOGUE

SUNDAY, JULY 21 (TWO DAYS LATER)

I slipped out of my room, carrying my new backpack, and tiptoed across the apartment. The long layers of my tulle skirt ruffled, but I didn't think Daniel or Madă could hear me over Daniel's snoring.

At least, I hoped they couldn't. I'd have a lot of explaining to do otherwise.

Maksim had been gone a lot these past two days, and I hadn't known why. Not at first. He stopped by for meals, to check up on me, but then he would leave again... and then I started finding notes all over the apartment.

They started with an "idea" he had, and as bits and pieces came to light—through the notes—I finally understood what he wanted to do.

What he was *asking* if we could do.

Which appeals to you most for a wedding? (you can only choose 1)
_ Extreme stress

_ Feeling overwhelmed
_ Complex logistics
_ Legal complications
_ Just you and me

As soon as I had the front door locked, I unzipped my backpack and pulled out my sneakers. They were pure white canvas, and I'd laced them up with white ribbon I'd found at a nearby shop.

I stuffed my feet into ankle socks—also white—and slid on the shoes. Then I dug through the backpack, searching for a very specific note.

My lips quirked as I came across the one about the shoes.

Wear whatever shoes you like. Whatever is most you. That's what I'll be doing.

"That's what I did," I whispered through a grin.

I kept digging until I found the note I was looking for.

Meet me at the park. Sunday @ sunrise.
Wearing white is encouraged.

I folded the note, hurried down the stairwell, and cut over to the door. Recycling bins overflowed around the entrance. Mailboxes lined the walls.

Wet pavement marked my path the entire way, and dull gray clouds threatened to break open again. I shouldered my backpack, gathered my skirt, and did my best to avoid the puddles.

Drops landed on my head as I crossed over to the park. Humidity threatened to curl my hair, which I'd straightened and swept into an updo. That'd been first thing this morning, while it'd been raining, and before dawn had ever broken. I even put on a little makeup—though, most of that went to covering up the marks on my throat.

"Don't think about that," I said. "Focus."

The drops tapered off as I followed the walking trails. Elderly men gathered by a park bench. They noticed me, and one of them tipped his hat.

I smiled and nodded, still holding up my skirt, and continued past them.

Three figures waited under a tree. One of the forms stood tall and lean, his shoulders straining against a collared shirt and beige suit jacket. Belted chinos the color of his jacket rested on his hips.

My attention drifted to his feet, and tears shimmied into my eyes. He'd worn white athletic shoes.

"Qui se ressemble s'assemble." Dom's voice streamed through my mind. *"Those who resemble assemble."*

Sadness pressed against my heart. Dom was the reason I'd learned that French proverb. It was going to be part of my vows because of him.

I wish you were here, Dom.

He'd been so angry with Maksim, but he'd been manipulated into those feelings. In the end, I think he realized his error. And if he were here now, he would have understood why I had to do this.

"Je t'adore, mon amie..." His voice rushed in, and it took everything I had not break down.

"I love you, too, friend," I whispered. A tear escaped at the very moment another raindrop landed on my head.

The two men standing by Maksim wore white robes embroidered with gold crosses. They nodded in my direction.

Maksim turned, and his expression softened. "Hi."

"Hi." I reached into my backpack and pulled out a bouquet of white roses with baby's breath. I tucked Maksim's note into the ribbon, then reached into the bag again.

Dad's crucifix lay on the bottom. I scooped it up and started forward.

Maksim's eyes glimmered. "You look beautiful," he said as I stopped beside him.

"Really?" I tossed my backpack by the tree. "This top is just a t-shirt, and I got the skirt at a thrift store."

"And the shoes?" He craned his neck, peering past the layers of tulle. "I'm a fan."

"Thanks." A smile played across my lips. "I like yours, too."

He winked, and my pulse trilled.

Icons of Jesus, the Virgin Mary, and a saint I didn't recognize hung from the tree. The priests faced that direction and started singing. Chanting? They took turns, one of them singing a line and the other answering.

My ears tuned in to their accents. I perked up. "They're singing in Romanian," I whispered.

Maksim grinned.

The song transitioned into a reading, and that was when the men faced us again. The head priest finished speaking and extended his hand.

Maksim passed him a ring. I caught a glimpse and lost my breath. It was a diamond-and-sapphire-crusted wedding band.

I gazed up at him. "Where did you get that?"

"I've had it." His mouth hitched. "Told you. I had plans."

A tear slid out. "I still need to get yours."

"I know. Don't worry." He reached over and brushed away the moisture. "We'll sort it out."

The priest turned toward me. Maksim intervened, shaking his head and explaining. The priest nodded and turned away.

"Hey, wait. I did bring something." There was only one jewelry store in Gentilly, and they didn't have much selection. So instead of getting a ring, I had replaced the chain on Dad's crucifix and decided to give him that instead. As a placeholder.

I tapped the priest's shoulder. He turned around, and I showed him the crucifix. He drew back, surprised, as I pointed at Maksim. "For him."

The man studied the crucifix, then shrugged.

Maksim sent a questioning look to me. "That's your father's."

"I know. But he would have wanted you to have it."

Maksim's eyes went damp as the priest blessed him, crossed him, and then draped the necklace over his head. He did the same to me using the wedding band.

When he finished, he placed the ring partway onto my finger. Maksim took my hand and slid it down until the glittery band rested against my engagement ring.

The second priest walked forward, holding a long silver contraption strung with bells. He proceeded to swing it. The bells jingled. Fragrant smoke filtered out of a central compartment.

"There's typically a lot more to the ceremony," Maksim whispered, "but they agreed to do a pared-down version. We're almost finished."

After putting the bells away, the head priest addressed Maksim.

"Could we do this part in English?" Maksim nodded toward me. "For Kat's sake?"

"Why, yes. Of course." The priest closed his bible. "I have a simple question, which I would like you both to answer. Why are you here?" He gestured toward Maksim. "If you would go first, please."

Maksim's smile vanished. "I've prepared vows. Are you asking me to recite them?"

"I'm asking *why* you prepared those vows."

Maksim looked like a deer in the headlights. His attention flicked to me, and he cleared his throat. "I know what I'm committing to, and I know why. But my preparation extended only to the former."

"I understand this question can be intimidating. But you are pledging, before God and men, to give all of yourself to this woman"—the priest gestured toward me—"and to become one with her. It's my belief that the 'why' is often more pressing than the 'what,' for if you cannot explain the reason *behind* your commitment, you will not be able to do all that is required to *meet* that commitment."

"Fair enough. But we have a complex history." Maksim motioned between us. me. "So parts of my answer may sound strange to you."

"God knows, son." The priest smiled, waiting.

Maksim pushed out a breath and faced me. "When Ștefan first spoke with me about you, it was for the purpose of investigating and—ultimately—spying on you."

The priest's smile slipped away. He divided a quizzical look between us.

"Initially, I didn't think there was anything remarkable about you—but I was wrong about that, and I realized it the first time I dreamed about you. In the dream, I was extremely protective of you." His gaze wandered over my face. "You were crying. Someone had hurt you, and I burned with rage. I wanted to kill the man... But do you know what you said to me?"

All I could do was blink. He'd never shared this before. Any of it.

"You took my hand, and you said, 'We just have to run.' And we did. Our strides were perfectly instep, and I felt that I could run forever with you... and when we finally stopped, the injury to your cheek was healed." A smile tugged at his lips. "Then you said to me, 'See? If we hadn't run, we wouldn't have known what happens next.' I love you, *dragă mea,* and I cannot bear to miss out on what's next—whether it's good, bad, or something in between. I have to know what it is, and I'll pay any price to find out." He covered his heart and then raised his hand. "I vow before God and these men to love and protect you, to lay down my life for you, to never stop fighting for you, until the day I die."

Two streams spilled over. The second priest passed me a tissue.

"That was... interesting." The head priest smiled through his clear alarm. "Uh, and now I ask this same question of you, dear." He gestured to me. "Why are you here?"

I took a deep breath and exhaled. *Here we go.*

"*Qui se ressemble s'assemble.*" *Kee suh rrey-SUHM-bluh sah-SUHM-bluh.*

My French, as usual, was terrible. But I had been practicing all night, and I inflected my very best accent.

Maksim's mouth settled into a gentle, expectant smile. "Birds of a feather flock together."

"That's right! That's the exact right translation. But I didn't know that at first, because when I learned the proverb—when Dom shared it with me—he was talking about our clothes and how we had dressed alike. But I think the meaning runs deeper than that.

"You and I resemble each other in ways that are beyond superficial. We understand each other on a deeper level because of the common thread running through our lives—the fact that your parents and my dad are dead because of Vladimir."

I didn't need to look at the priest to know he was going into shock. I could sense it.

"You were robbed of your family," I continued, "and all the amazing things you would have experienced with them... and so was I. We have that in common at our core. We understand heartache. We're familiar with pain.

"But we also think alike. Sometimes we dress alike." I extended a foot, indicating our shoes. "But even if we didn't, I want you to know that I love you. I've loved you from the beginning, back when I didn't want to, back when I was afraid and in complete denial."

He looked down, hiding a tear that slipped out.

"I don't think I've ever told you, have I?" I dabbed at my own eyes. "That I love you?"

He looked up, eyes still moist. "That's the first time."

"I told Dom that I love you. I've admitted it to Brandy and Dave. But I've never said it to *you* because I was scared. But I'm not scared anymore. For better or worse, 'til death do us part, we're in this together. That's my vow to you—that I'm in this with you, and that I want *you* to be in this with *me*."

A breeze blew over us, rustling our hair and clothes. Maksim captured one of my bronzy tendrils and twisted it between his fingers. His gaze wandered the planes of my face before settling on my mouth.

He glanced at the priest. The man said something in Romanian.

Maksim's attention returned. "He says I may kiss the bride."

My heart broke into a gallop. I lifted my gaze as he eased closer.

He leaned in, and the space between us evaporated. Our lips connected. Our tongues brushed. Our hands found each other, and we kissed like we'd never kissed before. Like we might never kiss again.

The park, the priests, Paris, the entire world disappeared until the only thing left was us. *Just you and me.*

I SHOULDERED MY BACKPACK AND WAVED. "THANKS again!"

The priests waved back as they headed out of the park.

"Okay, spill." I took Maksim's arm. "How'd you find Romanian Orthodox priests in Paris?"

"A Romanian Orthodox church. There happens to be one here." He picked a path and led me that way. "Normally, they would never perform an abbreviated ceremony, but some of their members had dire financial needs, and they've been praying for the funds to arrive."

"Uh-oh. You're not paying in cryptocurrency, are you?"

"Two years ago, I opened a safe deposit box, and it contains a significant amount of cash—one of the many reasons I wanted to come here." He flagged me with both eyebrows. "Not because of Marie."

"Are you sure?" I twisted up a grin. "Not even a little bit because of her?"

"That was more about Julien." Maksim's mood sank. "But even then, I wouldn't have brought you here if I had thought you were at risk."

"I know." I eased closer. "I'm sorry. I was just teasing."

"It's all right." He covered my hand and gave a tender squeeze —but I wondered if maybe it wasn't all right. He hadn't taken the paternity test yet. That had to be weighing on him.

"Anyway," he continued, "I told the priests I would happily meet the needs of their congregation, but that I had a dire need of my own."

A group of men bowled a silver ball over a patch of grass. I'd been watching their game until Maksim said that.

"You mean... this?" I met his gaze. "Us? Getting married was the dire need?"

"Absolutely." He smoothed a flyaway that had come loose from my updo. "I need you the way I need food and water. More. I could go without those things, but I cannot go without you." He placed a tender kiss to the top of my head. "Being with you fully, completely, is my most dire need."

My tummy fluttered. I soaked in the sensation. Feeling his touch never lost its luster—but a stray thought interrupted my bliss.

"What about Daniel and Madă? All they've been able to talk about is a big Romanian wedding. Brandy should have been my maid of honor. I would have asked Dave to be a bridesman. And what about Levi—?"

"I've thought of these things. Believe me." Maksim reached up, about to rake at his hair. He lowered his hand and rubbed his thigh instead. "We'll do a big ceremony, I promise, and we'll ensure everyone can be there. But something like that will take time. The logistics will be complicated."

"Because Vladimir is still at large?" I clutched his arm. "Daniel said he's probably not in Paris, but how can we be sure?"

"Vladimir wouldn't linger after an assassination attempt, especially with all the press coverage. That won't stop him forever, but it will keep him away for now." Maksim's eyes grew distant. "Raul and Renan are surely on the run. Vladimir will soon begin smoking them out."

"I don't know what that means."

"Cutting them off from contacts, forcing them to take bigger risks and venture out from their safe haven. Vladimir won't stop until they have nowhere else to turn. I'm deeply concerned for—"

Someone called out.

Maksim and I looked up to find a man jogging toward us. Maksim stepped in front of me.

I peeked out from behind him. The guy seemed pretty average —skinny, workout clothes. He couldn't be one of Vladimir's security guys.

Could he?

The man passed a piece of paper to Maksim, and nausea sloshed through me.

Maksim grilled him. The man's confusion heightened until he was holding up both hands in innocence. He mentioned *la blonde*, and Maksim's face blanched.

The man turned and jogged out of the park.

I touched Maksim's arm. "Are you okay?"

"No." He rubbed his forehead.

"I heard him mention a blonde. Do you think the note is from—?"

"I don't know." For the first time that morning, he shoved a hand through his hair and raked until every lock was out of place.

"Marie was being questioned by the police," I said. "They found phone calls between her and one of Vladimir's men."

"I think she was being blackmailed like Dom." He scanned the immediate area. "The man said she was crying, begging him to deliver this along with an apology. Supposedly, the apology was for both of us."

An ache penetrated my chest. "Was she apologizing for something she *did?*" I glanced around. "Or something she's *doing?* Should we be worried?"

Maksim stiffened. His eyes flashed to mine, and I knew he hadn't thought of that.

I gulped. Oh, no. No. Please.

He rushed to open the note. His face went from pale to ash gray.

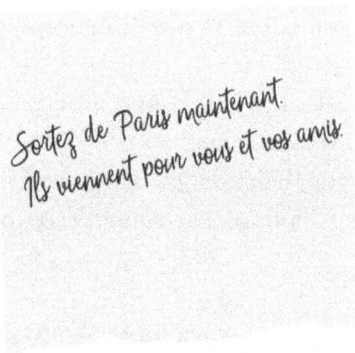

"Maksim? What's it say?"

"'Get out of Paris now. They're coming for you and your friends.'"

Reviews are incredibly helpful. If you enjoyed the characters, story, or anything else, Ellis and the artists who worked on *Dawn to Dusk* would be grateful for your review or rating. We simply can't compete with the big publishers otherwise.

LinkTr.ee/ReviewD2D

Stay tuned for *Dawn to Darkness: The Awaken Saga, Book 3* and a novella (Book 1.5) about what happened to Kat and Maks between the first two novels.

You'll get all the latest news and inside information by joining **Ellis' Extraordinary Readers Club!** It's FREE, and you'll be given access to free books by other amazing authors, as well as bonus material from The Awaken Saga—deleted scenes, character art + more!

SubscribePage.io/JoinReadersClub

You'll also receive *The Heart of Euroland,* the real life, award-winning story about the house fire that gave Ellis a debilitating case of writer's block and sent her on a journey to find inspiration.

Become an Extraordinary Reader today and get your free copy of ***The Heart of Euroland*** — now being turned into a full-length novel!

FROM THE AUTHOR & ILLUSTRATORS

Note from the author, Ellis K. Popa

Artists' work may not align with popular taste, yet that does not diminish its value. As long as it carries the emotions and messages they want to share it's undeniably a piece of art.

Krystal 1204.

Note from Krystal_1204

Krystal's work can be found in the limited editions of *Dawn to Dusk* and *Awaken the Dawn.*

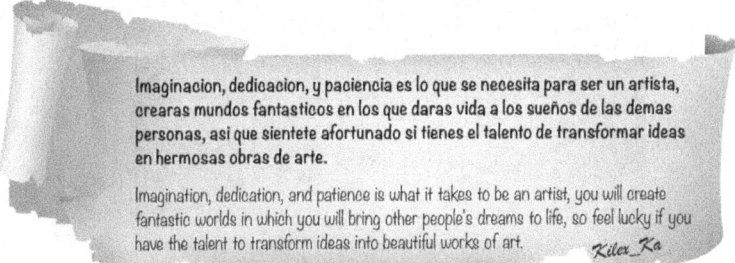

Imaginacion, dedicacion, y paciencia es lo que se necesita para ser un artista, crearas mundos fantasticos en los que daras vida a los sueños de las demas personas, asi que sientete afortunado si tienes el talento de transformar ideas en hermosas obras de arte.

Imagination, dedication, and patience is what it takes to be an artist, you will create fantastic worlds in which you will bring other people's dreams to life, so feel lucky if you have the talent to transform ideas into beautiful works of art. *Kilex_Ka*

Note from Kilex_Ka

Kilex's work can be found in the limited edition of *Dawn to Dusk*. He created the custom artwork at the front of both editions and the cover art for the ultraspecial photography edition.

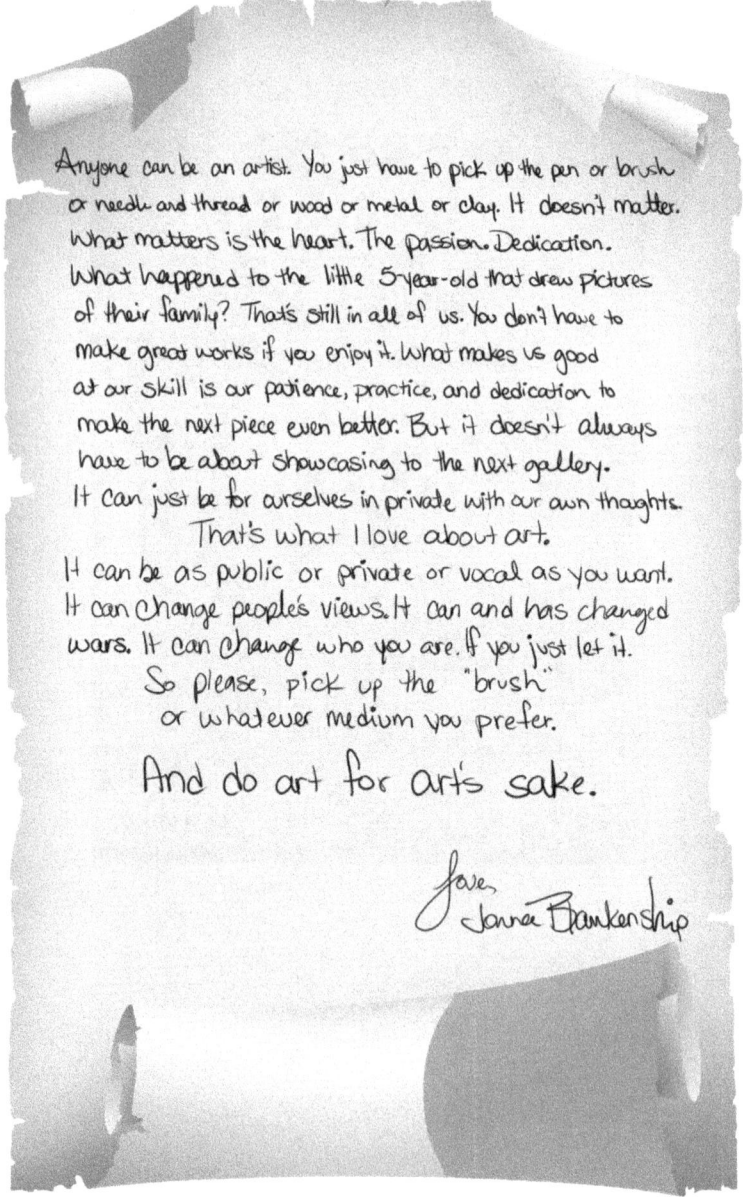

Anyone can be an artist. You just have to pick up the pen or brush or needle and thread or wood or metal or clay. It doesn't matter. What matters is the heart. The passion. Dedication. What happened to the little 5-year-old that drew pictures of their family? That's still in all of us. You don't have to make great works if you enjoy it. What makes us good at our skill is our patience, practice, and dedication to make the next piece even better. But it doesn't always have to be about showcasing to the next gallery. It can just be for ourselves in private with our own thoughts.
        That's what I love about art.
It can be as public or private or vocal as you want. It can change people's views. It can and has changed wars. It can change who you are. If you just let it.
        So please, pick up the "brush"
        or whatever medium you prefer.

And do art for art's sake.

                    love,
                    Jonna Blankenship

Note from Jonna Blankenship

Jonna's work can be found in the standard and limited editions of

Dawn to Dusk and *Awaken the Dawn.* She created the clue art and some of the limited edition art in both books.

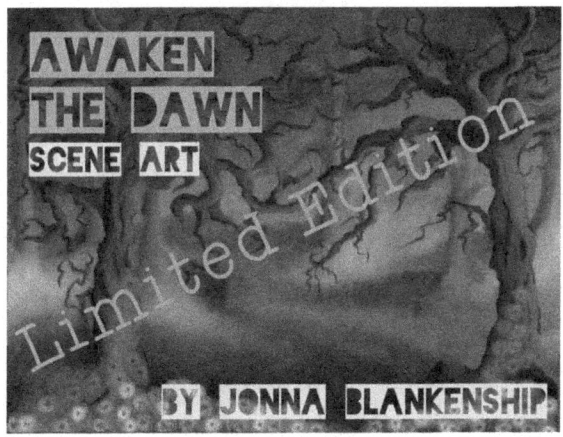

"*Maksim*" *(oil on canvas) by Jonna Blankenship*

The limited edition is only available during certain times of the year (through Kickstarter campaigns or giveaways).

To be notified of the next availability, be sure to join **Ellis' Extraordinary Readers Club**. IT'S FREE, and you'll receive access to FREE and DISCOUNTED books by other amazing authors!

SubscribePage.io/JoinReadersClub

KICKSTARTER BACKERS

There's a very special group of people I want to thank. They don't work for And Fire Books, but they took a chance on us and invested in *Dawn to Dusk* while it was still in production.

In exchange for backing the project, they received access to limited edition books and book-themed merch. We even named some of the places and characters after many of them (an extraspecial bonus we awarded during the *Dawn to Dusk* campaign).

To all the Kickstarter Backers, I want to personally thank you from the bottom of my heart. Without your support, this book would not have made it through final production. *Dawn to Dusk* is here because of you...

1. Bethany Oakes
2. Cathie Griffin
3. "L"
4. Wanda & Marty Northrup
5. Elizabeth Williams & Tom Noll
6. Marie & Howard Carter
7. Bee Blessed Farms
8. Vannessa Goodwin
9. John Benedict
10. The Johnson Family
11. Michael & Betsy Heilman
12. Shirlee & Eric Ross

13. Sabrina Laforest
14. The Wolf Family
15. Jennifer Corry
16. Anonymous - "Old" Friend
17. Ludi Acevedo
18. Lee & Cherilyn Hext
19. Shirley A. Cool Cochran
20. Heather Harwood
21. Karisa Moore
22. Jerome
23. Barbara & Paul Kiehl
24. B. Blue
25. Melinda Colt (Doamnă Anca)
26. Dave Elias
27. The Ferrymans
28. George Clark
29. Kelly Dalton
30. Chris Rottmair
31. Lana Allison & Harriett Fox
32. Brianna O'Keefe
33. Andy Dlugos
34. Angel Campbell
35. Linda Gentles
36. Julie Brinkley (Reading on the Brink)
37. Bob Fendt
38. Suzie Remmers
39. Nicole Williams
40. Christian Rockwell
41. Bethany & Deshawn White
42. Krissy Baccaro
43. Jonna Blankenship
44. Jenny Coyne
45. Breyce Neal
46. Jacque Turner
47. Issachar Wine

48. Suzy K.
49. LZ
50. Patrick O'Donnell
51. Caitee Cooper
52. David Neth of DN Publishing
53. DEDICATION: Kupo
54. Olivia
55. Neveah
56. Katie Bell
57. Damien Todd

THE D2D TEAM

A very big THANK YOU to these folks who assisted with various aspects of *Dawn to Dusk*.

Whatever your contribution, please know how grateful we are for your help, support, and input. We couldn't do this without each of you...

Andy K. - ARC team
Bethany O. - beta reading, first-look feedback, coaching & professional consulting
Bob F. - early reading, ARC team
Brian E. - computer/technical consulting
Cathie G. - ARC team
Chris E. - beta reading, computer/technical consulting
Hope G. - ARC team
Jenny C. - ARC team
Jonna B. - beta reading, illustrations, first-look feedback
Julie B. - ARC team
Katie D. - ARC team
Lauren R. - early reading
Nevaeh K. - book wrapping, early reading
Nicole W. - event scheduling, beta reading, first-look feedback
Olivia A. - book wrapping, early reading
Sabrina L. - ARC team
Stephanie B. - ARC team
Tambi S. - early reading

Vinné S. - ARC team

EDITING & PROOFREADING

L.C. Charles - Editing
Alexandra Ott - Proofreading & Foreign Language
Crystalle at Victory Editing - Proofreading & Final Checks

CREATIVES

Jonna Blankenship - clue & scene art (standard and limited editions)
Krystal1204 - scene & character art (limited edition)
Kilex_Ka - scene & character art (limited edition) + custom artwork for bookplates (all editions)
RedXDesigner - Trailer #1
Ray Morgan - Trailer #2
Nicole Love - book-themed reels & mini trailers
Adrijus at Rocking Book Covers - cover design

About the Author

When Ellis isn't moonlighting as a coffee *aficionada*, you might find her adventuring through Transylvania, doing photoshoots in Old Town Bucharest, or otherwise trying to talk her husband into moving to Eastern Europe. She's a lover of history with a penchant for World War II and the Cold War, and her favorite places are Wallachia in beautiful Romania and the Dalmatian Coast of Croatia.

(She's also an award-winning writer and budget-minded travel expert.)

@EllisKayeCreates